Praise for *Tales for Fairies*

"Alba Morollón Díaz-Faes makes a much-needed and welcome contribution to fairy-tale studies! Historicizing English-language gay and queer retellings across media from the 1990s to the 2010s, this study highlights how these fairy tales activate queer wonder, repurpose queer monsters, and navigate the changing challenges of mainstream culture."

—Cristina Bacchilega, professor emerita, University of Hawai`i at Mānoa, and coauthor of *Justice in 21st-Century Fairy Tales and the Power of Wonder*

"An exquisite blend of sociohistorical criticism, queer theory, and close reading, *Tales for Fairies* pulls at the queer threads of fairy-tale history and examines closely the overlooked, explicitly queer retellings of recent decades in the strange and fluid genre of fairy tales. This provocative, fabulous book is an exciting addition to the nascent field of queer fairy-tale studies."

—Christy Williams, author of *Mapping Fairy-Tale Space: Pastiche and Metafiction in Borderless Tales* and coeditor of *Marvels & Tales: Journal of Fairy-Tale Studies* (both Wayne State University Press)

"I have hoped for a book that might tackle the breadth of emergent queer fairy-tale creation, aided by the LGBTQIA+ rights movement and technological innovations. Finally, that book has arrived in *Tales for Fairies*. I am overjoyed! Not unlike a witch's potent brew, the right ingredients are poured into this concise, deftly written analysis by Díaz-Faes. She keenly historicizes contemporary queer fairy-tale projects of reclamation and revision and provides illuminating, highly creative, and politically potent examples from the queer counterpublics of international authors, artists, and fans working to reveal the fairy tale's always-ready queer potential. Just to name a few: Peter Cashorali's revolutionary 1990s anthologies of gay fairy tales for men; cartoonist José Rodolfo Loaiza Ontivero's queer Disney parodies; and Alexis Isabel Moncada's wildly popular X campaign, #GiveElsaAGirlfriend. Díaz-Faes's readings of these and many more recent incursions prove techno-capitalism to be a perverse playground for creatively subverting the demonization of difference. The princess is no longer asleep, nor is she following the straight path to crappy endings. The princess read *Tales for Fairies*, and she's headed to the drag ball."

—Kay Turner, coeditor of *Transgressive Tales: Queering the Grimms* (Wayne State University Press)

TALES FOR FAIRIES

The Donald Haase Series in Fairy-Tale Studies

Series Editor

Anne E. Duggan, Wayne State University

Founding Editor

Donald Haase, Wayne State University

A complete listing of the advisory editors and the books in this series can be found online at wsupress.wayne.edu.

TALES FOR FAIRIES

Tracing Queer Fairy-Tale Retellings

ALBA MOROLLÓN
DÍAZ-FAES

WAYNE STATE UNIVERSITY PRESS
DETROIT

ISBN 9780814350423 (paperback)
ISBN 9780814350430 (hardcover)
ISBN 9780814350447 (ebook)

Library of Congress Control Number: 2025933903

Cover illustration and design by Brad Norr Design.

Published with the assistance of a fund established by Thelma Gray James of Wayne State University for the publication of folklore and English studies.

Wayne State University Press rests on Waawiyaataanong, also referred to as Detroit, the ancestral and contemporary homeland of the Three Fires Confederacy. These sovereign lands were granted by the Ojibwe, Odawa, Potawatomi, and Wyandot Nations, in 1807, through the Treaty of Detroit. Wayne State University Press affirms Indigenous sovereignty and honors all tribes with a connection to Detroit. With our Native neighbors, the press works to advance educational equity and promote a better future for the earth and all people.

Wayne State University Press
Leonard N. Simons Building
4809 Woodward Avenue
Detroit, Michigan 48201-1309

Visit us online at wsupress.wayne.edu.

CONTENTS

INTRODUCTION

> Supernatural agency and the pleasure of wonder are interwoven in the character of fairy tales.
>
> —Marina Warner, *Once Upon a Time*

> Queering is at its heart a process of wonder.
>
> —Jeffrey J. Cohen, *Medieval Identity Machines*

The Case of "The Queer Minstrel"

In 1819, the Brothers Grimm added the tale "Der wunderliche Spielmann" to the second edition of their book, *Children's and Household Tales*. This tale's title has been variously translated as "A Miraculous Fiddler," "The Strange Musician," and "The Queer Minstrel." All variations include fitting terms: the protagonist is indeed somewhat miraculous, strange, and queer. In the story, he plays his violin in the forest, attracting the attention of various animals. However, he is not looking for an animal audience and so, displeased, he lays traps for them, capturing them one after the other. He is only happy when a woodcutter arrives, drawn by his wonderful melody. "At last comes the right companion," he says. At that point, the animals manage to free themselves and rush to attack the minstrel, who is protected by the woodcutter. The minstrel plays one last time for his human companion in thanks, and then he is on his way.

This strange little tale of pleasurable encounters in the forest and of fleeting, anonymous camaraderie between two men exemplifies the potential of the classic fairy tale for queerness. It is queer in the way Kay Turner and Pauline Greenhill indicate—in the "nineteenth-century usage of the word, to mean odd, strange-making, eccentric, different, and yet attractive" (4)—but also in the twenty-first-century sense: meaning everything not cisheteronormative, particularly as the tale focuses on male companionship between the musician and the woodsman. "The Queer Minstrel" also sidesteps genre expectations in that it disavows the marriage plot: the happy ending that most reinforces the connection between fairy tales and heteronormativity. It is perhaps the enduring connection between heteronormative endings and fairy tales that has so delayed the recognition of the genre as a fertile site for queer readings. However, as Turner puts it: "Even if many tales hurtle headlong toward normative reunion, marriage, and stability, often the route navigates a topsy-turvy space filled with marvels, magic, and weird encounters that don't simply contradict the 'normal' but offer, or at least hint at, alternative possibilities for fulfilling desires that might alter individual destinies" (248).

Some would argue that "The Queer Minstrel" is not, in fact, a fairy tale: it is an animal tale under the Aarne–Thompson–Uther folktale classification system. There are some tales, however, that come closer to what most people understand as fairy tales and still follow the sinuous, queer routes to normative happy endings that Turner mentions in the previous quote. Most notably, there are many maiden-knight tales in which young women cross-dress for various reasons and often end up in heterosexual royal marriages. Such is the case of Giovanni Francesco Straparola's "Constanza / Constanzo" and Marie-Catherine d'Aulnoy's "Belle-Belle or the Knight Fortuné," both of which contain cross-dressing knights who perform exceptional deeds and rise through the ranks, become the king's favorites, are eventually revealed to be women, and ultimately marry the king. However, none of these cross dressing tales (nor "The Queer Minstrel," for that matter) have infiltrated the contemporary fairy-tale canon, which mostly eschews tales that foreground gender-nonconforming protagonists.

It is thus understandable that, for the average reader, fairy tales would have remained exclusively cisheterocentric texts, and that even fairy-tale scholars might have taken longer than expected to start interrogating the normative surface of the genre. Even the budding subgenre of queer retellings that has flourished since the 1990s has been mostly overlooked by scholars, even though it offers an immediate, effective, and context-specific challenge to the genre's apparent cisheterocentrism. This study thus examines retellings in English from the 1990s to the

2010s that have received little or no scholarly attention, and it will analyze the strategies for genre queering they deploy. I argue that these works do not break with a heterocentric fairy-tale tradition but instead exist on the same discursive continuum—they amplify the queer echoes already present in the genre and are tethered to one another by a queer chain of retelling. Additionally, contemporary retellings are as impacted by their creators' sensibilities and varying sociohistorical contexts as their pretexts. Fairy tales are not only wondrous tales of magic and escapism that adapt to fluctuating and strange desires but also potent historical documents. By applying a sociohistorical approach to queer fairy tales, this study offers an in-depth analysis of the many intersections between these tales and the cultural, political, historical, and social elements surrounding their production. This study also draws from various queer theories to evaluate the techniques that queer retellings use to reflect, reinforce, subvert, or question shifting attitudes toward lesbian, gay, bisexual, transgender, queer, and intersex (LGBTQI) people—as these works converge with historically salient events and tendencies, such as the AIDS crisis, the mainstreaming or assimilation of queer identities, and the migration of queer communities to online spaces. In short, this study traces the emergence, evolution, and sophistication of the queer fairy-tale retelling subgenre, to offer a roadmap of the queer uses of the fairy tale in contemporary society.

Queer, Queering, Fairy Tales

Queer is commonly used to refer to those identities, sexualities, practices, and bodies that resist normative constructions, many of which are popularly grouped under the initialism LGBTQI, to which sometimes a plus sign is added (LGBTQI+).[1] Queer theorists expand its meanings: according to David Halperin, queer is everything that "is at odds with the normal, the legitimate, the dominant" (8); and for Judith Butler, it is that which exists outside of the "heterosexual matrix," that is, the "grid

1 The acronym, in one of its most popular forms, stands for lesbian, gay, transgender, bisexual, queer, and intersex. The plus sign at the end of the acronym represents the broad spectrum of identities and bodies that exist outside of societal norms, including pansexual, genderqueer, asexual, and more.

of cultural intelligibility through which bodies, genders and desires are naturalized" (*Gender Trouble* 194). For his part, Steven Angelides defines *queer* as "an umbrella category for the sexually marginalized" situated in a "no-man's land beyond the heterosexual norm" that challenges "the familiar distinctions between normal and pathological, straight and gay, masculine men and feminine women" (168–71). Eve Kosofsky Sedgwick understands the term more broadly as an "open mesh of possibilities, gaps, overlaps" (*Tendencies* 8), and Mary McIntosh considers it a defiant term: "defined more by what it is against than what it is for" (365).

Queer can also be used as a verb. I understand *queering* as a critical process that would entail challenging and breaking apart conventional categories (Doty xv), to which end one would need to "unpick binaries and reread gaps, silences and in-between spaces" (Giffney and Hird 5). It would not do to overlook or downplay the connection between queerness and nonconforming sexualities and identities, so, much like Lewis Seifert, I also understand *to queer* as: "to make strange by accentuating what departs from normative social expectations . . . thus exposing the notions of 'normal' gender and sexual identities as myths (albeit powerful ones)" ("Introduction" 16). Following this, throughout this study I embrace the indefinite, unstable, and expansive umbrella term *queer* to signify everything and everyone outside of the cisheteronorm, and the power of *queering* to disrupt, disturb, and deconstruct that which is perceived as natural, or normal—particularly regarding gender and sexuality within the fairy tale.

These flexible understandings of *queer* are particularly useful when applied to the fairy tale. As Jennifer Orme points out, this indefinability, "the shifty instability of the term *queer*" is "one of its few stable aspects" ("Happily" 148), which can also be said of the term *fairy tale*: yet another slippery umbrella term often redefined and used to refer to various things. As fairy tales are told, retold, adapted, rewritten, and reimagined in a variety of forms—from short stories, to novels, films, video games, and commercials—what makes a fairy tale a *fairy tale* becomes increasingly unclear. The genre is, in other words, constantly queered, made progressively stranger and more unpinnable. Somewhat paradoxically, it is the plasticity of the fairy tale, its ability to adapt its essence indefinitely—in short, its potential for queering—that has ensured the genre's survival. Furthermore, despite the ubiquitous normative endings, the strange world of the fairy tale is also necessarily queer: it operates following the unknowable rules of wonder and exists at the crossroads of fantasy and reality, where normalcy and all its agents are banished.

It would be disingenuous to insist that the fairy tale is inherently queer without also acknowledging that, at least in its canonical forms, the fairy tale is part of a heterosexist corpus that works to preserve what Adrienne Rich called *compulsory heterosexuality*, by which non-heterosexual experiences are deemed abhorrent or "rendered invisible" ("Compulsory Heterosexuality" 26). While interspecies tales like Jeanne-Marie Leprince de Beaumont's "Beauty and the Beast" and transspecies tales like Hans Christian Andersen's *The Little Mermaid* retain an underlying, strange queerness, they are nevertheless drawn to the orbit of heterosexuality: the Beast becomes a man who establishes a heterosexual relationship with Beauty, and the little mermaid transforms into a woman to seduce the prince. Problematizing the exclusion of non-heterosexual identities from the fairy-tale canon, which for so long has been "used to enshrine heterosexual love" is one of the main foci of this study (Seifert, "Introduction" 18).

Re-Vision of the Fairy-Tale Canon

This study primarily but not exclusively focuses on retellings of canonical fairy tales in the Western European tradition. This choice has to do with the usual limitations of any research project, but it is also due to the current state of the object of study, the contemporary queer fairy tale in English, which largely references pretexts from the European canon.[2] Of course, there is no such thing as an official fairy-tale canon, but a loose, *de facto* canon soon emerges for those who work with the genre. I use this concept along the same lines as Tom Shippey, for whom the canon is this "rather small core group of familiar stories" that tend

2 This is not necessarily exclusive to queer retellings. Fairy tales from Western Europe form the basis for many of the retellings that have come out of Europe and North America during the twentieth and twenty-first centuries. This is a testament to their enduring cultural currency in the global north, despite continued efforts to open the canon to multicultural versions, of which Angela Carter's fairy-tale anthologies are good examples: *The Old Wives' Fairy Tale Book* (1990) and *Strange Things Still Sometimes Happen: Fairy Tales from Around the World* (1993).

to get retold, adapted and collected most often (161). In his experience, this includes "Bluebeard," "Snow White," "Cinderella," "Little Red Riding Hood," "Sleeping Beauty," "Rapunzel," "Beauty and the Beast," "The Frog Prince," and "Snow White and Rose Red" (161). This core group amounts primarily to tales penned by the Perrault–Grimm–Andersen trinity, many of which were further established as canonical and further reshaped by Disney's adaptations. Consequently, and going by my own experience with retellings and collections, I include "The Little Mermaid," "Little Thumb," "Puss in Boots," "The Ugly Duckling," "The Snow Queen," and "Hansel and Gretel" in the list of canonical tales.

As noted, most of these canonical tales stick to stricter normative scripts, but many still contain nonconforming encounters, attachments, and pathways that invite queer readings. For instance, both the interspecies "Beauty and the Beast" and Andersen's coming-of-age tale of "The Ugly Duckling" contain themes of alterity that can easily be understood in queer terms, if one is so inclined. The pervasive, cross-media, and historically expansive presence of classical tales allows for a deep feeling of familiarity, which might complicate approaching them from a completely "strange" perspective. Adults might not exactly remember how a particular tale goes, and children might only know Disney renditions of "Cinderella" or "Sleeping Beauty," but as Cristina Bacchilega notes, we "respond to stereotyped and institutionalized fragments of these narratives, sufficiently for them to be a good bait in jokes, commercials . . . cartoons, and other elements of popular and consumer culture" (*Postmodern*, 2). Many of us will need to lift the confounding veil of familiarity, reassess and deconstruct our assumptions of what a fairy tale is (or is not), and reconsider how the laws of wonder operate and what can be expected of them. In other words, critics and retellers both perform an act of *re-vision*, to use Adrienne Rich's term ("Writing as Re-Vision," 18), to see the old fairy tales with fresh eyes, abandoning naturalized associations that might hold us back in our way to probe the queer depths of the fairy tale.

Furthermore, critics and retellers often also navigate external challenges. Pauline Greenhill explains that the mere indication that such tales could be read queerly might be met with a great degree of resistance, as one is perceived to be "sullying these allegedly innocent stories by suggesting they might not be always resolutely heterosexual" ("Sexualities").

In our time, the fairy tale approximates a sacred cultural institution, generally associated with sanitized plots, conservative morals, and cisheteronormativity—reimagined as a genre for children and whittled down to a handful of canonical tales that (at least superficially) support this narrow vision. Thus, queering these tales—both in the sense of critical reassessment and creative retelling—can still be considered taboo and perceived as a threat to this day. For instance, Disney's *Beauty and the Beast* live-action remake (2017) showed a sidekick character, LeFou, dancing with another man in a blink-and-you-miss-it scene, which was meant to imply he was non-heterosexual. This insignificant moment led to screening cancellations in some cinemas in the United States, as well as general displeasure and threats of censorship in countries with anti-gay policies, such as Russia. In 2020, a Hungarian retelling for children which inscribed queer identities became the target of homophobic politicians. The illustrated anthology was aptly named *Meseorszag mindenkie*, or *A Fairy Tale for Everyone*, and was intended for educational use and thus purposefully diverse, including a lesbian Snow Queen. The collection shot to attention when the leader of the extreme-right party Mi Hazánk (Our Homeland), Dóra Dúró, shredded the book in a press conference, denouncing it as "homosexual propaganda" (Gallant). When asked about the controversial book, Prime Minister Viktor Orban said: "Hungary is a patient, tolerant country [toward] homosexuality. But there is a red line that cannot be crossed, and this is how I would sum up my opinion: Leave our children alone" (qtd. in Haynes).

These examples of ferocious backlash are illustrative of the risks one runs when queering such esteemed texts, and it makes it even more remarkable and deserving of attention when creators and critics are bold enough to queerly *re-vise* the fairy tale. At the same time, the Hungarian example also brings some measure of hope for the future of the queer fairy tale and its increasing influence: after the institutional pushback, the collection sold 30,000 copies, and the publisher sold the rights to publishers in countries like Sweden and Poland, and to publishers like HarperCollins in the United States (Gallant).

A New Frontier for Fairy-Tale Studies

Fairy-tale scholars have only recently begun to address a twofold issue: both the queer potential of the genre, and the silencing of queer identities, themes, and desires in the canon. At the time of writing, there are only two book-length texts on the queering of fairy tales: Kay Turner and Pauline Greenhill's *Transgressive Tales: Queering the Grimms* (2012), and Anne Duggan's *Queer Enchantments: Gender, Sexuality, and Class in the Fairy-Tale Cinema of Jacques Demy* (2013). Moreover, Duggan herself points out in the introduction to *Queer Enchantments* that a cursory search in the MLA International Bibliography of combined keywords such as *queer*, *fairy tale*, *lesbian*, and *homosexual* returns a total of nine relevant articles (11). Duggan wrote this in 2013, but over ten years later, a similar search in the same database returns around twelve more articles, in addition to the eight articles comprising the 2015 special issue in *Marvels & Tales*, titled *Queer(ing) Fairy Tales*, which considered both historical fairy tales and contemporary retellings. There is a palpable growing interest in the intersection of queer theories and fairy-tale studies, but this approach is still in its infancy.

My study contributes to this inchoate academic approach to the genre, which has taken a surprising amount of time to take. This is particularly shocking if we consider the key role that feminist critics and gender theorists played in shaping the fairy-tale studies field into what it has become, with its focus on the sociohistorical context of fairy tales, the critique of the canon, and the recovery of lesser-known stories (Haase, "Feminist Fairy-Tale Scholarship" 16). Early feminist critics such as Marcia R. Lieberman identified classical and canonical fairy tales as texts that perpetuate myths about gender, often overstating the power fairy tales had as socializing tools for girls. These early, somewhat superficial criticisms of the genre soon gave way to a more nuanced discussion that would complicate the perception of the fairy tale as uniform in its representations of gender. Given the impact of feminist theories on queer theories and the relative continuity between them, an obvious next step following feminist criticism of the genre would have been to question the representations of identity and desire, which, as noted, are so seemingly cisheterocentric in the fairy tale. However, looking at the rather meager existing collection of texts about the queering of fairy tales, it is clear this line of inquiry has taken around forty years to gain any traction. I suggested some provisional explanations for this delay previously: the heterocentric alibi of the happy ending might have concealed the queer gaps in the tales, as might have the unexamined assumptions we have inherited about the genre, although one should not discount the fear of pushback.

Even though all the aforementioned reasoning is as true for critics as it would be for retellers, queer retellings of fairy tales have been around much longer—meaning, in this case, revisions containing explicitly non-cisheteronormative identities that engage critically with the canon. In fact, one of the earliest examples of retold feminist fairy tales, Anne Sexton's 1971 *Transformations*, also contains the first queer retelling of fairy tales: in her poem "Rapunzel," Mother Gothel and Rapunzel have a sexual relationship. However, this early example did not immediately elicit widespread queer engagement with the genre. Chapters 1 and 2 retrace the steps the genre took until queer retellings of fairy tales began to crop up in a noteworthy capacity from the mid-1990s onward.

The trend began in 1995, when Peter Cashorali published *Fairy Tales: Traditional Stories Retold for Gay Men*. Speaking of the increasing popularity of queer theory, this was also the year in which Lauren Berlant and Michael Warner declared: "Queer is hot" (343). This suggests a certain level of simultaneity between queer fairy-tale retellings and queer theory, but not with fairy-tale scholarship. In turn, this contradicts Stephen Benson's observation that there has been an "extraordinary synchronicity" between fairy-tale retellings and fairy-tale scholarship from the seventies onward (5). Benson, however, puts forward a compelling reason behind the synchronicity he describes:

> It is perhaps unsurprising to find scholarly work mirrored in the parallel world of contemporary fiction, given that a number of the writers have themselves written about the fairy tale: Carter in her collections of fairy tales, Atwood and Rushdie through a host of literary essays, and most recently Byatt, a former academic whose attention to developments in literary history and theory have made particularly interesting her occasional essays on the fairy tale and related subjects. (6)

To my knowledge, retellers of queer fairy tales have rarely written about the genre—apart from Cashorali, who has discussed using the fairy-tale mode to help his psychotherapy patients, and Neil Gaiman, who has written several newspaper articles on fairy tales but has never remarked on their queer potential. However, neither has written academically on the matter. Thus, the lack of creators-turned-academics (or vice versa) in the queer retelling subgenre points to another possible explanation for the delay in academic engagement with the queer fairy tale.

As it were, after 1995, queer retellings developed rapidly. Chapters 3 and 4 detail how the new millennium brought an increasing number of retellings with a queer slant. The number of queer retellings had become comparatively large by the 2010s, when the first book-length academic approaches to the queer fairy tale were being published. These retellings appeared in such a wide range of media—including mainstream television and various online platforms—that it has become virtually impossible to keep track of them all. The impetus behind the present study is the increasingly urgent need to catch up with this quickly emerging and presumably unstoppable subgenre.

Fairy LGBTales

Queer fairy tales in their retold form and queer criticism of the genre have been somewhat out of step with each other since the early 2000s. This study aims to address this issue not by offering an exhaustive report on queer fairy tales to date, but by spotlighting several mostly unstudied texts that have quietly yet steadily chipped away at the monolithic, cisheterocentric image of the fairy tale, carving out space for queer identities, sensibilities, desires, and bodies.

Although an increasing number of individual academic articles offer suggestive readings of queer retellings, this project aims to be the first study dedicated to mapping out the evolution of queer fairy-tale retellings in English—understood in this case to mean retellings that consciously inscribe explicit LGBTQI identities and desires. This would set it apart from other mentioned book-length studies, like Turner and Greenhill's, which includes a section on rewritings but mostly focuses on ways to read the traditional Grimm tales queerly, or Duggan's, which focuses on the films of a single creator: queer French director Jacques Demy.

Contemporary reimaginings of fairy tales have received several names. Bacchilega, echoing Rich, called them *re-visions* ("Cracking the Mirror," 2) and Vanessa Joosen compiled a useful list of other common terms, which includes "transformation, anti-fairy tale, postmodern fairy tale, fractured fairy tale and recycled fairy tales" (9). I think all these terms are equally valid, if somewhat vague at times. However, for the sake of simplicity and neutrality, and to account for the fact that the continued popularity of the genre hinges on a constant retelling that binds the tales to one another in a narrative chain, throughout this study I will refer to them as *retellings* like Joosen does. Retelling, in fact, stands at the heart of the fairy-tale genre: even fairy tales we consider classics nowadays are the product of retelling, either based on other written sources (fairy tales or not) or untraceable oral ones. We might not all agree on whether all writing is rewriting, but all fairy-tale telling is, after a fashion, retelling.

In this study, however, I concentrate primarily on contemporary queer retellings rather than on classical fairy tales that can be read queerly, or fairy-tale-inflected original contemporary fiction. This is because I consider them to be a significant site for representing, reconstructing, and "disidentifying" cultural images of sexual and gender identity. I use the term *disidentification* following José Esteban Muñoz's definition:

> Disidentification is about recycling and rethinking encoded meaning. The process of disidentification scrambles and reconstructs the encoded message of a cultural text in a fashion that both exposes the encoded message's universalizing and exclusionary machinations and re-circuits its workings to account for, include, and empower minority identities and identifications. Thus disidentification is a step farther than cracking open the code of the majority; it proceeds to use this code as raw material for representing a disempowered politics or positionality that has been rendered unthinkable by dominant culture. (31)

Even though fairy tales do contain possibilities for queer identifications (as suggested previously), they have been largely appropriated by a dominant, cisheterocentric culture. Thus the fairy tale is a prime site for queer disidentification *because* of its normative, exclusionary associations, not despite them. The retold queer fairy tale effectively decodes the exclusionary machinations of the hegemonic fairy tale; it reroutes its workings to include minoritarian identities and returns an updated version of the genre in which queer identities and bodies are explicitly represented—whereas before such a thing was unthinkable. Through the mechanisms of disidentification, the retold queer fairy tale offers a third option beyond the complete disavowal of fairy tales or assimilation into their cisheteronormative matrix—namely, "a partial disavowal . . . that works to restructure it from within" (Muñoz 28)—and eventually, the reclamation of the genre for queer people.

To trace the different ways in which creators infiltrate the fairy tale to restructure it queerly, I will concentrate on texts in English from the 1990s to the 2010s. While some queer retellings in other languages and from other places exist (see Joosen 114), the great majority of examples I have encountered are in English, and so these are the focus of my study. Furthermore, while many of the chosen retellings are novels, short stories, and other written works, the queer fairy tale has also shown a remarkable tendency toward medial diversification. This study therefore also considers graphic novels, TV shows, paintings, and YouTube videos to account for the plurality, liveliness, and creative possibilities of the subgenre.

Structure of the Study

This study includes an important sociohistorical component. I follow Jack Zipes's influential approach to the fairy tale, which, since the 1979 publication of his book *Breaking the Magic Spell*, has shaped the way Anglophone scholars study the genre. Zipes devised a more historically grounded method than those used by earlier scholars, who would depend on formalist methodologies, often drawing from folklore studies (for instance, inspired by Vladimir Propp's *Morphology of the Folktale*). In this book, Zipes urges readers to critically engage with the genre without letting themselves get distracted by its deceptive simplicity, and to reach beyond its magical surface to "grasp the socio-historical forces" at the root to better understand fairy tales in light of their ideological connections to the time and place of their production (Zipes xi). To this end, the first chapter, "Queering the Fairy-Tale Tradition: Queer Possibility in Fairy-Tale History," traces the evolution of the genre from its identifiable origins to the 1990s. This approach draws attention to several traditional fairy tales that problematize the contemporary understanding of the genre as uniformly cisheteronormative, thus allowing for a sense of continuity between historical tales and their modern queered versions and leading to a better awareness of the role queer retellings play within the genre.

In keeping with this, each of the following chapters focuses on a period from the 1990s to the present, analyzing the retellings from each period against the cultural tensions that inform them. Thus, the second chapter, "Tales for Fairies: Building Identity and Community Through 1990s Gay Fairy Tales" focuses on the first three book-length texts to retell fairy tales for gay men: *Fairy Tales: Traditional Stories Retold for Gay Men* (1995) and *Gay Fairy & Folk Tales: More Traditional Stories Retold for Gay Men* (1997) by Peter Cashorali, and *Happily Ever After: Erotic Fairy Tales for Men* (1996), the erotic anthology edited by Michael Ford. I posit that the publication of these texts at this time resulted from the convergence of several factors such as the development of gay literature (particularly short fiction), the establishment of infrastructures and audiences that would support this kind of literature, and a need to memorialize and regroup after the worst years of the AIDS crisis. I argue these fairy tales were thus used to rebuild a coherent gay community at a moment when wondrous and imaginative possibilities were needed.

The third chapter considers a range of texts from the mid-2000s to the late 2010s, including short novels, comic books, and TV shows. It explores the tension between assimilationist and subversive queer tendencies (as represented by fairy-tale heroes and monsters) during a period when queerness was being absorbed into the mainstream after the visibility that the AIDS crisis granted LGBTQI people. This chapter, titled "Heroes vs. Monsters: Monstrousness, Monstrosity, and the Normalization of Queerness in Modern Fairy-Tale Retellings," tackles Cathrynne M. Valente's "Bones Like Black Sugar" (2006), Jim C. Hines's *The Stepsister Scheme* (2009), Lauren Beukes's *Fairest Vol. 2: The Hidden Kingdom* (2013), Neil Gaiman's *The Sleeper and the Spindle* (2013) and the ABC show *Once Upon a Time* (2011–18). This chapter argues that the fairy tale, due to its strange nature and allegiance to dark desires, remains a fertile site for the endangered, potentially subversive queer monster.

The fourth chapter, "Queer Fairy Tales 2.0: Parodying the Disney Paratext from Online Counterpublics," focuses on the way creators who have grown up in the new millennium (and thus have experienced the normalization of queerness) contest the cisheteronormative, Disneyfied fairy tale. It analyzes several parodies originating online—namely Tim Manley's *Alice in Tumblr-Land* (2013), Brittany Ashley's *Lesbian Princess* (2016), Todrick Hall's music video parodies, and José Rodolfo Loaiza Ontiveros's paintings—and explores how these creators utilize camp to undermine the hegemonic discourse of Disneyfied fairy tales.

The wide variety of texts used throughout this study aims to paint a clear, if necessarily incomplete, picture of the contemporary queer fairy tale as it emerges, advances, and matures into a subgenre closely related to queer identities and discourses. Paying close attention to historical contexts, wider cultural trends, and critical discussions surrounding the production of these texts, moreover, aims to broaden our understanding of what the fairy tale is, what it has been, and where it is headed. Primarily, this study challenges the idea of the fairy tale as a univocal whole and blows it open, revealing it as a multifaceted, contradictory, and strange genre filled with queer possibilities.

I

QUEERING THE FAIRY-TALE TRADITION

Queer Possibility in Fairy-Tale History

Queer retellings of fairy tales seemingly provide a radical break from, or an outright rejection of, the genre's apparent conservative history. The fairy tale is, after all, a genre popularly associated with antiquated morals, sanitized narratives, and clichéd plots: peasants turned kings, passive princesses, magical objects, impossible quests and, at the end of it all, fairy-tale weddings that ensure a heterosexual happily-ever-after. However, the eventual emergence of queer retellings of fairy tales is linked to the genre's attachment to non-normativity and its complex, shifting history. This chapter explores the historical context of fairy tales in their Western European branch—their evolution and mutation, from the traceable beginnings of the genre to the present day, not to free the queer fairy tale from the genre's history, but to explore the fairy tale's complexities, contradictions, and ambiguities—all of which have ultimately given way to the queered fairy tales of the present.

The fairy tale is a hybrid genre that has developed throughout history by borrowing from other genres, which have, in turn, been contaminated by the fairy tale. It is a genre that makes itself remarkably diverse by crossing borders and historical periods, even if we try to limit ourselves to the Western European branch. As Marina Warner puts it, "fairy tales migrate on soft feet, for borders are invisible to them, no matter how ferociously they are policed by cultural purists" (*Once Upon a Time* xv). Furthermore, it is a genre that is commonly thought to have its origins in a distant, hazy oral tradition. Folklorists like Alan Dundes maintain that fairy tales are "an oral form," referring to figures such as Charles Perrault or the Brothers Grimm as retellers—"men of letters, often with a nationalistic and romantic axe to grind" (Dundes 259–61). For scholars like Dundes, literary tales could never be genuine fairy tales, though he recognizes their influence. Fairy-tale scholars like Jack Zipes, on the other hand, tend to acknowledge the probable primacy of the oral fairy tale but are not dismissive of other forms to which the fairy tale might have migrated. For these fairy-tale scholars, fairy tales remained fairy tales when written down, both by people who wanted to preserve tales they perceived as traditional (such as the Brothers Grimm), and by writers who devised their own tales (like Hans Christian Andersen). The literary fairy tale began to branch off from genres like the *lais* in the tradition of Marie de France and chivalric romances between the fourteenth and fifteenth centuries, and it established itself as a literary genre by the sixteenth and seventeenth centuries (Zipes, *Tradition* xi). To complicate matters further, from that point on there was a "vigorous two-way traffic of oral and literary tales" (Davidson and Chaudhri 2). Both the genre's hybridity and the large scope of its influence contribute to the fairy tale's complexity, and its oral origins lay an unsteady foundation upon which everything else is built.

However, the object of this chapter is not to untangle the intricate, confounding web of the genre's origins. The intention is, rather, to explore tales by canonical or influential fairy-tale writers that, while not necessarily nor purposefully queer fairy tales—that is, tales written with the intention of representing sexual and gender minorities—still present instances of recognizable queer dissonance. This approach aims to complicate "straight"-forward understandings of the fairy tale, a genre that is largely misunderstood in part because it is so often reconstructed through a contemporary, "Disneyfied" lens. In other words, this chapter queers the history of the fairy tale, both in the sense of drawing attention to its least normative elements and of deconstructing some of the most deep-seated, naturalized assumptions about it. Indeed, the fairy tale, seemingly familiar but unknown to many, manages to appear universal and timeless while simultaneously concealing "its artistic constellations and . . . basic history and ideology" (Zipes, "Media-Hyping of Fairy Tales" 213). As we will see, a close look at the genre's historical connections and influences reveals that the flat, simplistic image that is so popularly associated with the fairy tale is merely an illusion.

Much like there are misconceptions about fairy tales, there are many misconceptions about queerness, sexual identity, and gender identity—concepts that are often understood as natural in the present day but have rather ambiguous histories. The late nineteenth century saw the rise of the medical study of sexuality and gender, and, importantly, of sexual pathology, which codified "sexual perversions" and ushered in a paradigm shift in Western understandings of sexuality as identity (Chaperon 277a). As Michel Foucault outlined in his much-quoted first volume of *The History of Sexuality*:

> Homosexuality appeared as one of the forms of sexuality when it was transposed from the practice of sodomy onto a kind of interior androgyny, an hermaphrodism of the soul. The sodomite had been a temporary aberration; the homosexual was now a species. (43)

Foucault meant that, although people engaged in homosexual sex acts and had homosexual relationships prior to the nineteenth century, *sodomite* was not an ontological category. The term *homosexual*, a neologism coined by author Karl Kertbeny in 1869 to challenge the stigma of older terms, was, much like racial and ethnic typologies, a category under which people could classify themselves or others. Foucault also famously popularized the story of Herculine Barbin, an intersex person assigned female at birth in 1838 France, who was later legally reclassified as male by a court of law. Barbin's memoire marked a point of departure for discussions of sex and gender in history. In the introduction to her memoire, Foucault maintains that categories of "true sex" were not operative until the modern age, and that intersex people could freely choose their sex, inhabiting, like Barbin, a "happy limbo of non-identity" ("Introduction" xiii). In *Gender Trouble* (1990), Butler criticized Foucault for his "romanticized" view of Barbin's tragic life, noting that Barbin was, in reality, prosecuted and punished for her ambiguous identity, and identified resolutely as female by her own account (120). That same year, Sedgwick's *Epistemology of the Closet* (1990) also criticized Foucault's overly linear historicization of the understanding of gender and sexuality. Sedgwick instead suggests privileging "plural, varied, and contradictory" historical understandings of same-sex relations and gender identity (*Epistemology* 48).

This glimpse at some salient theoretical discussions exemplifies the complexities inherent to the historical categorization of people, representations, and desires in societies without the modern binarisms of heterosexuality and homosexuality, cisgender and transgender. Most of the texts discussed in this chapter predate the widespread sexological discourse of the nineteenth century, and as such unfold in a different social reality in which both sexuality and gender identity might have been perceived in rather different terms. For instance, James Brundage writes that in medieval Europe, marriage was "the sole setting for legitimate sex," which would exclude all other sexual activity from being sanctioned on the same level—be it "homosexual or heterosexual, mercenary or gratuitous, long-term or short-term, solitary or social" (24). Furthermore, and as we will explore in this chapter, women cross-dressing as men was a recurrent plot in literature in premodern times, including fairy tales, as "it was not considered to have anything to do with [sexuality or gender identity] unlike the case in the twentieth century," and thus was much less provocative (Bullough 9). Seeking to sidestep the "anxieties of anachronism" (2), to use Claude J. Summers' words, my identification of "moments of queer dissonance" in fairy tales will be from the perspective of the present-day reader, with her present-day understanding of gender and sexuality, but not necessarily from that of the tales' contemporary reader or writer. Thus, I aim to uncover the gaps in the text in which the strange and unpredictable operate, from where to rediscover the surprising, excessive, fantastic visions that are intrinsic to the genre, and which extend a queer invitation across time and space.

Although it might seem counterintuitive, many of the genre's elements can resonate with present-day queer audiences. As Seifert notes, the fairy tale works well with "the camp aesthetic that is exploited in many gay and lesbian circles" ("Gay and Lesbian Tales" 401). After all, fairy tales in their many forms routinely make use of recognizable stock characters, such as brave princes, beautiful princesses, and evil old hags—all of which are excessively gendered, stereotypical, exaggerated, and theatrical, often following predictable scripts to such an extent that they border on self-referential and parodic. While such obviously manufactured representations will not bring attention to gender and sexuality constructions or defy the status quo on their own, they have the potential to appeal to queer audiences who are accustomed to finding and creatively reimagining the fabrications of a dominant cisheterocentric culture in dissidentificatory processes. Furthermore, the fairy-tale world, at once fantastic and mundane, "creates a paradox that opens the door . . . to an unsettling of what is normal" (Seifert, "Introduction" 19). The marvelous condition of the fairy-tale world throws together everyday elements with the magical, and a queer space emerges at the intersection of the two in which they can happily coexist. In Stith Thompson's words, the fairy tale produces an indefinite "never-never land" (8). This concise description cuts to the center of the genre, as the fairy tale produces not only a queer space of wondrous possibilities, but also queer temporalities that challenge normative, linear, "straight" time. As Elizabeth Freeman writes, queer temporalities "are points of resistance to this temporal order that, in turn, propose other possibilities for living in relation to indeterminately past, present, and future others" (*Time Binds* xvii). Although fairy-tale critics have demonstrated that queerness in fairy tales exists independent of normative markers like the heterosexual happy ending (see for instance Turner and Greenhill 3; Seifert, "Introduction" 18), the formulaic parenthesis of tales, so often associated with the cisheteronorm, offers reduced, queer notions of time. "Once upon a time" and "and they lived happily ever after," for instance, situate these tales in a perpetually decentered, unpinnable, and dislocated time frame where normative advancement becomes impossible. In Jack Halberstam's terms, they exist in a "queer time" in which notions of past, present, and future are diminished (*In a Queer Time and Place* 4–10). Moreover, although fairy tales have some sort of internal progression that would seem to be linear (from rags to riches, from peasant to royal), the path to narrative resolution is often not straight. We find all manner of plot points that confound linear progression and complicate what Freeman calls *chrononormativity*—the organization of human bodies in relation to time, from childhood to adulthood to death, through marriage and reproduction (*Time Binds* 3). These plots might involve genre staples such as impossible transformations from human to animal or vice versa, false deaths, and queer attachments that defy normative kinship (including interspecies romances). For the trained eye, it becomes readily apparent that the fairy tale has multiple entry points from which it can be queerly interrogated.

This chapter explores the evolution of the genre from its literary origins to the present, demonstrating that notions of gender, sexuality, and normativity are not as stable as commonly assumed in traditional fairy tales. This examination traces the birth of the literary fairy tale in sixteenth-century Italy, exemplified by the tales of Giovanni Francesco Straparola and Giambattista Basile, through its full generic autonomy in seventeenth-century France, with the influential works of Marie-Catherine d'Aulnoy and Charles Perrault. The golden age of fairy tales in the nineteenth century is explored through the tales of the Brothers Grimm and Hans Christian Andersen, and the modernization of the genre is unavoidably explained using Disney's fairy-tale productions. Finally, the countercultural, feminist retellings of the twentieth century are analyzed, particularly those that first inscribed queer sensibilities and made inroads for a queer re-evaluation of the fairy tale. In this way, I aim to better understand how the cisheterocentric image of the genre became so firmly lodged in our collective imagination and contribute to dismantling it by unearthing the queer tensions that have always been present in the many forms of the fairy tale.

The Beginning of a Literary Genre: Italian Forefathers and French *Counteuses* and *Conteurs*

In the European tradition, fairy tales began appearing sporadically in Italian collections from the fourteenth century onward (Zipes, *Tradition* 507), but it was not until the sixteenth and seventeenth centuries that the genre "reached full literary autonomy" (Canepa, *From Court to Forest* 16). This began with two important early modern Italian works that will be discussed in this section: Giovanni Francesco Straparola's *Piacevoli Notti* (1550–52) and Giambattista Basile's *Il Pentamerone: Lo Cunto de li Cunti* (1634). Some French writers turned their attention to the fairy tale by the end of the seventeenth century. Writers analyzed in this chapter, like d'Aulnoy and Perrault, drew heavily from Straparola and Basile and borrowed plots and themes from popular genres that had come before, like epic poems and *lais*, and completed the road toward the generic independence of the fairy tale with their resulting works. All these writers slowly constructed a model that bears significant influence on present-day understandings of the genre, though, as we will see, many of their tales might challenge assumptions about what the fairy tale is—or is not.

Despite Basile's *Pentamerone* being the first collection containing only fairy tales, Straparola was the first author to write fairy tales in a vernacular style that made them acceptable for the educated classes (Zipes, *Happily* 17–18). Straparola's *Piacevoli Notti* (*The Pleasant Nights*) contained seventy-three *novelle*, or novellas, of which thirteen can be said to qualify as fairy tales. Among them, we can find some of the first written versions of fairy tales that are still well known, such as "Donkeyskin" / "All-Kinds-of-Fur" (called "Tebaldo and Doralice" in Straparola's collection), and "Puss in Boots" ("Constantino Fortunato"). Straparola himself is a rather mysterious figure who was only known as the author of a poetry collection published years before writing *Piacevoli Notti*, but this later work was undoubtedly popular among his contemporaries. This is evident from its translation into several languages and its influence on several major fairy-tale writers, including Basile, d'Aulnoy, Henriette-Julie de Murat, Perrault, and the Brothers Grimm. However, *Piacevoli Notti* has since fallen into relative obscurity, possibly because these tales, much like Basile's, are rife with perverse and nonconforming desires, which can be provocative for present-day audiences used to bowdlerized fairy tales. A good example is "The Pig Prince," which was retold by d'Aulnoy as "Prince Marcassin." Animal bridegroom tales like this one are staples of the genre from a present-day perspective—particularly through the popularity of "Beauty and the Beast"—but "The Pig Prince" remains a particularly shocking version of this tale type.

In the story, a royal couple longs for a son. While the queen sleeps in the garden, three fairies appear, and each bestows a gift on her and her future son. The last fairy, in the tradition of contradictory fairy characters, also curses the child to be born in the shape of a pig. The child-pig is raised as a human, but he retains many of his piggish tendencies, such as rolling in mud on any occasion. As he grows older, he begins to ask his mother, the queen, for a human wife. She finally finds him the eldest daughter of a very poor family, promising them riches in exchange for consenting to the beastly marriage. When confronted with her horrible pig husband, the new bride resolves to kill him, but the pig prince learns of her plans and brutally attacks her on their wedding night, delivering "such savage blows on the breast with his sharp hoofs that he killed her instantly" (Straparola 276). This happens again when the pig prince marries the second sister. The tale thus challenges expectations of romantic resolution after the fairy-tale wedding, instead positioning the hero as a serial killer akin to villainous Bluebeard figures. When it comes time for the third sister to marry the prince, she is not put off by his animal shape, and in fact welcomes his advances: "he got up and kissed her on the face and neck and bosom and shoulders with his tongue, [and she returned] his caresses, thereby arousing in him a warm love for her" (Straparola 277). After this encounter, the prince sheds his pig skin to reveal his true human form and the two live happily together. The heavily implied bestiality serves as the final loyalty test for the third wife. Textually, she is rewarded for her accepting nature, but she can also be read as having strange sexual appetites, which highlights the double-voiced nature of fairy tales. "The Pig Prince" thus revels in provocative desire while also serving as a prime example of arresting, surprising temporalities or queer becomings that challenge chrononormativity, as the pig child, born to human parents, eventually grows into a human man (through multiple marriages, murders, and cross-species sexual activity) and openly confounds normative development.

Another Straparola tale that invites queer readings is "Constanza / Constanzo" (or "Constanza, the Girl-Knight"), a cross-dressing maiden tale whose queer elements might be more readily recognizable as such for present-day readers. The title already anticipates some of the most obvious queer elements: a princess named Constanza disguises herself as a male knight and flees her kingdom to escape an arranged marriage she feels is below her station. Constanza, now responding to the name Constanzo, travels to a neighboring kingdom, where the king, "finding himself greatly pleased by the appearance of the youth" (Straparola 508), enlists his services as an attendant. The queen is also moved by his looks and falls in love with him immediately. However, Constanzo spurns her advances. The tale does not provide insight into how Constanza/Constanzo feels about this predicament, but the reason behind Constanza/Constanzo's rejection is that "being a woman like herself, she could not possibly satisfy the [queen's] unbridled lust"

(Straparola 509). Constanza/Constanzo thus turns the queen down due to their supposed inability to satisfy her rather than the knight's personal lack of desire, which points to somewhat more fluid boundaries in Constanza/Constanzo's sexuality. Soon after, the scorned queen convinces the king to send Constanzo away to capture a dangerous satyr, expecting Constanzo to die. Against all odds, Constanzo manages to capture the magical creature, who eventually reveals Costanzo's true identity and that many of the queen's ladies-in-waiting are actually young men. All instances of queerness and gender nonconformity are unveiled and ultimately eradicated when the king orders the queen and her cross-dressing lovers to be burned and "fixes" Constanza's fluctuating gender by marrying her.

Cross-dressing maiden-knight narratives that ultimately reassert heteropatriarchal order through the marriage plot are not uncommon in the medieval and early modern periods,[1] and, in fact, this very tale was later rewritten by both Basile ("The Three Crowns") and d'Aulnoy ("Belle-Belle ou le Chevalier Fortuné"). Furthermore, two contemporaries of d'Aulnoy, Marie-Jeanne Lhéritier and Henriette-Julie de Murat, also penned maiden-knight tales in which gender and sexuality are at least momentarily troubled. However, this tale type has failed to infiltrate the present-day fairy-tale canon, which has remained largely cisheteronormative. This might be because present-day readers will associate cross-dressing with queerness, nonconforming gender, and variant sexuality. Catherine Craft-Fairchild notes that acceptance of cross-dressing plots "dwindled as the eighteenth century drew to a close" (177).[2] This coincides with what Thomas Laqueur has identified as the evolution

1 There are numerous examples of these narratives: Thirteenth-century French romance *Silence* has a similar plot to "Constanza / Constanzo," only the princess is raised as a boy. Two *chansons de geste*, *Yde et Olive* (thirteenth century) and *Tristan de Nanteuil* (fourteenth century), also feature cross-dressing heroines, but they are magically transformed into men by the end of the story. This plot point is reminiscent of Ovid's transformation of Iphys (eighth century). There is also, famously, Viola in William Shakespeare's *Twelfth Night*, whose story presents a similar structure to Straparola's tale.

2 Cross-dressing elements at the theatrical level remained popular in the nineteenth century and beyond in fairy-tale British pantomimes, which famously revel in the carnivalesque. Pantomimes would routinely cast cross-dressing actresses to

from the "one-sex model" to that of the "two-sex model" (6). In this new model, women were not seen as a lesser version of men anymore, but instead as an opposite category of human. In Craft-Fairchild's words, this would mean that cross-dressing women would be seen as "violating the boundaries between separate spheres," and thus, as a threat rather than as attempting to climb up the "chain-of-being" (177).

Similarly to Straparola's *Piacevoli Notti*, Giambattista Basile's work is fairly unknown among contemporary audiences. However, his *Il Pentamerone: Lo Cunto de li Cunti* (*Pentamerone: The Tale of Tales*) contains the first literary examples of some of the best-loved tale types such as "Sleeping Beauty," "Rapunzel," "Cinderella," and "Hansel and Gretel." Published posthumously in five volumes between 1634 and 1636 and written in the local Neapolitan dialect instead of the learned Tuscan, its intended audience was most likely "the small courts in which [Basile] served" (Canepa, "From Court to Forest" 291). The decision to write this collection in Neapolitan can be linked to the orality of fairy tales. The tales in *Pentamerone* are narrated by old women (and one young heroine posing as an old woman), which would have furthered the illusion of orality, since old women were seen as the traditional fairy-tale storytellers. The collection is framed by a tale about Princess Zoza, whose quest is to break the fairy spell on the cursed Prince Tadeo by filling a pitcher with her tears. Exhausted from crying, Zoza falls asleep just before finishing this task. A slave girl adds the final teardrops, completing the task and claiming credit for freeing the prince, for which he marries her. Zoza then enchants the new princess to crave stories while she is pregnant, and several old women are invited to the castle to tell her tales. Zoza, disguised as one of these old women, infiltrates the palace and tells the story of the deceiving queen. This reveals the queen's real identity, and Tadeo has the queen killed by burying her from the neck down. He then marries Zoza. This tale is an amalgamation of several tale types, such as ATU 425, "The Search for the Lost Husband," and ATU 559, "Making the Princess Laugh (The Dungbeetle)," and contains elements from *The Arabian Nights*. Present-day readers may also see it as a gender-bending "Sleeping Beauty," since Zoza—a particularly active princess who takes

play the principal boy (who would seduce principal girls) and cast cross-dressing men to play the figure of the Dame (see Schacker 53–59).

on a semi-Scheherazadian role—goes on a quest to revive a passively waiting prince.

Overall, and despite the violent end of the slave girl-turned-queen, the frame tale is relatively tame compared to others in the collection. As mentioned, the first literary examples of some contemporary favorites come from *Pentamerone*, but Basile's versions are quite different from what most people have come to associate with these fairy tales. For example, the Cinderella character in "The Cinderella Cat" murders her stepmother by breaking her neck with the lid of a chest, for which she seems to feel little to no remorse. Similarly, the tale "Sun, Moon, and Talia" is a version of "Sleeping Beauty," but the eponymous Talia falls "dead to the ground" when a piece of flax gets under her fingernail, rather than simply falling asleep (Basile 414). Her distraught father abandons her body in a locked palace, where she is found by another king. The king thinks her asleep and tries to wake her up. She does not respond, but the king is so inflamed by her beauty that he carries her to bed and picks "the fruits of love" (Basile 414). As a result of this rape, Talia gives birth to twins who eventually revive her. After some trials and tribulations, she marries the rapist king. This tale presents a different challenge to chrononormativity, offering an arrested temporality to the arresting one of the "Pig Prince." In this tale, death—which forecloses narrative progression—is ephemeral, reversible, and thus disruptive of normal temporality. Moreover, the necrophiliac eroticism that often underlays sleeping beauty stories appears at the textual level, and yet by the end of the story, the deviant king slots tidily and without resistance into the hero position. It is not surprising that both the death and the ensuing rape would be omitted in versions that have remained more popular. Both Perrault and the Brothers Grimm soften the princess's death into a long magical sleep, and the German brothers—writing for a bourgeois readership—eventually include a magical reviving kiss, which is now so closely associated with the tale.

Despite the general lack of familiarity with *Pentamerone*, the collection had numerous Neapolitan editions and was translated into several languages, particularly during the nineteenth century. Even the Grimms regarded the stories as "the basis of many others" (Grimm, *Household Tales* 482). Nonetheless, by the time *Pentamerone* was published, the following stage in the development of the genre was nearing and the fairy tale was about to flourish in French literary salons. During the first years of the salon period, aristocratic and upper-class men and women gathered in literary salons to discuss manners, ideas, literature, and, most relevantly, to swap tales for entertainment. Of the *conteurs*, only Charles Perrault had any lasting significance, and his name "has become practically synonymous with the term *conte de fée*" (Zipes, *When Dreams Came True* 13). Similarly to their male counterparts, and despite their popularity during their lifetimes, most of the *conteuses* fell into obscurity after their deaths—except for d'Aulnoy, the most prolific and best-known among them, who was still being published and read well into the nineteenth century and who coined the term *conte de fée*.

It is important to note that although Perrault and the other male *conteurs* frequented these literary salons, they were eminently female spaces. All-male societies, such as the *Académie Royale des Inscriptions et Belles-Lettres* and the *Académie des Sciences*, were prolific in France during the second half of the seventeenth century. Excluding women from important intellectual networks became the norm, and one that was sanctioned by the king himself. Louis XIV had become progressively more despotic and turned to religious conservatism under the influence of his second wife, Madame de Maintenon, who, alongside François Fénelon, argued that the restoration of an aristocracy fallen into moral decline required women to "turn away from the pleasures of mondain life . . . to take on instead the duties of domesticity" (Seifert, *Fairy Tales, Sexuality, and Gender in France* 902). The literary salons thus offered an intellectually enriching haven for women who were increasingly excluded from the public sphere, and the fairy tale provided a suitable medium to express their dreams and frustrations. Their affinity for the genre is reflected in the number of fairy tales they wrote: the *conteuses* penned "two-thirds of all the fairy tales in this period" (Seifert, "Marvelous in Context" 922). This phenomenon might have to do with the fact that the fairy tale was believed to be a predominantly female genre. For example, the Abbot of Villiers contemptuously referred to it as "women's province" (qtd. in Bottigheimer, *Framed* 76), and Perrault's collection, *Histoires ou contes du temps passé* (*Histories or Tales of Times Past* 1697), had the alternative title *Contes de ma Mère l'Oye* (*Mother Goose Tales*).

At first glance, many of the tales written by women contain elements that would not surprise present-day audiences, such as fairies, beautiful princes and princesses, and plots that champion true love. However, the tales are very much a product of their time. Beneath the innocuous surface of the fairy tale, seventeenth-century writers often inserted surreptitious criticisms of court life while simultaneously validating and encouraging aristocratic modes of conduct (Teverson 88). For example, contrary to Straparola's tales, in which lower-class protagonists are commonplace, most characters in French *contes de fées* are of noble extraction. Such is the case of d'Aulnoy's tales. Marcy Farrell notes that "no peasants rise to power in these tales" (29), even though d'Aulnoy's writings do contain subversive undercurrents that challenge certain social norms. An aristocrat writing for an upper-class audience, d'Aulnoy does not seek to completely upend the status quo with respect to social class, but rather to represent alternative avenues to happiness for women like herself.

Marie-Catherine d'Aulnoy was born either in 1650 or 1651 to an aristocratic family from Normandy (Jasmin 61). Many of the details of her life are speculative, but it is known that she was married at just thirteen to a significantly older man, François de la Motte, Baron d'Aulnoy. The marriage was reportedly an unhappy one, which possibly colored some of her later writing. A dramatic turn saw d'Aulnoy involved in a plot to accuse her husband of *lese majesté*, a crime against the dignity of the king "which carried the death penalty" (A. Duggan, "d'Aulnoy" 80). Although she fled France, d'Aulnoy settled back in Paris in the 1690s, where she entered the salon scene and eventually opened her own. From her return to France until her death, d'Aulnoy enjoyed a successful literary career, writing memoirs, historical novels, and, of course, fairy tales.

Her first fairy tale is also the first literary fairy tale to be published in France. It appeared in 1690 as part of her popular novel, *L'Histoire d'Hypolite, comte de Duglas* (*The History of Hipolytus, Earl of Douglas*). "L'Île de la Félicité" ("The Island of Happiness" or "The Island of Felicity") features a protofeminist, all-female island that remains untouched until Russian prince Adolphe convinces the gentle wind, Zephyr, to carry him over to the hidden world. The tale presents a utopian society free of men, where learned women coexist under the peaceful rule of the fairy princess, Félicité. This peace is disrupted by Adolphe's arrival, as he and Félicité fall instantly in love, and Adolphe enjoys the pleasures of the island for 300 years. Adolphe breaks away from this arrested temporality when he realizes he has not accomplished anything in his life in terms of heroic deeds. He leaves the island to search for military glory, only to be caught and killed by Father Time. When she learns of his death, Félicité, heartbroken, closes the doors of her palace forever. The tale ends on a bleak note that reveals the fragility of love, particularly when faced with the demands of chrononormativity.

After "L'Île de la Félicité," d'Aulnoy developed a taste for fairy tales and went on to publish many more: *Les contes de fées* (*Tales of the Fairies* 1697) contained four volumes of fairy tales, and so did her second collection, *Contes nouveaux ou les fées à la mode* (*New Tales, or the Fashionable Fairies* 1698). Her stories are generally characterized by the pursuit of true love, which might seem conservative to present-day readers. However, as Marina Warner notes, women were often forced into loveless marriages, and the fact that some of the *conteuses*' tales championed the freedom to choose a lover demonstrates that "the French wonder tale was fighting for social emancipation and change" (*Wonder Tales* 9). d'Aulnoy also tends to place relatively complex female characters at the center of the action: fairies that resemble powerful courtiers and thus can use their powers for good or evil, cruel or benevolent queens, and beautiful princesses who are not always submissively virtuous. For instance, in her tale "Finette Cendron," the Cinderella character, while resembling other passive Cinderellas, also violently decapitates an ogress in the middle of the tale. In "La Princesse Belle-Étoile et le Prince Chéri," a tale of hidden noble identities, we find a protagonist who first falls in love with a character she thinks is her brother (the beautiful Prince Chéri, who is actually her cousin), and is later tasked with saving him and her two biological brothers, thus positioning her as the chivalric hero within the story. The three men fail to retrieve a magical bird with the ability to reveal their real heritage, but Belle-Étoile, cross-dressed as a knight, manages to save them all, restore them to wealth, and marry Chéri.

Such cross-dressing tales allow the exploration of female power fantasies in exclusively male contexts or roles, but much like in previous Italian tales, they also open gaps that invite queer interrogation. For instance, d'Aulnoy's "Belle-Belle ou le Chevalier Fortuné" ("Belle-Belle or the Knight Fortuné")—most likely a retelling of Straparola's "Constanza / Constanzo"—is a particularly interesting tale in terms of gender and sexual non-normativity. Unlike "Constanza / Constanzo," "Belle-Belle" features three extraordinary noblewomen rather than just the one, who in this case cross-dress to fill in for their elderly father, who is called to present himself before the king. Each sister is more virtuous and skilled in traditionally male areas than the last, but the two elder sisters refuse to help a fairy in disguise on their way to the castle. The fairy shouts out to them "Good-bye, disguised beauty!"—thus making them believe they are not able to pass for men, which forces them to turn around and forfeit the ruse (d'Aulnoy 175). The youngest sister thinks herself better suited for the task since she is taller and better at riding and hunting, but it is her kindness toward the fairy that ultimately allows her to succeed. The fairy rewards her good deed with magical gifts: an enchanted talking horse that can see the future and a disappearing chest filled with beautiful garments, swords, and gold. With the help of this disguise, Belle-Belle, now responding to Fortuné, both passes for a man and becomes the most exceptional knight in the realm. He proves himself to be the bravest, the most loyal, the best at jousting and hunting, and the best-looking: "'Have you ever seen a cavalier more handsome, better built, or more handsomely dressed?' they cried out" (d'Aulnoy 178). Fortuné is only revealed to be a woman at the very end, when he is falsely accused of attempting to rape the queen and is swiftly sentenced to death: "The guards tear open his beautiful robe and, without the protective layers of well-chosen clothing, Belle-Belle's 'alabaster bosom' is uncovered" (d'Aulnoy 204). Gender is as fluid as in "Constanza / Constanzo," but "Belle-Belle" delves deeper into the psychological depths of the cross-dressing protagonist. In the tale, Fortuné is uncomfortable with the amount of female attention he gets both from ladies at court and from the queen herself, but he does not mind it when he becomes the king's "beloved favorite" (d'Aulnoy, "Belle-Belle" 204):

> He had become very appreciative of the king's merits and became more attached to him than he had wanted. "What's my fate" he said. "I love a great king without any hope of his loving me. Nor will he ever know what I'm suffering." (185)

The pronouns and names referring to Fortuné remain male while the protagonist is wearing his male attire. Thus, the previous excerpt could read like a gay man's love confession, including the angst over apparent sexual incompatibility. There is room to read Belle-Belle/Fortuné as a transman, although a genderfluid interpretation might fit better here: after all, the protagonist is comfortable living as a woman, but is also willing to remain a man forever, and Belle-Belle/Fortuné performs both genders with equal dexterity and ease. At the end of this particularly queer journey, Belle-Belle/Fortuné marries the king, like Constanza/Constanzo, which similarly fixes Belle-Belle's gender identity presumably for good.

d'Aulnoy and other women writers used the realm of the fairy tale as a metaphorical extension of their salons, in which they could explore power fantasies in "idealized feudal and matriarchal worlds," while Charles Perrault imbued his tales with bourgeois sensibility and used the fairy tale to settle literary, political, and ideological disputes (A. Duggan, "Feminine Genealogy" 200). Born in 1628 to a bourgeois family, Perrault grew up surrounded by like-minded people, became involved in courtly and bureaucratic life, and gained recognition as a poet when he composed odes to Louis XIV and his reign. He was also involved in one of the most intense literary debates of his time. The *Querelle des Anciens et des Modernes* (*Quarrel of the Ancients and the Moderns*) pitted the Ancients, who contended writers should imitate classical authors, against the Moderns, who contrarily praised the writers of the century of Louis XIV. The Moderns were led by Perrault, who questioned the necessity to imitate classical authors and their genres following two main strategies: first, he "conflated scientific progress with literary and artistic progress to argue for the superiority of the Moderns" (A. Duggan, "Perrault" 739), and second, he considered women to be the gauge for literary judgment. Perrault maintained that women possessed an innate good taste that allowed for the recognition of artistic quality and that the Ancients' insistence on erudition was "a form of exclusion, a self-interest on the control of literary judgments" (Seifert, "Storyteller's Voice" 16).

In fact, Perrault's fairy tales can be seen as conscious, modern reworkings of fables, which Ancients like La Fontaine valued for their classical and "immutable superiority" (Seifert "Storyteller's Voice" 15). While *conteuses* like d'Aulnoy wrote long, novella-like tales, Perrault wrote concise tales closed by morals, thus structurally likening them to fables. Perrault, however, believed his fairy tales were morally superior to fables because they were polished versions of the peasant's old wives' tales (Seifert, "Storyteller's Voice" 14). Indeed, the fairy tale seems like the natural choice of genre for a Modern like Perrault. After all, women—able to recognize artistic value through an innate, non-erudite quality—were seen as the primary storytellers in the form of old wives and governesses, as well as the main audience for fairy tales.

Perrault's use of the fairy tale had other effects beyond furthering a literary feud. He wrote eleven different fairy tales in his life: "Sleeping Beauty," "Little Red Riding Hood," "Bluebeard," "Puss in Boots," "Cinderella," "Riquet with the Tuft," "Little Thumbling," "Griselidis," "The Ridiculous Wishes," "Donkeyskin," and "The Fairies." Since at least half of them have entered the contemporary fairy-tale canon (albeit with some modifications due in part to Disney's early adaptations of his tales), it is unsurprising that Perrault's take on gender roles should become seemingly intrinsic to the fairy tale. However, his representations of gender are personal and highly dependent on context. For example, when it came to his male characters, Perrault favored representations of men inspired by the *bourgeoisie*: intrepid male characters were the heroes of tales such as "Little Thumbling" and "Puss in Boots," and they often succeeded thanks to their superior intellect, eloquence, and diligent spirit. These characteristics are nowhere to be found among Perrault's female characters. As Seifert maintains, "Perrault's appropriation of the peasant and the salon female communities in his tales does not affirm the status of women in society" ("Storyteller's Voice" 17). Quite the opposite: Perrault constructs his ideal woman through his tales, revealing that this ideal woman should be beautiful, gracious, helpless, submissive, and exceedingly passive. Perrault often writes heroines whose saintlike patience is eventually rewarded within the narrative and later lauded in the paternalistic moral. Moreover, his versions of some tale types are almost completely stripped of female agency, such as his Cinderella character who, unlike d'Aulnoy's or Basile's, does not indulge in violent rebellion. Some heroines stray from the narrow moral path Perrault delineates, but they are swiftly punished: Little Red Riding Hood is devoured by the wolf, and Bluebeard's wife's curiosity proves almost fatal—and would have, were it not for her brothers, who save her at the last minute.

Perrault's tales may seem antithetical to non-normativity and subversiveness, as they are so attached to what we could consider traditional gender roles and strict morality. Nonetheless, his "Sleeping

Beauty," although not as disturbing as Basile's "Sun, Moon, and Talia," still presents evident interruptions to chrononormativity that invite queer readings (see Seifert, "Queer Time" 27–29). Furthermore, while Perrault did not write any cross-dressing maiden tales—the tale type that most obviously lends itself to queer interpretations—he did introduce the most recognizable cross-dresser in fairy-tale history into the canon: Little Red Riding Hood's wolf. He is a murderous villain who is seductive and deadly to both grandmother and granddaughter and who, by impersonating the human grandmother, violates both male/female and human/animal boundaries. As such, he anticipates the queer monster archetype that will become popular and will be queerly appropriated from the twentieth century onward, as we will see in chapter 3. Beyond this, Perrault's morals often offer contradictory and ambiguous readings. For example, "Cinderella" placed great emphasis on her dresses—fairy gifts that allowed her to charm the prince, much like Belle-Belle's superior garments had charmed the women at court. However, the first moral seems to contradict the fairy tale: "it's kindness more than dress / That can win a man's heart with greater success" (Perrault 454). This first moral is then contradicted by a second one: "It is undoubtedly a great advantage / To have wit . . . and other worthwhile talents . . . but all of these might prove useless . . . without godfathers or godmothers" (Perrault 454). These multivocal messages can complicate interpretation and open the tales up to irony.

Perrault's tales and fairy-tale model remained enormously popular in the following centuries, with multiple reprints and countless adaptations, even if the potential for ambiguity was often downplayed as the tales were adapted into different formats or edited upon reissue or translation. The Grimms regarded his stories as the most beautiful among the French tales, and quite unfairly referred to d'Aulnoy as Perrault's "inferior imitator" (Grimm, qtd. in Harries 22). From a present-day perspective, it may seem like d'Aulnoy lived in Perrault's shadow, as she is considerably less well known. However, her tales were still translated and reprinted for a long time after her death. Besides enduring popularity in France, many of her writings were extremely popular during the eighteenth century in England. d'Aulnoy was still known for her fairy tales in the nineteenth century, although they circulated in different formats, such as chapbooks or individual tales, often under different names and stripped of their historical context (M. Palmer 230–50). During the eighteenth century, the genre's "aristocratic roots" were progressively forgotten as the fairy tale shifted toward the "complex of bourgeois Christian values" that would become central to nineteenth-century literature for children (Seifert, "Fairy Tales of France" 181).

The Golden Age of Fairy Tales: Brothers Grimm, Hans Christian Andersen, and the Nineteenth-Century Imagination

The nineteenth century was a particularly fertile period for European fairy tales. At the time, a sense of urgency brought about by an increasingly urban and literate population inspired several folklorists to collect an oral tradition that was perceived as endangered, sometimes also encouraged by their nationalist agenda. In Russia, for instance, Alexander Afanasyev collected 600 Russian folktales and fairy tales, and Peter Christen Asbjørnsen and Jørgen Engebretsen Moe collected their *Norwegian Folktales* in the wake of Norway's independence. Undoubtedly, these folklorists and many others were modeling themselves after the Brothers Grimm, whose 1812 fairy-tale collection *Kinder- und Hausmärchen* (*Children's and Household Tales*) was a part of their project to recover a common national heritage for German-speaking people. Following in the steps of these popular collections, many writers offered their own interpretations, sometimes drawing from old folktales or making use of fairy-tale motifs to fashion new ones. Such is the case of writers like George MacDonald, Lewis Carroll, Oscar Wilde, and, of course, Hans Christian Andersen—a key writer who, with the Brothers Grimm and Perrault, was instrumental in establishing the twentieth- and twenty-first-century fairy-tale canon.

Jacob and Wilhelm Grimm were born in Hanau in 1785 and 1786, respectively, and grew up in a Calvinist family that would ensure they "set high moral standards for themselves" (Zipes, *Enchanted Forests* 2). They attended a high school in Kassel alongside children of aristocratic families, an experience that both drew them closer and made them "acutely aware of class injustice and exploitation" (Zipes, *Enchanted Forests* 3). The memory of an idyllic, pastoral childhood, as well as the middle-class ideals of labor and betterment instilled in them by their family later informed their fairy tales. Once at the University of Marburg, the Grimms, now law students, became protégés of Professor Friedrich Karl von Savigny, through whom they would meet Clemens Brentano and Achim von Arnim. Brentano and Arnim were involved in a burgeoning Romantic movement that campaigned to unify Germany by establishing a common cultural heritage. Arnim and Brentano encouraged the brothers to start collecting German tales, an endeavor that eventually culminated in the publication of the Grimms' *Children's and Household Tales*.

The Brothers Grimm made a distinction between oral and literary fairy tales and claimed that the tales they collected in *Children's and Household Tales* were spontaneous creations, relayed to them by "illiterate or semi-literate peasants" (Stein). Their intention was to capture the true national spirit of the German folk by preserving traditional tales. The distinction between oral tales and literary fairy tales was made to set their collection apart from other, less authentic contemporary collections. Folklore was thus equated with authenticity, authenticity with orality, and orality with the purest form of fairy tales. However, scholarship shows that their informants were mostly middle-class or aristocratic friends: well-read women like the Wild sisters and the Hassenpflug sisters contributed many tales.[3] Even Dorothea Viehman, the only informant they mentioned and who was characterized as "a peasant woman" was most likely a middle-class woman of Huguenot descent (Hettinga 139). Moreover, the brothers subjected their collection to an intense editing process: instead of just transcribing the tales, they would often make modifications in content and style. Indeed, from 1812 to 1857 there were seven editions of *Children's and Household Tales*, "each one different from the last, until the final, best-known version barely resembled the first" (Zipes, "Saved"). As a result, the Grimm tales are regarded less as the product of oral tradition and more as "a historical phenomenon that documents the appropriation of oral tradition" by middle-class literary

---

3 Although this reaches beyond the scope of this chapter, it must be noted that German-speaking women were not only oral tellers of fairy tales but also writers. See Shawn C. Jarvis and Jeannine Blackwell's 2001 anthology *The Queen's Mirror: Fairy Tales by German Women, 1780–1900*, or Julie L. J. Koehler, Shandi Lynne Wagner, Anne E. Duggan, and Adrion Dula's 2021 anthology *Women Writing Wonder*.

men for the sake of constructing a coherent nationalist myth (Haase, "Framing" 61).

Over the years, the brothers added and removed tales according to several factors. For example, tales like "Puss in Boots" and "Bluebeard" were removed from the collection because they were derived from Perrault's versions and were thus considered to be too French. Other tales were removed for being too gruesome, such as "How Some Children Played at Slaughtering," a tale with two versions in which children murder their playmate. However, some tales that included instances of violent justice were left in: villains in "Cinderella" and "Snow White," for instance, are brutally punished—Cinderella's birds peck out the evil stepsisters' eyes, and the Evil Queen is made to dance to death while wearing red-hot iron shoes. Who the villains were in the story was also not incidental. The editing process worked to progressively exculpate father figures and shift the blame onto female characters. "Hansel and Gretel" includes an example of this: in the 1810 manuscript of the story, the mother convinces the father to abandon their children in the forest to avoid starvation, and, in subsequent editions, the *step*mother is increasingly cruel and the father increasingly reluctant and caring. More egregious still are the collection's antisemitic representations. In the story "The Jew in the Brambles," the protagonist uses a magic violin to torture a Jewish man, making him dance in a thorny underbrush. This attack is completely unprovoked, but it is later legitimized by the narrative when the Jewish man is discovered to be a thief and is hanged for it. Shockingly, the Grimms thought this tale to be so relevant that they included it in the small edition of 1825, which contained only fifty tales and was intended for children.

Not all the brother's editorial choices would be so appalling or foreign to present-day audiences. The Brothers Grimm cultivated a distinct literary style that removed the specifics of time, place, and narrator to make their stories more universal; they turned cruel mothers into more palatable evil stepmothers and misbehaving fairies into witches. They also consistently weeded out sexual elements from the tales. For example, "The Master Hunter," which was relayed to the Grimms by Viehman, featured a princess sleeping naked in a tower and a protagonist who rapes and impregnates her. Reminiscent of Basile's "Sun, Moon, and Talia," this story was relegated to the notes section in the second edition, and the tale that substituted it featured "a fully clothed princess and a young man who stands as a model of restraint and decorum" instead (Tatar, *Hard Facts* 7). Earlier versions of tales were generally shorter, less polished, and considerably more ambiguous (and strange) as a result, whereas the heavily edited versions are more homogenous and straightforward.

This is not to say that the resulting edited versions were free of queer undertones.[4] For instance, "The Frog King, or Iron Heinrich" (yet another tale of animal husbands and arresting queer temporalities) contains, beyond the well-known plot of the transformed frog, a coda-like section in which the king's faithful servant is given surprising importance. He is both the only character with a name, highlighting his relevance, and the only one whose feelings are described with intensity: he is said to have placed iron bands around his heart when the king was transformed "to keep it from bursting in grief and sorrow" (Grimm "The Frog King, or Iron Heinrich"). Heinrich's attachment to the king far surpasses that of his wife, the princess, who is scarcely mentioned. In fact, the tale's closing lines center on the depth of Heinrich's queer devotion:

> The prince heard a cracking sound and thought that the carriage was breaking apart, but it was the bands springing from faithful Heinrich's heart because his master was now redeemed and happy. (Grimm "The Frog King, or Iron Heinrich")

Thus, heterosexual love—which presumably stands at the center of the tale—is secondary in intensity to Heinrich's queer affections in this significant tale, which the Grimms placed first in their collection across all editions. Moreover, ending the tale by placing the focus on Heinrich's

4 Joosen notes that "in a few rare instances, critics have attributed Jacob Grimm's lifelong bachelor status to suppressed homosexuality" (111), but this has not significantly impacted readings of the Grimms' fairy tales. This might be due to the collaborative nature of the collection and the fact that Wilhelm was the main brother in charge of editing the tales, which could have obscured any personal, queer traces inserted by Jacob. At the time of writing, however, this is only conjecture, and Jacob's possible queerness (which would also include asexuality, not just homo- or bisexuality) is not as visible in the brothers' collection as Andersen's is in his tales, as will be discussed later.

love for the king suggests that this reunion is the true "happy ending," rather than the (mentioned only in passing) heterosexual union. When examined, the tale challenges genre-specific heterocentric expectations.

Cross-dressing tales can also be found in the Grimms' collection, even though, as previously noted, cross-dressing narratives were comparatively less well-received by the nineteenth century, as ideas about gender categorization were shifting and female transvestites elicited increasing unease due to their "sexual and social ambiguity" (Craft-Fairchild 178). An example of this tale type is tale number 67 of the seventh edition, "The King with the Lion," also called "The Twelve Huntsmen," which, like other tales discussed in this chapter, involves cross-dressing women—twelve of them, to be precise. Interestingly, this tale begins where so many other fairy tales end: a prince and a princess are in love and about to get married. Before that can happen, the prince's father, on his deathbed, makes the prince promise to marry a different princess of his choosing. When the prince becomes king, he summons the princess his father wanted him to marry. His first fiancée, waiting for him in her kingdom with only a ring to remember him by, hears the news and asks her father to provide her with her eleven maidens who look exactly like herself. All twelve women then dress as huntsmen and ride to the palace, where the princess asks her former bridegroom for a position for all of them. The king does not recognize her, but "because they were such handsome people, he gladly granted the request and welcomed them to his court" (Grimm, *Household Tales* 223). Just like in Straparola's "Constanza / Constanzo," the king is swayed by the cross-dressers' looks, which could indicate queer desire. Also like in Straparola's tale, there is a truth-telling magical creature—in this case a lion—who alerts the king of the women's deception: "You believe you've employed twelve hunters, but they're actually twelve young women" (Grimm, *Household Tales* 224). The lion then instructs the king to put them through foolproof tests to reveal their true identities: he tells him to spread peas on the floor (women's steps would be too light to crush them), and to display spinning wheels in the room (since women would supposedly find them irresistible). Both tests fail because a servant overhears and tells the hunters, who step firmly on the peas and manage to stop themselves from inspecting the spinning wheels. The princess is only discovered because she faints when she hears her beloved's new fiancée is on her way. The tale concludes with the cross-dressing princess and her king in a traditional heteronormative marriage. However, it must be noted that the women in the tale, much like in d'Aulnoy's "Belle-Belle or the Knight Fortuné," perform extraordinarily well as men—so much so that only a magical creature is able to see through their deception. Thus, such representations reveal male/female and man/woman as permeable rather than hermetic categories, and these categories as performatively constructed, following Butler's understanding of gender as something we do, "something that one becomes—but can never be" (*Gender Trouble* 143). In other words, this tale, as well as the other cross-dressing tales analyzed in this chapter, depicts gender as a ritual action rather than an ontological category, and these maiden-knights as particularly apt at acting out their different genders.

Inspired by the economic success of their translated collection into English, which was bowdlerized, illustrated, and intended for children, the brothers released the *Kleine Ausgabe*, or "small edition," in 1825. This small edition, designed to be more marketable, featured a selection of fifty stories illustrated by their brother, Ludwig Grimm. This edition, while not as successful as the English translation, paved the way for fairy tales to enter "the middle-class nursery as sanctioned texts," thus completing the transformation of the fairy tale into a genre for children (Teverson 113). Indeed, it is around the same time when Hans Christian Andersen began writing fairy tales: in 1835 he would publish his first collection *Eventyr, fortalte for Boern* (*Fairy Tales, Told for Children*). His oeuvre ranged from novels to travel writing and from poetry to plays, but nothing would be as well remembered or as instrumental to the advancement of children's literature as his four fairy-tale collections.

Andersen intimately identified with fairy-tale characters, as demonstrated by the title of his second memoir: *Mit Livs Eventyr* (*The Fairy Tale of My Life*, 1855). He was born in 1805 to a poor family in Odense, Denmark, and decided to travel to Copenhagen as an adolescent to try various artistic pursuits with little luck. Despite multiple setbacks, Andersen was tireless in his pursuit of fame and success, and his determination "eventually did make an impression on various philanthropic gentlemen" (Zipes, *Misunderstood Storyteller* 6). Thanks to their patronage, he was able to attend ballet school and take singing lessons, but it soon became obvious to everyone that he was not meant for the stage. Even his first attempts at writing were a failure—one of his patrons, Jonas Collin, who would become a father figure to him, insisted Andersen required further schooling (Zipes, *Misunderstood Storyteller* 6). Collin sent seventeen-year-old Andersen to a school in Slagelse and put him in a class with eleven-year-olds. His schooling was a precondition to joining the Collin family, and, although he finally managed to pass the university admission test, he would remember his school years as some of the darkest of his life (Sorensen 167).

When he first started writing fairy tales in 1835, Andersen often reworked traditional folk tales by adding his own artistic flair. Such is the case of "Little Claus and Big Claus" or "The Princess and the Pea," which he first heard "from his grandmother in the spinning room at the Odense asylum" (Wullschlager 144). Even when he moved on to write original fairy tales, his debt to the oral tradition was evident. As he wrote to Henriette Hank in 1835: "I have started some 'Fairy Tales Told for Children' and I feel I have succeeded . . . [I] have written them exactly the way I would tell them to a *child*" (qtd. in Wullschlager 144, emphasis in original). His style is markedly different from that of the Brothers Grimm. Whereas the Grimms regularly used conventional "Once upon a time"-like structures, Andersen's style was more direct and spontaneous, as in the opening of "The Tinderbox:" "A soldier came marching down the road: Left . . . right! Left . . . right!" (Andersen 1). To present-day readers, this might not seem in any way extraordinary, but that is because children's literature has followed in Andersen's trail:

> We accept imaginative, anarchist stories as the basis of all good children's books . . . But when Andersen wrote his first fairy tales, children's books were not expected to be about enjoyment: they were usually formal, improving texts which highlighted a moral and were meant to educate, not amuse, young readers. (Wullschlager 145)

Understandably, Andersen faced considerable criticism at the time of publication. Reviewers deemed his tales unacceptably informal and borderline immoral for children. However, readers had no such qualms: the collection sold well and was quickly translated into several languages, expanding its reach well beyond Denmark's borders (Teverson 121).

Andersen was keenly aware of the fact that he personified the modern narrative of upward social mobility. In 1844, he wrote to Edvard Collin: "Twenty-five years ago . . . I arrived with my small parcel in Copenhagen, a poor stranger of a boy, and today I have drank chocolate with the Queen" (qtd. in Wullschlager 1). Though successful, Andersen remained forever ambivalent about his split identity and never felt at ease in his own skin. Feeling like an outsider is a recurring theme in Andersen's fairy tales, which are often told through the eyes of the dispossessed, the neglected, and the innocent—usually children. Although Andersen did not seek to surround himself with children and remained unmarried and childless his whole life, this focus could have stemmed from his own childish disposition. As contemporary critic Georg Brandes remarked: "Indeed, he did become a great man. But he did not become a man. There was not the slightest glimmer of manliness in the soul of this child" (Brandes 104). Andersen exorcised other personal demons through his tales: he poured his many insecurities about his physical appearance[5] into his semi-autobiographical animal fable, "The Ugly Duckling." Furthermore, Maria Nikolajeva notes that the tale is "a poignant account of the road from humiliation through suffering to well-deserved bliss," which echoes Andersen's famous quote: "First you must endure a lot, then you get famous" (Nikolajeva, "Andersen" 14). Scholars, nonetheless, tend to become entangled in another issue that colored Andersen's writing and caused him much anguish: his sexuality.

The mystery of Anderson's sexuality has been the subject of ongoing discussion among academics since at least 1901, when a Danish writer first brought the topic up in a German magazine (D.C. Frank and J. Frank 11). Yet, there is no consensus. In *The Life of a Storyteller*, Wullschlager details his (likely not consummated) love for various men and women. Zipes considers that Wullschlager spends too much time "trying to prove his homosexuality" and notes that biographers such as Bredsdorff or the Franks deny he was gay (*Misunderstood Storyteller* 143). The Franks

---

5 His issues with his self-image (and other aspects of his life) are well documented in Andersen's personal diaries and much of his correspondence, all of which have been preserved. For example, Jackie Wullschlager's biography, *Hans Christian Andersen: The Life of a Storyteller* (2001), makes extensive use of them.

write that "the only evidence [for his homosexuality] comes from a literal reading of the . . . overheated language of the nineteenth century," only to later add: "As an older man, [Andersen] was occasionally infatuated with men as well as women . . . but Andersen's virginity . . . remained intact" (D.C. Frank and J. Frank 11). In my view, this back-and-forth is only sustainable because of a strictly binary understanding of sexuality and the misconception that if desires are not physically acted upon, they are not indicative of sexuality—particularly, of course, when that sexuality is nonconforming. This recalls Sedgwick's sarcastic enumeration of reasons why queerness is elided or disregarded when discussing historical figures, and which includes the following points:

> 1. Passionate language of same-sex attraction was extremely common during whatever period is under discussion—and therefore must have been completely meaningless. Or . . .
> 7. There is no actual proof of homosexuality, such as sperm taken from the body of another man or a nude photograph with another woman—so the author may be assumed to have been ardently and exclusively heterosexual. (*Epistemology* 52–53)

Despite the heated conversations about Andersen's sexuality, at least one of his tales is consistently read in relation to queerness: *The Little Mermaid*. A sentimental tale about unrequited love written in 1837, *The Little Mermaid* is perhaps one of the best-known tales for children, which was further canonized by Disney's 1989 adaptation. The eponymous mermaid is fascinated by the human world but must wait until she is fifteen to go to the surface. Once she is of age, the little mermaid visits the surface, saves a prince's life after a storm, and instantly falls in love with him. She then learns about the concept of immortal souls. As her grandmother explains to her, a mermaid can live up to 300 years, but "when we die, we shall never rise again" (Andersen 66). In contrast, humans have souls that live eternally. Since the only way for a mermaid to gain a soul is to marry a human, the mermaid becomes fixated on marrying the prince. The motif of the pagan mermaid versus the Christian prince had already been used by writers like Fouqué and Goethe, but Andersen toned down the religious themes and highlighted the mermaid's self-sacrifice and suffering instead. This is particularly evident when the mermaid visits the sea witch to get her legs, the process of which is described in minute and gruesome detail:

> I will mix you a potion . . . Your tail will divide and shrink, until it becomes what human beings call "pretty legs." It will hurt; it will feel as if a sword were going through your body. All who see you will say that you are the most beautiful child they have ever seen. You will walk more gracefully than any dancer; but every time your foot touches the ground, it will feel as though you were walking on knives so sharp that your blood must flow. If you are willing to suffer all this, then I can help you. (Andersen 68)

As payment, the sea witch cuts out the mermaid's tongue, and so she enters the human world—desperate, disabled, and in excruciating pain. This story, generally considered to contain several autobiographical elements, has been interpreted as a tale about the sacrifices a lower-class person must endure to access close-knit upper-class circles (Zipes, *Misunderstood Storyteller* 36–38). It has also been argued that it is a misogynistic tale that demonstrates Andersen's fear of female sexuality, "and a desire to counteract that fear by promoting self-sacrifice and silent suffering as ideals for female behavior" (Teverson 126). However, it must be noted that Andersen would often identify with his female characters, and Wullschlager reads *The Little Mermaid* as a response to the wedding of Henriette Thyberg to Edvard Collin, with whom Andersen was in love. Edvard Collin is thus cast as the selfish prince who marries another despite the mermaid's adoration. "This is surely how Andersen identified with the tale," Wullschlager writes, "allying himself in his bisexuality to the mermaid's sense of being a different species to humankind" (167). Wullschlager also notes that the little mermaid has long been considered a homoerotic character (167), and it is certainly a tale that resonated with Wilde, who wrote *The Fisherman and His Soul* in 1891 as a response. Indeed, *The Little Mermaid* has the power to resonate with a transhistorical queer experience, as it is a tale of unrequited love and longing; of otherness and the search for identity; and of infiltrating a repressive society from the margins—but ultimately failing as an unassimilable outsider.

Tellingly, Andersen's tale ends sadly, with the mermaid sacrificing herself rather than killing her prince.

Beyond purely autobiographical interpretations, the tale allows for a multiplicity of readings. The mermaid is a liminal figure as a monstrous half-human and half-fish whose very existence disrupts culturally established gender and sexual binaries. Furthermore, although beautiful and feminine from the waist up, the mermaid possesses an "impenetrable tail" that prevents her participation into normative, heterosexual economies (K. Simpson 58). She is also a character who, following in the footsteps of other transformation-inclined figures in fairy tales, challenges chrononormative development and exemplifies the genre's penchant for queer becomings. Unlike earlier fairy-tale characters, the mermaid reveals much more interiority, allowing for more complex readings. Leland Spencer finds parallels between the transspecies fairy tale and the performance of transgender identity. His interpretation is particularly suggestive when it comes to the mermaid's body-related dysphoria: "Despite the cost and the pain, the mermaid chooses to change her body to enable the identity performance she desires," is an idea further underscored at the end of the story, when the mermaid gives up her "life rather than returning to a body that feels wrong to her" (Spencer 117–18). Transgender people, particularly children, have often identified with the transspecies mermaid. As a testament to this, the leading organization in the United Kingdom for transgender and gender-diverse children and teens is called Mermaids.

Andersen wrote many other fairy tales that have since become children's classics, such as "The Emperor's New Clothes" and "The Snow Queen."[6] By 1843, however, he was writing for a mixed audience, "remembering the Father and Mother often listen, and you must also give them

6 This is another fairy tale with considerable queer potential. For example, Greenhill has investigated how the underlying queerness in "The Snow Queen" has been translated to the screen (see Greenhill "'The Snow Queen': Queer Coding in Male Directors' Films," and "Team Snow Queen"). Furthermore, Disney's *Frozen*'s (2013) equivalent to the Snow Queen, Elsa, has been read as queer, and her song, "Let It Go," has been interpreted as a coming out anthem both by conservative detractors and by LGBTQI supporters. T. Kingfisher's 2016 novel *The Raven and the Reindeer* offered a lesbian retelling of the fairy tale.

something for their own minds" (Andersen, qtd. in Wullschlager 228). This approach was imitated by authors like Carroll and Wilde, and by others in the twentieth century like C. S. Lewis and Philip Pullman, whose book *Northern Lights* clearly echoes "The Snow Queen" (Teverson 124).

Both the Brothers Grimm and Andersen have left an indelible mark on the fairy tale, and they have certainly shaped present-day perceptions of the genre, particularly across Europe and North America. Their fairy tales are still being translated and printed in collections for children, although often with numerous amendments so that the resulting product is an adapted, sanitized version that often omits the context and forgoes the nuances of the pretexts. This simplification and alteration trend continues into the realm of film, where adaptations, notably by Disney, have significantly influenced the reconstruction of the fairy-tale genre:

> [T]he film adaptations of the classical tales by Andersen as well as those by Brothers Grimm and Charles Perrault have become better known than the classical texts, which, in comparison, have virtually lost their meanings due to the fact that the films have replaced them (Zipes, *Misunderstood Storyteller* 104).

However popular these adaptations are and however many misconceptions they may have spread about the genre, it would be a mistake to think that the adaptations completely annul their pretexts. As future chapters reveal, many twentieth and twenty-first century readers and writers find a gateway in these films, through which a breadcrumb trail leads back to Andersen, the Brothers Grimm, Perrault, and other foundational storytellers.

Fairy Tales for Modern Times: Disney, Feminist Retellings, and the Advent of Queer Fairy Tales

The twentieth century was a prolific period for fairy tales, comparable to previous golden ages, such as those in seventeenth-century France and nineteenth-century Germany. Technological developments—especially cinema, but also the internet—only contributed to the spread, globalization and institutionalization of fairy tales, particularly as a genre for children. As Seifert notes, "[b]eyond the continued production of . . . tales for children, without doubt the most important development was the appearance of The Walt Disney Company's fairy-tale film, which reshaped cultural expectations for the genre" (Seifert, "Sex, Sexuality" 851). These Disney-influenced "cultural expectations" have to do with form, content, and ideology, and are upheld to this day. In other words: Disney's fairy-tale films have greatly contributed to notions about what a fairy tale looks like, how it should develop, and what morals underlie each story.

In the 1970s, after Disney had already released three of its fairy-tale films to international success, this underlying ideology came under scrutiny. In 1970, Alison Lurie wrote "Fairy Tale Liberation," in which she claims that fairy tales are the source of strong female characters who could serve as role models for children. This elicited a rebuttal from Marcia R. Lieberman. Her article, "Some Day My Prince Will Come: Female Acculturation through the Fairy Tale" (1972) directly addresses the influence Disney had on popularizing a fairy-tale corpus that perpetuates harmful stereotypes for women (Lieberman 283–84). According to Haase, this debate worked as the seed for modern-day fairy-tale studies ("Feminist Fairy-Tale Scholarship" 15–16). In the space between the publication of Lurie's and Lieberman's texts, Anne Sexton published *Transformations* (1971). Sexton's collection, which contained a few Grimm tales rewritten as poetry, kickstarted a trend to retell fairy tales from a feminist perspective. This practice blossomed at the fringes of mainstream culture and inspired contemporary writers such as Angela Carter and Margaret Atwood. It also influenced following generations of fairy-tale creators and further shaped the emerging field of fairy-tale studies. Queer retellings appeared at the same time as feminist retellings, albeit more discreetly. However, they did not immediately gain the same degree of traction among writers or scholars as feminist retellings did, and they became significant in number and relevance only in the mid-1990s (a phenomenon that is more deeply explored in chapter 2). Nonetheless, this section explores early queer retellings, as they serve as an appropriate bookend to a twentieth century filled with saccharine, conservative fairy tales and countercultural reactions to them.

In 1937, Disney released *Snow White and the Seven Dwarfs*, which was based on the Grimms' version of the tale. Its early success marked the beginning of a lifelong love story between the company and fairy tales. To this day, The Walt Disney Company has released a total of nine animated films directly inspired by fairy tales: *Snow White* (1937), *Cinderella* (1950), *Sleeping Beauty* (1959), *The Little Mermaid* (1989), *Beauty and the Beast* (1991), *Aladdin* (1992), *The Princess and the Frog* (2009), *Tangled* (2010) and *Frozen* (2013). Several other Disney films are based on fairy-tale-like narratives, such as *Pinocchio* (1940) or *Peter Pan* (1953), and, perhaps more interestingly, some stories, myths, and legends have been widely relabeled as fairy tales as a result of Disney's magic touch. In this way, the legends of King Arthur and Hua Mulan[7] are routinely referred to as fairy tales, and revisions of both are often included in collections of fairy-tale retellings.[8]

Apart from the connection between Disney and fairy tales, there is also an undeniable connection between Disney and childhood, which has indirectly furthered the association between childhood and fairy tales. Known popularly as "Uncle Walt," Disney "provided a father-like, protective role to people living in uncertain times during the mid-twentieth century" (Wills 27).[9] Thus, Disney products easily entered millions of households. Shrouded as it was in its trademark innocence, the company often went unquestioned by consumers—after all, a spoonful of sugar *does* help the medicine go down—but Disney products have never been ideology-free. As Wills points out, Disney pushed several conservative social values, such as absolute morality, a Protestant-like work ethic, and traditional gender roles (Wills 104–5). The studio's first feature film, *Snow White*, serves as a good example of the ideological

---

7 Disney released animated films about both legends: *The Sword in the Stone* (1963) and *Mulan* (1998).

8 For example, Tim Manley's *Alice in Tumblr-Land: And Other Fairy Tales for a New Generation* (2013) features retellings of both, Cameron Dokey's *Once Upon a Time* series includes a retelling of Hua Mulan (*The Wild Orchid: A Retelling of "The Ballad of Mulan,"* 2009), and Michael Buckley's *The Fairy-Tale Detectives* (2005) features King Arthur as a character.

9 Interestingly, his initial intention was not to create products for children. Indeed, *Snow White*, in which the Evil Queen is a memorably sinister figure, caused a slight controversy in the United Kingdom. The film was deemed too scary for British children, and an age-sixteen rating was initially suggested (Wills 11), but this was just a small bump in an otherwise smooth road toward global takeover.

underpinnings of Disney films. The Evil Queen is the antithesis to passive Snow White: she presumably rules her kingdom, is proactive and independent, and wields incredible magical powers for nefarious purposes. Snow White, on the other hand, only possesses the considerably more harmless ability to communicate with forest creatures and to sing wistfully of the day her prince will come to rescue her from her lackluster life. She also behaves like the ideal "angel in the house," taking care of seven infantilized dwarves who live in a strictly homosocial environment but lead wholly desexualized lives. With time, Disney's monopoly on childhood entertainment led to increased mistrust among critics, and, since The Walt Disney Company had lain the foundations of its mouse empire upon European fairy tales, the scrutiny sometimes extended to the genre as a whole.[10] The representation of gender in fairy tales—by Disney and other storytellers—became a particularly contentious point in the 1970s, when second-wave feminists committed themselves to critically assessing cultural representations of gender. The 1960s gave way to several social movements around the world, such as the civil rights movement, the student insurrection of 1968, the gay and lesbian liberation movement, and, of course, the women's liberation movement. It was against this backdrop of social vindication and change that the conversation about representations of gender in fairy tales took hold.[11] It began when Lieberman responded to Lurie's rather inaccurate assertion that fairy tales are "one of the few sorts of classic children's literature of which a radical feminist would approve." Lurie argues that little girls can

10 The popularity of Disney was not the only reason fairy tales were scrutinized. Fairy tales had been popular in nurseries and schools for over a century, and had been used both to convey subversive messages, as is the case of Soviet fairy tales under Communist rule (see Nikolajeva "Fairy Tales in Society's Service"), and to serve dominant ideologies, as was the case in Nazi Germany (see Zipes, "The Battle over Fairy-Tale Discourse" 2006). As such, they were regarded as powerful socialization tools.

11 Simone de Beauvoir anticipated feminist critique of fairy tales back in 1949, when she wrote in *The Second Sex* that "[w]oman is the Sleeping Beauty, Cinderella, Snow White, she who receives and submits. In song and story the young man is seen departing adventurously in search of a woman; he slays the dragon, he battles the giants; she is locked in a tower, a palace . . . a captive, sound asleep; she waits" (271–72).

easily find examples of active and resourceful women in the genre, while Lieberman believes these tales socialize them into passivity:

> Only the best-known stories, those that everyone has read or heard, indeed, those that Disney has popularized, have affected masses of children in our culture . . . The "folk tales recorded in the field by scholars," to which Ms. Lurie refers . . . are so relatively unknown that they cannot seriously be considered in a study of the meaning of fairy tales to women. (Lieberman 383–84)

As seen in previous sections, Lurie was right to point out that some fairy tales do deviate from normative or traditional representations of gender, but Lieberman was also right to emphasize that those tales were not well known, especially in the 1970s, and thus had very limited influence on children. Questioning the process of canonization of certain fairy tales over others is commonplace in modern fairy-tale scholarship, as is the focus on sociohistorical context and the recovery of lesser-known tales—especially those by women writers.

After the Lurie-Lieberman exchange took place, many other feminists joined the conversation, often echoing Lieberman's arguments and similarly overstating the power that fairy tales (or any other genre, for that matter) could have over society. However, the ball was already rolling, and by the end of the decade, critics began to offer more nuanced, if disparate, analyses: "from the literary . . . the psychological and the sociological, to the philosophical and spiritual" (Haase "Feminist Fairy-Tale Scholarship" 21). In 1979, Carolyn Heilbrun proposed that fairy tales "must be transformed by bold acts of reinterpretation" (155), and, as if conjured, Angela Carter published *The Bloody Chamber* that same year. In fact, Carter's collection so transformed fairy tales and the field of fairy-tale studies that Bacchilega speaks of a "post-Angela Carter . . . culture" in which "the fairy tale's gender and sexual politics are investigated rather than universalized or simplified" ("Economies of Desire" 81).

The Bloody Chamber and Other Stories contains ten fairy-tale retellings. Carter claimed to be in the "demythologizing business," and she indeed worked with myths in earlier novels such as *The Passion of New Eve* (1977), but she found more enjoyment in fairy tales, which were, in comparison, "a much more straightforward set of devices [and] much easier to infiltrate with other kinds of consciousness" (Carter, "Notes" 38). And infiltrate the genre she did: she wrote violent, dark, sexually charged fairy tales for adults—a far cry from Disneyfied interpretations of the genre. The first retelling in the collection, "The Bloody Chamber," follows the structure of Perrault's "Bluebeard" fairly closely, only it is told from the heroine's point of view rather than by a detached third-person narrator. However, having a voice does not save her from being victimized. Similar to Perrault's tale, the protagonist is married to a sadistic, wealthy man who, unbeknownst to her, has killed all his previous wives. Perrault's tale was famously gruesome, but Carter's gothic language adds to the horror and brings the underlying eroticism of the tale to the surface. For example, the Marquis gives the protagonist "a choker of rubies, two inches wide, like an extraordinarily precious slit throat," which foreshadows the macabre end the Marquis has envisioned for the protagonist (Carter, *Bloody Chamber* 6). When he takes her virginity, the Marquis kisses the rubies before he kisses her mouth, and the many mirrors in their room reflect a suggestive image that brings sexuality and violence against women to the fore: "A dozen husbands impaled a dozen brides while the mewing gulls swung on invisible trapezes in the empty air outside" (Carter, *Bloody Chamber* 14).

As discussed by Orme, Carter's retellings were accused by early critics, such as Patricia Duncker, of not being revisionist enough or "queer enough" (Orme, "Mouth to Mouth" 122), and of merely "rewriting the tales within the strait-jacket of their original structures" (Duncker 73). Similarly, the seductive way in which abuse and violence are described made some critics, like Avis Lewallen, feel uneasiness "at being manipulated by the narrative to sympathize with masochism" (Lewallen 151). To be sure, most of Carter's retellings deal with the intertwined themes of female sexuality and violence against women in ways that some might find fetishistic, and "The Bloody Chamber" deals extensively with the objectification of women. However, her project is multifaceted in that it approaches gender and sexuality in varied ways, thus resisting simplistic moral positioning. For example, one of Carter's retellings of "Red Riding Hood," entitled "In The Company of Wolves," features a Red Riding Hood who carries a knife and thus is "afraid of nothing" (*Bloody Chamber* 114). This protagonist is a willing participant in the wolf's scheme, to the point of overlooking the clattering of her grandmother's bones under the bed. In the end, instead of reenacting the role of passive victim that fairy-tale tradition has routinely casted her in, the girl acts out her sexual desires, and thus she "offers herself as flesh, not meat" (Bacchilega, *Postmodern* 63).

As it were, the sensuous and confronting retellings by Carter drew many other writers to fairy tales. Feminist writers in particular questioned the limited and limiting closures of the happily-ever-afters, the marriage as ideal ending, and the timeless and enchanted quality of classical fairy tales. Revisionists often anchor their tales to a specific moment and often write sequels or prequels to the well-known stories. For instance, Maxine Kumin's "The Archaeology of a Marriage" (1978) is a sequel to "Sleeping Beauty," in which the protagonist wakes up when she is fifty only to find that disenchantment follows her happily-ever-after:

> Was it her fault he took so long
> to hack his way through the brambles?
> Why didn't he carry a chainsaw like any sensible woodsman?
> Why, for that matter, should any twentieth-century woman
> have to lie down at the prick of
> a spindle etcetera etcetera. (3)

Feminist retellings also continued to dismantle representations of "patriarchy's ideal woman"—that is, the sleeping princess in distress, displayed in a glass coffin like a beautiful object suspended in time (Gilbert and Gubar 41). Many of the earlier retellings were simple role reversals without much added depth, which elicited some criticism, even within retellings like Sara Maitland's "The Stepmother's Lament:"

> There's this thing going on at the moment where women tell all the old stories again and turn them all inside-out and back-to-front—so the characters you always thought were the goodies turn out to be the baddies, and vice-versa, and a whole lot of guilt is laid to rest: or at least this is the theory. I'm not sure myself that guilt isn't just passed on to the next person, *in tecta*, so to speak. (222)

Some stories went further—not merely to shift the blame, but to add nuance to famously polarized narratives. Such is the case of Maitland's short tale, which is told from Cinderella's stepmother's perspective. The tale is sympathetic to the stepmother, but it does not rewrite or downplay the abuse she subjected Cinderella to: "I was not innocent, and I have grown out of innocence now and even out of wanting to be thought innocent. Living is a harsh business" (Maitland 222). Indeed, the fascination with villains, heroines, and the distance between the two is recurrent in retellings. Margaret Atwood's "Bluebeard's Egg" blurs the line between antithetical character types, playing with perspective and ambiguity so that, by the end of the short story, the reader cannot be sure who the Bluebeard figure is: the protagonist, her husband, perhaps both, or neither. Retellings in the post-Carter years demonstrate a readiness to challenge the entire basis of fairy tales, and feminist retellings are a sustained effort to reveal gender roles as culturally specific constructions, rather than natural occurrences.

Emergent during the 1970s, popular during the 1980s, and ubiquitous by the 1990s, feminist retellings and feminist critique of fairy tales had lasting effects, even outside of literary circles. In the 1990s, Disney was experiencing a "Disney Renaissance"—a golden age of successful films that marked the company's return to fairy-tale narratives after a break of thirty years. This renaissance produced some comparatively active fairy-tale heroines, such as Belle in *Beauty and the Beast* (1991), a curious social outcast who loves reading, and Jasmine in *Aladdin* (1992), a woman who rejects arranged marriages and escapes to explore the world. Disney sought to capture and hold the imagination of the world, and as such, it had to appeal to shifting views and values in society—which, in this case, meant acknowledging the feminist criticism of previous heroines like Cinderella and Snow White. As markers of further, if slow-moving, progress, the company revealed its first Black princess, Tiana (*The Princess and the Frog*), in 2009, and the exceedingly popular *Frozen* in 2013. In particular, *Frozen* shows remarkable self-awareness: when the younger sister, Anna, falls instantly in love with a prince she wishes to marry, her sister, Queen Elsa—who is herself unmarried and often interpreted as queer by fans—responds that Anna cannot marry a man she has just met (unlike every other Disney princess before her, is implied). Furthermore, at the end of the film, the spell-breaking love characteristic of fairy tales is not romantic love, but rather the love between the two sisters. However, if Disney is lagging behind in one area, arguably far behind all others, it is in non-heterosexual representation. Love is a central theme for the company, and it is shown to take all kinds of forms, from friendship to romantic love to love among family members, but explicit homosexual love is conspicuously absent from all major Disney products.[12]

Perhaps not coincidentally, queerness is also virtually absent from earlier feminist retellings of fairy tales. This was, in fact, one of Duncker's criticisms: she contends that Carter "still leaves the central taboos unspoken. She could never imagine Cinderella in bed with the Fairy Godmother" (75). Indeed, while feminist writers exposed the gender constructions entrenched in the genre, constructions about sexuality often went unexamined. Marriage was questioned, happily-ever-afters were deconstructed, and eternal love was dethroned, but it was rarely recognized that marriage, happily-ever-afters, and eternal loves were almost always heterosexual in nature. Even in the 1980s, when feminists acknowledged the failure of the movement to include "issues of race and class, and of sexual inclination," queer fairy tales were thin on the ground (Joosen 111). Some exceptions to this deficit from the 1970s and 1980s include texts by feminist writers who had some personal experience with queerness, such as Anne Sexton, Suniti Namjoshi, Olga Broumas, and Jeanette Winterson.

Anne Sexton's *Transformations* was published in 1971. This was one of the first collections of fairy tales published in the style of feminist retellings. One of the poems from this collection, "Rapunzel," "offers a literary precedent for lesbian readings of the fairy tale" (Kapurch 438). The poem opens with a contemporary scenario, like all tales in the collection: "Many a girl / had an old aunt / who locked her in the study / to keep the boys away. / They would play rummy / or lie on the couch / and touch and touch. / Old breast against young breast" (Sexton 35).[13] The incestuous undertones carry over to the retelling, in which Mother

12 Some minor exceptions are the character LeFou in *Beauty and the Beast*'s 2017 live-action remake, and the background lesbian kiss in *Toy Story*'s spin-off, *Lightyear* (2022).

13 The very first lines are "A woman / who loves a woman / is forever young" (Sexton 35), which is echoed (likely by chance) in Disney's 2010 adaptation of "Rapunzel,"

Gothel keeps Rapunzel captive and develops a sexual relationship with her: "As she grew older Mother Gothel thought: None but I will see her or touch her" (Sexton 40). However, the relationship is doomed to fail as soon as the prince inevitably appears. Rapunzel falls in love and marries him:

> They lived happily as you might expect proving that
>   mother-me-do
> can be outgrown . . .
> The world, some say, is made up of couples.
> A rose must have a stem. (Sexton 42)

The poem thus preserves the traditional happy ending of the pretext and underscores both the pressures of chrononormativity and the compulsory heterosexuality of fairy tales ("A rose must have a stem"). It also perpetuates the narrative of fleeting lesbianism, presented here as a phase that can be outgrown by young girls but must be endured by lovelorn older women, witches all, whose hearts just shrink "to the size of a pin" (Sexton 42). Marilyn Farwell characterized this poem as a "radical retelling" whose conclusion "appears to be that the lesbian story is ultimately unimaginable" (Farwell 44). However, as Stephen Burt points out, Sexton routinely "ruins the happy endings" and shows that "heterosexual fulfillment is always a poor, guilty and tainted goal" (Burt 136).

Unhappy endings are the norm in Sexton's retellings, as they are the norm across the few queer retellings published during the 1970s, 1980s, and beyond. As such, it may be more productive to regard this phenomenon not in relation to feminist fairy-tale revisionism or even Sexton's oeuvre but rather to queer literature at large. As Jeff Nunokawa points out, "the dominant media has always pictured gay people as 'deathbed victims'" (371). In this way, there always was a "requisite unhappy ending" (Bronski 155), and, even before AIDS, a "veritable epidemic of gay deaths" in literature (Pearl 9). Another early writer of queer fairy-tale retellings, Suniti Namjoshi, certainly contributed to the body count in

---

Tangled. In the animated film, Mother Gothel keeps herself young by using Rapunzel's magical hair.

her *Feminist Fables* (1981). For example, her retelling of "The Beauty and the Beast,"[14] appropriately titled "A Moral Tale," features a lesbian protagonist who has grown up reading stories that, much like most canonical fairy tales, "made it clear that men loved women, and women loved men" (Namjoshi 23). Faced with a representational void, the protagonist aligns her identity with marginalized nonhumans, thus explicitly highlighting the queer undertones of this type of hybrid fairy-tale character: "The only story that fits me at all is the one about the Beast" (Namjoshi 23). The girl's parents, who presumably grew up hearing the same stories, are not pleased—not because they "disapprove of homosexuals as such" but because society does, which, in turn, they claim, is the cause of unhappiness for homosexuals (Namjoshi 23). As Joosen points out, the tale shares Lieberman's "conviction that children's literature has an enormous impact" on shaping women's self-image (115). The protagonist imagines that Beast does not turn into a human as a consequence of being loved by Beauty, but rather that its monstrous, queer love for Beauty is what makes him a beast. The only possible ending for a beast so unassimilable into a strictly normative society is its eradication, a fate that the protagonist follows, for which she is blamed in the moral: "she had been warned and she hadn't listened" (Namjoshi 23).

Problematic, narrow morals like the ones Namjoshi criticizes in her fables are further deconstructed in the brief retellings Jeanette Winterson inscribed in her novel *Sexing the Cherry* (1989). She uses the Grimms' tale, "The Twelve Dancing Princesses," to imagine twelve alternate endings for various types of fairy-tale women, thus democratizing exclusionary endings—particularly those that treat heterosexual marriage as the ultimate achievement. As the eldest sister mentions, if they all eventually

---

14 "Beauty and the Beast" easily lends itself to queering. Beyond the inherent queerness of a transspecies romantic tale, queer people have long been associated with monstrosity, vilified, and pushed to the margins of society. Jean Cocteau's 1946 film *La Belle et la Bête* is an early example of a retelling that subtextually explores the tale's queer potential, particularly through the solitary, and demonizes Beast, who was played by Cocteau's male lover. As we will see in following chapters, the relationship between the beast and homosexuality was further explored in the 1990s, explicitly in, for example, Peter Cashorali's *Fairy Tales: Traditional Stories Retold for Gay Men* (1995), and implicitly in other cases, such as Disney's *Beauty and the Beast* (1991).

find fulfillment in their lives, it is "not with [their] husbands" (Winterson 48). It is actually with other women that some of the sisters find temporary happiness. For example, one of the princesses lives happily with her husband—who is revealed to be a woman—in an isolated, drafty castle until they are discovered. Another sister finds a better ending for herself: she falls in love with a beautiful mermaid, a testament to the lasting queer appeal of Andersen's tale, and moves to the bottom of a well, where they live "in perfect salty bliss" (Winterson 48). Yet another of the dancing princesses, perhaps in conversation with Sexton's retelling, falls in love with Rapunzel. She is not an old witch, and Rapunzel is not a child, but Rapunzel's family twists their story and reimagines them as such because they are angry at Rapunzel's refusal to marry a prince. This prince is unconventional in his own right, and "had always liked to borrow his mother's frocks" (Winterson 52). In fact, his cross-dressing abilities allow him to infiltrate their tower and cruelly put an end to their story: "he carried Rapunzel down the rope he had brought with him and forced her to watch while he blinded her broken lover in a field of thorns" (Winterson 52).

Winterson imagines a wider range of outcomes for her queer characters, but out of all the early retellings of fairy tales that offer queer reinterpretations, the poetic renditions by Olga Broumas in *Beginning with O* (1977) are certainly the most optimistic. The collection is entirely dedicated to articulating lesbian subjectivity by retelling classic myths, legends, and fairy tales. It is also in direct dialogue with Anne Sexton's *Transformations*. For example, her poem "Snow White" blurs the line between mother and lesbian lover in continuity with Sexton's "Rapunzel:" "All through the war we slept / like this, grand- / mother, mother, daughter. Each night / between you, you pushed and pulled / me, willing / from warmth to warmth" (Broumas 59). More explicitly referential still is her own take on Rapunzel, which reproduces the opening lines of Sexton's poem: "A woman / who loves a woman / is forever young." In this double retelling of both the Grimms' and Sexton's versions, Rapunzel presumably addresses Sexton's Mother Gothel and urges her to "Climb / through my hair, climb in / to me, love" (Broumas 59). In contrast with Sexton's tale, which presented lesbian love as something to outgrow, Broumas defends it as something not only normal but coveted and desirable:

How many women
have yearned for our lush perennial, found themselves pregnant,
and had
to subdue their heat, drown out their appetite. (59)

Writing in response to Sexton and to fairy tales at large, Broumas's retelling argues that the happily-ever-after, this "lush perennial," is not accessible through heteronormative unions. In fact, that sort of ending only inhibits women's appetite, which remains drowned out but perhaps not wholly gone. Broumas's Rapunzel, contrary to Sexton's, manages to avoid the trappings of chrononormativity and to salvage her hunger. The ending verses are celebratory and erotic: "I'll break the hush / of our cloistered garden, our harvest continuous / as a moan" (Broumas 60). Harries explains that Broumas shatters the cloistered hush of Sexton's version, and I would add, of the fairy-tale canon, by rewriting as natural that which "has been written off as 'unnatural' or perverse" (150).

However, the defiant and optimistic tone of Broumas's collection was far from the norm among queer fairy-tale retellings, which often adhered to popular representations of queerness, regularly ending in tragedy. Outside of the genre, the imaginary connection between perversity, unnaturalness, and homosexuality was hardly banished during the twentieth century. It is perhaps due to this enduring connection that queer retellings of fairy tales have been slow to become popular and are so scarce when compared to feminist retellings: the genre, after an intense process of Disneyfication, is largely considered to be only for children, for whom "perverse" storylines are not suitable. Tellingly, the queerest characters in the most mainstream fairy-tale products—namely, Disney films—are often villains. Gender nonconformity is consistently exploited in the animated films to subtextually indicate monstrosity and alterity in the villains, from *Aladdin*'s theatrical, kohl-wearing Jafar, to *The Princess and the Frog*'s Freddie Mercury-like Dr. Facilier—although the most overt example might be *The Little Mermaid*'s Ursula. As Laura Sells explains, "Ursula was modelled on the drag queen Divine, while the voice and ethos belong to Pat Carroll [and] both of these character actors are known for their crossdressing roles" (182). This is thus the final layer that fairy-tale revisionists and critics must peel away: not only to question the apparently heteronormative texts but also to question the hesitancy to actively, openly queer a genre that is so ripe for it.

Conclusions

While writing about fairy tales in 1984, Duncker said that, for all its attachment to feudalistic structures and "apparently unalterable social realities," the genre also unlocks "an unstable world" where magic "translates, fragments, inverts" (71). Her conclusion was that fairy tales are ultimately sexist and inescapably conservative, influenced by a canon- (and Disney-) given vision of the genre, but Duncker was already, unknowingly, pointing to the queer possibilities within the fairy tale. The "fantastic inverted world" of the fairy tale she describes—"a world of extremes, excess, and inversion of dailiness" (Duncker 71–72)—indeed lends itself to transgressions of all kinds, strange becomings, fluid identities, nonconforming desires, and surprising temporalities. As a testament to this, despite its apparent normativity, the fairy-tale genre boasts numerous beastly love stories (like Straparola's "Pig Prince"), kings with uncommon tastes (like the necrophiliac monarch in "Sun, Moon, and Talia"), gender-bending women (like in d'Aulnoy's "Belle-Belle"), and species-defying characters (*The Little Mermaid*), among others. As such, the genre offers a multitude of vantage points from which to disturb its apparently cisheteronormative surface.

The following chapters explore retellings of fairy tales from the mid-1990s onward that capitalize on the genre's naturally queer disposition. That was when the most popular collection of queer retellings to date was published: Emma Donoghue's *Kissing the Witch* (1997), which offered a lyrical, timeless challenge to the genre from the perspective of (mostly queer) heroines in a series of intertwined retellings. However, Donoghue was explicitly following in the steps of writers like Carter, Broumas, Sexton, and Winterson (Donoghue, "Interview" 174), and thus is indebted to a feminist fairy-tale tradition in which queer perspectives remained sidelined, marginalized, and treated as an afterthought. My focus instead will be on mostly understudied texts that do not fit neatly within that genealogy, and that offer mostly context-specific contestations to the cisheterocentric fairy tale. I will then trace their evolution as they emerge, flourish, diversify, and receive critical attention as queer texts in their own right, rather than as isolated examples within the feminist fairy-tale tradition. Working from a contemporary perspective, these queer retellings will not merely gloss over the genre's history but delve deeply into it, challenging pervasive myths and revealing the potential of the fairy tale, which, beneath its façade, embraces unspeakable, puzzling, and wondrous scenarios where the strange and queer are largely the norm.

2

TALES FOR FAIRIES

Building Identity and Community Through 1990s Gay Fairy Tales

> That there have been other unions like ours is obvious, but we are unable to draw on their experience.
>
> —F. O. Matthiessen, a letter to his lover, Russell Cheney

> [A]s the infected population grew, it became clear that gay men were everywhere . . . Part of the shock of AIDS was thus the shock of identity.
>
> —Paula Treichler, "AIDS, Gender, and Biomedical Discourse"

In the nineties, fairy tales appeared to be everywhere. The Walt Disney Company had regained its position as the primary provider of children's entertainment with its official return to fairy tales in the form of *The Little Mermaid* (1989) and *Beauty and the Beast* (1991). The genre was used in commercials for major brands like Cheerios and Levi's (Wittwer). It had also gained ground in the literary field with the feminist retellings of Tanith Lee, the edited collections of Terri Windling and Ellen Datlow, and the works inspired by the genre, such as Neil Gaiman's *Stardust* (1998) and Philip Pullman's *Northern Lights* (1995). All around the world, fairy-tale figures, symbols, and themes were often used as an easy shortcut for evoking wonder and romantic love. For instance, the following exchange in the film *Pretty Woman* (1990) refers to the classic fairy tale that structures the film's plot:

KIT: Maybe you guys could, like, get a house together and buy some diamonds and a horse; I don't know—it could work, it *happens*!

VIVIAN: When does it happen, Kit? When does it happen? Who does it really work out for? . . . You give me one example of someone we know that it happened for . . .

KIT: You want me to, like, give you a *name*, or something?

VIVIAN: Yeah, I'd like a name.

KIT: Oh, *God*, the pressure of a name . . . Cinde-fucking-rella!

In popular culture, fairy-tale love was unattainable and exceedingly idealized. At the same time, it was aspirational—the epitome of romance—and invariably heterocentric. Heterocentric portrayals of desire were hardly unique to popular representations of fairy tales, but tireless repetition reinforced the connection between the genre and heterosexuality. Mention of a "fairy-tale wedding," for example, or a "love story worthy of a fairy tale," would most likely only bring heteronormative images to mind. By the 1990s this was nothing new, but in the decade in which the AIDS crisis had pushed people out of the closet and into the streets, or at the very least into the mainstream, the love that dare not speak its name demanded to, finally, be spoken about—even in fairy tales.

This chapter will explore three works that tested the boundaries of the genre, which for so long excluded queer identities, by unapologetically articulating the gay male experience through fairy-tale retellings: Peter Cashorali's *Fairy Tales: Traditional Stories Retold for Gay Men* (1995) and *Gay Fairy & Folk Tales: More Traditional Stories Retold for Gay Men* (1997), and the erotic anthology edited by Michael Ford, *Happily Ever After: Erotic Fairy Tales for Men* (1996). As these are the first collections to explicitly acknowledge and explore gay desires through the fairy tale, we will see how they challenged deeply entrenched heterocentric lessons in an effort to reclaim the genre for the gay community, as well as how they deployed the fairy-tale model to contribute to the very constitution of this gay community—a group whose identity has, historically, often relied on reading practices.[1]

1 I privilege the term "gay" throughout this chapter—to mirror both period usage and the texts' own audience—even where "queer" might appear elsewhere.

As established in the previous chapter, queer retellings of classical fairy tales appeared sporadically before the 1990s, beginning in 1971 with a queer retelling of "Rapunzel" in Anne Sexton's *Transformations*—which also kickstarted feminist retellings of fairy tales in English. However, whereas feminist retellings exploded in popularity in the 1970s and influenced all kinds of mainstream fairy tales, interest in queering fairy tales remained remarkably sparse. The reason might lie within the different political and critical currents that gave way to, or at least facilitated, the appearance of both kinds of retellings. By the 1970s, the second wave of feminism was underway—the first having occurred some seventy years earlier. In other words, there was already a feminist tradition to inform the ideology behind feminist retellings, a thriving political community of feminists who could potentially be interested in retellings, and a history of female identities being questioned, reconsidered, and variously articulated in literature, politics, and media.

Gay and lesbian liberation movements (and gay and lesbian studies) emerged in the late 1960s in the wake of second-wave feminism and the Black Power movement and were thus comparatively young. Gay liberation in the United States is commonly understood to have begun in 1969, with the Stonewall Riots (see Adam 75–76). These protests marked a change in the way LGBTQI people related to the establishment and to each other, unified by an increased feeling of shared identity. In the years surrounding the riots, gay writing and publishing flourished significantly (Pearl 6). As Seifert rightly points out, "it is this context that explains the fairly recent appearance of gay and lesbian fairy tales" ("Gay and Lesbian Fairy Tales" 401). The dates certainly fit for the first queer retellings by Sexton and Broumas, both published in the 1970s, but this explanation does not account for the significant slump in production of queer fairy tales from then until the mid-1990s. Winterson and Namjoshi published their queer retellings in the 1980s, but these remained isolated outliers, and it was not until the last decade of the twentieth century that there seemed to be noteworthy interest in writing queer fairy tales, both as retellings and as original stories (Joosen 114). As we shall see, queer retellings emerged when queer literature had evolved to make space for them, and queer writing—and its publication—was contingent on the degree of LGBTQI political organization, cultural representation, and social acceptance, particularly in the United States, where the texts analyzed were first published.

Early Years of the Gay Community and the Significance of an Emergent Gay Literature

Pro-homosexual organization did not start with the Stonewall Riots, nor did it begin in the United States, despite the primacy of North America in narratives of contemporary LGBTQI history. The first organization of this type to be recognized in the United States was the Society for Human Rights—founded by Henry Gerber in 1924—and it was inspired by the remarkably advanced German gay movement, which had emerged in the late nineteenth century (Rupp, Roth, and Taylor, 665).[2] The Society for Human Rights was short-lived, however, and it wasn't until the 1950s that the first homophile societies emerged: namely, the Mattachine Society (a society of gay men founded in Los Angeles in 1950) and Daughters of Bilitis (a society of lesbians founded in San Francisco in 1955). These early examples of LGBTQI organization emerged in fraught postwar years. Joseph McCarthy's anticommunist campaign targeted homosexuals or suspected homosexuals in the 1950s, which led to extensive firings and confinement in prisons and mental institutions (Adam 60). This rushed in an anti-LGBTQI "Lavender Scare" that rivaled the better-known anticommunist "Red Scare" in scale (Rupp, Roth, and Taylor 665; Simpson and McDaniel x). The homophile groups thus adopted an assimilationist strategy, by which "gay identity, culture, and values would be disavowed (or at least concealed) in return for the *promise* of equal treatment" (Adam 64, emphasis in original).[3] Though cautious in their approach, homophile groups still cultivated an identity centered around same-sex desire and pioneered efforts at reform—these were,

---

2 For more information about early gay and lesbian organization around the world, see Barry Adam's "Early Movements and Aspirations" in *The Rise of a Gay and Lesbian Movement* (1983). For an overview of the early movement in Germany, see Ralph Dose's *Magnus Hirschfeld and the Origins of the Gay Liberation Movement* (2014).

3 The homophiles' assimilationist approach was replicated by similar groups throughout western Europe. This was done out of necessity during the postwar years, which proved to be worse for queer people than the war itself (see Adam 64–68).

effectively, the beginnings of an organized gay community in the United States. The gay and lesbian liberation movements of the 1960s and 1970s both continued their labor and were the radical answer to the homophiles' (real or perceived) conservatism, whose "patterns of recruitment, organizational goals, and . . . the assumption that women and men are fundamentally different" had prevented achieving a truly diverse and inclusive movement (Rupp, Roth, and Taylor 665).

A shift toward radical activism was already taking place by the mid-1960s, informed by a growing anti-establishment sentiment and New Left ideals of forming an egalitarian, participatory democracy. In particular, many feminists and gay liberation activists, radicalized in Black student organizations, distanced themselves from the civil rights movement, less interested in being accepted by a system they regarded as profoundly and structurally heterosexist, racist, and militarist. Both formations established consciousness-raising groups (see Adam 76–77) that would draw attention to the commonality of their struggles through personal storytelling, as explained in this excerpt from the New York Gay Liberation Front journal, *Come Out!*:

> A consciousness-raising group is a group of gay people who have regular sessions together. By consensus a topic is selected for each session. Each member of the group contributes her personal experiences relating to the chosen topic. When all of the testimony is heard, the group locks into the similarity in the experiences related by all the members . . . A gay person begins to see that his personal hang-ups . . . are indeed the same . . . that other gays were also afraid to divulge. (Gavin 19)

Construction of a unifying identity through storytelling practices was thus central to the mobilization of gays and lesbians in the 1970s. So was their oppositional relationship with authority and normative society, as conflict with authority in particular was exacerbated by mounting tensions with the police, who would routinely harass queer people and raid gay bars.

These increasingly adversarial relationships came to a symbolic climax due to the Stonewall Riots. On June 28, 1969, following a violent police raid of the Mafia-run, illegal gay bar the Stonewall Inn, riots erupted on and around Christopher Street in Greenwich Village. Although not the first of their kind, the events at the Stonewall Inn received unparalleled attention from the media, who may have been tipped off by gay activists (Crage and Armstrong, 737). For three days, thousands of queer people turned up at Christopher Street to "celebrate and demonstrate the emergence of Gay Power," facing the police's violent repression with a newfound sense of collective consciousness (Teal 7). It is notable that the riots were spearheaded by underrepresented factions of the community who were frequent targets of police abuse, such as street queens, transwomen of color, and butch lesbians[4]—a fact often underreported. The riots, furthermore, precipitated the creation of the Gay Liberation Front in New York and other equally radical groups across the country. These groups promoted sexual freedom, the creation of alternative and underground institutions, the practice of coming out as gay, and "direct action in the form of public protest" to transform society (Rupp, Roth, and Taylor 669).

A new openness in homosexual life followed the events at Stonewall, allowing for a small industry of gay publications to thrive in the 1970s, which coincided with the first queer retellings of fairy tales by Sexton and Broumas. This is not to say that gay writing began in the 1970s. As Jonathan Katz notes, "a number of fictional works with major or minor male homosexual themes began to be published in the U.S." in the 1880s (657). Some notable gay and lesbian fiction was published in the war and postwar years prior to Stonewall, during what Evert Van der Veen has called the "hiding" period of gay publishing (15–21). Examples of works published in this period include Patricia Highsmith's *The Price of Salt* (1952), James Baldwin's *Giovanni's Room* (1956), and Christopher Isherwood's *A Single Man* (1964). However, some scholars place the emergence of the new gay novel in 1978 (Bergman, *Gaiety* 9–10; Gambone 3). This year saw the publication of Larry Kramer's *Faggots* and Andrew Holleran's

4 The gay and lesbian liberation movements were more diverse in class and race than the homophile groups and were more likely to feature women in prominent roles. However, there was no shortage of friction between men and women. Some groups were consistently marginalized, such as bisexual or transgender people, which led to the formation of alternative groups. The interests of cisgender white gay men remained at the core of the gay liberation movement (Armstrong 199).

Dancer from the Dance, and for Edmund White both novels "documented the new gay culture that had been spawned by liberation, prosperity and societal tolerance" (1991). The 1970s and early 1980s were years of comparative prosperity: gay and lesbian groups proliferated, as did gay neighborhoods, and institutional presence and visibility increased exponentially (Rupp, Roth, and Taylor 672). Broumas's *Beginning with O* (1977), with its remarkably sanguine tone, is a natural product of what was then a new era. It is also clearly a direct response to Anne Sexton's darker *Transformations* (1971). Both works were recognized for their literary quality,[5] and they could have inspired further queer approaches to the fairy-tale genre, but they did not. One contributing factor to this could be the confessional, poetic nature of both collections, which was not the most popular mode of fairy-tale storytelling.[6] Another factor could be that both collections were somewhat cautious in their attempts to queer the fairy tale. After all, *Beginning with O* included numerous revisions of Greek myths alongside some retellings of fairy tales, and *Transformations* included only one retelling that could be considered openly queer. Comparatively, Carter's *The Bloody Chamber* served as a comprehensive stylistic roadmap for future writers who would question the fairy tale from a feminist perspective. The influence of her work can be found in fairy-tale retellings to this day. Notably, short fiction—a format traditionally favored by fairy-tale writers and revisionists—was still developing in the gay and lesbian publishing scene in the 1970s at a pace that likely stalled the appearance of queer retellings in prose. Once queer short fiction began to develop, however, it grew rapidly, encouraged by the creation of specifically gay and lesbian literary journals like *Christopher Street* (1976–95) and gay and lesbian literary anthologies, which reached new publics and reaffirmed an existing interest in homosexual narratives (Gambone 3–4). When gay writer Christopher Bram's first story was picked up by *Christopher Street*, he thought: "I can write about

5 Broumas's *Beginning with O* received the Yale Younger Poets Prize. Sexton, who had won the Pulitzer for Poetry years before, published *Transformations* to considerable popular acclaim (Trinidad).

6 This is not to say that fairy tale retellings did not appear in poetic form. Sara Henderson Hay's *Story Hour* collection was published in 1963—even earlier than Sexton's.

being gay and get published. I can write about what's important to me and succeed as a writer" (qtd. in Gambone 95).

The increasing popularity of gay literature, buoyed by local, specialized press and bookstores, and even by mainstream publishers (see Gambone 3–5), influenced the formation of an emerging gay community. The community differs from other minorities in that gay people are not necessarily born to gay parents, or even have gay relatives, so people often grow up in isolation from other members of the group, and are thus disconnected from a shared history and culture.[7] For this reason, a number of critics (N. Miller 476; Bergman, *Gaiety* 10; Dyer 1) have identified reading practices as the bridge between individual and community, and some have even characterized gay people as an imagined community of readers, structured through relevant literature and the imagined social space it generates (Pearl 7; Rodríguez 397).[8] Literature—cheaply produced, easily hidden, and transportable even to remote rural areas—could thus "assist in the construction of gay identities where other socializing influences are absent" (Rodríguez 409). Bergman highlights the dependence of gay youth on literature as a source of identity when he remarks homosexuality was "a literary construct to many gay people" (*Gaiety*, 6), a sentiment echoed by Richard Dyer, who maintains that because gay people "grew up isolated not only from our heterosexual peers but also from each other, we turned to the mass media for information and ideas about ourselves" (1).

However, gay representation in mass media was mostly negative, which, for Corey Creekmur and Alexander Doty, meant that "gays and lesbians often found their cultural experience and participation constrained and proscribed by a dominant culture in which they are generally ignored or oppressed" (1). In this sense, literature produced by gay authors was often the only medium through which people could

---

7 Furthermore, both the Nazis' efforts and, later, the communist and capitalist elites' "willful forgetting" (Adam 54), did much to sever the gay community from its early history, making the gay and lesbian liberation movements of the 1970s appear as uniquely contemporary occurrences.

8 I refer here primarily to a gay male community, and mostly to white gay men, at that. Other members of a broader LGBTQI community might not, historically, have found the same amount of solace and sense of community anywhere, not even in literature.

encounter subversive images of homosexuality and was thus key to piecing together a communal identity. Both the Mattachine Society and the Daughters of Bilitis, for example, included queer book review columns in their political magazines (*Out* and *The Ladder*, respectively) alongside discussions of the rights of sexual minorities, which points to the importance of literature for the constitution of an emergent LGBTQI community. Bergman goes as far as to say literature "has been of greater importance for gay communities than for any other ethnic, national, or religious group," given the particular atomism of gay people (Bergman, *Gaiety* 10). However, race, class, and ability differences, among other factors, limited the effectiveness of gay literature as an intersectional tool for identity formation for all gay people. Perhaps Bergman's statement should be qualified to acknowledge that, at least for middle-class, able-bodied white gay men (and, to a lesser degree, lesbians),[9] literature provided images upon which to model their identity. Thus, during the 1970s, increasingly available literature played a central part in producing and maintaining relatively stable gay identity, if not a perfectly inclusive one. As the decade came to a close, literature and culture remained crucial for the transmission of gay history and identity, particularly as the shadow of AIDS loomed.

The AIDS Crisis and Its Effects on Gay Identity and Gay Literature

As early as 1981, young men in U.S. urban areas were falling ill with and quickly dying from an unknown disease. Most of these men identified as gay, so the disease was unofficially called "gay pneumonia," "gay cancer," and—foreshadowing the intense moralistic rhetoric that would accompany the epidemic—the Wrath of God Syndrome (Treichler 198). The official name eventually became the somewhat less problematic but still inaccurate Gay-Related Immune Deficiency. This changed only when the growing number of infections made it impossible to ignore that other

9 Sheila Liming claims that literature "has long served as a vessel by which lesbian women might come to terms with their identity and has helped to contextualize lesbianism more broadly [but] it has done so through a rather meagre ration of lesbian texts and authors" (86).

groups, such as hemophiliacs, heroin addicts, and Haitian immigrants, were being affected. Despite increasing evidence that the disease was not limited to gay men—including large numbers of heterosexual men and women in Asia, Africa, and Latin America—the public, and even medical researchers, often clung to early assumptions, which severely pathologized gay men (Wald 219). This has been understood in the context of the rise of a New Right, a countermovement that sought to mobilize against social change and sexual liberation (Capitanio and Herek 1130–40). Years after the American Psychiatric Association declassified homosexuality as a mental illness, conservative sectors finally found a new, tangible way to demonize a group whose "disordered" lifestyle was framed as a threat to the heterosexual majority. Their rhetoric, at best, characterized HIV/AIDS as a natural consequence of queer people's moral corruption, and at worst imbued HIV carriers with a perverse intentionality to spread the disease (Wald 230).

Anti-gay stigma and discrimination certainly increased in this period, but the AIDS crisis galvanized the LGBTQI community when it could have easily destroyed it. After all, all kinds of LGBTQI people—upper class, lower class, artists, writers, politicians, Black, White, famous and anonymous people alike—were dying in large numbers. Yet the community, whose networks had been strengthened during the days of gay and lesbian liberation, responded with an unprecedented, unified rise in civic engagement to address the multifaceted challenges that ensued. For instance, cisgender lesbians, who were less directly affected by the disease, played a crucial role in providing services to people with HIV/AIDS and mobilizing the community when the government failed to provide proper care or to recognize the severity of the epidemic (Rupp, Roth, and Taylor 672).[10] Many of the early battles fought by the community were about seemingly ordinary issues, such as hospital visitation rights, "taking time off to be with loved ones who were sick and dying [and]

10 President Reagan did not address the matter publicly until 1985, five years after the first diagnosed cases and thousands of deaths in the United States. The inaction and overt hostility of the government only encouraged the political mobilization of LGBTQI activists. For more information, see Jennifer Brier's *Infectious Ideas: U.S. Political Responses to the AIDS Crisis* (2009) and Deborah B. Gould's *Moving Politics: Emotion and ACT UP's Fight Against AIDS* (2009).

claiming insurance benefits" (Picard). Eventually, organized efforts were made to further HIV/AIDS research, treatment, and anti-discrimination policies. AIDS irreversibly changed the landscape of LGBTQI life—and death—and it may have stalled the fight for equality. However, as the crisis advanced, LGBTQI activists were compelled to develop more sophisticated and efficient strategies for affecting change. AIDS activism also set the stage for queer theories by radically challenging understandings of identity, power, and community. Furthermore, AIDS activists' direct action, resistance to complacency,[11] and coalitional (as opposed to separatist) politics were replicated by queer activists in the 1990s. Ultimately, the visibility that both the disease and the activism surrounding it granted these groups had the somewhat ironic consequence of making LGBTQI people a familiar—if not necessarily accepted—fixture of public American life.

The AIDS epidemic also had a grotesquely ironic effect on gay literature. At the same time AIDS claimed the lives of numerous gay writers, gay literature blossomed like it never had before, during what Neil Miller has described as "The Gay Fiction Boom of the 1980s" (444). White offers a poignant personal account of this time:

> I left [the Violet Quill, a gay writing group] in 1983, when I moved to Paris. When I came back to the States in 1990 this literary map had been erased. George Whitmore, Michael Grumley, Robert Ferro and Chris Cox were dead; Vito Russo was soon to die . . . Many younger writers had also died; . . . Tim Dlugos, Richard Umans, Gregory Kolovakos, the translator Matthew Ward and the novelist John Fox (who'd been my student at Columbia). My two closest friends, the literary critic David Kalstone and my editor, Bill Whitehead, had also died . . . For me these losses were definitive. The witnesses to my life . . . were gone. The loss of all the books they might have written remains incalculable. (White)

Literature flourished despite this huge creative and human loss. Perhaps it was due to increased visibility and interest, even from straight

11 Consider Queer Nation's slogan "We're here, we're queer, get used to it" ("Queer Nation Manifesto").

audiences, or perhaps it was that AIDS had forced queer people to confront matters of love, life, death, and identity—"the very preoccupations that have always animated serious fiction and poetry" (White). Nonfiction gay literature was also urgently produced and consumed, often proving to be the only reliable source of information for the community during the crisis (Pearl 3).

The sheer amount of AIDS fiction (which was often, but not always, gay) can be daunting, but Monica Pearl offers a useful periodization through which to understand the general trends. She divides the period into four parts: first, pre-1988 literature, which produced novels concerned "with instruction [rather than] with aesthetics" (Pearl 4) that are now mostly out of print; second, literature from 1988 to 1995, which was characterized by the publication of novels "formative to the canon of AIDS literature" (Pearl 4), during a period in which the disease had become an everyday reality for many in the community; third, literature from 1995 to 2001, during which the "pharmaceutical threshold" transformed AIDS into a chronic illness rather than a death sentence (Pearl 1–2); and finally, literature published after 9/11, which marked a change in what "America conceives of as the enemy, which shifted to some extent from internal nemeses . . . to external ones" (Pearl 211). The books used in this chapter—Cashorali's *Fairy Tales* and *Gay Fairy & Folk Tales*, and Ford's anthology, *Happily Ever After*—were all published after this "pharmaceutical threshold" in rapid succession. While they would not technically qualify as AIDS literature, HIV/AIDS (and mortality) is one of the most recurrent themes in these stories—even the erotic ones. This fact ties the texts to a particular historical moment and demonstrates how deeply the trauma of AIDS had permeated both everyday life and the imaginative spaces of gay people, even finding its way into largely escapist fairy tales.

Constructing Community Through Reclaimed Gay Fairy Tales

The three texts analyzed here are rather different from one another. The most obvious difference is that Cashorali's publications are both single-author collections, and Ford's anthology has multiple authors. They have different publishing backgrounds as well: whereas Ford's anthology was published by Masquerade, a small New York imprint that specialized in LGBTQI erotica, Cashorali's collections were published by Harper-Collins and Faber & Faber. Furthermore, Cashorali's first collection was popular enough to warrant a sequel, and both of his collections were reviewed in mainstream magazines such as *Publisher's Weekly*. The appeal of *Happily Ever After* is understandably narrower since it contains explicit gay erotica. Nonetheless, a companion anthology of lesbian fairy tales also edited by Michael Ford was published in the same year, titled *Once Upon a Time: Erotic Fairy Tales for Women*.[12]

Despite these differences, there are more elements of these works that tie them to each other than set them apart. Particularly, the fact that these are works written (and edited) by gay men, intended for gay men, and closely connected to the realities of gay men in the mid-1990s. This is noteworthy because these works are the first ones to revise the fairy-tale genre from an openly (male) gay perspective in English. The Abbot of Villiers remarked that fairy tales were "women's province" (qtd. in Bottigheimer, *Framed* 76), pointing to the feminine associations with the genre in seventeenth-century France—a notion which seems to have carried over to Michael Ford's days. As he explains, his initial plan was to put together a lesbian anthology of retold fairy tales because he thought men would have little interest in the genre: "Fairy tales have always seemed to me to appeal on a deep level more to women than to men, and the most interesting characters in the tales are women" (Ford, "Introduction" 2). To his surprise, he found the men he surveyed had strong reactions to certain fairy-tale stories from their childhoods. The intensity of these gay men's connections to their favorite childhood fairy tales resulted in his anthology comprising twenty-eight stories across more than 400 pages, making it "much longer than I ever expected it to be" (Ford, "Introduction" 3). Despite contemporary interest shown by the LGBTQI community and beyond, Ford's anthology and Cashorali's collections are both currently out of print and rather difficult to find. This additional commonality between them is likely because most themes tackled in each publication's stories are largely historically specific, as are the humor and cultural references. This is especially true when compared

12 For more information on this collection, see Jeana Jorgensen's 2008 article, "Innocent Transformations: Female Agency in Eroticized Fairy Tales."

to Donoghue's *Kissing the Witch*, a more lyrical and timeless work that revises the genre from a female, queer perspective. Perhaps unsurprisingly, some of the stories in Donoghue's collection are still considered a prime example of queer retellings of fairy tales. Their literary quality notwithstanding, in what follows, I contend that Cashorali's and Ford's works are significant and valuable as historical documents that capture the anxieties and desires of mid-1990s gay men, explored openly for the first time through the fantastic mode of the fairy tale.

This engagement with the genre was radical at the time and questioned by some (as a reviewer in *Publisher's Weekly* put it, "do we really need a 'Jack and the Penis?'"), but was a natural development at this juncture. Gay literature—specifically short stories—developed greatly during the AIDS crisis.[13] This, together with the fact that genre fiction such as fantasy and science fiction began to make space for queer identities in the 1980s (Levy 395), prepared readers to receive queer approaches to fairy tales. Furthermore, in the mid-1990s, after the "pharmaceutical threshold" of AIDS, the first gay epics appeared, including Felice Picano's *Like People in History* and Ethan Mordden's *How Long Has This Been Going On?* (Pearl 5). This suggests an awareness of gay history, or perhaps a need to historicize gay existence: after the urgency of the first AIDS decade, there was a need to regroup, to memorialize, and to rebuild. It is in this context that the community-forming fairy tales of Cashorali and Ford, quite literally, came out.

Fairy tales were used to assist in the construction of national identities—particularly in the nineteenth century, as discussed in the previous chapter—and generated especially fertile ground for other community-construction efforts. Thus, in the same way that the Grimms employed fairy tales to provide the German people with a source of collective identity, so did Cashorali's and Ford's retellings contribute to the creation of a coherent identity for gay men, with obvious differences in reach and lasting impact. Robert Kopcke engages with this idea in the foreword he wrote for *Fairy Tales*, in which he places Cashorali in line with the likes of Wilhelm and Jacob Grimm: "Cashorali follows in a long

13 As Sharon Oard Warner wrote in 1993: "What I know about AIDS—about living with it and dying from it—I have learned from literature, from novels and poems and essays, and, most of all, from short stories" (491).

line of storytellers before him [and he speaks] the truth of his community, my community, by telling the stories that follow" (Kopcke VIII). Some, as Brian Walker puts it, might regard the comparison of the gay community to a nation as "nothing more than a parodistic mimicry of 'real' [nations]" (Walker 518), but this both overestimates the depth of traditional nations and underestimates the depth of gay culture.[14] Gay people might not have a distinct cuisine or architectural style, but they do have a culture, a common history, and institutions. Since they are not concentrated territorially,[15] Walker compares gay people to other nonterritorial diaspora nations (Walker 537–43). Walker does not advocate for the separatism of a gay and lesbian state, but instead defends queer people as a culturally distinct group with a nation-like sense of peoplehood:

> Bit by bit an imaginary community was created through which gay people could link up their local experiences of violence and harassment with the experiences of other gay men and lesbians . . . and come to see themselves as a people set apart. (Walker 523)

Germany, much like the gay community, is an "imagined community," as described by Benedict Anderson, since both are socially constructed communities where individuals will never meet most members of their group but still perceive (or imagine) a kinship to them (Anderson 6). Anderson places special importance on "print languages" when it comes to the origin of national consciousness, as they create "unified fields of exchanges and communication" (44). This aligns with the Grimms' nation-building fairy tales, and with literature's central role in constructing a gay community—in many ways an imagined community of readers—by serving as a "unified field of communication" through which

14 An early example of queer nationalism was the direct-action organization, Queer Nation (formed in 1990), whose manifesto called to the creation of a queer nation in which a community, unified by their difference, could reclaim their history, culture, and space: "Let's make every space a Lesbian and Gay space. Every street a part of our sexual geography . . . A city and a country where we can be safe and free and more" ("Queer Nation Manifesto").

15 Except possibly in localized queer enclaves or neighborhoods such as San Francisco's Castro Street.

isolated individuals could articulate their subjectivity and connect to a common identity.

Naturally, Ford's and Cashorali's campy, demystifying retellings seem like departures from the Grimms' serious approach to fairy tales. Although the Grimms edited their tales extensively, their goal was to provide a common cultural heritage for the German people. Cashorali and Ford do not attempt to unearth a cultural heritage gay people might have been severed from; they do not, for instance, attempt to rediscover and collect lesser-known fairy tales that contain moments of queer tension. They do, however, engage with a hidden heritage by finding fissures in classic fairy tales and teasing out the queerness lurking just below their apparently heterocentric surface. By retelling these tales for gay men, the authors amplify their latent queerness, make it the center of their plots, reimagine wonder, and invite gay readers to reconsider the genre and their place in it. In fact, the blurb in Cashorali's *Fairy Tales* identifies the gay community as a group who "have longed since childhood to find images of themselves in their bedtime stories," and Cashorali as the one who has finally provided such images.

Thus, Cashorali's and Ford's works can be seen as self-aware, tongue-in-cheek, and campy, yet still devoted efforts to reclaim the fairy-tale genre. In doing so, they reclaim fairy-tale aesthetics, themes, forms, plots, and the genre's potential for community construction. As will become evident, their tales deploy recurring themes—such as the HIV/AIDS crisis, homophobia, gay subculture, community formation, and identity—to provide a coherent narrative of gay experience, making literature once more a nodal point for the gay community.

Peter Cashorali's *Fairy Tales: Traditional Stories Retold for Gay Men* and *Gay Fairy & Folk Tales: More Traditional Stories Retold for Gay Men*

Cashorali's collections contain thirty stories in total: seventeen in *Fairy Tales* and thirteen in *Gay Fairy & Folk Tales*. He uses various sources, from Alexander Pushkin's *Bajka* to the Brothers Grimm's *Kinder- und Hausmärchen*, and he is careful to reference his inspiration for each retelling. His scope is broad. For instance, he lists collections of Arabic folktales and Chinese fairy tales among his sources, although in keeping with the focus of this study, the only retellings analyzed here will be European fairy tales, with a particular emphasis on canonical tales. That said, the distinction is not always clear: Cashorali often cites several sources as the inspiration behind his apparently composite retellings. These sources, however, are always thematically linked. For instance, his story "Rumpelstiltskin" notes the Grimms' version as a source alongside the Icelandic legend "Who Built Reynir Church?" (*Fairy Tales* 43), which also features a trickster-like character who offers his magical help in exchange for a firstborn—a condition only reversible if the protagonist can guess the trickster's name. In practice, his stories usually use one, rarely two, of the many listed sources as the main model for his retellings. His "Rumpelstiltskin" follows the Grimms' version closely that the supposed influence of other tales is negligible. Thus, Cashorali's careful recording of his sources can be considered a scholarly exercise in connecting his stories to other tales and traditions, or a simple suggestion for further reading.

Cashorali's erudite approach to sourcing stands in stark contrast to the general tone of his retellings, which is light and humorous. He focuses on the challenges of mid-1990s gay men, but instead of adapting these issues so that they blend in with a recognizable fairy-tale world (or the opposite: instead of updating fairy-tale elements so that they work in a contemporary setting) he creates a dissonant liminal space in which all elements—contemporary, wondrous, and archaic—coexist. Author Douglas Sadownick's blurb in *Fairy Tales* points to this: "The contemporary . . . edge of his work shows that we queers are living in a new myth, weirdly futuristic and archaic at the same time." Cashorali's stories indeed appear weirdly, *queerly*, outside of time, neither past, future, nor present, in an echo of the genre's typical "never-never land" setting. In many ways, Cashorali's stories seek to imitate traditional fairy tales. Indeed, his stories open with vague structures that do not seem out of place in the genre, like "There was once a young man" (*Fairy Tales* 13) and "Long ago and very far from here" (*Gay Fairy & Folk Tales* 3). They take place in vaguely named locations, such as the "Endless Forest" (*Fairy Tales* 1), and are populated by kings, princes, and peasants, yet they still seem to unfold in a distinctly contemporary, affluent, and urban milieu. An example of this scrambled temporality is the retelling "Rumpelstiltskin," in which the protagonist, Steven, works a very physical job in a medieval windmill during the day, and at night, his uncle the miller takes him to "coffeehouses and the theater and gallery openings, where Steven met the miller's friends" (Cashorali, *Fairy Tales* 43). This discordant juxtaposition of elements emulates the traditional fairy tale's mix of everyday elements and magic, and, although it is jarring—or perhaps because it is—it contributes to the parodic tone of his retellings.

Cashorali's use of jarring narrative techniques inevitably draws the reader's attention to the fact that these retellings are artificial constructions. As a result, reader immersion takes second place to the obvious didactic drive of Cashorali's tales. Overt didacticism and artificiality are some of the most common criticisms leveled at retellings of fairy tales (Joosen 102), but, in the style of queer writing, Cashorali embraces "affectation and false creation as means in themselves" (Geczy and Karaminas 1), and he makes no attempt to conceal that he is using the fairy tale as the vehicle for life lessons for gay men. Kopcke writes in the introduction that the stories contain "lessons that bear repeating to everyone, but especially to men in the gay community" (Kopcke viii). For instance, several stories deal with homophobia, internalized and otherwise, some work to contest the dominant narratives of HIV/AIDS, and others aim to help readers navigate specific pockets of gay subculture.

Homophobia

Internalized homophobia is particularly central to "King Crossbill," a retelling of the Grimms' "King Thrushbeard." Cashorali uses one of the most recurring queering devices in retellings: he swaps genders. He turns the heroine into a hero—a strikingly handsome young man named Christopher—as arrogant as the Grimms' protagonist, who, in this case, has very specific motives for his behavior:

> It happened that many young men would also sigh when he passed. Though he didn't like to admit it . . . these were the sighs that sounded sweetest to his ear . . . he certainly saw no reason to let anyone else bring it to his attention, and he used his fists to change the topic of conversation whenever it came up. (*Fairy Tales* 13)

The psychological angle in this story is not surprising, though it is a departure from classical fairy tales, which are generally devoid of psychological complexity and interiority. Cashorali is a psychotherapist by trade and considers fairy tales a valuable tool for discussing "the psychic development of the personality" (Cashorali qtd. in Dubin). In fact, he has used the fairy-tale mode to help his patients understand and work through their issues (Cashorali, "Fairy Tales in Therapy"), a practice that may have been influenced by Bruno Bettelheim's *The Uses of Enchantment: The Meaning and Importance of Fairy Tales* (1976). By employing fairy tales as therapeutic tools, Cashorali aligns himself with Lieberman's belief that fairy tales are "training manuals for girls" (Lieberman 395). He extends their influence to gay men and turns Lieberman's accusation on its head: in Cashorali's hands, fairy tales are a means for correcting society's exclusionary lessons rather than sexist tools of oppression. In this tale, for instance, Christopher's personal journey is intended to help gay men dismantle the negative self-images imposed by a homophobic culture.

At the beginning of the story, Christopher reacts violently every time his sexuality is at risk of being disclosed, even to himself. Unlike other gay youths, he has ample opportunities to explore his sexuality, as "many young men" pursue him, but fear and self-loathing make him lash out at them instead. This is the case even when a proposition comes from a powerful king whose offer he rudely rejects: "'That's you,' he growled. 'King Crossbill.' By which he meant the bird's beak wasn't straight, and neither was the king" (*Fairy Tales* 14). After this encounter, Christopher is forced to work for a beggar. As the beggar's apprentice, Christopher must do some jobs he finds demeaning and "effeminate," such as flower arranging. The beggar responds to his complaints by flexing his biceps and asking, "Does this look effeminate to you?" (*Fairy Tales* 18), then hitting him across the face and finally ordering him to make sure his bouquets are extraordinarily dainty. The beggar, transformed into Christopher's mentor, shifts between rough masculinity, effeminacy, and back, forcing Christopher to question his deep-seated prejudices and the very stability of binary gender expression. At the end of the tale, Christopher must clean the palace ballroom before a party but is not done in time, and he looks on as the guests arrive.

The scene that follows is a vibrant tableau upon which traditional boundaries of gender and social hierarchies are visibly dismantled in a deliberate inversion of the normative structures observed throughout the narrative:

> Beautiful women in glittering gowns walked in arm in arm, and handsome men in tuxedos kissed one another hello; handsome women in tuxedos kissed one another hello, and beautiful men in glittering gowns walked arm in arm. (*Fairy Tales* 19)

This scene cuts diagonally across the gender binary, the sexual divide, and even class difference—one of the village boys, Christopher's former admirer, is invited to the ball: "Alex, whom he'd knocked down . . . Alex, who seemed was a guest of honour here" (*Fairy Tales* 20). The ballroom scene's challenge of external hierarchies brings to mind a different kind of ballroom scene: ballroom culture, a primarily African American and Latino drag subculture in which queer people "compete . . . in ways that emulate the archetypal traits of a gender, sex, or social class that is not theirs—or battle through a dance known as voguing" (Rio 122). Christopher's experiences leading up to and within the ballroom illustrate a profound transformation, reflecting Malcolm Rio's assertion that drag ballroom spaces represent a "fabulous and ingenious form of queer, racial, and spatial alterity" (Rio 123). In this context, Cashorali's ballroom scene creates an agentive space where norms are reshaped and reimagined.

At the end, and following the fairy-tale plot, the king appears and reveals himself to be both the one Christopher nicknamed King Crossbill and his mentor, the beggar:

> "I did this because I love you and because I saw how much you would need to learn before you finally came out." (Cashorali, *Fairy Tales* 20)

The final lesson in the Grimms' tale is humility, freely—and at times cruelly—dispatched by a king who marries the protagonist in the end. Here, the lesson in humility comes paired with a lesson on acceptance of oneself and others. Christopher, moreover, does not marry the king. Instead, the king resumes his role as mentor, guiding Christopher as he takes his first steps into the queer world the king has opened to him.

The power imbalance of the pretext is thus not replicated in Cashorali's version, as the story champions queer kinship and community belonging over a more traditionally romantic fairy-tale ending.

Comparable lessons on homophobia appear in other tales, such as "The Queer Garment" or "Romaine." "Romaine" is a retelling of Basile's "Parsley" and the Grimm's "Rapunzel," in which the eponymous boy is exchanged as a newborn for a head of romaine lettuce. The witch figure who raises the protagonist is an ogre who represents hegemonic and toxic masculinity. As such, he wants to raise Romaine to be "an ogre, like me" (Cashorali, *Fairy Tales* 55), so he discourages Romaine's effeminate tendencies and forces him to play with "butch" toys in his tower. There is ambiguity in the story, which otherwise does not invite dissenting readings: at some point, the ogre confesses he finds Romaine secretly fascinating "because he was so unlike everything the ogre knew" (*Fairy Tales* 55). This curiosity is never acknowledged again, nor is it implied elsewhere, but it opens a small fissure in the text that suggests repressed queer desire. Inevitably, Romaine grows up and lets a prince climb up his hair and into his bed. The ogre finds them together and declares: "That's the most disgusting thing I've ever [seen]!" (*Fairy Tales* 58). When the ogre's attempts to model Romaine into his hypermasculine image fail, he declares him "no ogre" (*Fairy Tales* 58) and throws Romaine out of his tower—an act that echoes homophobic parental rejection.

Cashorali's "The Queer Garment," a retelling of Andersen's "The Emperor's New Clothes," explores a different facet of homophobia. In this tale, the emperor is obsessed with appearing straight, even though, much like King Crossbill's palace, his realm is distinctly queer:

> Neither the emperor nor his ministers—nor any of his subjects, for that matter—were straight. But the emperor had gotten the idea into his head that this was the proper way to appear and act, and nothing could dissuade him from it. (*Gay Fairy & Folk Tales* 16)

The kingdom's famously cunning tailors contrive to create an outrageously flamboyant suit for the emperor and tell him that, to anyone who is straight, "it will look entirely straight. But to anyone who isn't, it will look very queer indeed" (*Gay Fairy & Folk Tales* 19). This false promise is a commentary on queer clothing codes. Queer sartorial codes have historically been used to resist normative gender expectations and to signal sexual identity within and outside the in-group. Several codes emerged in the 1970s, such as the elaborate hanky code, which allowed gay men to convey sexual preferences (Cage 41–44), and the appropriation of ideal representations of American masculinity in the "clone style" (Hobson 75), which favored butch images such as the construction worker, the lumberjack, and the cowboy. These identifying markers could be worn outside the physical confines of gay subculture, since some of these codes—particularly the clone style—could pass as straight while still signaling homoerotic interest to informed observers. Similarly, the tailors in Cashorali's story promise the emperor a magical outfit that will conceal the wearer's homosexuality to the heterosexual (or heterosexual-acting) onlooker but will reveal queer erotic possibilities to those who can see them.

Outwardly queer tendencies, and particularly effeminacy, are forbidden in the realm, so everyone who sees the emperor wearing his bright pink suit remarks on how straight-looking it seems. As one minister remarks, "Sober? Why, it looks positively funereal" (Cashorali, *Gay Fairy & Folk Tales* 19). The clone style was subversive, with its exaggerated parodying references to stereotypical masculinity, but the ability of clones to blend in with normative society gave them a degree of passing privilege that feminine gay men lacked. Many such clones adopted a hypermasculine style as a rejection of feminized gay stereotypes (Levine 58). Thus, Cashorali's story criticizes this brand of homophobia within the gay community: the emperor lives in a realm reminiscent of a gay enclave populated entirely by queer subjects, making laws that force everyone to conform to heteronormative, hypermasculine appearances feel strikingly out of place.

When the emperor goes on a walk to show everyone "what a man should look like" (*Gay Fairy & Folk Tales* 21), his subjects fearfully pretend not to see the outfit, except an old man, who sees the flowery embroidery and cries out: "It's a pansy, a splendid pansy!" (*Gay Fairy & Folk Tales* 22). Whereas Andersen had the eyes of a child pierce through the tailors' deceit, Cashorali has the obvious observation (with the word "pansy" carrying a double meaning) come from an old man whose "eyesight wasn't all it had once been" (*Gay Fairy & Folk Tales* 22). Andersen's Romantic, prepubescent child derives wisdom from lack of experience, but Cashorali queers this dichotomy between innocence and experience by situating the ironically clear-eyed old gay man as the mouthpiece of simple truth. As in the original tale, his remark breaks the "spell," and everyone, including the emperor, comes to embrace diverse self-expression.

Mortality, HIV, and AIDS

Cashorali tends to resolve his narratives in the inviolable happy ending that has become fundamental to fairy tales. Strict gender and sexual boundaries become a thing of the past, everyone learns the most important lessons, and real conflict magically removes itself from Cashorali's queer utopias. One theme, however, resists these neat happy-ending closures in Cashorali's tales, and that is mortality, always—explicitly or not—linked to HIV and AIDS. Many of Cashorali's death-themed retellings are based on obvious sources, such as the Grimms' "Mary's Child" or "Godfather Death," both of which already include themes of mortality. Cashorali's version of "Godfather Death," for example, takes place in a kingdom beset by a devastating, unnamed epidemic that affects the king's son. In the original Brothers Grimm tale, the king and princess fall merely ill, but Cashorali alludes to HIV/AIDS by mentioning a widespread and unnamed epidemic. As Sharon Oard Warner argues, most early AIDS fiction did not "even mention [the disease] by name," a disease with no name to go with the love that dare not speak its own (S. Warner 491). At the root of that avoidance was a fear of alienating the presumed heterosexual reader, but also the concern that addressing such a transient topic would curtail the work's lasting importance (S. Warner 491–93). Cashorali, of course, introduces numerous similarly transient social issues in all his tales, and he includes recognizable references to HIV/AIDS in at least six of them. He only refers to HIV/AIDS openly in "Rumpelstiltskin," revealing some reticence to address it directly.

While Cashorali's retelling of "Godfather Death" is otherwise quite like the Grimms', its protagonist is particularly fixated on saving the prince, defying his godfather, Death, three times. Death is considerably more lenient in this version than in the pretext and does not kill his godson for his repeated defiance. Instead, he delivers an ominous send-off: "I wash my hands of you. From now on, you're on your own" (*Fairy*

Tales 132). His godson returns to his prince's bedside, but the story does not conclude with a conventional happily-ever-after; it stops without making any promises about the lovers' future. In the context of the AIDS crisis, who would not have wanted to permanently cheat death for their loved ones? Cashorali, however, may have been reluctant to offer a fantastical solution to a very real tragedy.

Some retellings draw from sources whose connection to the theme of mortality is more tenuous, or altogether absent. Cashorali inserts HIV/AIDS in retellings of the Grimms' "Rumpelstiltskin," Perrault's "The Master Cat, or Puss in Boots," and Andersen's "The Ugly Duckling." Cashorali's approach to HIV/AIDS in "Rumpelstiltskin" is particularly direct, aiming to address and correct ignorant narratives about the disease. As in the Grimms' version, the protagonist is visited by the well-known imp, but the situation is quite different: the imp reveals to the protagonist a way to tame an angry prince, and the price he asks for in return is the protagonist's happiness, to be paid in a year's time. The protagonist desperately accepts these terms, and after a year of living happily with the prince, the imp reappears to tell him he is HIV-positive. As his happiness vanishes, Rumpelstiltskin offers the protagonist a final way out:

> I could make you a special, one-time-only offer. If you can tell me, in these next three nights, three guesses per night, why you're positive, what that means for you as a person, I'll give you enough happiness to live a good life. (Cashorali, *Fairy Tales* 50)

This provides Cashorali with the perfect opportunity to voice and challenge recurring homophobic arguments, as the protagonist repeatedly answers incorrectly: "I'm positive because . . . God thinks I'm a bad person? Sex equals death? Too many poppers? . . . [it is] nature's way of telling me I'm not what she had in mind?" (*Fairy Tales* 50). At the end of the third night, as in the Grimms' tale, he finds the correct answer: "It's just a virus I was exposed to. A terrible one, but just a virus" (*Fairy Tales* 52). Cashorali is thus contesting the dominant, moralistic, and negative—"if not annihilative"—representation of HIV and AIDS, instead to advance what Thomas Yingling called "a discourse of empowerment, meaning, and possibility" (101). The protagonist ultimately does get enough happiness back to live a good life, which approximates the happy ending without promising utopian happiness.

Cashorali's versions of "Puss in Boots" and "The Ugly Duckling" approach the HIV/AIDS crisis from the perspective of those who love and care for people with AIDS. In his version of "Puss in Boots," titled "Penny Loafers," AIDS is the catalyst that compels the disenfranchised protagonist to ask the resourceful Puss in Boots character for help:

> There was once a young man . . . who fell in love with a furniture maker . . . And for quite a long while, they were very happy. But George became ill, and after getting worse, getting better, and then getting much worse, he died. He died at ten o'clock in the morning and didn't leave a will. (Cashorali, *Fairy Tales* 133)

The story addresses some of the issues that gay men faced during the AIDS crisis. When someone died in the United States without having written a will, the surviving same-sex partner had no legal right to inheritance. This lack of inheritance rights, along with other marital rights afforded to heterosexual married couples, accelerated the fight for marriage equality. The situation became even more emotionally and materially fraught when the deceased partner's blood relatives opposed the relationship, which is the case in "Penny Loafers." In the story, "At ten forty-five, his three sisters who hadn't spoken to him in many years arrived at the door . . . and by the time the sun set, George's lovely house was empty" (Cashorali, *Fairy Tales* 133). Cashorali's story denounces the hypocrisy of relatives who scorn gay family members in life, but in death suddenly remember that "blood is thicker than water," and often entirely overlook the labor and suffering of their relative's partners and caregivers (Cashorali, *Fairy Tales* 133).

The effects of AIDS on caregivers are similarly explored in "The Ugly Duckling," a retelling of Andersen's story. Andersen's "The Ugly Duckling" easily lends itself to queering: it is a tale about the queer outsider who eventually finds a community in which he fits. Cashorali, however, takes the story in an unexpected direction. Although the beginning is similar enough, with a duckling who feels like he does not belong until he finds he wants to be like the beautiful swans who sometimes visit his corner of the pond, the story shifts into a narrative about friendship and endurance. The duckling finds the swans beautiful, but a drab blue loon approaches him, and an unlikely and lasting friendship blossoms. The loon begins to feel increasingly tired, raising immediate concern: "Everyone knew there was an illness going round . . . that it was almost always fatal, and one of the symptoms was fatigue" (*Fairy Tales* 120). As the loon's health deteriorates, the self-involved duckling, "who had never taken care of anyone" (*Fairy Tales* 120) must step into the role of caretaker.

Like many caretakers of people with AIDS, the duckling faces the looming reality of a loved one's shortened lifespan, with the ensuing "pressurized perception of the world" (R. Levin, Buckingham, and Hart 74). As such, he departs from a chrononormative life and instead experiences *queer time*, a term coined by Jack Halberstam, which initiates "once one leaves the temporal frames of bourgeois reproduction and family, longevity, risk/safety, and inheritance" (Halberstam, *In a Queer Time and Place* 6). Blurring the boundaries of normative time also allows for a particularly surprising ending:

> Then the duck, who was neither a duckling nor ugly any longer, gathered some food . . . and brought it back to their nest.
> And that
> is where the two of them are
> right now. (Cashorali, *Fairy Tales* 123)

Past, present, and future are flattened in this ending. Although the stair-like formatting of the text suggests movement or progression, there is no indication that time passes, and the excerpt is devoid of any of the markers of life—including, perhaps, the most defining and most universal one that threads through the tale: death. By disengaging the characters from normative temporality, Cashorali also disentangles them from normative narrative expectations, eschewing both the finality of tragedies and the utopian orientation of fairy tales[16] in favor of an ephemeral instant, forever suspended in time.

---

16 Some German folktales end on the phrase "if they have not died, they are still alive," as an alternative to "and they lived happily ever after." The former ending can be found in some of Cashorali's tales, the Grimms' "Foundling-Bird," and in other traditional tales like "The Enchanted Princess" and "The Tale of the Silver, Golden

The Margins of Gay Subculture

Even though happy endings are not absolute in AIDS-related tales, they contain a certain undercurrent of immediate, achievable contentment, if not hope, with its connotation of futurity. This contentment in Cashorali's retellings is related invariably to community in its many forms, as previously isolated characters come to find love, friendship, a general sense of belonging, or all three. Given the nature of the tales, this community is subcultural and almost always gay. In most cases, the community depicted is quite uniformly white, middle-class, and homonormative, but there are some stories in which Cashorali explores some of the subcultures within the gay world that have historically been positioned against hegemonic models of gay culture. This is the case in his retelling of "Hansel and Gretel," which features drag queens, and his retelling of "The Beauty and the Beast," which includes nods to BDSM[17] and leather culture.

Cashorali's retelling of "Hansel and Gretel" is based on the Grimms' story of the same name. It features the two siblings, who are eventually abandoned by their parents in the middle of the forest where, as prescribed by the pretext, they find the candy house. Instead of the traditional witch, a beautiful woman emerges from inside:

> She had big bouffant hair the colour of moonlight and a wrap of white fur, and when the lights hit her long dress they broke into a thousand pieces and danced. She wasn't young at all. (*Fairy Tales* 38)

The mysterious figure invites them inside. While Gretel is reluctant and distrustful, Hansel feels an instant connection to the woman. Though only the façade of the home is made of candy, it is "much, much larger on the inside than on the outside" (*Fairy Tales* 39). Such indications of magic are further confirmed when the woman and Hansel sit down to talk:

---

and Diamond Prince"—both of which can be found in Kurt Ranke's *Folktales of Germany* (1966). Queer temporalities are, once again, evidently rather pervasive in the genre.

17 This acronym stands for a combination of different sexual practices and activities: bondage/discipline, dominance/submission, and sadomasochism.

> "Do you like magic?" And, without waiting for an answer, she opened a jar of cream, smoothed some on her face, and wiped it off with tissue. "Now . . . Who shall I be?" She took out pencils and brushes and . . . with just a few strokes she gave herself a completely different face. (*Fairy Tales* 39)

While Cashorali's retellings are fantastical and full of unexplained wonder, traditional fairy-tale magical powers are largely absent from his stories. In fact, Cashorali most closely approximates the idea of magic when addressing the transformative abilities of drag queens, as seen in the previous example.

In addition to the witch in "Hansel and Gretel," his retelling of the "Sleeping Beauty" tale, "The Beauty in the Mountain of Ice," also casts the thirteen fairies as drag queens:

> Curious about what was up there, he climbed the stairs [and saw] a balding, middle-aged man . . . Now, this man was the evil thirteenth fairy, who had removed all her makeup, taken off her wig, and exchanged her lovely gown for a wrinkled seersucker suit. (*Gay Fairy & Folk Tales* 24)

The witch in "Hansel and Gretel" and the evil fairy in "The Beauty in the Mountain of Ice" are the only two characters who are openly drag queens. The fact that they are both villains recalls Disney's tendency to convey moral deviance and monstrosity through gender nonconformity. This reading is undercut when it is implied that the other twelve (good) fairies in "The Beauty in the Mountain of Ice" are also drag queens, and Hansel, who is cast as the hero of "Hansel and Gretel," ultimately becomes a drag queen himself.

The drag queen witch in "Hansel and Gretel" attempts to groom Hansel to be her successor, which raises a homophobic alarm in Gretel: "We have to escape . . . She's turning you into her" (*Fairy Tales* 40). The homophobic connotations become even clearer when Gretel thinks that "the lady was eating Hansel a bit at a time" (*Fairy Tales* 40). This echoes not only the cannibalism of its source material, but also common moral panic rhetoric that equates homosexuality with monstrous appetite and queerness with sexual predation.[18] Gretel's homophobic anxiety about her brother being "turned," assimilated or otherwise consumed by the gay world is framed within an overarching rivalry between the cisgender girl and the woman-in-performance, the biological sister and the potential chosen family. The narrative ultimately favors Gretel when she tricks the vain witch into stepping into the oven and burning to death.

This normative narrative turn, which eliminates the gender-nonconforming character, is challenged at the end, when Gretel finds her brother in the witch's dressing room, completely transformed:

> [As] he passed the triple mirror he saw her . . . and oh, she was beautiful. When Hansel smiled with joy to see her, she smiled back, and when he raised his hand to his face, the lady raised her hand in farewell. (Cashorali, *Fairy Tales* 42)

In a way, it is Hansel who effectively consumes the witch, who appears for the last time as his reflection before she dissolves into the nowhere space within the mirror. The drag queen witch remains an ambiguous figure in this story, cast as the villain but also as an affirming model of identity for Hansel. One can go further to say that she is the embodiment of Hansel's queer future and must be absorbed by him for his journey of self-discovery to be complete. The witch's ambiguity is further compounded by the uncertainty surrounding her status as a drag queen: she is said to transform into several movie stars in the style of a drag queen impersonator, but there is no moment where her gender performance breaks down, unlike the example cited earlier, in which the evil fairy of "The Beauty in the Mountain of Ice" is surprised while out of character. Although transgender people can and do perform drag,[19] the witch's seamless gender presentation raises questions about her (and, by

---

18 The connections between monstrosity/monstrousness and queerness will be further explored in chapter three.

19 A heated discussion on the boundaries of drag was sparked in 2018 by television personality and famous drag queen RuPaul, who remarked that he would not allow post-transition transwomen to participate in his reality show, *RuPaul's Drag Race*. He eventually reconsidered this position (see S. Levin).

extension, Hansel's) gender identity, which might be better addressed in a transgender reading of the story.

If drag queens represent the most feminine end of the spectrum of gay culture, leathermen occupy the opposite end as ultra-masculine BDSM enthusiasts "who wear distinctive black leather outfits, military-style leather caps . . . and leather harnesses" (Weems 480). In Cashorali's version of "The Beauty and the Beast," the Beast is depicted as a leatherman. His retelling follows the version included in Andrew Lang's *The Blue Fairy Book*, which is an abridged version of Madame Gabrielle de Villeneuve's romance novel published in 1740 (Griswold 93). Villeneuve's story formed the basis for the best-known version of the tale: Jeanne-Marie Leprince de Beaumont's 1756 adaptation, which in turn inspired later versions, including Disney's 1991 animated film. Cashorali, as usual, follows a familiar script but turns the female protagonist into a man:

> His name was Buddy, but because, as even his father had to admit, he was much prettier than boys usually are, everyone called him Beauty. (*Fairy Tales* 21)

Although reimagined as a boy, Beauty retains the characteristics that made the female Beauty desirable: he is gentle, pure of heart, cheerful, and, of course, beautiful. But these are not prized masculine qualities, and he is seen as lesser than his brothers.

As in the source material, Beauty is fond of flowers. When his father asks him what he would like from a business trip, Beauty requests a flower. Stopping at a beautiful penthouse, the merchant stays the night and finds an exquisite dark orchid that "looks like a bruise" (*Fairy Tales*, 25), foreshadowing the sadomasochistic elements that emerge later in the story.[20] At that moment, an alarm goes off—"like the roar of an angry animal" (*Fairy Tales* 24)—and a man in a leather outfit seizes the merchant:

---

20 This also calls to mind Proust's image of a bee fertilizing an orchid when describing gay sex between two characters in *Sodom and Gomorrah* (1922), which incidentally is in keeping with the botanical/zoological theme of Cashorali's retelling.

> Now, the huge irritated someone was wearing nothing except a costume made of leather straps and steel rings. Because the merchant had seen harnesses like that only on horses and dogs, he concluded that he was in the grip of a beast. (*Fairy Tales* 24)

Interestingly, the merchant's impression of animality is what initially casts the leatherman as the Beast in the narrative. This dehumanization is reminiscent of attitudes about the sexually nonconforming. In this case, his non-normativity is twofold, as the Beast belongs to a kinky subset of the gay community (Eynat-Confino, 93). Like monsters, queer people have historically been seen as living proof of the dangers of deviating from the norm. Thus, it is not surprising that many queer people should have resonated with the monstrous, interspecies fairy tale, leading to many a queer revision: from Jean Cocteau's 1946 film *La Belle et la Bête*, to Namjoshi's 1981 "A Moral Tale," to Donoghue's 1997 short story "The Tale of the Rose." Even one of the most popular versions among younger audiences, Disney's 1991 *Beauty and the Beast* has a discernible queer undercurrent. Howard Ashman, who was the lyricist for the film and an HIV-positive gay man who died before its release, greatly identified with the Beast. This sense of kinship reflected in his lyrics for the film. As his partner Bill Lausch remarked:

> Gay people will always identify with someone who's on the outside, who is feared and misunderstood . . . We respond to being perceived as ugly, as a monster. People are afraid of what they don't understand—that's actually in the lyrics of one of the songs. (Lassel 77)[21]

After the first meeting with the Beast, Cashorali's story unfolds in a familiar manner: the father vows to send his younger son to the Beast's place in exchange for his freedom. Beauty goes willingly, knowing himself to be a disappointment to his father. Once he is at the Beast's

---

21 Lausch was referring to the lyrics of the appropriately named "Mob Song," which plays when the villagers are getting ready to kill the Beast: "We don't like/ what we don't understand/ in fact it scares us/ And this monster is mysterious at least" (*Beauty and the Beast*).

penthouse, the Beast reveals to him what the terms of their domestic discipline arrangement will be: "During the day . . . your only responsibility will be to take care of my orchids . . . At night, after you've eaten, your only responsibility will be to make me happy" (Cashorali, *Fairy Tales* 26–27). Cashorali thus brings the sexual innuendo of Beauty's captivity to the forefront: in his retelling, the transaction is openly sexualized but also framed within the ritualistic and honest approach to sex particular to BDSM culture (Bauer 147). After each sex session, Beast asks Beauty a question originally posed in de Villeneuve's version of this story: "Beauty . . . do you love me?" (Cashorali, *Fairy Tales* 27). To which Beauty answers: "No, I don't love you . . . How could I? You're a Beast" (*Fairy Tales* 27).

This is how Beauty spends his days: at night, he performs his sexual ritual with Beast, which culminates with the same question-and-answer sequence, but during the day, he is allowed to explore the penthouse. He takes care of the plants and eventually finds the library, where he discovers a passion for reading and learning. For Beauty, the penthouse soon becomes the site of personal growth rather than a prison, where his queer curiosity gets to thrive far away from his repressive, heterocentric family home. At the end of the story, Beauty comes back from visiting his family and sees the Beast, standing before him for the first time under the light of day:

> To his amazement, the person . . . wasn't a beast at all, but the handsomest man he had ever seen. "Beast . . . Were you under a spell all this time?"
>
> "No . . . You were. Now the spell is broken, and you're free. You can leave or stay." (*Fairy Tales* 34)

By peeking beneath the illusion his father had cast, Beauty breaks down ontological barriers: "I want to stay with you . . . On one condition . . . That tonight, after dinner . . . you'll be Beauty, and I'll be the Beast" (*Fairy Tales* 34). Beauty breaks free from the spell of his father's heterocentric vision, which had distorted the queer unknown into something ugly, monstrous, and scary. In doing so, Beauty steps outside of the passive role traditionally assigned to him in fairy tales.

Michael Ford's *Happily Ever After: Erotic Fairy Tales for Men*

Michael Ford's collection contains twenty-eight stories, each written by a different author. The collection is aptly named: it features erotic reimaginations of fairy tales, in which the obligatory happy ending is sometimes a traditional romantic conclusion. Even when that is not the case, the sexual slant of the retellings guarantees that there is at least *one* kind of happy ending, which playfully fulfills the narrative requirements of the genre. Unlike in Cashorali's books, the collection does not feature careful annotations of interconnected sources, but each story is prefaced by a short epigraph in which each author introduces their retelling. Through these epigraphs, authors draw from an ample range of sources and traditions, from Native American myths to Middle Eastern folklore, although this section will analyze stories rooted in the Western European tradition.

Ford writes in the introduction that fairy tales are not only entertaining stories for children but "treasure chests of information that taught us, knowingly or not, about love, life and what was expected of us" (Ford 1). His understanding of fairy tales thus mirrors Cashorali's, as he takes them to be teaching tools that would, among other things, prime little boys and girls for their assimilation into an exclusively heterosexual society. However, Ford emphasizes that these little boys and girls have the capacity to be dissenting readers:

> What more beautiful image is there than of a father reading his son the same stories his father read to him as a boy. Little does he know that . . . his little man is dreaming of the prince who will take him in his arms, wondering exactly what the Big Bad Wolf would do if he ever caught the naughty little pigs, or learning that the forbidden desires of the darkened woods can bring all kinds of pleasures. (Ford 2)

Thus, the authoritative, didactic, and prescriptive role of traditional stories is challenged in this understanding, and fairy tales are recast as the landscape in which the specter of sexually nonconforming desire first takes hazy shape. The very acknowledgment of sexuality of any kind in children goes against childhood's "freshly scrubbed face" image, which Ford urges readers and writers to question primarily by reaching "beneath the deceptively simple" stories told to children, to find "the hidden truths flowing below" (Ford 3–4).

According to Eric Tribunella, rediscovering childhood texts through the lens of sexual adult experience taps into the "carnivalesque pleasure [of] adult nostalgia, revelry in the taboo, and exertion of adult agency over the artifacts of childhood" (Tribunella, "Kiddie Lit" 136). Since the connection between fairy tales and childhood has become inescapable, the practice of eroticizing fairy tales carries a unique, illicit appeal, as it targets the ultimate "artifact of childhood." Such reinterpretations are not exclusive to postmodernism.[22] Heterosexuality is still the more common configuration of erotic retellings, but the retellings in Ford's collection go a step further in reveling in the taboo by being exclusively and explicitly queer. Therefore, much like Cashorali's stories, Ford's collection works as an antidote to normative society's oppressive narratives. Perhaps even more than Cashorali's collections, Ford's anthology is framed as an attempt to retroactively reclaim childhood—not for other queer children, but for the child-selves of its readers and writers. These sexualized stories turn back to that remembered and perhaps partly imagined past, a period of solitude, invisibility, and confusion, overwriting it with the promise of what the authors know lies beyond. In Tribunella's words, it is a kind of "cultural therapy" ("Older Children" 629). As the following sections show, Ford's "cultural therapy" tackles themes that overlap with those found in Cashorali's collections, such as diverse gay identities, the HIV/AIDS crisis, and the journey to queer belonging, revealing a common thread of experience for gay men in the mid-1990s.

Gay Identities

As Simon Sheppard writes in the epigraph to his retelling "The Ugly Duckling," queer people learn early that "identity is complex," with many layers and intersections that might require understanding "coming out" as "a succession of self-defining moments," and not a single event (Sheppard 91). People may also come out in increments at various points in

22 See for instance *Fairy Tales for the Disillusioned: Enchanted Stories from the French Decadent Tradition*, edited by Seifert and Gretchen Schultz (2016).

their lives to different groups of people, narratively creating a "temporal trajectory within which [periods] of disclosure [follow periods] of repression" (Halberstam, *In a Queer Time and Place* 36). If queer temporalities exist independently from normative time, coming-out moments might substitute or overshadow some normative landmarks of life experience. For instance, while reaching the age of majority might be an important milestone for many people, coming out of the closet might be a more significant moment for queer individuals. Living in the closet can push back a lot of the experiences nonqueer people first encounter during adolescence, such as first loves and early sexual experiences, which further reinforces the impression that queer people live out of step, perhaps even out of time, outside the bounds of chrononormativity. Heather Love highlights how queer people embrace this backwardness as a key feature of queer culture—"in celebrations of perversion, in defiant refusals to grow up" (Love 7). However, the succession of coming-outs that Sheppard describes suggests a progressive unfolding of identity that both mimics a normative growing-up process and offers an alternative to it. The following analysis will illustrate how stories in Ford's collection explore the characters' awakening to new parts of their identity, and how identities shift and are reorganized in relation to queer time and queer space.

Many of the stories collected in *Happily Ever After* depict BDSM sex in one way or another, which is also a common theme in Cashorali's less explicit collections. Robin Bauer points out that Western BDSM culture has its roots in post–World War II biker clubs comprised of homosexual war veterans who would replicate military discipline in their sexual practices (Bauer 143). As a result, BDSM has been closely linked to the gay community from its modern beginnings. However, BDSM remains a marginal sexual practice even within the gay community, often necessitating its own distinct coming-out process (Bauer 142). In Ford's collection, BDSM themes often emerge in retellings where the pretexts suggests a dominance-and-submission dynamic or another form of power imbalances, such as William Mann's "Jack and the Beanstalk," in which a boy is trained by a giant to be a good submissive partner, and Michael Lassell's "The Three Bears," in which the Goldilocks character engages in a sexual encounter with the three "bears"—a reference to the gay slang term.

They also emerge, interestingly, in retellings of tales in which identity is a central theme, such as "The Frog King," or, predictably, "The Ugly Duckling." Andersen's "The Ugly Duckling" is a tale that tackles identity, alterity, and belonging head-on, as seen in Cashorali's version. Sheppard's version of the tale taps into this potential for queering by emulating a coming-out narrative, but adds a slight twist to it:

> Once upon a time, a man named Swann looked into a mirror and did not much like what he saw there. For you see, the man in Swann's mirror was decidedly middle-aged. (Sheppard 91)

The appropriately named Swann[23] must come to terms with aging in a commercial gay scene that greatly privileges youth and, as Rebecca Jones writes, is "even hostile to older age" (23). In this context, "older age" can mean just barely "over thirty" (R. Jones 23), and Swann spends several years rejecting his own aging process. He desperately latches onto the artifacts of youth by turning "his cap back-to-front" (Sheppard 92) when young people start doing it, and by peppering "his earlobes with new holes" (Sheppard 92) when that seems like the fashionable choice, which echoes the "defiant refusal" to grow up mentioned by Love (7).

Eventually, the dissonance between his inner image and the image others perceive becomes too great to ignore:

> Castro Street on a sunny Saturday was a place for the young and beautiful . . . youths showed off their nipple rings, nose rings, navel rings, and rings God knew where else, putting Swann's few pathetic earrings to shame. *He's old. He's ugly*, Swann thought he heard them say. (Sheppard 92)

San Francisco's Castro Street is depicted here as a distinctly queer space in that it is (apparently exclusively) populated by queer men, but also in that queer desires have seeped into the public sphere, refashioning the rules of normative society so that youthfulness and a queer interpretation of male beauty reign supreme. These social rules are, however,

---

23 This might be a layered reference: one to Andersen's swan, and the other to Proust's Charles Swann, who has been read as queer.

still narrow and exclusionary, and, because he does not fit the paradigm, Swann feels increasingly out of place.

He tries the sex club, the gym, and the gay bar in search of a pocket within the queerscape that would accept him, but he is repeatedly rejected. Swann heads home by way of a cruising area where men seek anonymous sex, and while he is rejected by many men, until one boy calls out:

> "Hello, Daddy," the tall, skinny boy said. *Daddy! Was he really that old, then? Daddy!* At first, Swann thought he should feel insulted. But he didn't . . . He felt something entirely new. (Sheppard 95)

Swann and his new lover have sex in a public space, in front of appreciative onlookers, and they never exchange names. Their encounter defies regulated heteronormative expectations, which sanction only one-on-one, private, (hetero)sexual encounters, usually within a monogamous relationship. The roles of daddy and boy that these characters assume create a scenario in which incestuous taboo and the power differential of an intergenerational relationship are consciously harnessed for erotic purposes, which sets them further apart from the norm. This proves to be a transformative experience for Swann, who sees his identity reshaped as he learns to "see himself in the mirror of the boy's desire" (Sheppard 96). At the end of the story, Swann comes out as a leather daddy, which opens new possibilities of kinship for him: "Saturdays on Castro Street, he nodded at other men who looked like him: handsome, balding men who carried themselves well in their leathers" (Sheppard 96–97). Sheppard's story thus reroutes the traditional path to happiness and fulfillment, which would include marriage and the promise of reproduction in the heteronormative trajectory, while he highlights less-common ways of belonging within a queer space.

Jesse Monteagudo's "The Prince and the Pauper," which follows Mark Twain's novel but also inserts some Cinderella elements, shares several themes with Sheppard's story, though its protagonist and overall message stand in stark contrast. The protagonist of Monteagudo's story, Tom Conte, a twist on the original pauper's name, Tom Conty. Conte is a common Italian name, but it also means "tale" in French, reinforcing the story's fairy-tale connections. Unlike Swann, Conte is exceptionally attractive—just like men who walked up and down Castro Street in "The Ugly Duckling"—and he has no trouble commanding attention in the same spaces Swann was invisible:

> Tom had a body that wouldn't quit, both on the job by day and at the hottest gay discos and sex clubs by night. Then he was a prince, worshipped by every man, approached by only a few. (Monteagudo 284)

Conte is, as befits his character, "a pauper" (Monteagudo 284), but as soon as he enters a queer space, this side of his identity fades away and he is worshipped like "a prince" (Monteagudo 284). This is especially true in the sex club, where all markers of wealth or lack thereof are stripped away along with clothing.

In his epigraph, Monteagudo argues that the gay world shakes up the normative hierarchy, so that wealth and class "are less important than youth and beauty" (Monteagudo 283), a sentiment already reflected in Sheppard's retelling. This leveling of the playing field allows the pauper and the prince to interact as equals when they first meet: "Tom approached his twin, aroused by the opportunity to make love to himself" (Monteagudo 286). However, this narcissistic fantasy dissolves as soon as they are done having sex and they step outside of the liminal, magical space of the sex club. Outside, all the material differences between them are thrown into sharp relief:

> As the two men dressed, Tom began to notice the differences between Ed Tuttle and himself. Instead of the old T-shirt and jeans that Tom wore, Ed put on an expensive outfit. . . . Astonished by the contrast, Tom followed his new friend to the parking lot, where Ed's Rolls Royce awaited them, a new model bearing the license plate PRINZ ED. Once in the car, the men drove . . . toward Ed's penthouse apartment. (Monteagudo 286).

Once the spell breaks, neither can go back to the illusion of equality that marked their first meeting. The "prince," Ed Tuttle, is revealed to be the closeted heir to a great fortune, which places him far away from Tom's less-than-privileged reality. The power of the gay world to upend hierarchies proves limited, as Ed remains closeted to avoid losing his position within the family business. Their relationship seems doomed until Ed's father dies, freeing him to live openly as a gay man and to pursue his love for Tom. Tom thus follows the well-trodden rags-to-riches path that reveals him as a Cinderella figure.

Monteagudo describes the restructured hierarchy of the gay space and illustrates how gay desire's transformative power "helps us transcend the boundaries of race and class" (Monteagudo 284).[24] However, this assertion ignores racial and class tensions within the gay community, which has historically been overrepresented by middle- and upper-class, city-dwelling white men. It is telling that the author (a Latino man) chose two white-coded men as the protagonists of his story, who met in a high-cost sex club that restricted access to people with fewer economic resources, and who managed to reach happiness—while Ed Tuttle retained his economic status—via normative channels of inheritance. As Monteagudo puts it, "while our desire can get us through the night, we need more than our libido in order to make it past breakfast" (Monteagudo 284). In Monteagudo's narrative, gay desire can momentarily overturn hierarchy, but only inside queer spaces; beyond their borders, both characters are forced back under more powerful social structures of power.

HIV/AIDS as Magical Condition

Ford's erotic collection does not avoid the topic of HIV/AIDS—in fact, the themes of death and sex are sometimes intimately intertwined. The treatment of the crisis in these stories is not significantly different from that of Cashorali's tales, particularly when it comes to avoiding the disease's name. Of all twenty-eight stories, only Robert Thompson's "The Traveling Companion" mentions AIDS by name. A key difference between these collections is the prominent role of magic in Ford's treatment of the epidemic. For instance, in Bruce Benderson's "Pinocchio in the Port Authority," Pinocchio is a hustler who meets the famous Blue

---

24 This is reminiscent of Edward Carpenter's assertion when writing about cross-class, homosexual relationships in *The Intermediate Sex*: "Eros is a great leveler" (114).

Fairy. Besides enabling a facile double entendre, the Blue Fairy is revealed to be under a debilitating spell:

> The Blue Fairy had been lithe and attractive just a few months before and had loved every kind of pleasure—dinner parties and clubs, sex and leather. Then a spell had begun to transform him into an unwell, emaciated man. (11)

Here, AIDS is a magical malady—mysteriously contracted and transmitted—so that not even the powerful Blue Fairy is immune to it.

Historical overreaction to the transmission of HIV/AIDS can be understood in the context of the law of magical contagion (Rozin, Markwith, and Nemeroff, 108). This principle states, "when two objects touch . . . they pass properties to one another" (Rozin, Markwith, and Nemeroff, 1082). A 1989 study by Rozin, Nemeroff, Wane, and Sherrod concludes this was a deeply entrenched belief among Americans. Magical contagion was considered positive if the contact was between an object and a revered or loved person, but negative if the contact was between an object and a despised or feared person (367–70). When it came to the issue of HIV/AIDS, Rozin, Markwith, and Nemeroff find that, besides an excessive fear of contagion through non-risky contact, people morally objected to any kind of contact with the affected—a fear of stigmatization by association (108).

The exact process of contagion in "Pinocchio and the Port Authority" is unknown, and Pinocchio sees a kindred spirit in the gaunt Blue Fairy: "there was a look of purity to his ravaged body. In fact, it seemed worn and polished down into simple, elongated curves, much like Pinocchio's" (Benderson 11). Pinocchio's status as a marginalized, homeless sex worker negates any potential stigmatization that could arise from associating with a person with AIDS, and the fact that he is made of wood makes him immune to diseases of the flesh. "How wonderful," the Blue Fairy thinks at some point, "to be made of wood and never have to worry about getting sick" (Benderson 11). HIV/AIDS is ultimately transmitted through mysterious magical means in "Pinocchio in the Port Authority."

D. Travers Scott's "Hansel and Gretel" comes closer to depicting the less literal "magical contagion" that Rozin, Markwith, and Nemeroff describe:

> A terrible plague and famine gripped the land, filling their every day with suspicion and fear. No medicine could prevent or cure the plague. Some people died immediately . . . others wasted away over years . . . The sickness spread from person to person through the slightest touch: brushing shoulders, holding hands, kissing, embracing . . . Children learned to walk without the guidance of parents' hands. Over the years, the disease had forced lovers to stay virgins. (Travers Scott 312)

Whether this AIDS-like plague is transmitted through physical contact or by supernatural means is unclear, but in this story, all human contact leads to death. This pushes people to extremes: they stop touching each other completely and close themselves off to the world. Hansel and Gretel are gender-nonconforming siblings who grow up in this repressive world. Hansel is shy and likes reading fantasy novels in secret, while Gretel prefers weightlifting to books. They both practice their hobbies far away from their parents' judgmental eyes, as they assume Hansel is the one exercising and Gretel the one reading. This creates a strong bond between them that eventually takes a desperate, incestuous turn:

> Once he had confessed to Gretel, and she to him, of his constant aching, his lonely hunger. They decided that night to risk the plague and touched each other, exploring their bodies together. . . . Strangely, they found no relief, only more frustration and loneliness. (Travers Scott 314)

The hunger of the pretext is transformed into hunger for contact in Travers Scott's retelling. This hunger is not sated by their touch, perhaps because they are siblings, or because both are dreaming of lovers of the same gender, "Hansel imagined her as a man, a powerful stranger who could take Hansel . . . to a far-off land where there was no plague and an equally powerful sister for Gretel" (314). Ultimately, their defiant non-normativity is the catalyst to their abandonment in the forest: their parents become suspicious that the siblings have contracted the plague because Hansel is too thin, "no matter how much he eats or exercises" (315), and that Gretel must have fallen sick as well because they spend so much time together. Thus, homophobic parental rejection emerges in this story just as in Cashorali's "Romaine"; however, here Travers Scott incorporates the HIV/AIDS stigma, with its connotations of moral transgression and a perhaps justified fear of magical contagion.

It is interesting to note that both Travers Scott's and Cashorali's retellings set the cabin in the woods as the site for a kind of reaffirming but also annihilative queer self-discovery, harnessing a particular blend of desire and fear that characterizes the Grimms' version of the tale. Much like in the Grimms' story, Hansel and Gretel will find the specific kind of nourishment they crave in the house in the forest:

> Out into the pale moonlight stepped two of the most beautiful people Hansel and Gretel had ever seen: a man and a woman, both completely naked. . . . Without a word, each embraced a child, encircling them with their arms, flooding their cold bones with warmth and rejuvenating their dry, starved skins with velvety caresses. (Travers Scott 319)

In this retelling, the witch figure is split into two characters to accommodate both gay and lesbian desire. This is particularly salient since this is the only tale (in Ford's and Cashorali's collections both) to explore lesbian sexuality—which is understandable, given the intended audience of these works—but this omission becomes even more conspicuous when readers realize this is also one of the only stories to feature lesbians at all. Lesbians are otherwise absent, even in retellings set in environments where diversity could be expected, such as gay neighborhoods.

Similar to Hansel and Gretel's first enchanted encounter with the candy house in the pretext, the siblings' initial wonder fades when they discover the horror that lurks within. The beautiful beings claim that they are free of the plague and have purified their house so that it "heals all who pass through its doors" (320). These claims seem to offer a magical cure for AIDS, a trope that Benderson and Cashorali carefully avoid in their tales. However, the story takes a dark turn. While the siblings are distracted by their sexual encounter with the two witches—an experience they perceive as "a physical engorgement, a seven-course feast after years of famine" (320)—the house itself is preparing to consume them:

> The room had changed. The walls and ceiling had moved closer. . . . Most horrifying was the fireplace, burning bright blood-red. A fireplace no longer, it yawned: a huge fleshy mouth, opening wide to reveal a wet, quivering throat pulsing with luminescent red veins. (320)

The anthropophagous house pushes the Freudian concept of the unhomely to new extremes, shattering the illusion of the safe, familiar space of the home (made doubly safe by its magical prophylactic properties) to reveal something monstrous and deadly. This house is reminiscent of other horrifying fairy-tale houses, such as Baba Yaga's chicken-legged hut, and the sea witch's house in Andersen's *The Little Mermaid*, which was made from the bones of shipwrecked human victims. The witches' house in this retelling is also made up of the bodies of previous victims that were fed to the cabin in exchange for its magical protection. Both siblings soon realize the doorknobs are closed fists, the door jambs are writhing legs, the knots in the wood are vigilant eyes, and the floor is an ambiguous sexual organ, "hairy and spastic" (321). The abject house thus blurs the boundaries between the inanimate and the living, between object and subject.

Perhaps the most frightening aspect of the house is its single-minded hunger, which mirrors and distorts the queer hunger that drew the two siblings there, adding a cautionary dimension to the retelling. The witches keep the siblings captive and attempt to extract fluids from them to "empower their hungry home-beast with a double dose of deflowering" (322). Yet, having spent their entire lives denying their physical needs, the siblings are able to resist. Meanwhile, the house claims other victims, whose disembodied parts are added to its hybrid frame:

> Hansel and Gretel would hear the screams of a new victim who had realized the witch and warlock's secret too late. Soon new faces, arms, and legs would appear in the body of the house. (323)

As in the original tale, Hansel and Gretel eventually trick the house into devouring the witches. The house collapses, letting out a "death-howl of an agonized beast" (326), then disappears into the ground.

They travel west, drawn by a hopeful light—a symbolic contrast to their dark and repressive birthplace in the east:

> Standing in the clearing where the house-beast and its evil lords had once been, they squinted up into the brilliant sun at songbirds swooping by overhead. To the east rose the dark hills of the land of their birth. To the west rose purple-green mountains of unknown lands. They smiled and continued their journey forward. (327)

"The West" is a significant concept for queer people, figured as an Edenic alternative to their ostensibly rural, intolerant places of origin. The dream of the idealized West, famously popularized by The Village People's gay anthem, "Go West," which described the 1970s "gay flight" to California, collapsed in the following decade when HIV/AIDS ravaged these enclaves of sexual freedom and social acceptance (Alwakeel 85–88). Hansel and Gretel, however, flee from an AIDS-like plague that ravages their heteronormative homeland. Revising the tale from a mid-1990s perspective, Travers Scott thus reroutes the trajectory of the epidemic and restores the dream of the Edenic queer West, allowing the two queer characters to escape unscathed toward the untouched promised land of Hansel's daydreams.

Queer Belonging

The central theme of Travers Scott's "Hansel and Gretel" is a desire to belong—to find a place where one's difference is celebrated rather than feared or despised—and a hope that such a place exists. Freeman defines queer belonging as a "longing to be, and be connected" ("Queer Belongings" 299), which suggests that connecting with others reaffirms one's existence. Recognizing that others share some of our experiences makes our own difference more legible, more coherent, and thus more real. This, in turn, explains the success of consciousness-raising groups in uniting gays and lesbians in the 1960s.

Belonging is hardly a thematic oddity in narratives that grapple with nonconforming, minoritarian identities. This same yearning for queer belonging appears in most stories analyzed in this chapter and across all three collections. Queer belonging is a central theme in the "Hansel and Gretel" and "The Ugly Duckling" retellings in Ford's collection. It is a prominent theme in Tom Bacchus's "Lily Boy," a composite retelling of several tales about miniature people, such as the Grimms' "Tom Thumb" and Andersen's "Thumbelina," both of which feature childless parents who wish for a child, however small. In Bacchus's story, the protagonist is found inside a lily in a clearing, and so he is named Lillo. Lillo never grows to be taller than an "impressive" seven inches (Bacchus 339), a tongue-in-cheek reference to an above-average penis size. His disabled status, deviant physiology, and nonconforming size put him in constant danger of being devoured, stomped on, kidnapped, or exploited for others' benefit. This sense of alterity extends to his sexuality, and the intersection of his disability and sexuality drives his need to belong.

Although he begins a rather unlikely sexual relationship with his attractive (full-sized) cousin, who is presumably bisexual, his cousin soon marries a woman. Feeling sad, Lillo wanders away from the village and follows "the path through the forest to a place that, although he did not remember having visited, felt familiar and safe" (349). This "familiar and safe" place is, of course, the liminal forest clearing where his mother first found him, and it is where Lillo later finds his people:

> "Have you been enjoying yourself in the human world?" said another creature . . . he was no taller than Lillo. The boy was caught between shock and joy. He had never seen anyone his own size. . . . These were . . .
>
> "Fairies."
>
> "Yes, all of us." (350)

Lillo discovers that there is an "us" that includes him, and the story could end neatly and happily, with Lillo finding his queer kin. However, the story delves into the complexities of balancing two separate families, as Lillo keeps his relationship with the fairies a secret from his parents. This is reminiscent of queer people who maintain a biological family and a chosen queer family and might feel split in their loyalties, remaining "some of one, some of the other" (Bacchus 351).

Most retellings follow similar structures to that of "Lily Boy," in which the protagonist's final queer belonging is part of the story's denouement. This is because queer belonging in these stories either mirrors or approximates the happy ending of the pretext. To find a departure from this script, then, one must look for retellings of fairy tales that do not feature a happy ending. Such is the case in Kyle Stone's "Aquamarine," a retelling of Andersen's famously tragic *The Little Mermaid.* Stone's retelling is a neat mirror image of Bacchus's "Lily Boy" in that it charts an opposite narrative path, from queer belonging to loneliness and abjection. It might not be entirely coincidental that they appear side-by-side in the anthology. The story begins under the sea, where human rules do not apply:

> Down there beyond the reach of men live the water people, who are neither male nor female, human nor fish, but a wonderful combination of all four. Their country is full of beautiful plants and flowers, and the sun floats down in bars of shimmering gold. All manner of amazing creatures live there, too. They glow every color of the rainbow and a lot more besides that we have no words for. (Stone 353)

Beyond its normative monarchical order, the underwater world is fantastically queer, inhabited by hybrid creatures of ambiguous gender and taxonomy. It is truly beyond the reach of men—not only physically, but conceptually—so that even the colors down there have no human name. The little mermaid character, Clare, is referred to as a "he" and has a father, but all other characters are spoken of in gender-neutral terms. His father used to have a partner, and Clare has several siblings of unspecified or unknowable gender. Clare's budding queer curiosity leads him to spy on his siblings, and one day he finds two of them "entwined in an upside-down embrace" (353), which offers a blurry glimpse into how the rules of togetherness operate under the sea. This nebulousness and queer ineffability extend to other elements of underwater life. When Clare begins to develop, he feels he is transforming into an indescribable "something 'other'," which is, for him, "inexplicably exciting" (353–54). This likens Clare to many other fairy-tale characters—beyond the little mermaid—who grow up refusing to abide by chrononormative rules, instead following an unpredictable path of queer becoming.

When a statue of a human man floats down to his garden, Clare realizes that simply becoming a grown-up merperson will not be enough for him. This "something other" he is becoming will require crossing species lines:

> Clare let his breath out in a long sigh and knew at last what he had been longing for. "I want to be a man," he said, but his tutor had fallen asleep again, which was probably just as well. He would merely say what was plainly evident: Clare was a sea prince. He would never be a man. (355)

Stone amplifies the transgender undertones in Andersen's story and adds a twist: in Stone's retelling, Clare's transition is clearly positioned against his "queerer" original state. Clare belongs to a hybrid genderqueer species but seeks to align himself with a binary-oriented, monospecific identity. Clare's journey echoes that of an intersex person, whose body is deemed incomprehensible in a mostly binary society and is typically surgically altered to conform to a binary mold.

In love with a human prince, Clare makes his way to the cisnormative human world through magical means and pays the same price as the little mermaid: he loses his voice and feels excruciating pain when he walks on his newly formed feet. Therefore, Stone keeps disability central to his narrative,[25] adding another layer of alterity to queer, transgender, and transspecies Clare. Alterity does not hinder love, however, and the human prince quickly falls for Clare. They live blissfully together until a beautiful princess catches the attention of the bisexual prince and he marries her. Bacchus and Stone imagine similar points of inflection in their narratives, but while Lillo's heartbreak prompts the discovery of his fairy kin, Clare, having rejected his queer homeland in favor of "the world of men, where there are laws that regulate love" (Stone 366), dies by suicide by jumping into the sea.

There is an undeniable political message in a story about a queer creature that enters the cisheteronormative world only to be destroyed, but the prince presents another political dimension of the tale:

---

25 For a disability-focused discussion about *The Little Mermaid*, see Lori Yamato's 2017 article, "Surgical Humanization in H. C. Andersen's 'The Little Mermaid.'"

> "But my dearest boy, a prince must marry. If I could follow my heart, perhaps I would marry you." He smiled. "But you know as well as I do that the law of the land will not allow such a union." (Stone 366)

Here, legal safeguards for queer rights serve as a countermeasure to their annihilation. This speaks to another aspect of queer belonging as described by Elizabeth Freeman, who understands it not only as the mentioned "longing to be" and connect, but also as a desire to "be long" ("Queer Belongings" 299). That is to say: to extend beyond one's limited existence, seeking to have something "queer exceed its own time" (299). Although Freeman seeks nonconforming ways of "being long," Stone's narrative call for legally regulated kinship (perhaps marriage) has the potential to extend beyond its own time, reaching "a hand across time and touch the dead or those not born yet" (299). The search to belong somewhere queer and to "be long" in a queer way underlies all three short story collections. These queer cultural artifacts long to exist, reaching back into the past to correct the bedtimes stories told to the authors' and readers' child-selves, while also reaching into the future and expressing their reality, needs, and desires to those who might be waiting to listen.

Conclusions

Cashorali's collections and Ford's anthology both strive to reclaim the fairy tale for gay men on multiple levels. They demystify the centuries-old genre, imbue it with the immediacy of contemporary issues and language, and inject it with large doses of campy humor to weave gay subjectivity and culture into the fairy tale. Published at a historical junction in which gay writing and genre fiction had evolved enough to allow reimaginings of children's literature, all three collections place queer characters at the center of the narrative, making them as present and principal as heteronormative characters. This approach attempts to address both the invisibility of queerness in canonical fairy tales and the broader subordination of LGBTQI characters in culture and media. Frequent retellings of certain fairy tales, such as "The Ugly Duckling" or "Hansel and Gretel," reveal that various queer authors have independently and concurrently recognized and teased out the potential for queer readings within those tales. The overlapping themes in all three collections—whether the AIDS crisis or the personal need to belong in a community—reflect shared experiences of marginalization among gay men in the mid-1990s. The three texts consistently articulate issues through fairy-tale retellings that, when put side-by-side, create a clearly defined image of gay identity and community. As such, these authors present a coherent proposal for a dialectically constructed gay community, embedded within their fairy-tale vessels.

It is, however, an imperfect and necessarily incomplete depiction of the gay community. With few exceptions, gay men are represented as cisgender, white, middle-class, and sexually active, making their only "difference" their non-normative sexuality. While undoubtedly revolutionary, these retellings remain mostly blind to racial, class, and gender identities, which ultimately undermines their potential to effectively challenge systems of power. This is not to say Cashorali's and Ford's figurations of community are invalid—these retellings approach gay experience from extremely personal points of view. As Cashorali writes, his stories were directly based on his own and his friends' experiences of homosexuality, and most authors in Ford's anthology take similarly intimate approaches to their retellings, as indicated in their epigraphs (qtd. in Dubin). However, in their desire to make their own experiences visible within the genre, these writers also erase large swathes of the gay community, particularly as the collections carry generalizing subtitles such as *Erotic Fairy Tales for Men* and *Traditional Stories Retold for Gay Men*.

As Bacchilega puts it, fairy tales are "ideologically variable desire machines" (*Postmodern* 7), a claim she later added nuance to:

> For some, fairy tales instigate compensatory escapism, while for others they offer wisdom; alternatively, fairy tales are seen to project social delusions that hold us captive under their spell; or else they promote a sense of justice by narrating the success of unpromisingly small, poor, or otherwise oppressed protagonists. (*Transformed* 4).

For Bacchilega, the fairy tale has variable meanings, uses, and potential to effect change, depending on our own understanding of the genre. The queer fairy tales of the 1990s are strangely situated as all the above;

they are repositories of contemporary wisdom and escapist fantasies (not without limitations), and also utopic, comforting narratives that foreground subversive desires. As Bacchilega implies, the fairy tale contains all these possibilities, even in its most classical iterations. For instance, the Grimms' "Hansel and Gretel" reflects the drama of famine and the danger of trusting apparently kind strangers but also addresses children's primal appetites and fantasies of excessive consumption, as well as a fear of being dehumanized and turned into food. At the same time, it depicts the impossible architecture of candy houses, which simultaneously serve as condensations of desire and adumbrate the threshold to horror. At a time when AIDS had ravaged the gay community, the fairy tale's queer and contradictory desires—of excess, transformation, the challenge of hierarchies; of belonging; of mundane and ineffable pleasures both—offered uniquely productive spaces for gay writers. Its realms of wonder, along with its capacity to construct or magically regenerate community, became powerful tools for reimagining queer identity.

3

HEROES VS. MONSTERS

Monstrousness, Monstrosity, and the Normalization of Queerness in Modern Fairy-Tale Retellings

> Fairy tales do not give the child his first idea of bogey. What fairy tales give the child is his first clear idea of the possible defeat of bogey.
>
> —G. K. Chesterton, *Tremendous Trifles*

> Monster Theory . . . Thesis Two: The monster always escapes.
>
> —Jeffrey Cohen, *Monster Theory*

Classic fairy tales contain famously polarized narratives, with a clearly delineated axis of good and evil and characters that must fall on one side or the other. The conflict between good and evil gives shape to the genre in its most popular form: heroes vanquish monsters in countless scenarios, beautiful princesses prevail over ugly witches, kind and clever younger brothers succeed where their cruel older siblings fail, and so on. It is a genre expectation that the righteous and deserving triumph over their rival, the villainous monster, and that the monster is suitably punished for their misdeeds:

> The wicked woman uttered a curse. . . . At first she did not want to go to the wedding, but she found no peace. . . . When she arrived

> she recognized Snow-White, and terrorized, she could only stand there without moving.
>
> Then they put a pair of iron shoes into burning coals. They were brought forth with tongs and placed before her. She was forced to step into the red-hot shoes and dance until she fell down dead. (Grimm, "Little Snow-White")

The punishment of the monster signals a return to normalcy, the eradication of the chaotic other by normative forces, and the restoration of the status quo. Even if, as Duncker points out, the fairy tale favors plots of individual upward mobility, "the hierarchies remain resolutely intact" (71). In tales where the status quo is momentarily troubled by a protagonist who challenges their social station—for instance, by seeking wealth despite being born a peasant, or by dressing as a male knight despite being a woman—the final reward often involves the assimilation of the transgressive protagonist into normative institutions such as royalty, usually through the equally normative institution of marriage. Thus, heroism is ultimately aligned with the norm, and antagonistic figures represent the non-normative, the outsider, and the queer—all of whom must be eradicated.

Drawing an explicit parallel between fairy-tale monsters and queerness, Dallas Baker has noted that antagonists work as obstacles for "the heteronormative narrative trajectory" (80), and the death of the monster "precedes a heterosexual union or reunion . . . and thus this punishment can be seen as a necessary precursor to heterosexual fulfillment" (81). The scene of the queen's demise cited previously, in which she is made to dance to death while wearing blistering iron shoes—on the same day of Snow White's wedding, no less—is a fitting example of Baker's suggestion.

Although the narrative function of queer monsters in fairy tales is primarily an obstacle to normative fulfillment, particularly in canonical stories, how these monsters are realized varies—they are revealed through a manifestation of monstrousness, monstrosity, or a combination of the two. As Alexa Wright describes, the terms "monstrosity" and "monstrousness" are often used interchangeably but mean different things (3). Monstrousness "encapsulates the impossible, dreadful, amoral, inhuman, unspeakable, and even unthinkable qualities that lie at the periphery of human identity" (Wright 3). In other words, it is an abstract, intangible, and moral quality. Fairy-tale monstrousness can be found, for instance, among the incestuous kings who try to marry their daughters, such as the one in Perrault's "Donkeyskin," or with the beautiful but murderous stepmother in the Grimms' "Little Snow-White." Monstrosity, on the other hand, is "the tangible means by which the unspeakable and threatening force of the monstrous is brought into being" (Wright 3). It is a physical manifestation of monstrousness. Witches and ogres in fairy tales are often both physically repulsive and morally twisted, such as the cannibalistic witch in the Grimms' "Hansel and Gretel" and the ogre in Basile's "The Flea."

All these monsters share an oppositional relationship with the tale's hero, who must vanquish them. The pervasiveness of this opposition makes it a frequent target of deconstruction in contemporary fairy-tale retellings. In addition to this trend, which reimagines fairy-tale monsters and heroes, many contemporary retellings also remove the heterosexual union and, at times, the romance plot from the narrative, thereby reducing the monster death requirement if we follow Baker's formula. Queer retellings, which inherently reject the heterosexual prerequisite of the fairy tale, would seem the least likely to demand the queer monster's punishment. However, many twenty-first century queer retellings maintain a relentless attachment to the thematic tensions between the virtuous hero and queer monster, even if the categories themselves are muddled: heroes are neither entirely normative nor free of *abjection*,[1] and monsters, though sometimes still presenting physical monstrosity, might not be all that monstrous.

This chapter focuses on texts from the mid-2000s onward to coincide with a noticeable increase in the number, variety, and sophistication of queer fairy-tale retellings in English. It analyzes Jim C. Hines's

---

1 I use the term *abject* in this chapter along the same lines as Julia Kristeva, who defined it in *Powers of Horror: An Essay on Abjection* as that which induces horror because it disturbs normative understandings of "borders, positions, rules" (4). As such, it threatens to collapse the boundaries between self and other, clean and filthy, living and dead, et cetera.

The Stepsister Scheme (2009), Neil Gaiman's *The Sleeper and the Spindle* (2014), Catherynne M. Valente's "Bones Like Black Sugar" (2006), Lauren Beukes's *The Hidden Kingdom* (2013), and the ABC TV show *Once Upon a Time* (2011–18). Following the first community-constructing efforts in the 1990s, we will situate these queer fairy tales within an ongoing conversation around the normalization and deradicalization of queerness, which has gained traction since the early 2000s, particularly in cultural representations. Ultimately, this chapter will investigate the prevalence of the queer monster in these retellings, its merging with the fairy-tale hero, and the meaning of such monstrous resiliency when mainstreaming queerness seems to have eradicated all the queer monsters.

No More Queer Monsters?

In a 2011 article, Sam Miller declared "there are no more queer monsters" (222). He was referring to the horror genre, not fairy tales, but the two are intimately connected: as Karra Shimabukuro and Kara Andersen state, the constant "violence in fairy tales seems to make a horror/fairy-tale match-up an inevitable conclusion" (93). The genres are similarly well-stocked with queer villains, even if monsters in horror are somewhat more explicit about their queerness. The fairy tale features the famous cross-dressing wolf in the Grimms' "Little Red Cap," but most villains in canonical tales usually allow for more symbolic queer readings. The evil stepmothers in "Snow White" and "Cinderella," for instance, are queer insofar as they stand in the way of heteronormative fulfillment, and the witch in "Hansel and Gretel" queerly opposes "reproductive futurism" by attempting to eat the two children (Edelman 3).[2] In contrast, horror offers early literary examples like Sheridan Le Fanu's lesbian vampire in *Carmilla* (1872), who makes romantic advances toward the female

2 For Edelman, *reproductive futurism* argues that political organization is ultimately driven by the promise of creating a better future for children. Thus, the future itself is symbolized by the child and is linked to heteronormativity, rendering all alternative (queer) modes of kinship futureless. The witch in "Hansel and Gretel" opposes reproductive futurism. She is childless, shows no interest in procreation, and threatens to eat the children (who are quite literally the results of reproduction), thus ultimately precluding the possibility of a future.

protagonist and exclusively feeds on young women, and Oscar Wilde's notoriously queer monster in *The Picture of Dorian Gray* (1890).

Horror film history is also densely populated by queer monsters, including two of the most iconic villains: cross-dressing, murderous Norman Bates in *Psycho* (1960), and (potentially) transgender serial killer Buffalo Bill in *The Silence of the Lambs* (1991). Whereas *Psycho* did not receive much negative press from gay and lesbian groups at the time of release, *Silence of the Lambs* faced widespread backlash. *Silence of the Lambs* was released between two other films featuring queer killers, *Cruising* (1980) and *Basic Instinct* (1992), all of which were boycotted and protested by LGBTQI activists. In the case of *Silence of the Lambs*, some groups, such as ACT-UP, threatened to disrupt the Oscars ceremony (Bloomer). These reactions were byproducts of increased political organization during the AIDS crisis but also involved a targeted effort to enter the cultural mainstream—or, at the very least, to correct "damaging" representations of queerness. For Miller, it is precisely this fight for positive representation—particularly in mainstream American culture—that has brought about the death of the queer monster: representation has led to normalization, normalization has defanged the monster, and, as a result, queerness "is no longer frightening" (226).

Eradication of the Queer Threat Through Normalization

Jordan Schildcrout points out that negative representations of queerness, including queer monster-villains, have long supported equally negative attitudes about gender nonconformity and sexual non-normativity (2). Influencing mainstream representations of minorities has become a major front in the fight for equality in America. To this end, the Gay & Lesbian League Alliance Against Defamation (GLAAD) was founded in 1985, modeled after other lobbying groups such as the National Association for the Advancement of Colored People and the Anti-Defamation League (Schildcrout 2). GLAAD has monitored mass-produced popular culture since the late 1980s. If the organization perceives a particular product featuring negative representations of queer people, they can put pressure on "creators, sponsors and consumers" (Schildcrout 2) to eliminate the defamatory images or at least publicly acknowledge them as harmful. As Schildcrout writes:

> Representations of "normal" and even exemplary LGBT people are lauded and affirmed, and negative representations are thus positioned as hindrances to the goals of acceptance and assimilation. (2)

Representational politics are part of a broader discussion about the assimilation, mainstreaming, and normalization of queerness—a debate that deeply divides queer groups. LGBTQI movements have never been monolithic, as evidenced from the early homophile days described in the previous chapter. As historian John D'Emilio posits, LGBTQI movements have historically been sorted into opposing categories: "those who pursued mainstream methods of lobbying, education, and negotiation" against "those who urged more militant, confrontational tactics," and "those whose work gave priority to opening up mainstream institutions to gays and lesbians" against "those who valued the building of almost 'nationalist' communities" (85). GLAAD belongs to a neoliberal mainstreaming strand, which favors, in Lisa Duggan's words, "politics compatible with a corporate world order" (42). As such, it seeks to normalize queerness not through "any political analysis or critique of oppression" (S. Miller 223) but through the recasting of previously threatening individuals as harmless, even coveted, consumers—in this case, within the ever-growing media market. Though this lobbying style is specific to American culture, the conversation about positive representation has crossed borders, possibly due to the American preeminence in the global media market and the worldwide emergence of LGBTQI politics. For instance, in the "BBC 2017/18 Equality Information Report," the British public service broadcaster remarked that they were aware "the diversity of production teams and who our audience see and hear in our programs is vital to how we reflect modern Britain" (BBC 81), and for that reason they were committed to having an "8% LGBT on screen portrayal including some lead roles" by 2020 (BBC 81).

Mainstreaming queerness through access to normative institutions, such as marriage and the military, continues to be a central issue for LGBTQI activist groups globally. In the 1990s, this focus on mainstream equality was interpreted as a conservative turn in LGBTQI activism[3] and was immediately criticized for "taming or [domesticating] the radical potentials of queer desires, practices and institutions" (Manalansan 78), and for excluding identities and bodies that did not satisfy established hegemonic values—that is, individuals who are less "palatable," less easily homogenized, and less compliant with cisheteronormative expectations. As Miller reminds us, the normalization project has "primarily benefited white people who conform to a mainstream understanding of masculinity or femininity" (S. Miller 228).

The possible consequences of attempting to tame queerness have since spread to different facets of culture: In a 2003 publication, Halperin voices his concern that queer theory, which derived its power from confrontational postures and "its shocking embrace of the abnormal," would be so effortlessly, even eagerly, absorbed into institutions of knowledge (341). As queer theory was increasingly accepted across new disciplines, Halperin observes that it became "harder to figure out what's so very queer about it" (342). By the turn of the twenty-first century, B. Ruby Rich declared that New Queer Cinema (NQC),[4] a term she had coined a decade earlier, was over (18). She believed that the radical style, aesthetics, and preoccupations of NQC had been absorbed into the mainstream, resulting in narratives and characters that were no longer threatening to audiences (18).

However strongly critics opposed the normalization—or perhaps the deradicalization—of queerness, it has proven to be an unstoppable process. As of 2024, twenty-three years after the Netherlands became the first country to implement marriage equality, thirty-six countries

3 Compare to the Gay Liberation Front (an admittedly radical group), which in 1970 had proclaimed about the system and all its institutions: "it's not a question of getting our share of the pie. The pie is rotten" (Wittman).

4 New Queer Cinema was a movement led by independent queer filmmakers that emerged in the 1990s, particularly in the United States and the United Kingdom, and produced films that featured radical representations of queerness. Films such as Todd Haynes's *Poison* (1991) offered images of queerness that would reject hegemonic attitudes and promote positive representation, as Michelle Aaron writes: "no longer burdened by the approval-seeking sackcloth of positive imagery, or the relative obscurity of marginal production, films could be both radical and popular, stylish and economically viable" (3).

recognize same-sex marriage, and nearly as many explicitly allow joint same-sex adoption—expanding legal equality while integrating queerness into the framework of respectable family structures. Queer theory remains widely used in academia, and films that depict largely positive images of queer people were recently nominated for the Academy Award, such as *Moonlight* (2016) and *Call Me by Your Name* (2017), with *Moonlight* winning the coveted award for Best Picture. For its part, GLAAD announced in 2015 that it would discontinue its Network Responsibility Index, which for nine years had monitored the quality, quantity, and diversity of LGBTQI representation on American television, as all networks were deemed "adequate" or better (Goodman and Adam). This suggests that nonconfrontational images of queerness are being produced and widely consumed, but also that there is an increasing mainstream acceptance of queerness—even if that queerness must smooth rough edges to fit within the straitjacket of normalcy or must be ironed down into homonormativity. The question remains, to echo Halperin: if queerness must be somewhat de-queered to be accepted into the mainstream, what, if anything, is so very queer about it anymore?

In the face of the rapid advance of LGBTQI rights and the growing strength of the normalizing discourse, the process of de-queering has faced both resistance and support among queer people,[5] for whom normalcy holds a unique appeal. As Michael Warner declares, who can blame them "if the alternative is being abnormal, or deviant, or not being like the rest of us?" (*The Trouble with Normal* 53). In other words, if the alternative to being normal in a society that favors a binary worldview is to be a monster, it is not surprising that many would support the normalization of queerness, rejecting any association of their identity with abjection.

Monstrous Potential

The relationship between queerness and monstrousness—or, more specifically, between the homosexual and the monster—has a long history.

5 For more information on both positions, see Andrew Sullivan and Urvashi Vaid's books, which mirror each other: *Virtually Normal: An Argument About Homosexuality* (1995) and *Virtual Equality: The Mainstreaming of Gay and Lesbian Liberation* (1995).

Jack Halberstam situates the first signs of a shift in emphasis in the 1890s: the monster, always standing for a fluctuating "other," often represented a marginalized class, race, or nationality, but this period saw the monster signifier expand to include representations of non-normative sexuality and gender as well (*Skin Shows*, 64–77). In 1890, Oscar Wilde published *The Picture of Dorian Gray*, which was used as evidence against Wilde in his 1895 trial for homosexual activity (Halberstam, *Skin Shows* 84). This is not to say that queer monsters did not exist before this point: as mentioned, less explicitly queer monsters are a staple of fairy tales. However, there was a marked increase in the cultural association between monstrousness and queerness—an association that has been linked to "the hegemonic installation of psychoanalytic interpretations . . . which understand . . . monstrosity as sexual pathology" (Halberstam, *Skin Shows* 24). The legislation criminalizing homosexual sex and the medicalization of homosexuality, which were enacted toward the end of the nineteenth century and the beginning of the twentieth also contributed to this trend (Halberstam, *Skin Shows* 65–69). According to Foucault, the medicalization of homosexuality worked both to restrict normative sexuality and produce perverse sexualities (*History of Sexuality* 44). In other words, the establishment of the norm creates the monster. Once the boundaries of acceptable sexuality are firmly defined, the monster outcast emerges as the embodiment of the perverse in its mutating form.

Like Halberstam, who analyzes the late nineteenth century through the anxieties projected onto the monster signifier, Jeffrey Cohen defends reading cultures "from the monsters they engender" in his foundational essay, "Monster Culture: Seven Theses" (3). Writing in 1996, Cohen asserts that the monster "polices the border of the possible" (12), whether in the intellectual, the geographic, or sexual realm. Whether or not we accept Halberstam's thesis that shifting the boundaries of acceptable sexuality in the nineteenth century generated a recognizable queer monster, it is undeniable that the figure of the queer monster was firmly established by the twentieth century. This development was at least partly driven by a growing Hollywood cinematic convention that implicitly associated all queerness with monstrosity—and, under the Hays Code, did so explicitly (S. Miller 221). Officially known as the Motion Production Code, the Hays Code was a series of guidelines enforced from 1934 to 1967 that dictated there would be no immorality in film. While homosexuality was not explicitly mentioned, the code mandated that only "correct standards of life" be depicted and that "sex perversion or any inference to it [was] forbidden" (qtd. in Bresler 174–76). This left filmmakers with little room to explore nonconforming sexualities and gender identities. Even queer creators, such as director James Whale in *Bride of Frankenstein* (1935), had to encode queerness as terror-inducing monstrosity or monstrousness to evade censors.

Harry M. Benshoff historicizes cinematic queer monsters in his book *Monsters in the Closet: Homosexuality and the Horror Film* (1997), arguing that they are largely derogatory representations, with queer identities and desires both displaced onto and contained within a monstrous signifier doomed to annihilation. Brent Hartinger expressed a similar sentiment in 2008:

> Literally all the big-budget Hollywood movies until, perhaps, *Philadelphia* in 1993, that featured major gay male characters portrayed them as insane villains and serial killers. Worse, these movies often played on the audience's fears of gay people and discomfort with behaviors that violate gender norms, using people's prejudice to make them hate the villain more, and make the audience feel better when the hero finally vanquishes them (usually violently killing them). (Hartinger qtd. in Schildcrout 3)

For critics like Hartinger, the problem arises when the monstrous queer is the only visible representation of queer people—when their sole narrative role is that of a sexually transgressive monster, existing to briefly threaten the status quo before being eradicated by the normative hero in a comforting narrative resolution.

However, Cohen recognizes another side to these conservative narratives. If the monster contains the ineffable—all that is transgressive, threatening, and different—then monster narratives offer unique opportunities to safely experience the pleasure of all those forbidden desires, at least momentarily. The monster stands just beyond the boundary of the acceptable, and its capacity to instill horror is directly proportional to its otherness. Yet the same otherness that repels us can also attract us. As Cohen writes:

> The monster is continually linked to forbidden practices, in order to normalize and to enforce. The monster also attracts. The same creatures that terrify and interdict can evoke potent escapist fantasies; the linking of monstrosity with the forbidden makes the monster all the more appealing as a temporary egress from constraint. This simultaneous repulsion and attraction at the core of the monster's composition accounts greatly for its continued cultural popularity. . . . We distrust and loathe the monster at the same time we envy its freedom. (16–17)

For many queer people, the queer monster is, in fact, a source of dissident pleasure. Despite the conservative slant of many queer monster narratives and the overt prejudices they may perpetuate, queer monster tropes have been reappropriated, their grotesque forms transformed, and their horrors deployed against a dominant heteronormative culture. In Miller's words, the queer monster "not only provides an opportunity to identify with someone . . . it also allows us to vicariously live out our rage against a social order that oppresses us" (S. Miller 221). Several films from the NQC movement exemplify this phenomenon, but the most striking example of cathartic, anti-heteronormative, queer monster rage from this period is Gregg Araki's *The Living End* (1992), in which two HIV-positive gay men embark on a killing spree across America. Another queer monster who has captured the imagination of queer spectators is the cross-dressing murderer and parody of Dr. Frankenstein, Frank "N" Furter, from the cult classic *The Rocky Horror Picture Show* (1975). Among other transgressions, Frank "N" Furter seduces a heterosexual couple, creates a beautiful, muscley monster, and cooks and eats his (presumed) ex-lover. Even queer-coded Disney villains have been eagerly welcomed into queer circles. For instance, *The Little Mermaid*'s monstrous Ursula has been described as "the diva that launched 1,000 drag costumes" (Lang).

The monster has long perpetuated narratives of abjection, exclusion, and fear, often at the expense of misunderstood and misrepresented minorities. Nonetheless, even monsters produced within the normative order can offer queer people subversive modes of self-identification. In the right hands, they can be reimagined as fantasies of destruction and revenge against the oppressor. For Schildcrout, these demonized monsters "probe the darker anxieties and fears that can affect queer lives . . . including victimization from homophobia, the oppression of the closet, and the devastation of AIDS" (Schildcrout 4)—perhaps in ways that queer heroes never could. Even if concerns about positive representation could kill off the queer monster forever, its potential for subversion, confrontation, and even liberation may very well ensure its survival.

Navigating Fairy-Tale Dichotomies in Contemporary Retellings

The texts analyzed in this chapter were all released between 2006 and 2018. I identify 2006 as the moment that definitively opened the genre to queerness in fairy-tale retellings. The previous chapter identified the mid-1990s as the point in which the first small wave of gay and lesbian responses to the fairy tale emerged. It can be interpreted as a "wave" because queer retellings from that period share thematic links, including comparable views on sexuality, identity, and historically specific issues. Notably, between 1996 (when Michael Ford's *Happily Ever After* was published) and 2006 (when the first edition of JoSelle Vanderhooft's *Sleeping Beauty, Indeed* was released), few queer fairy-tale retellings appeared in either the independent or mainstream literary scenes.[6] However, from 2006 onward, countless retellings have been published.[7] This significant

---

6 *Shrek* (2001) is somewhat of an exception. Unquestionably a film of wide mainstream appeal, it contained a cross-dressing wolf (from "Little Red Riding Hood") and a transgender-coded evil stepsister (from "Cinderella"), although both were minor characters.

7 Author Malinda Lo recorded the number of YA books published by major publishers that contained queer characters. Her study, which analyzed books from 2003 to 2014, found that there was a "high point" in 2007 when twenty-five books were published containing at least one openly queer character. The number remained relatively stable in the following years. While not directly related to queer fairy tales (although Lo published her queer Cinderella retelling, the YA novel *Ash*, in 2009), these findings point to a shift in mainstream interest, which could have affected queer fairy tales as well and precipitated the boom in the following years. It could also be incidental—as she says, just "a blip in the radar" (Lo).

boom in production is due to the resurgence in fairy-tale popularity,[8] the growing visibility of queer identities and desires in the media, and the increasing number of avenues for publishing queer-focused material—including new possibilities for self-publishing and the relatively democratic nature of internet-based fiction.

The great diversity in the themes, media, intended audiences, and production values of these retellings makes it difficult to treat them as a homogenous body, yet they all belong to what can be described as the "sophistication period" of queer fairy-tale retellings. As products of a particular moment in time, these texts are relevant to the ongoing conversation about the deradicalization of queerness, particularly as it intersects with representation. As outlined in this chapter, the tensions between normative and disruptive positions have permeated multiple cultural layers, particularly in the Western, Anglophone world. Previous sections have drawn several conclusions—namely, that a correlation exists between exemplary (or heroic) queer characters and normative or mainstream positions, suggesting that queer heroes function as conformist representations. Along similar lines, the queer monster could align with subversive, non-assimilationist positions, making it a more ideologically incisive figure. However, one can make the opposite argument: queer monsters may perpetuate negative stereotypes, reinforcing conservative narratives of queerness, while queer heroes may be seen as breaking away from age-old prejudices, rendering them the more revolutionary representations of queerness.

While this chapter does not seek to reductively categorize contemporary queer fairy-tale heroes and monsters as either "good" or "bad" representation, all possible interpretations presented here are relevant to the analysis of these texts and are considered. As this chapter details, these retellings weave a complex queer net around the categories of hero and monster. The queer characters discussed here are all protagonists or co-protagonists of their own stories, embark on a quest or journey, and are positioned at the narrative center in such a way that compels the reader or viewer to empathize with their plight. In that sense, they

8 To the question, "Are fairy tales back in fashion?" Gaby Wood answered, "The recent success of Disney's films *Frozen* (2013) and *Maleficent* (2014) seems to point to something."

are all heroes. However, they also embody some degree of monstrosity, monstrousness, or both—an otherness that sets them apart from an established norm. In this way, they can also be read as monsters.

Bearing in mind that these categories are by no means fixed, the chapter uses them as a flexible framework. The section "Heroes" focuses on Jim C. Hines's *The Stepsister Scheme* (2009) and Neil Gaiman's *The Sleeper and the Spindle* (2014). The queer protagonists in these texts are primarily heroic: they are LGBTQI versions of existing fairy-tale protagonists, retaining their adventurous, brave, and beautiful qualities, even as their narratives are at times haunted by the specter of the queer monster. The section "Monsters" analyzes "Bones Like Black Sugar" by Catherynne M. Valente (2006), Lauren Beukes's *Fairest Vol. 2: The Hidden Kingdom* (2013), and the ABC TV show *Once Upon a Time* (2011–18). The characters in this section are similar to the ones in the "Heroes" section in that they are fairy-tale protagonists reimagined as queer. However, they are also openly, explicitly, physically, and often morally monstrous.

Thus, this chapter analyzes how these texts, which exploit the most horrific elements of the fairy tale to varying degrees, reimagine the fairy-tale dichotomy of the hero and the monster, to what extent they collapse it, reproduce it, or deconstruct it. Then, we observe how this changed relationship ties in with the normalizing trajectory of queerness in culture and where it positions contemporary queer fairy tales in the debate of representational politics.

Heroes

Male fairy-tale heroes take many forms. Tatar explains that folklorists tend to divide male heroes into "active heroes and passive heroes, formal heroes and ideal heroes, tricksters and simpletons, dragon slayers and male Cinderellas" (Tatar, *Hard Facts* 86). The hero is recognized as such not because he sticks to a single archetype, but because he is the focus of the narrative and, ultimately, he "embodies the superior terms of [good vs. evil] dualisms as he adventures forth on his quest and encounters evil monsters, dragons, witches and the like" (Hourihan 2). Thus, the hero is defined by his position within the story and in opposition to the enemies he must defeat.

Male fairy-tale heroes are also defined in contrast to their rather more passive female counterparts. Compared to their male heroes, fairy-tale heroines exist within a more restricted range of roles—particularly in canonical tales. Many female fairy-tale characters have been defined as "innocent persecuted heroines" (see Bacchilega, "An Introduction," and S. Jones), who must endure debasement and pain while demonstrating industry and piety to earn their happy ending—or even their status as heroes. Straying from the marked path of virtue might put them at risk of becoming monsters. Among the characters that fit the archetype described by Bacchilega and Jones are Snow White, Cinderella, and Sleeping Beauty, all of whom are reimagined in the following analyses of their respective queer retellings. However, as will become evident, the new versions of the well-known characters largely reject the "innocent persecuted heroine" archetype. At some point, they draw closer to the figure of either the male hero or the queer monster, wedging themselves in an in-between space that stretches the boundaries of established categories.

Jim C. Hines's The Stepsister Scheme

The plot of Jim C. Hines's *The Stepsister Scheme* is based entirely on the subversion of the persecuted princess archetype. This young adult (YA) novel begins immediately after the traditional ending: a Cinderella-type protagonist has recently married Prince Charming. However, within the first few pages, she finds out that her husband has been spirited away to Fairyland by her abusive stepsisters, and that she must team up with Snow White and Sleeping Beauty to rescue him. From the beginning, this retelling grants the princesses agency, reversing their traditional roles from helpless damsels in distress to powerful rescuers. It also interweaves fairy-tale fragments in a postmodern-pastiche and deconstructs the happily-ever-after trope.

Happily-ever-afters are notoriously fragile—as countless retellings, feminist and otherwise, have revealed—because they depend entirely on the story ending at just the right moment. *The Stepsister Scheme* easily dispels the mirage of the happy ending by beginning the story soon after the fairy-tale wedding. The action unfolds immediately, as the protagonist must save herself from an assassination attempt by her stepsister, Charlotte. She is helped by Talia, named after Basile's "Sun, Moon, and Talia," who, in this universe, is better known as Sleeping Beauty. Talia introduces the protagonist to Snow (White, naturally), who explains that both women work for the prince's mother, the queen. What follows is an inverted fairy tale in which three princesses rescue a prince.

The premise of the novel allows for a dense layering of intertextual references. This mix includes, among others, the tales of Cinderella, Snow White, and Sleeping Beauty. However, even when reconstructing the Cinderella story, Hines does not limit himself to using only one source. Cinderella is called Danielle in reference to the 1998 film *Ever After*. She enlists the help of birds, like the Grimms' Cinderella (and, famously, Disney's), and she receives her glass slippers from a wish-granting tree inhabited by the spirit of her mother, also in keeping with the Grimms' version. Hines also preserves the more gruesome elements of the Grimms' tale, and at times makes them even more horrific. In the original tale, Cinderella's helpful birds attack the stepsisters at her wedding; in Hines's novel, they kill the stepmother. When Charlotte attacks Danielle, Danielle notices her foot is bandaged and bloody from the time her stepmother "had cut away part of her heel in a deranged attempt to fit Charlotte's foot to Danielle's discarded slipper," again referencing the Grimms' version (Hines 10). Furthermore, when Danielle reflects on some palace rumors, Hines uses the opportunity to reference elements from Perrault's version of the tale that Disney later popularized:

> Within days of the winter ball, rumors had spread through the city, growing wilder with every retelling: she had snuck from her house to attend the ball—no, she had stolen a carriage—no, she had ridden within an enchanted pumpkin, drawn by giant mice. (3)

This also serves as a metafictional commentary on the nature of fairy tales—an element present, to some degree, in all retellings discussed in this chapter. Fairy tales, like the stories people tell in *The Stepsister Scheme*, have many coexisting versions that influence one another, are mixed and confused, and are often changed with each retelling.

However, within the universe of *The Stepsister Scheme*, some versions are more accurate than others. A significant portion of the plot involves untangling conflicting versions to uncover the characters' true backstories:

> "Sleeping Beauty?" Danielle turned to Talia . . . "Aren't you married?"
> "Hardly," said Talia.
> "But the stories, your prince awakened you with a kiss, breaking the fairy curse, and—"
> "Sometimes the stories are wrong." (Hines 32)

These classical fairy tales are inaccurate in at least one regard: the role the princesses play within the narrative Hines constructs. At the heart of the novel is a sustained, gender-queering role-reversal. All three princesses are the heroes of their story, and their unique skills are essential for surviving their journey into treacherous Fairyland and rescuing the prince. Their role is, just like that of traditional heroes, constructed in opposition to the passive princess—a role, in this case, fulfilled by Danielle's husband. As Hourihan writes, "women in hero stories appear only in relation to the hero" (3). Correspondingly, Prince Charming appears in *The Stepsister Scheme* only at the end of the novel, when the three princesses finally breach the tower where he is held captive—an image that references the trope of the princess stuck in a tower, passively awaiting rescue. However, these simple inversions do not necessarily result in "demythologizing a romanticized image of fairy tales" (Bacchilega and Rieder 31), since the love between Danielle and her prince remains magical and everlasting.

Another significant way in which Hines transforms the princess archetype is by bringing their sexualities to the forefront. Talia, Danielle, and Snow still possess most of the qualities that Ming-Hsun Lin identifies in archetypal princesses; namely, nobility stemming from social, spiritual, or biological sources:

> Socially most are of royal birth or obtain royal status by marriage. Spiritually they are often pious and virtuous. Biologically they are usually young and beautiful. Their beauty is an expression of their inner positive qualities—an internalized form of nobility. (Lin 81)

All three are indeed beautiful, young, and of royal lineage. However, they are not perfectly virtuous or pious. For instance, Snow is depicted as an openly sexual, flirtatious, and exceptionally attractive woman:

> Though she looked a few years older than Danielle, her smooth, pale face evoked the innocence of childhood . . . a blue shirt draped her shoulders and made a half-hearted attempt to conceal the curve of her chest . . . though it would have had a better chance had she bothered to do up the laces. A polished silver pendant in the shape of a snowflake hung between her breasts. Danielle did her best not to look at it, or rather, at *them*. (Hines 28)

Even Danielle, who embodies heteronormativity—feminine, presumably straight, married to a man, and expecting a child—has somewhat ambiguous reactions to Snow's exuberant beauty. In the previous passage, her reaction could be interpreted as indicating queer desire.

All three protagonists can be interpreted as queer in that they reject their traditional gendered category. There are also queer undertones in the intense bonds Danielle develops with both Talia and Snow over the course of their adventure. However, no relationship in the novel is queerer than the one between Snow and Talia. Their interactions are marked by tension, the source of which remains undisclosed until the moment Snow is struck by a sleeping curse. Talia—miniaturized after eating shrinking spores, in a reference to *Alice in Wonderland*—wakes her with a kiss, to Danielle's absolute surprise:

> "What are you doing?" Danielle asked . . .
>
> Talia shook her head. . . . Planting one foot in Snow's right ear, she pulled herself up, grabbed a nostril for balance, and kissed Snow on the corner of her mouth. Snow's eyelids began to flutter. (Hines 283)

The tradition of the true-love kiss is not as prevalent in fairy tales as Disneyfied versions suggest: Perrault's Sleeping Beauty wakes after completing one hundred years of sleep; the Grimms' Little Snow-White revives when the poisoned apple is dislodged from her throat as a servant stumbles while carrying her glass coffin; and the frog from "The Frog

King" transforms back into a human only when a princess throws him against the wall in disgust. However, Hines engages with this Disneyfied tradition, making the significance of the kiss as clear to the reader as it is to Danielle: Talia is in love with Snow and may, in fact, be her one true love. Talia's feelings are further clarified after Snow wakes up and she cautions Danielle against revealing what she has done to save her:

> "Breathe a word about what really happened, and I'll kill you myself." Danielle looked at Snow, then back at Talia. There was a kind of weary resignation in Talia's dark eyes. . . . Snow clearly had no idea how Talia felt. (Hines 286)

Talia's feelings mark her as the "queerer" hero among the three, but her queerness, which was likely meant to be a straightforward subversion of heterocentric fairy-tale stereotypes, becomes something more complex than mere positive representation when her backstory is finally revealed. As mentioned, her character is named after Basile's Sleeping Beauty tale, and her past closely resembles that version of the tale:

> "I was awakened by the agony of childbirth," Talia said, "as my twin children were expelled from my womb. . . . My prince wasn't as kind as yours. . . . I'm sure he began by planting a royal kiss on my cold lips. That's what you're supposed to do, right? But it didn't work. I didn't open my eyes and fall madly in love with him. So instead, he indulged another fantasy." (Hines 276)

Talia's horrific rape is given an emotional weight that was missing in the original tale, in which "the very idea of 'consent' is deemed immaterial" (Short). However, since Hines reimagines her as queer, the rape carries the added connotation of "corrective rape"—a form of violence through which lesbians, unavailable to male desire, are "punished and/or violently recovered" (Gqola 9). As Paul Morrison observes, in the heterosexist imaginary, "gender trumps sexuality," and a "lesbian is, after all, a woman, and a woman is defined by her sexual availability to men" (5–6). Thus, Talia's unavailability may render her subject to "violent recovery" through rape. While this serves as a (somewhat oblique) commentary on a very real issue, the fact remains that the only openly queer woman in the narrative is also the only character who is sexually assaulted—a pattern reminiscent of many instances of homophobic victimization. It is also egregious, given her backstory, that Talia would impose her desires on a sleeping Snow. Even though she is excused as merely following fairy-tale rules, her actions thoughtlessly perpetuate the cycle of fairy-tale sexual violence rather than disrupting it.

This is further complicated by Hines's decision to relocate Talia's origin to a vaguely Middle Eastern kingdom. Talia wields a spindle-shaped whip, is described as having brown skin and dark eyes, and speaks with a musical accent that leads Danielle to guess she comes from "the Arathean Desert to the south" (Hines 4). By taking the story of the raped Sleeping Beauty, an Italian tale, and transferring it to a remote, heavily Middle Eastern–coded land, Hines shifts the narrative blame, as it were, away from Europe and the Global North. The new setting he creates—where such un-Charming, somnophiliac (or necrophiliac) princes can act out horrific fantasies—is thus safely removed from the center:

> The habitations of the monsters . . . (whatever land is sufficiently distant to be exoticized) are more than dark regions of uncertain danger: they are also realms of happy fantasy, horizons of liberation. Their monsters serve as secondary bodies through which the possibilities of other genders, other sexual practices, and other social customs can be explored. (Cohen 18)

Talia comes from an exoticized place where sexual excesses are permitted—both rape and, presumably, queerness. Thus, Talia, marked as monstrous by her nonconforming sexuality, her status as a racialized foreigner, and even as a rape survivor, becomes more intelligible to the norm, as she hails from one of Cohen's "dark regions of uncertain danger." In other words, reimagining a fairy-tale princess as queer may be more palatable when she is also a racial other who comes from a distant land infused with Orientalist stereotypes about Middle Eastern violent men and victimized women. The villains in the story are indubitably Danielle's evil stepsisters—both of whom are straight—but Talia's complex intersections and her rebounds into conservative monstrousness may ultimately undermine the subversive potential of her status as a queer hero.

Neil Gaiman's The Sleeper and the Spindle

The treatment of the queer hero is somewhat less complex in Gaiman's *The Sleeper and the Spindle*, a YA novella published in 2014 and illustrated by Chris Riddell. It tells the story of a young queen, inspired by Snow White, who, on the eve of her wedding, abandons her fiancé and sets out to rescue a sleeping princess, accompanied by her dwarven entourage. This text employs several of the same deconstruction and inversion techniques as Hines's, depicting an active, queer Snow White who has outgrown the constraints of her past and must bravely navigate a dangerous fairy-tale land to fulfill her quest.

As Paulina Palmer explains, classical fairy-tale heroines are "frequently relegated to the conventional heteropatriarchal role of trophy and object of exchange" (141), but the queen in *The Sleeper and the Spindle* thoroughly deconstructs that trope—arguably even more so than the princesses in *The Stepsister Scheme*. To begin with, she is queen in her own right; she does not ascend to the throne via marriage and, in fact, holds a higher station than her fiancé:

> She called for her fiancé and told him . . . that they would still be married, even if he was but a prince and she a queen, and she chucked him beneath his pretty chin and kissed him until he smiled. (Gaiman 16)

The role of the traditional princess—beautiful and patiently waiting—is thus played by the queen's fiancé, much like Prince Charming in Hines's novel was cast as the damsel in the tower. The queen aligns more closely with the male hero, or even Prince Charming himself: she is dashing, adventurous, athletic, and knightly, ready to ride to save a kingdom and wake the sleeping princess. She can also be read as recuperating the tradition of the cross-dressing maiden knight. Though nothing suggests she is cross-dressing according to in-universe rules, her heroic, armor-clad persona evokes Straparola's Constanza/Constanzo or d'Aulnoy's Belle-Belle/the knight Fortuné. In addition to being an excellent knight, her features befit a fairy-tale heroine: she is pale as snow, with "raven-black hair" (Gaiman 20) and cherry-red lips. However, her aesthetic deviates from the Disneyfied princess. Riddell's incredibly detailed illustrations introduce tension between text and image, walking the line between beauty and grotesquerie: tiny skulls adorn all her possessions, her long black hair falls limply around her broad forehead, and she is strikingly tall and thin—a combination of features which, when assembled into a single visual style, suggests monstrosity.

This gender-role-defying queen, who has built up a resistance to sleeping spells thanks to her fairy-tale background, enters a kingdom full of sleeping inhabitants who attempt to stop her:

> They were easy for the dwarfs to outrun, easy for the queen to outwalk. And yet, and yet, there were so many of them. Each street they came to was filled with sleepers, cobweb-shrouded, eyes tight closed or eyes open and rolled back in their heads showing only the whites, all of them shuffling sleepily forwards. (Gaiman 35)

If zombies are "the walking dead," the monsters in *The Sleeper and the Spindle* are "the sleepwalkers," juxtaposing the death-like sleep of fairy tales with zombie ethos. The swarm of sleepers is modeled after a zombie horde, "distributed and horizontal, but also driven by an invisible, intangible life force" (Thacker 182). The abject zombie swarm queers human life by being both human and no longer human, dead and animate, simultaneously inhabiting individual bodies and sharing an insect-like collective consciousness. However, unlike most zombie swarms, this one is controlled by a spider "at the center of the web" (Gaiman 59) that eerily speaks through them. The spider lures the protagonist closer with a request reminiscent of "Beauty and the Beast" tales:

> "Bring me roses," said the three bandits as they slept, with one voice, while the blood oozed indolently on to the ground from the stump of the fat man's arm. "I would be so happy if only you would bring me roses." (Gaiman 40)

Determined to rescue the sleeping princess, the queen cuts through the swarm and burns her way through a thick barrier of enchanted thorns. Finally, she enters the tower, where she finds a sleeping princess and a mysterious, senile old woman—the only conscious person in the kingdom. When the queen sees the young girl lying on the bed, she assumes what every knowledgeable reader will assume: that she is Sleeping Beauty. Following common fairy-tale logic, she kisses her on the lips to wake her up:

> "Somebody's got to do the honors."
> "I shall," said the queen, gently. She lowered her face to the sleeping woman's. She touched the pink lips to her own carmine lips and she kissed the sleeping girl long and hard. (Gaiman 49)

The kiss is not necessarily framed as romantic, and since neither the possibility of marriage to the princess nor true love is ever mentioned, it appears entirely divorced from personal desire. Instead, it serves only as a well-known remedy to a pervasive fairy-tale problem. However, there remains a distinct sensuality to the previous passage—especially in the book's accompanying illustration on pages 50 and 51—which draws on Disney's visual tradition and the company's iconic kissing scenes in classic films like *Sleeping Beauty* and *Snow White and the Seven Dwarfs*. It is worth noting that both women (created by a man and illustrated by another, both presumably straight) are depicted as conventionally feminine, particularly in this illustration, in which they kiss demurely but firmly on the lips. There is a pointed focus on their equally long, flowing hair, which intertwines on the sheets, suggesting sensuality. Notably, the queen's less normative features—her skeletal proportions, her goth aesthetic—are obscured in the illustration, due to perspective or conscious artistic choice on Riddell's part. She appears more conventionally beautiful, accentuated by a markedly feminine flower tucked behind her ear. Therefore, the kiss illustration, which might otherwise appear undoubtedly queer, relies on male fantasies about lesbians, wherein women retain normative feminine traits, presumably to appeal to straight men even as they engage in practices that would exclude them. These "lesbians-for-male-visual-pleasure"—as seen in pornographic films—are often hyperfeminine, sometimes sporting unlikely long nails. In *The Sleeper and the Spindle*, they have long flowy hair, which is surely an impractical feature for an adventurous queen. As such, the women in this story are rendered relatively nonthreatening, visually domesticated to soften the narrative's queerest moment.

The twist in the story occurs when, upon waking, it is revealed the sleeping beauty is, in fact, the witch who controls the murderous sleepwalkers and originally enchanted the entire kingdom. Thus, the deathlike sleep that prompted Talia to claim "To sleep is to be helpless" (Hines 227) and that has made a victim of her and so many other princesses before her, is entirely reimagined by Gaiman:

> "I slept, and they slept, and as each of them slept I stole a little of their life, a little of their dreams, and as I slept I took back my youth and my beauty and my power. I slept and I grew strong. I undid the ravages of time and I built myself a world of sleeping slaves." (Gaiman 52)

Gaiman queers fairy-tale sleep, transforming it from a passive state into one that is chosen and fiercely guarded by sleep-zombies. It is no longer a punishment inflicted on the heroine, but a way for the witch—the queer monster in the story—to regain her power. And the witch is undoubtedly a queer monster: she is beautiful, deadly, and seductive in the style of lesbian vampires, long a staple of literature. Much like these predatory monsters, who corrupt young, naïve, heterosexual women, the witch has stolen the youth and life of the girl she is impersonating—now the withered old woman. Moreover, upon waking, she attempts to seduce the queen with promises of unlimited power: "Love me. . . . All will love me and you who woke me must love me most of all" (Gaiman 55). This inversely echoes the "true-love kiss," as the kiss is meant to produce everlasting love. The queen is tempted, but her past experiences with her stepmother make her more resistant than most to magical lures. This wisdom transforms her history as a fairy-tale victim into a source of personal strength: "Learning how to be strong . . . had been hard; but once you learned the trick of it, you did not forget" (Gaiman 59). Ultimately, she allows the old woman to kill the witch, an act that, in turn, reveals the old woman as the hero of the story following traditional formulations, since she is the one to vanquish the kingdom's great evil.

The ending introduces a final series of inversions in Gaiman's tale. After her adventure, the queen sits thoughtfully under a tree, pondering her wedding. Finally, she concludes: "There are choices. . . . There are always choices" (Gaiman 63). She has the choice to reject heterosexual marriage—and with it, the constraints of a life of queenship she feels does not fit her. Instead, she chooses to continue adventuring with her group of dwarves, leaving behind the limitations of heteropatriarchal duty and all homonormative approximations, in favor of escaping "into the night" (Gaiman 66). The queerness of this open ending troubles the structure of the tale as well: the story becomes a capsized fairy tale, its structure flipped so that it begins with the wedding and ends with the hero going on an adventure. Fittingly, then, the queer monster dies at the hands of an unexpected hero, and the queer protagonist is allowed to continue—untethered, freed of her status as fairy-tale princess, queen, and even hero—into the dark beyond.

Monsters

As noted, the monster is created simultaneously with the norm: it guards the limits of the normative. Teratology scholars, such as Halberstam, usually analyze it in opposition to the non-monstrous. However, as Cohen reminds us, the monster is also a "harbinger of category crisis"; an inherently queer creation that refuses "easy categorization" and participation in the "classificatory 'order of things'" (6). Therefore, although monsters uphold the norm, they also inspire horror, as their very existence poses an unrelenting threat to normative distinctions (Cohen 6). It is not surprising, then, that such dangerous and ambiguous figures should eventually be domesticated. As Robin Wood writes:

> Otherness represents that which bourgeois ideology cannot recognize or accept but must deal with . . . in one of two ways: either by rejecting and if possible annihilating it, or by rendering it safe and assimilating it, converting it as far as possible into a replica of itself. (R. Wood 65–66)

The first option mentioned here can be found in classical vampire literature and film, as Benshoff and Sutton observe: they "reject and destroy the monstrous other," whereas the *Twilight* books and films would "work on the latter mode, rendering the [monster] safe by attempting to assimilate it to dominant values" (204). The assimilation process, which Tina Marie Boyer calls the "individualization" or "humanization" of the monster, has been on the rise since the early 1990s, particularly among monsters with humanoid features (15). For instance, angsty teenage werewolves star in MTV's hit series *Teen Wolf* (2011–17). In BBC Three's *In the Flesh* (2013–14), newly aware, medicated zombies must learn to "live" again, haunted by what they did as mindless monsters.

Predictably, the domestication of the monster has been compared to the domestication of queerness, as the threat of the "humanoid" queer persists (see S. Miller). In Butler's terms, these humanoid queers are unintelligible to the norm; "less-than-human" queers who have been extinguished through their successful assimilation (*Undoing Gender* 2). It is in this context that the following texts will be analyzed and narratively situated. We will see how the queer characters fall variously along the monstrous continuum. As protagonists of their own stories, they collapse the distance between hero and monster, yet they also maintain a threatening otherness that is controlled to varying degrees.

Catherynne M. Valente's "Bones Like Black Sugar"

The most disturbingly monstrous protagonist among the chosen texts is Gretel from Catherynne M. Valente's "Bones Like Black Sugar." The short story, which could also be characterized as a prose poem, is a dark sequel to "Hansel and Gretel," originally published in *Fantasy Magazine* and later compiled in JoSelle Vanderhooft's lesbian fairy-tale collection *Sleeping Beauty, Indeed*. The tale's unique tone is set in the opening lines:

> Why did I ever go back? Wasn't it enough that the eggs fried evenly in my iron pan, that the white edges crisped so prettily, like doilies . . . that the green trees stayed in their civilized trim, that they never again reached out for me as they did in those days, brackish arms a-bramble? . . . I have a house of my own, of wood and stone, with violets eating earth in the shadow of an iron-hinged door, and not a sparkle of sugar in any cupboard, on any tongue. (Valente 29)

Valente paints a haunting scenario in which both siblings have left behind the poverty of their childhood, built a house, and acquired all the things they used to lack. Yet, a traumatized Gretel is unable to forget the past. "I will never recover from this, I will never be well, I will never grow up" (31), she thinks, which recalls Love's queer refusal "to grow up" (7). However, in this context, Gretel's words reflect paralyzing trauma rather than queer defiance of normative maturity. The liberating space that could emerge within that house—she has, after all, "a house of [her] own" in an echo of Virginia Woolf's room—fails to materialize. Instead, the house proves to be a prison: "[Hansel] built a house around me, up, up, up, a house with no windows" (29).

In Gretel's eyes, Hansel is a double figure, both provider and warden. He brings the food, builds her house, yet also regulates her behavior, forbidding her from boiling "chocolate in a silver tin," or combing "honey from any hive" (30). As befits a tale rooted in the Gothic tradition, incestuous undercurrents run through the narrative. However, unlike in Travers Scott's "Hansel and Gretel" retelling, analyzed in the previous chapter, these tensions never break through the textual surface. Still, Gretel bows her head before Hansel "as before a husband," and describes how "he sleeps behind me, sleeps dead and sweat-pooled" (Valente 29–30). Hansel's controlling figure projects a twisted version of normative masculinity, transforming their relationship into a perverse replica of heteronormative domesticity.

This drives Gretel to leave the relative comfort of her home and retrace the steps of her childhood nightmare on a nightly basis, seeking the hut in the forest. What follows is an unsettling, nightmarish, fragmentary scene, stitched together in a textured filigree of compound words: "crumble-barren," "cinnamon-cinders," "sweetshop-graveyard" (Valente 31–34). When she finally finds it, what remains of the gingerbread house is a candied ruin, with "charred banisters of twisted liquorice and cherry-sticky stairs leading up to the star-bowels" (Valente 30). Its syrupy chaos stands in direct contrast to the manicured order of Hansel's house-prison, where, of course, all sugar is strictly forbidden. Whereas Gretel scours her house until her fingers are raw, the witch's hut is derelict, wall-less, roof-less, impossible to clean, sick with its "carbuncle-heart of sugar seething in its endless boil" (30).

At the center of the monstrous house awaits its monstrous stomach: "a good German oven. . . . Its cacao-grille throat-open,"[9] and sticking out of it, half-consumed, is the witch:

> Her candied pelvis caught on the broiling pan, fleshless arms stretched out in supplication, frozen in the grace of a ruined arch, the skeleton of an angel consumed, angles all wrong, ribs descending black as treble scales, femurs like cathedral columns dripping with honey-gold. (Valente 31)

Gretel sees the body of the witch as a desecrated holy building. Continuing with the religious imagery, she picks up the bones and deposits the witch on an altar-like bed. The grotesque ritual carries strong wedding night connotations: "It would be poetic to carry her up the stairs, a dead bride" (32). With no need for further normative ceremony, however, Gretel simply rearranges her bones "like runes," as if for a spell or religious ritual, and the witch comes back to life:

> And under my arms there is flesh. . . . Under my lips there are lips like floss, and my eyelashes beat against warm skin. . . . She smiles at me, she smiles at me and the belly under my hands is Turkish delight, she smiles as if I had never pushed her. . . . She smiles like erasure. (Valente 32)

This is the turning point in the story, where Gretel's sanity and stream of consciousness begin to unravel. Now grown up and trapped in marriage-like duty to her brother, she deeply regrets her role in murdering the witch. Unable to move on, Gretel imagines the ways in which her past could be erased or rewritten. In Gretel's mind, the witch would find her a child again, "student-bright" (32), ready to learn from her and be like her. The alternative reality she charts is kinder and more forgiving, with everyone scrubbed clean of blame.

---

9 This image recalls Travers Scott's depiction of the anthropophagous house, which connects these queer retellings: "A fireplace no longer, it yawned: a huge fleshy mouth, opening wide to reveal a wet, quivering throat pulsing with luminescent red veins" (320).

However, a wishful reimagining of the past soon becomes a dark litany of transgressive desire, which in the style of all things queer, is "scary, perhaps unspeakable, unimaginable . . . certainly not for the faint of heart" (Pasquesi 120):

> and punish me, punish me, I ought to be punished, I ought to be burned, I ought to have gone into the oven with you, into the fire, into the red and the ash . . . and my skull ought to have shattered on the stone where my fontanel must have been, and the shards of it, the shards of it ought to have mingled with yours when the leaves fell, ought to have been indistinguishable, ought to have, ought to have. (Valente 33)

The narrative grows increasingly repetitive and frantic, and in that moment of desperation, Gretel wishes for an intermingling of their flesh in a perverted version of sex, melted together into the oven and burned like martyrs or sinners.[10] Gretel imagines a radical mode of togetherness, an inventive vision of intimacy between the witch and herself. In short, Gretel envisions a twisted queerness to offset the twisted heteronorm her brother has built around her. During that feverish ritual in the broken church with her dead bride, Gretel finds freedom from her life with Hansel, who would forbid her to "stretch taffy between [her] fingers for the village children" (Valente 29–30). This suggests he suspects that Gretel's lurking monstrousness mirrors that of the witch. Spiraling, Gretel finally pleads for the witch to eat her:

> Devour me now as you promised, swallow me, I am offering it . . . take me up into your iron pot and I will boil for you, if you ask it . . . my love, you promised to destroy me. (Valente 33)

10 This is reminiscent of Turner's reading of the Grimms' "Frau Trude," in which he states: "Associated in Christian tradition with martyrdom, purification, and transformation as well as evil and damnation, fire, the tale's central motif, grounds 'Frau Trude' in familiar religious binaries" (Turner 260). In fact, "Frau Trude" shares many elements with "Bones Like Black Sugar," since both stories deal with themes of desire, transgression, queer kinship, and monstrous consumption between a young girl and a witch.

This returns the retelling to its pretext, recuperates its hunger, and complicates the villain-victim binary. While Warner maintains that cannibalism in fairy tales is tied to the fear of losing personal identity (see M. Warner, *Six Myths of Our Time*), Gretel desires to escape her identity through cannibalism—to be consumed by the witch, to be remade by her and be one with her in a distorted echo of the Eucharist. This act both absolves the cannibalistic witch of blame and positions Gretel as a willing disciple. However, the story forecloses the possibility of a queer transubstantiation, concluding with the horrific image of Gretel holding a corpse under the moonlight, the illusion shattered, the witch's "dead mouth yawning at the moon" (Valente 34). Yet, this ending does not completely preclude a queer, monstrous future for Gretel. In fact, it draws attention to the loose grasp Gretel has on her own monstrousness, which threatens to crack the walls that contain her.

Lauren Beukes's The Hidden Kingdom

A case of uncontained physical monstrosity and, to a lesser degree, moral monstrousness, appears in *Fairest Vol. 2: The Hidden Kingdom*. The volume, written by Lauren Beukes and illustrated by Iñaki Miranda, belongs to the comic book series *Fairest*, a spinoff of Bill Willingham's *Fables* series. The main series follows various fairy-tale characters who have been expelled from their Homelands and must establish themselves in the human world—specifically, in a hidden community located in New York City known as Fabletown. *Fairest* comprises five volumes and one standalone issue, each dedicated to a female fairy-tale character.

The Hidden Kingdom follows Rapunzel, who travels to the Japanese version of Fabletown after receiving a mysterious letter containing just two words: "your children" (Beukes ch. 1). Rapunzel understands this to mean her twins, to whom she was also a mother in the Grimms' version of the tale, but who, in the *Fables* universe, were stolen at birth. As the story unfolds, it is revealed that she has traveled to Japan before: "I came here to erase myself" (Beukes ch. 2). The text thus unravels two timelines simultaneously: one set in the present, and another recounting her first visit to the Celestial Palace centuries ago. The Celestial Palace serves as the Japanese equivalent to the Homelands, where folklore creatures—the yokai—once lived before they, too, were driven out and expelled to

Tokyo. Thus, the text transplants characters from the European fairy-tale tradition (who are also, via the *Fables* series, from the United States) and drops them into a darker Japanese mythical landscape—a world populated by ghosts, demons, and all manner of nightmarish creatures, all rendered in colorful detail by Miranda.

Thus, the totality of the text is geographically recentered, bringing this monstrous "dark [region]" (Cohen 18) into focus—its dangers not uncertain but lovingly depicted—in contrast to the vague descriptions offered in *The Stepsister Scheme*. As Wright argues, "once it can be symbolized, monstrousness loses its terrible power" (4). Something truly monstrous is that which remains invisible, unimaginable, and "cannot be situated" (Wright 18). By making the monsters so visible, Beukes and Miranda may, in fact, be diminishing their monstrousness, rendering their grotesque monstrosity a natural part of the landscape. For instance, the initial image of Mayumi—a character based on the Kuchisake onna, a traditional spirit in Japanese folklore who is recognizable by her cut-open mouth and who relentlessly seeks vengeance—is confronting, but by the end of the issue, readers have grown accustomed to her broken face and pointed teeth.

Rapunzel's visual descent into the grotesque is particularly striking, potentially due to her status as a well-known fairy-tale character and her initially familiar, wholesome image. It is revealed that when the Celestial Palace was attacked, she was thrown into the well alongside dead bodies and left to die. However, as an immortal *fable*, she did not: "The others started to rot. The maggots set in. I ate my own hair, I couldn't consider the alternatives. It broke something in me" (Beukes ch. 4). Unlike Gretel, Rapunzel could not consider the possibility of cannibalism, which might make her comparatively less monstrous. However, in this case, cannibalism would have been necessary for survival, rather than an act of ritualistic transubstantiation aimed at incorporating the other. By eating her magical hair, however, Rapunzel invites another kind of monstrosity: she creates magical bezoars[11] which pull her out of the well.

11 A bezoar is medically defined as "a ball of swallowed foreign material most often composed of hair or fiber. It collects in the stomach and fails to pass through the intestines" (*MedlinePlus*). When these bezoars extend through the intestines, it is called, interestingly, *Rapunzel's syndrome*. Historically, however, they were believed

FIGURE 1. Still from *Ringu* (1998), depicting Sadako climbing out of the well. Sadako is a vengeful ghost who kills anyone who watches her cursed tape. After emerging from the well in the recording, she breaks through the television screen and kills the viewer. In *The Hidden Kingdom*, Rapunzel climbs out of her own well in a similar manner—wild-looking, splattered with blood, and ready for revenge.

The bezoars—here sentient creatures—help Rapunzel kill her enemies, but they eventually escape her control and wreak havoc in the Celestial Palace. One image in the comic book of Rapunzel emerging from the well is a reference to Japanese horror film *Ringu* (*The Ring*, 1998) and stands in stark contrast to traditional representations of fairy-tale princesses (see figure 1).

However surprising the image may seem, the connection between Sadako/Samara and Rapunzel has been imaginatively drawn by Walter Rankin, who wrote in 2007:

> Both are changelings taken from their original homes by foster mothers who ultimately abandon their daughters when they find that they cannot control them. Rapunzel and Samara are isolated from the outside world as they get older. They reach out through

to have magical or curative properties and were depicted as such in Wilde's *The Picture of Dorian Gray*.

> the media of their time, whether by song or video, as they try to save themselves. And, yes, their hair serves as a defining physical characteristic for each of them, from Rapunzel's golden locks to Samara's ebony tresses. (75)

The disquieting juxtaposition of both characters ought not to be so shocking, particularly if we consider the well, as Rankin does, as an "inverted tower" (77). Thus, in *The Hidden Kingdom*, Rapunzel, as a Sadako/Rapunzel hybrid, plunges from her fairy-tale tower into her death well, where her monstrosity finally breaks free.

Each issue's cover illustration reflects the progressive decomposition of Rapunzel's character. The first one presents her as innocent, pure, beautiful, and surrounded by animals, but the next cover progresses into darker territory, depicting her splattered with blood and as a screaming skeleton, recognizable only by her golden hair. Even her hair, the most recognizable symbol of the Rapunzel character, can be linked to monstrosity. Warner explains: "Maidenhair can symbolize maidenhead—and its loss too, and the flux of sexual energy that this releases" (M. Warner, *From the Beast to the Blonde* 374). Rapunzel's excessive hair thus serves as a marker of excessive sexuality—uncontained, unpredictable, and even dangerous. In the Grimms' story, her prince climbs her hair to breach the tower and impregnate her. Likewise, in *The Hidden Kingdom*, her hair grows whenever she has sex—a feature she incidentally uses to escape a tower. It is fitting, then, that her murderous bezoars, which the text refers to as her "monstrous children," should come out of her excessively "sexual" hair in a corrupted version of birth-giving (Beukes, ch. 4).

This potential for monstrosity, inherited from the Grimm tale and fully realized at the Celestial Palace, is what ultimately enables Rapunzel's queerness. She is portrayed as heterosexual in the majority of the series, but in *The Hidden Kingdom*, she falls in love with the kitsune Tomoko—a fittingly monstrous partner, half woman, half man-eating fox.[12] The book's back cover, which highlights this central relationship, is notoriously filtered through a male, heterosexual gaze, much more

---

12 Kitsunes in Japanese mythology are magical foxes. They can be wise, good, or mischievous, and they possess the ability to shapeshift into humans or humanlike creatures.

obviously than the illustration of the kiss in *The Sleeper and the Spindle.* The two lovers appear in a sexualized, improbable position: Rapunzel, naked but covered by her hair, has her head thrown back, while Tomoko, barely shielded by a kimono, looks provocatively at the viewer. This imagery taps into stereotypical male fantasies, as Tomoko appears to be beckoning an onlooker to join in their lesbian encounter. While their relationship within the book is treated with sensitivity by Beukes, this initial image by Miranda has the potential to shape the reader's perception, rendering their relationship transient, unserious, and ultimately less threatening.

Rapunzel and Tomoko's relationship develops at the Celestial Palace, which positions itself as considerably more open to queerness than the Fabletown in New York. Fabletown remains invariably heterocentric despite being populated by impossible magical creatures. As one disgruntled review observes:

> In all of these worlds, in stories with talking animals and fantastic worlds, there doesn't seem to be any gay or lesbian characters. . . . For as many stories about people being transformed into animals, objects and even plants, both purposefully and in some cases against their will, transgender doesn't come up at all either. For a universe [in which magic is commonplace] switching genders hasn't come up at all. (Cox)

Thus, the exotic Celestial Palace is aligned once more with other queer, monstrous, distant lands, such as the desert land Talia hails from in *The Stepsister Scheme.* As such, it serves as a foil to its more restrictive, normative, and moral counterpart, Fabletown. Predictably, Rapunzel's queerness and monstrosity are forbidden to leave the confines of the exotic land of dark desire. Tomoko begs Rapunzel to stay with her and suggests that Rapunzel forget who she is, indicating that being with Tomoko is incompatible with remaining the traditional Rapunzel figure:

> "Easy things: forgetting, falling back into her arms, letting go. I'm so tempted. . . . Or I could do what I have to do and face the dog of my past" (Beukes ch. 6)

The cover for the last chapter foreshadows the ending, depicting a warrior-like Rapunzel, fierce but whole again. Ultimately, Rapunzel chooses to return to Fabletown with Joel, who is in love with her and with whom she occasionally shares a sexual relationship. With normativity reasserted, Rapunzel pulls away from a queer, temporary, and exoticized fantasy, located in an "other" world. Now resembling a traditional fairy-tale heroine once more, Rapunzel effectively gives up her monstrous queer past to focus on her heterosexual present. However, this conservative "happy" ending is undercut by the volume's final lines: "there's plenty of time to think about the future, about the possibility of coming back" (Beukes ch. 6). Her monstrosity is imperfectly confined within the Celestial Palace, leaving open the possibility of return—should Rapunzel choose to embrace a queer future.

ABC's Once Upon a Time

The final analysis in this chapter focuses on a character who may best exemplify the domestication of the queer monster: Little Red Riding Hood, known as "Ruby" or "Red" in the television show *Once Upon a Time*. The show's premise is like that of *Fables*: several fairy-tale characters have been transported to the human world but have forgotten who they truly are. They stand frozen in time, unable to move forward or return to their homeland. In other words, they unknowingly eschew chrononormativity and are stuck in queer time. The show aired on ABC, a subsidiary of The Walt Disney Company, and is heavily influenced by Disney in its selection of characters, the narrative trajectory of their backstories, and their visual representation. For instance, Belle, from *Beauty and the Beast* is named after the 1991 animated Disney version and wears the iconic golden dress in season 1, episode 12, "Skin Deep." However, *Once Upon a Time* also features characters from tales Disney has not reimagined, such as Rumpelstiltskin, portrayed as both a villain and a tragic antihero, and Little Red Riding Hood, whose representation will be analyzed primarily through two episodes: season 1, episode 15, "Red-Handed," and season 5, episode 18, "Ruby Slippers." Existing outside of the Disney Princess pantheon ostensibly frees Red from representational constraints—at least while she inhabits the human world—allowing her to embrace a more transgressive look. She wears revealing clothing, heavy makeup, and red extensions in her hair. More significantly, she is freed from narrative constraints, and she is revealed to be a werewolf in season one and bisexual in season five.

As Brittany Warman writes, "Red's werewolf nature [is] a coded depiction of her then latent but later confirmed bisexuality" ("Wolf" 2). As with the other monsters (and even heroes) analyzed in this chapter, monstrosity and queerness are inextricably intertwined in Red from the very beginning of the show. "Red-Handed" is the first episode in the show to focus on Red, who lives and works with her grandmother—with whom she has a complicated relationship. The source of intergenerational tension between them is, in true fairy-tale style, the grandmother's desire to police Red's sexuality and Red's desire to break away from that control. This leads to a good amount of bickering whenever Red flirts with customers:

> GRANNY: For another thing, *Liza*, you dress like a drag queen during Fleet Week.
>
> RED: And *you* dress like Norman Bates' mother when he dresses like Norman Bates' mother. (*Once Upon a Time*, "Red-Handed")

This exchange invokes queer monstrosity in both grandmother and granddaughter. Red is likened to drag queens—monstrous representations of femininity (or failed masculinity with monstrous results)[13]—while Granny is compared to Norman Bates, the monstrous cross-dresser from *Psycho*. The reference to a monstrous cross-dresser, incidentally, conjures yet another monstrous cross-dresser: the wolf from the Grimms' "Little Red Cap," who famously eats the grandmother and then dresses in her clothes to deceive the little girl. Consuming the grandmother is, of course, a transformative process, merging the grandmother and the wolf into one. Thus, the previous exchange functions as foreshadowing for not only Red's but also Granny's status as a queer werewolf.

"Red-Handed," like *The Hidden Kingdom*, follows two narratives: one set in present-day Storybrooke, and one revealing the characters'

---

13 Furthermore, the "Liza" probably refers to Liza Minelli, a notorious gay icon.

past in their fairy-tale land. Red is quite different in the flashbacks: innocent, obedient, and visually resembling traditional depictions of *Little Red Riding Hood*, with pure-white skin set against a blood-red cape, a symbol of her imminent passage from childhood to womanhood. As Zipes writes, "Little Red Riding Hood" is the "most provocative fairy tale in the Western world" (*Trials and Tribulations* 343), underpinned by themes of maturity, violence, and "the regulation of sex roles and sexuality" (124). These themes carry over into "Red-Handed." In the flashbacks, Red longs to be with her boyfriend, but her grandmother strictly forbids her from going out at night. The town has been plagued by deadly wolf attacks during what townspeople call "wolf's time." As Warman suggests, *wolf's time* alludes to "Moon Time, a phrase often used for the period when a woman is menstruating" (Warman, "Wolf" 6), reinforcing the theme of impending sexual maturity that is central to many "Little Red Riding Hood" tales, symbolized by the red cape. However, in "Red-Handed," the cape takes on a different role as a tool of societal control: it is revealed to be what keeps Red from turning into a werewolf, explaining her grandmother's anxiety when she discovers Red has left it behind to run away with her boyfriend. By the episode's end, Granny finds Red in the forest, back in her human form—next to the dismembered body of her boyfriend.

This is not the first text to draw the somewhat obvious connection between lycanthropy and menstruation, nor is it the first "Little Red Riding Hood" retelling to merge the figures of the girl and the wolf into one lycanthropic character. For instance, *The Company of Wolves*, a 1984 film based on Angela Carter's retelling, does both. However, "Red-Handed" is unique in its incorporation of queerness to this mix. Although it will not be explicit until the fifth season, as Warman contends:

> [The werewolf/Red is] a dangerous creature who terrorizes normative society and destroys the possibility of heterosexual love . . . in keeping with heterosexual fears regarding queer sexualities. ("Wolf" 7)

Red embodies the stereotypical, predatory queer monster, one who threatens heterocentric structures and even murders the innocent heterosexual love interest. However, Red is unaware of her condition, as her grandmother, a former werewolf herself, has kept the truth from her "for her own good." This revelation exculpates Red, framing her monstrousness as incidental: she is a blameless victim of her monstrosity, a character to whom monstrosity happens, rather than a character who knowingly perpetrates monstrous acts. Granny later reveals that Red's mother was also a werewolf and, although she thinks her dead, Red finds her mother in season 2, episode 7, "Child of the Moon." In this episode, Red also discovers that her mother belongs to a werewolf commune that hates humans. A genealogy of queer female monsters is thus established: first, her grandmother, who would forever suppress her monstrous side; second, her mother, who would embrace her monstrosity and use it against the established norm; and finally, Red, who, as a heroic monster, will be "assimilated to dominant values" (T. Sutton and Benshoff 204).

Red embodies the humanized or individualized monster Boyer describes (15). Somewhat ironically, Red's complete assimilation coincides with the discovery of her nonconforming sexuality. By the fifth season, she has learned to control her monstrosity and can transform strategically with the help of the magic cape, which reimagines her monstrosity as a superpower. However, she still has not found her place and continues searching for her pack. This is when she meets Dorothy from *The Wizard of Oz*, and they form an immediate connection. In the episode "Ruby Slippers," Dorothy falls victim to a sleeping spell, and Red is the only one who can wake her with a "true love's kiss." From episode one, *Once Upon a Time* establishes true love's kiss as a powerful form of light magic and the most effective curse-breaker. It is used more than fifteen times over the course of the show's seven seasons, but "Ruby Slippers" marks the only instance where a same-sex couple attempts to invoke the highly normative magic of true love.

For Warman, Red's explicit bisexuality "distances the show significantly from Disney's . . . notoriously heteronormative politics" and characterizes *Once Upon a Time* as "unconventional and progressive" ("Wolf" 9). However, Red's status as an utterly defanged monster, combined with the simultaneous reveal and assimilation of her queerness through the exclusive rite of the "true love's kiss," undermines this reading. The show oscillates between characterizing Red as both normative and other, as both monster and hero, but her ambiguity is stabilized into a homonormative approximation to dominant values—specifically, monogamy and socially acceptable togetherness—by pairing her with Dorothy. As a queer monster, Red is never entirely "normal," but she ultimately settles exceptionally close to the heteronorm, and her alterity remains just barely, harmlessly, marked.

Conclusions

When Sam Miller wrote about the death of the queer monster in horror, he was referring primarily to mainstream cinema, as a few queer monsters remained in independent gay films such as "*HellBent* (Paul Etheredge, 2004) [and] Bruce LaBruce's *Otto; or, Up with Dead People* (2008)" (S. Miller 228). This divide between independent and mainstream cinema is not replicated in fairy-tale revisions: the most mainstream of them all, *Once Upon a Time*, maintains its queer monster roots, even if the monster is presented here as a (mostly) successfully domesticated other. This is unsurprising, given that the show is intended for younger viewers and, despite The Walt Disney Company's conservative slant, more subversive forms of queerness are less likely to feature in that type of text, if at all. Texts for children generally "meet standards of acceptability that preclude overt sexual content" (Kenney 171). Heteronormative sexuality is naturalized, made innocuous, and thus commonly found in these texts, whereas nonconforming sexuality is automatically perceived as sexual or sexualized, making it considerably rarer (Kenney 171). *Once Upon a Time* is intended for a young audience, but not necessarily for young children (it was classified *PG* in the United States and as 12+ in countries such as the United Kingdom or Spain), which may explain the show's timid yet present inclusion of queerness.

Queer heroes are more commonly found in retellings intended for young adults, such as *The Stepsister Scheme* and *The Sleeper and the Spindle*. Relatively free from the conservative constraints of texts intended for children—especially from the 2010s (see Town 18–22)—the YA genre is a fertile site for narratives of empowerment. As Terry Norton and Jonathan Vare argue, queer YA literature "may not eliminate homophobia nor alleviate the risks stemming from it, [but] well-written books may help subvert the culture of silence still current in many school environments and offer a supportive framework for self-understanding by gay and lesbian teens" (23). Thus, these texts favor positive representations of queerness, providing affirming examples for young queer readers. Nonetheless, a closer examination of Talia's plot in *The Stepsister Scheme* raises an issue: despite presumably good intentions, the novel perpetuates negative stereotypes about sexual and ethnic minorities once Hines's narrative choices are considered alongside the real-world implications of Talia's intersectional identity. On the other hand, although *The Sleeper and the Spindle* is arguably haunted by the creators' male gaze and perpetuates the normative death of the queer monster, it also features a fully realized queer hero. Therefore, the queer monster does not "stand alone in the field of representation," and the text avoids universalizing associations of queerness with alterity (Schildcrout 3). Additionally, the narrative resists overly homonormative closures. Rather than conforming to classical fairy-tale endings, the retelling ultimately offers an escapist queer fantasy, wherein the final heroic reward is freedom from the normative institutions of marriage and royalty.

Comparatively, texts intended for adult readers are generally allowed to represent a wider spectrum of queer identities, so "Bones Like Black Sugar" and *The Hidden Kingdom* both spotlight truly monstrous queer characters. Perhaps because it is the most independently produced among the texts analyzed, "Bones Like Black Sugar" allows Gretel's uncomfortable, unassimilable monstrousness to roam free. Her descent into monstrousness unfolds unapologetically before the reader, and the narrative never softens the nightmarish scenario nor offers any comforting resolutions. For its part, *The Hidden Kingdom* presents grim visuals, featuring a particularly ghastly reimagining of Rapunzel—a character who embodies a strange combination of the traditional fairy-tale princess, a murderer, a savior, a mother of monsters, and a vengeful spirit akin to *Ringu*'s Sadako. However, this graphic novel exposes a problem that might emerge as queer fairy tales evolve, enter the mainstream, and target broader markets beyond their current niche audiences. As nonqueer creators engage with the subgenre, they may over-prioritize nonqueer audiences and, in doing so, fail to inscribe queer sensibility within their work.

As these diverse texts suggest, the fairy tale has an unflinching affinity for the queer monster—arguably even more so than the horror genre. This affinity is so strong that it makes its way into shows intended for young audiences, embedding queer monstrosity and monstrousness within the most heroic queer protagonists. Seemingly rigid fairy-tale categories become porous in these retellings, allowing the monster to flow through them. When retellings do not structure their plots around the traditional tensions between hero and monster, they internalize this conflict within the protagonist's body, producing monstrous heroes or heroic monsters who must learn to navigate or control their fragmented identity. This positions the fairy tale as an equally valid site for aspirational, normative, comforting narratives, and horrific, subversive, or otherwise defiant ones.

Marina Warner writes that the fairy tale's wonder mode elicits "dread and desire at once, attraction and recoil, producing a thrill, the shudder of pleasure and of fear" (*Wonder Tales* 3). This claim mirrors Cohen's description of monsters as creatures that terrify but also evoke "potent escapist fantasies" (17). Fairy tales and monsters are inescapably linked by their capacity to simultaneously attract and scare, captivating audiences with their odd, appealing, otherworldly, and even off-putting qualities. Thus, the wondrous fairy tale emerges as a natural habitat for the monster outcast in all its forms—even the most provocative. This explains why the endangered, dissident pleasure of the queer monster remains present in contemporary fairy tales, even as it has become increasingly rare in other genres. In fact, Miller, at the same time as he was mourning the queer monster's demise, remarked that it "might come strutting [back] at any moment" (S. Miller 231). Perhaps it never left. Perhaps it was just waiting to be found, in true horror fashion, in the most unexpected place.

4

QUEER FAIRY TALES 2.0

Parodying the Disney Paratext from Online Counterpublics

In 2001, DreamWorks released the computer-animated film *Shrek*, a postmodern fairy-tale parody that challenges the cultural and corporate monopoly of Disney. The film inverts characters from various fairy tales, legends, and children's stories—many of which appear in Disney adaptations—and infuses them with pop culture references and adult humor. The titular Shrek is a crude, fairy-tale-hating, swamp-dwelling ogre. Traditionally depicted as a monster and villain, he is recast as the hero of the story, exemplifying an increasingly popular narrative strategy (as demonstrated in previous chapters). Accompanied by his donkey sidekick, Shrek rescues a princess, deposes the authoritarian antagonist, and discovers that the princess transforms into an ogress at night. The story culminates in a fairy-tale wedding with said ogress—held in a swamp and set to the upbeat song "I'm a Believer" by Smash Mouth. This parodic engagement with Disney's fairy-tale conventions proved so popular that it grossed $120 million during its opening weekend (Bacchilega and Rieder 9). It also launched a lucrative franchise that includes three sequels, a television spinoff, numerous video games, and even a musical.

The film's incredible success demonstrates three things: first, the fairy tale is as pliable as ever, capable of being reinvented through technical innovation and genre mixing; second, the genre's appeal is not exclusive to children; and third that the fairy tale could easily, even productively, be approached from a place other than the sentimental nostalgia characteristic of the Disney paratext.[1] As Bacchilega and Rieder write, *Shrek* was also an effective contestation to Disney's "monopoly on the cinematic fairy tale" (30), influencing the production of other CGI films parodying fairy tales, such as *Hoodwinked!* (2005) and *Happy N'Ever After* (2007). Eventually, even Disney jumped on this trend and released *Enchanted* (2007), a film that mixes animation with live-action techniques and satirizes Disney's own fairy-tale codes (Bacchilega and Rieder 30). Since then, Disney's output has grown—if not parodic, then at least increasingly metareferential—reinforcing the company's approach to fairy tales at the same time as it demystifies it. For example, the 2014 live-action film *Maleficent*, a prequel to Disney's 1959 *Sleeping Beauty*, rehabilitates and recontextualizes the villain while also establishing Disney's version of Sleeping Beauty as canonical.

As much as all these films aim to revise fairy-tale conventions and adapt them to twenty-first-century sensibilities, none have meaningfully challenged their insistent heterocentrism—revealing major shortcomings in their potential to subvert. Bacchilega and Rieder, in fact, contend that both *Shrek* and *Enchanted*, as different as they are, show the same staunch allegiance to the romanticized fairy-tale plot:

> [While *Shrek* draws] on a satirical demystification of fairy-tale formulas and motifs already active in popular culture, the effect is merely humorous and transient because the alliance of fairy tale and romance still ends up shaping the stories' closure and emotional power. *Enchanted* seems to have learned from the Shrek films this dualistic strategy of initially parodying the idealization of romance . . . only to conclude by celebrating the same set of conventions. (30)

---

1 *Disney paratext* as used by Greenhill and Matrix (5–8) and explained by Ida Yoshinaga, refers to "the pervasive (collectively) canonical intertext generated by The Walt Disney Company's control of mass-produced, audiovisual fairy-tale representations from the twentieth century onward" (Yoshinaga). A typical Disney story includes a young girl who yearns for love, freedom, or status, and a villain who threatens or imprisons the protagonist, a young prince or love interest who rescues the protagonist, and a happy ending in which both young lovers get married (Yoshinaga).

The "set of conventions" of these authors doesn't necessarily include compulsory heterosexuality, but Linda Pershing and Lisa Gablehouse note that cisheteronormativity is certainly "presumed in *Enchanted*; viewers see no same-sex couples or alternative gender depictions" (147). Notably, gender nonconformity appears in the *Shrek* franchise in the figures of a cross-dressing wolf, a transgender-coded ugly stepsister (from *Cinderella*), and a lingerie-wearing Pinocchio. However, nonconforming gender expression or identity is always played up for (mostly horrified) laughs. To be fair, as everything is played up for laughs in the *Shrek* tetralogy, these jokes align with the franchise's general irreverence. However, the fact that the evil, vain, and laughable Prince Charming (voiced by gay actor Rupert Everett) is the closest approximation to a homosexual character reinforces the impression that the franchise treats gender and sexual non-normativity as something to ridicule or fear.[2] Disney, for its part, has consistently avoided including explicitly queer characters in its major fairy-tale releases—with the sole exception of 2017's *Beauty and the Beast* remake, in which the villain's sidekick, LeFou, is briefly shown dancing with another man, a moment intended to signal his queerness.

Disney, of course, is constrained by its own well-established codes and reputation, and its attempts to break away from that have remained mostly superficial. Changing too much or too fast would likely endanger the company's cultural position, which, as discussed in chapter 1, has long promoted conservative, child-friendly products;[3] in comparison, Zipes deems DreamWorks' *Shrek* "a delightful and hopeful anticipation of a de-Disneyfied world" that shatters "standard notions of fairy tales and normative standards of beauty, proper mating behavior, femininity and masculinity" (*The Enchanted Screen* 59). Yet, given that even DreamWorks has largely organized *Shrek*'s fairy-tale plots around heterosexual love (with the third film introducing straight love's most normative

---

2 In the NBC Halloween special *Scared Shrekless!* (2010), Charming appears in a parody of Psycho called "Boots Motel." He is depicted as a murderous cross-dresser in the style of Norman Bates, which brings us back to the previous chapter's discussion on the relationship between queerness and monstrousness or monstrosity, as well as the pervasive presence of the queer monster in fairy-tale retellings.

3 The company was accused, quite ironically, of being one of the main promoters of the "homosexual agenda" in America in the 1990s, when it introduced slightly more progressive internal policies like same-sex partner benefits (Sweeney 130).

product in the form of ogre triplets), one must question how possible it truly is to challenge the most entrenched fairy-tale codes from within American entertainment conglomerates, where creative freedom and even creators' ideologies are secondary to corporate and economic interests.

To this day, we must turn to independent producers to find fairy tales that effectively challenge cisheteronormative conventions. As the texts analyzed in this study show, almost all queer fairy tales are produced outside of the mainstream, or are, at the very least, relatively small projects—especially when compared to big-budget animated films. In previous chapters, we analyzed novels, novellas, poetry collections, short stories, comic books, and television shows, but, since the 2010s, a new kind of queer retelling has flourished and steadily gained momentum: the web-based queer fairy tale. This kind of retelling is not defined so much by its format as by its origin and the way it reaches new audiences. The internet provides several platforms for independent queer creatives to disseminate parodic contestations that, much like *Shrek*, seek to undermine Disney's hegemony—but unlike *Shrek*, explicitly address the problematic cisheteronormativity of the fairy tale.

This chapter thus analyzes texts that were created online and gained wider visibility through social media: Tim Manley's illustrated collection *Alice in Tumblr-Land* (2013); Brittany Ashley's web series *Lesbian Princess* (2015–16); Todrick Hall's music video parodies, such as "CinderFella" (2012) and "Cinderoncé" (2013); and José Rodolfo Loaiza Ontiveros's pop art illustrations. As this chapter shows, despite the medial diversity of these revisions, they all, invariably, identify Disney as the contemporary fairy-tale canon-maker; its adaptations are thus seen as authoritative versions to reference, resist, or otherwise undermine. We explore how these independent (or semi-independent) producers take commodified forms and tactically redeploy them to humorously undercut Disneyfied discourse. The resulting texts challenge centralized, mass-produced, corporate fairy-tale paratexts through a patchwork of small, politicized contestations emerging from queer online counterpublics.

Queer Online Counterpublics

Queer counterpublics are a kind of what Nancy Fraser terms "subaltern counterpublics," following the work of Gayatri Spivak and Rita Felski. These are alternative discursive spaces where members of subordinated groups "invent and circulate counter-discourses" (Fraser 67). Fraser developed this concept as a critique of Jürgen Habermas's idea of the singular public sphere—a space "made up of private people gathered together as a public and articulating the needs of society with the state" (Habermas 176). For Fraser, this is an idealized vision, since the unified public sphere has historically offered limited access to minorities, such as "women, workers, peoples of color, and gays and lesbians" (Fraser 67). These groups instead come together in counterpublics "to formulate oppositional interpretations of their identities, interests, and needs" (Fraser 67). As such, subaltern counterpublics act as "spaces of withdrawal and regroupment," where members of the group excluded from the public sphere can create a language to articulate their experience and construct their identities on their own terms (Fraser 68). They also serve a second function: as venues of "agitation, activism and contestation" (Boklage 120), from which members try to reach a wider audience and challenge the subordination of participants in the dominant public sphere (see M. Warner, *Publics*). For instance, the consciousness-raising groups discussed in chapter 2—in which queer people would get together to share their experiences and struggles to develop identity and community—are good examples of subaltern counterpublics, especially as they eventually helped to mobilize gays and lesbians. The LGBTQI organizations, neighborhoods, bars, clubs, bookstores, and so on that emerged in the second half of the twentieth century can also be described as counterpublics—or, more specifically, queer counterpublics (see M. Warner, *Publics*).

"Publics," as defined by Habermas, do not necessarily exist in a located, identifiable space, and neither do counterpublics. As Evgeniya Boklage contends, subaltern counterpublics are now practically synonymous with internet technologies (121). She argues that the internet has helped to bring about a decentralized communication network managed by civil society, thus restoring the possibility for participation, response, and relative control denied by old media. This is not to say that there are no limitations: although user-generated, bottom-up content has gained significant ground, it is still filtered through commercial and institutional frames—for example, by the use of platforms such as Facebook or YouTube. Still, the new media model facilitated by internet infrastructures eases one of the biggest impediments to the dissemination of counterhegemonic discourses emerging from queer counterpublics. According to Michael Warner, such discourse could "circulate up to a point, at which it is certain to meet intense resistance. It might therefore circulate in special, protected venues, in limited publications" (*Publics* 120). As seen in previous chapters, that was long the case of LGBTQI literature—and, longer still, queer fairy tales—which flourished alongside specialized publishing houses, circulated mostly in limited circles, and only marginally impacted the mainstream. Although still operating from within capitalistic frameworks, counterhegemonic discourse (queer and otherwise) has significantly benefited from the availability and increased reach of digital and online technologies.

The internet undeniably provides alternative avenues not only for the circulation of counterhegemonic discourses, but also for social networking, organization, political mobilization, and identity affirmation, among other functions. These possibilities are particularly attractive for LGBTQI people who, as detailed in chapter 2, have historically grown up in isolation from other queer individuals and thus have been disconnected from identity-forming referents, their own community, and so on. Online connection pathways can offset this historical isolation, leading Christopher Pullen to argue that the LGBTQI community is, in fact, "increasingly distanced from the need of a physical social space," as it forgoes the "physical and disconnected" in favor of the "virtual and immediate" (xi). As chapter 2 observes, gay people could be characterized as an imagined community of readers due to their reliance on gay literature for identity and community construction. This final shift away from the hold of the local—which situates the LGBTQI community as uniquely dependent on online counterpublics—ought to be seen as a natural development of that same tendency: after all, the LGBTQI community has, in many ways, become an imagined community of internet users.

Digital Fairy Tales

It follows that this subset of internet users would eventually use the potentialities of queer online counterpublics to produce revisions of fairy tales. This is due not only to the freedom and immediacy provided by such spaces to creatively explore marginal interests, develop distinctive contestation styles against dominant discourse, and build an audience of like-minded individuals, but also to the remarkable suitability of fairy tales for online platforms.

The fairy tale has migrated across mediums from oral forms to written ones and back with great success. It was used by early filmmakers such as Georges Méliès to explore new technical possibilities, and by early animators such as Lotte Reiniger, and has been adapted into forms as disparate as opera and video games. In short, the genre has repeatedly readjusted itself to fit a myriad of new media forms and frameworks of production, distribution, and consumption. However, it is the latest medium shift—the rise of internet technologies—that might have transformed it most significantly. As Jessica Tiffin writes, the twentieth-century commercial appropriation of the fairy tale:

> has perhaps blunted its aspect of communal *ownership*, despite its adoption of the mock oral-voice at times, but it has simultaneously ensured that the process of communal *experience* is enabled by new technologies of mass culture of mass production. (Tiffin 219, emphasis in original)

Indeed, internet technologies have expanded opportunities for communal fairy-tale experiences. The "fairy-tale web," as Bacchilega terms it, makes classical fairy tales from all possible traditions widely accessible (*Transformed* 3). For instance, several online resources compile and contextualize fairy tales:

- **D. L. Ashliman's Folktexts** (http://www.pitt.edu/~dash/folktexts.html): This resource collects numerous fairy tales and folktales edited and translated into English by Ashliman.

- **Norske Folkeeventyr** (http://runeberg.org/folkeven): This resource is sponsored by the Runeberg Project and hosts the classic Norwegian tales of Asbjørnsen and Moe.
- **SurLaLune Fairy Tales** (http://www.surlalunefairytales.com): This collection offers specially selected and translated fairy tales with hyperlinked annotations, illustrations, teaching guides, and discussion boards.
- **International Fairy-Tale Filmography** (http://iftf.uwinnipeg.ca): This resource is a growing, searchable database that indexes films worldwide and links them to the fairy tales or fragments they reference.
- **Fairy-Tale Teleography and Visualizations** (http://fttv.byu.edu): This indexed database of television shows features fairy-tale material, complete with visualization tools for exploring intertextual connections.

These platforms not only broaden access to primary texts but also introduce new methods of analysis—demonstrating how the fairy-tale web has reshaped both the object of study and the approaches scholars use to investigate it.

Internet technologies also restore the lost aspect of "communal ownership" of the fairy tale Tiffin mentions earlier—much as new media models address the limitations of old media—particularly insofar as the web favors practices of folk participation and bottom-up transformation.[4] A cursory Google search reveals intense engagement, especially with hypercommodified versions of fairy tales, such as those by Disney, which (despite copyright laws[5]) are routinely appropriated and challenged

4 Folklorists have recently discussed the necessity of studying "techlore," or internet folklore production, about which Trevor Blank writes: "Creativity is at the center of folkloristic inquiry, and the manifestations of online identity formation, artistic expression, folk religion, and the social dynamics of community construction are all important venues for analysis" (12).

5 Most of the examples listed are protected in the United States as "fair use" or "transformative use," but Disney has been, until very recently, notoriously intransigent when it comes to anything that would resemble copyright infringement (see Leonard).

in online forums. For example, internet users engage via cosplay and fan art (featured, for instance, on the art website DeviantArt); fanfiction (found on platforms such as Archive of Our Own); discussions (like those found in the DISboard forums); and video essays and song mashups (both of which are popular on YouTube). While Disney's filmic adaptations have been accused of attempting "to become definitive, thereby solidifying a single variant" (Koven 177), creators on online platforms forsake the single-variant model in favor of *bricolage*—to use Lynne S. McNeill's term meaning, "the construction of a personally relevant, pieced-together montage of meaning"—and thus their creations maintain the "dynamism of the folk process" (McNeill).

More relevantly still, online platforms extend the communal ownership of fairy tales to historically disenfranchised groups, such as LGBTQI people. Queer creators online have found a way not only to continue the reclamation of fairy tales begun in the 1990s, but also to appropriate the Disneyfied fairy-tale paratext and broadcast their sensibilities, cultural referents, and aesthetic preferences with unprecedented impact—often transcending, as we will see, the boundaries of queer online counterpublics.

Camping Up the Fairy Tale

Extremely diverse and multilayered, Disney revisions in the fairy-tale web—queer or not—are a complex international phenomenon. Creators' cultural and linguistic backgrounds intersect with these globalized, commodified fairy tales, and the resulting revisions interact in many ways at the vernacular level. Although not all these works are parodic in tone or intention, I consider *camp* to be the main language of queer counterpublics. It blends seamlessly with the wondrous mode of fairy tales—particularly in their Disneyfied versions. Thus, this chapter will focus on parodic revisions that work to *camp* the genre.

In *The Oxford Companion to Fairy Tales*, Ruth Bottigheimer distinguishes between fractured fairy tales and fairy-tale parodies: fractured fairy tales are "traditional fairy tales rearranged to create new plots with fundamentally different meanings or messages," while parodies "mock individual tales and the genre as a whole" ("Fractured" 209). The key difference, according to Bottigheimer, is that fractured fairy tales have a "reforming intent" and "seek to impart updated social and moral messages," whereas parodies, though closely related, do not. The parodies analyzed in this chapter contradict this distinction: while they indubitably mock Disneyfied fairy-tale codes, they also contain, at their center, "updated social and moral messages" with clear reforming intentions.

In that sense, the stories selected in this chapter follow Linda Hutcheon's conception of postmodern parody, characterized as "repetition with critical distance, which marks difference rather than similarity" (*Theory of Parody* 6) and is "resolutely . . . and inescapably political" ("Parody and History" 180). Like other postmodern parodies, these texts confront the "uniformization and commodification of mass culture" as they revise Disney tales, and do so, contradictorily, "from within" the same structures of commodified mass culture (Hutcheon, "Parody and History" 183). A defining characteristic of postmodernism, according to Hutcheon, is precisely that it is fundamentally contradictory:

> Its art forms (and its theory) use and abuse, install and then subvert convention in parodic ways, self-consciously pointing both to their own inherent paradoxes and provisionality and, of course, to their critical or ironic re-reading. ("Parody and History" 180)

Hutcheon expands on this contradiction in *The Politics of Postmodernism*, wherein she argues that "parody is doubly coded in political terms: it both legitimizes and subverts that which it parodies" (97). All Disney parodies mentioned—particularly the queer parodies analyzed in this chapter—are contradictory in this way and follow this model of legitimization and subversion: they acknowledge and reinforce the cultural monopoly of Disneyfied fairy tales while also questioning the absolute authority of these versions. Thus, as much as these parodies may appear complicit in certain structures of power, ultimately their "subversion is still there" (Hutcheon, *Politics* 102).

However, at the heart of most criticisms of postmodern parody is the claim that parody depends on already existing texts and thus runs counter to romantic notions of prized originality. Hutcheon nonetheless finds unique value in the parodic mode, as it "forces a reassessment of the process of textual production" (*Theory of Parody* 4). This reassessment is particularly useful for exposing the relationships of power within textual production—that is, who "possesses the original" and who only "possesses the parodic alternative" (Meyer 9). For Morris Meyer, only the dominant order can advance its own codes as the "original," and parody:

> becomes the process whereby the marginalized and disenfranchised advance their own interests by entering alternative signifying codes into discourse by attaching them to existing structures of signification. (Meyer 9)

Meyer's camp is synonymous with queer parody, and, for him, is the only way in which "the queer is able to enter representation and to produce social visibility" (Meyer 9).[6] Meyer wrote this in 1994, at a time when the debate around the normalization of queerness was gaining momentum. As covered in chapter 3, the mainstream assimilation of queerness has fundamentally shaped queer cultural and social visibility since the early 2000s. Thus, I would not claim that camp parody is the *only* means for queer social visibility nowadays—not even for queer revisions of Disney. These online revisions are as diverse as the people who produce them. However, I do consider camp to be the most salient mode for circulating counterhegemonic discourse in queer counterpublics; one later used to infiltrate the dominant sphere. In pre-Stonewall times, as Bergman notes, camp functioned as "an argot that provided an oppressed group some measure of coherence, solidarity, and humor" and a way "to talk to one another within the hearing range of heterosexuals who might be hostile to them" ("Introduction" 13). Camp thus became the language of queer counterpublics before their mass migration to cyberspace. Yet camp is not only coded queer language; it is also a queer aesthetic that seeks to "undermine the heterosexual normativity through enacting outrageous inversions . . . and gender codes" (Medhurst 279). It is irony, "theatricality and humor" (Babuscio 20).

6 Meyer was partly responding to Susan Sontag's 1964's "Notes on Camp." For Sontag, camp sensibility was detached, and thus depoliticized or apolitical, but Meyer sought to recover the politics of "Camp-as-critique" and the radical possibilities of "parodic intertextuality" (Meyer 9).

While fairy tales are notoriously heterosexual, they are also indubitably campy: they exaggeratedly and absurdly mix mundane elements and magic; are prone to outrageous, temporary inversions; and feature dramatis personae who are theatrical and almost parodic in their depthless characterization as gendered archetypes. Specifically, the Disney fairy tale routinely makes use of musical numbers, humorous animal sidekicks (some of which have been read as gay),[7] gender-non-normative villains, bright colors, and extravagant costume designs. My analysis of the following texts will consider the dual process of camping the genre as recognized by Anne Duggan, which can entail "both reading camp into the tale as well as infusing the tale with camp aesthetics" (*Queer Enchantments* 46). I will examine the ways in which queer online creators identify the camp undercurrents in these tales and how they reshuffle their elements to articulate counterhegemonic discourses. In this way, we will see how they claim ownership over the Disneyfied fairy tale—not by offering an authoritative substitute, but by advancing a myriad of personally relevant alternatives that unsettle Disney's monolithic paratext.

Tim Manley's *Alice in Tumblr-Land*

Within the corpus of texts examined in this chapter, Tim Manley's *Alice in Tumblr-Land* is the clearest example of how parodies that emerge within queer online counterpublics can later gain mainstream recognition. The illustrated book, published by Penguin in 2013, is based on Manley's Tumblr blog, "Fairy Tales for 20 Somethings" (http://fairytalesfor20somethings.tumblr.com), launched in 2012. Manley began his blog at the age of twenty-seven to post micro-tales poking fun at the urban, Millennial struggles with which he was grappling: "Fairy tales were a big part of the way I made sense of the world as a child, and so it seemed logical to return to them as I try to make sense of it now" (Manley, qtd. in Gray). This approach is reminiscent of the one taken in Cashorali's and Ford's collections. Fairy tales are treated by these authors as foundational

7 The American Family association called Timon and Pumbaa from *The Lion King* "the first homosexual characters ever to come to the screen" (qtd. in Sweeney 130). Even though they are not openly gay, Gael Sweeney's "*What do you want me to do? Dress in drag and do the hula?*" offers a convincing queer reading of these sidekicks.

texts containing important life lessons—specifically, Manley claims to better understand life through the simplified, allegorical lens of the fairy tale. However, unlike Ford and Cashorali, who tailored their collections to appeal to gay men in the 1990s, Manley has a broader audience in mind (although he identifies as bisexual). Tellingly, *Alice in Tumblr-Land*'s subtitle reads "and Other Fairy Tales for a New Generation."

Judging by these microstories, this "new generation" is primarily characterized by its complicated relationship with social media. For example, Cinderella is obsessed with the success of her photo blog; Little Red Riding Hood searches for love on OkCupid (where she receives insistent messages from wolves); and Sleeping Beauty, who is depressed and sleeps all day, only experiences the outside world through her Facebook feed. The centrality of social media is, of course, already advertised on the cover, which depicts Alice being sucked into the wondrous "Tumblr-Land." The cover's design mimics Sir John Tenniel's classic illustrations of Alice, and the word "Tumblr" retains the distinct typography of the social network's logo. These elements immediately mark this work as derivative and parodic and thus do not invite the reader to consider it a serious contender for a new canon of definitive fairy tales for a younger generation.

Tumblr is a microblogging platform founded in 2007 that allows users to share photos, videos, audio, text posts, and other short pieces of content. Manley's microparodies are tailored to fit this particular social network, in which images and short text combinations are well received. The tales retain the microtale format because the blog served as the basis for the book. The most significant difference is that Manley gives his characters a more traditional narrative arc in the book. Whereas his Tumblr posts were disconnected tales with no linear progression, *Alice in Tumblr-Land* follows several characters through adventures that reach some form of resolution. However, the blog's influence remains present in the book's format: the tales are presented in a nonconsecutive manner, with each installment interspersed with others—thus mimicking the spontaneous, decontextualized nature of social media posting.

Manley made use of the counterpublics side of Tumblr to viralize his project. Tumblr posts can gain broader visibility beyond one's social circle through a tagging and "reblogging" system that allows users to find relevant content and curate their blog in ways that reflect their interests, aesthetic preferences, identities, and political tendencies. In 2013, the social network's users leaned particularly young, with 40 percent of users in the 15–24-year-old bracket—making it a prime site for queer identity formation and performance (Dame, 23–25; Kohnen, 351–67; Zain). In 2017, the Daily Dot named it the safest space "for LGBT youth to hang online" (Fabian). Marty Fink and Quinn Miller argue that some of Tumblr's core features—such as its unstructured tagging system and visually aggregated posts—allow queer users to wrest their identities "out of a white, middle-class, cisgender (non-trans), mass-consumption paradigm" and build toward "an individually tailored, polyvocal, margin-based, and personalized form of distribution" (Fink and Miller 612). This description of the possibilities of Tumblr's interface aligns closely with queer fairy-tale parodies, which likewise attempt to wrest Disneyfied fairy tales away from the cisheterocentric, bourgeois center and move it toward more fragmentary margins—a connection Manley first articulated. He initially tagged his posts with popular, tangentially related terms such as "feminism" and, later, with tags like "gay" or "LGBT," progressively growing his audience by making his tales visible to different counterpublics within Tumblr (McNeill).

While Manley's project did not aim to offer exclusively queered versions of fairy tales, sexual and gender non-normativity appears throughout. As Manley mentions in an interview with the American LGBTQI magazine *Out*: "The characters' queerness came naturally . . . It's inevitable that a certain number of my characters would be queer, because that's what I see as true in life" (Manley, qtd. in Lambe). It follows that the generation at which this collection is aimed—those who entered adolescence at the beginning of the twenty-first century and thus experienced the progressive normalization of queerness firsthand—would generally expect normalized queerness in all aspects of their life, even in their fairy tales. Queerness is introduced in a fittingly casual manner. For instance, it is revealed that Cinderella divorced the prince soon after the end of the tale: "No, he wasn't secretly gay, just kind of a prick" (Manley, *Alice* 14). This at least opens the tale up to the possibility of queerness, directly contrasting its total invisibility in Disney fairy tales (even parodic ones like *Enchanted*). Cinderella even moves "back with her stepmother," which introduces new possibilities for intergenerational sorority and challenges the female rivalry embedded in the Disney paratext (Manley, *Alice* 14).

It becomes clear that this collection takes aim at the Disneyfied tradition. Although the illustration accompanying this Cinderella story fragment is monochromatic and sketchy—and thus does not particularly attempt to mimic Disney's visual style, unlike the works by Loaiza Ontiveros to be examined later in the chapter—the iconic Disney gown remains recognizable due to its shape, puffy sleeves, and voluminous skirt. Even Cinderella's hairstyle and gloves are similar, although she wears a more practical alternative to the glass slippers: "As a symbolic gesture, she vowed not to wear glass slippers, or any slippers, ever again. From here on out, all Crocs, all the time" (Manley, *Alice* 14). Cinderella is depicted walking down the stairs of a modern New York City apartment building—echoing the well-known image of her escaping down the palace stairs in the 1950 animated film—while her white Crocs peek from beneath the classic, extravagant gown. This juxtaposition of anachronous and modern elements, regal and kitsch styles, was already used in Cashorali's collections to similar effect: both authors exploit this contrast to produce incongruous, parodic images. Manley uses illustrations to amplify this parodic effect and to highlight what is already campy in the Disney images—in this case, the intricate, impractical gown and the theatrical escape down the palace stairs. Much like Cashorali, Manley wields affectation and conscious artificiality as tools for queer appropriation.

The effectiveness of these parodies depends almost entirely on the reader's familiarity with the Disney franchise. Manley's collection features some fairy tales that have not been adapted into Disney films—"Little Red Riding Hood," for example—but both visual cues in the illustrations (such as those described previously) and the selection of tales point to Disney as the primary referent. Characters such as King Arthur and Mulan appear in Manley's collection of "fairy tales for a new generation." Although Mulan embodies the cross-dressing maiden-knight fairy-tale trope, neither of these characters originates from what we would generally classify as fairy tales. They are instead drawn from legend—but because Disney made films about each of them, the power of adaptation and association has transformed their stories into fairy tales in the popular imagination. Curiously enough, Manley reimagines both Mulan and King Arthur as queer. Arthur—not yet king, working at an Applebee's and only unsheathing his sword, Excalibur, "if he wanted to be really dramatic when cutting a sandwich" (Manley, *Alice* 85)—is in love with his roommate, Lancelot, who, in turn, is dating Guinevere. This retelling taps into the legendary love triangle between Arthur, Lancelot, and Queen Guinevere, but it also recuperates the homosexual subtext between Lancelot and Arthur in T. H. White's *Once and Future King* (1958), upon which Disney's *The Sword in the Stone* (1963) is based. Since Manley uses Disney's version as a reference point, the queer element brings this web of intertextual connections full circle. For her part, Mulan in Manley's collection realizes he is a transman and eventually changes his name to Ping—an explicit intertextual reference to Disney, as Ping is the name Mulan chooses in the animated film when she disguises herself as a male soldier. Manley's tales about Mulan and Arthur become stories of difficult personal discovery, relayed in an ironically detached tone. For instance, Mulan is unsure whether he wants to identify as a man, although he likes dressing in men's clothes, until "one night at the movies she saw the line for the women's bathroom and was like, *Well* . . ." (Manley, *Alice* 111). On the one hand, one could interpret this as a perpetuation of transphobic narratives that reduce the transgender identity to an affinity for men's clothing, a feeling of disconnect from girls, and a desire to avoid the complications of being a woman. On the other hand, Manley surfaces the obvious transgender and queer undercurrents in Disney's *Mulan*—though the film tries hard to dispel queer anxiety through constant reminders of Mulan's "true" sex and by delaying her connection to the male love interest until after she is revealed to be a woman. Ultimately, Manley's retellings occupy the complex position of postmodern parodies: complicit with dominant values they inscribe, even as they subvert them (Hutcheon, *Politics* 102).

Similarly, Manley's retelling of "Rapunzel" reimagines her as queer but offsets this radical subversion with somewhat conservative humor. In his version, Rapunzel cuts her hair short, which causes everyone to think she is a lesbian, prompting her to wonder: "Is this still a thing—that only lesbians have short hair? Can't pretty much anyone have short hair now?" (Manley, *Alice* 155). Manley thus challenges the conflation of gender expression and sexuality, which Rapunzel experiences from both heterosexuals and lesbians. That is, she resists the dominant association of long hair with femininity and heterosexuality, and the opposing association of short hair with masculinity and lesbianism. However, Rapunzel ultimately confirms this conflation when she eventually begins dating a girl, which entails a complete rewrite of the Disneyfied paratext:[8]

> There was the story Rapunzel had expected for her life: a damsel in distress stuck in a tower, dreaming to be rescued [*sic*]. But then there was the one she'd made for herself: a bad bitch with a buzz cut, a hybrid car, and a hot girlfriend. She preferred the one she'd made. (*Alice* 233)

This conclusion foregrounds the contrast between traditional elements (the damsel in distress, the tower) and modern ones (the buzz cut, the car, even the openness of a lesbian relationship), and serves as a metafictional suggestion for fairy tales to come: new generations—particularly those congregating in online counterpublics that favor individually tailored content—would presumably choose the self-made, modern version over the expected, passed-down scripts of traditional tales. However, the emancipating final message is made less threatening to the status quo by the closing lines: "I will bravely face the future, a fearless warrior completely undeterred by whatever is to—WAIT, am I getting crow's-feet?!" (Manley 233). The fear of aging, and thus of losing worth in a patriarchal value system, situates Rapunzel once more within the boundaries of the stereotypical femininity expected of fairy-tale princesses and throws into question the lasting power of her rebellion.

Manley originally chose Tumblr as a platform for his retellings because he perceived it as particularly accessible: "There's no signup fee for Tumblr, and no laws on who can or can't post, and very few about what you can or can't post" (Manley, qtd. in McNeill). However, Tumblr

8 Although a Disneyfied paratext is undoubtedly referenced and challenged in this retelling, the actual Disney version of "Rapunzel" is not. *Tangled* was released in 2010, two years before Manley began his project, so it could have reasonably made the cut. However, since Manley was already an adult by the time the film came out, it is likely the Disney version did not have any significant impact on his perception of the classical tale, which exposes the generational limitations of Disney as a fairy-tale canon-maker.

was purchased by Yahoo in 2013, which ultimately exposed the limitations of such platforms in preserving counterhegemonic discourses and preventing independent, radical content creators from being silenced when corporate interests are at stake. After years of incremental changes and growing unease—particularly among Tumblr's queer constituency (see Fink and Miller 612–14)—in December 2018, Tumblr announced it would ban all adult content on the site. This decision led to the purge of thousands of blogs and the removal (i.e., censoring) of innumerable posts which were flagged as inappropriate (see Radulovic). This algorithm-driven, preemptive mass censoring has been accused of disproportionately targeting tags such as "trans," "lesbian," and "bisexual," even when posts did not contain adult material (see Brammer). This has severely challenged the rosy, optimistic vision Manley had of the platform in which he entrusted his queer parodies. Browsing through his "Fairy Tales for 20-Somethings" blog reveals that several of his fairy-tale posts have been flagged as inappropriate and are no longer accessible, even though his retellings did not contain explicit material. At the time of writing, his vision for parodic fairy tales—those that thrived thanks to Tumblr's open-access policy, its facilitation of counterhegemonic creativity, and its fostering of queer networks—can only be fully experienced in Penguin's conventionally published *Alice in Tumblr-Land*.

YouTube's Fairy-Tale Parodists: Brittany Ashley and Todrick Hall

Tumblr is not the only social network accused of unfairly censoring LGBTQI content. In fact, Tumblr's mass censoring reminded queer users of YouTube's "restricted mode" scandal, which took place in 2017. Explicit material is already banned on the platform, but the restricted mode—which is toggleable and can be turned off at any moment—aimed to filter out more mature content in YouTube in the style of parental controls. However, users soon realized that YouTube's algorithm flagged many videos with tame queer material as "mature" (see Hunt). This effectively rendered some videos with no sensitive material inaccessible to many YouTube users, particularly young ones, because they contained words like "lesbian" or "transgender" in their titles. Although YouTube reversed some restrictions, many videos with queer content are still restricted—including some fairy-tale parodies (Brammer). And there are quite a few parodies to choose from: Warman maintains that these are, in fact, the most common types of fairy-tale videos on YouTube (Warman, "YouTube"). On a platform that enables even amateur users to become video producers, Carol Vernallis suggests that the parodic or sardonic response works as a shortcut to reach and connect with an already primed audience: "your sarcastic take immediately places you in relation to a select group of viewers [as it] piggybacks on an already accrued attention" (Vernallis 146). The following section observes how Brittany Ashley and Todrick Hall navigate the platform's limitations and exploit its technical features to communicate their queer criticisms, using the momentum of the Disneyfied genre to appeal to a wider digital audience.

Brittany Ashley's Lesbian Princess

This web series, released serially from 2015 to 2016, was produced by Ashley while she was working for BuzzFeed—which effectively meant she ceded the rights of her videos and their concept to the digital media company. As such, unlike other creators analyzed in this chapter, she does not fully qualify as an independent creator, but her case illustrates a particular set of problems faced by creatives working with emerging media platforms. *Lesbian Princess* began as a standalone video satirizing Disneyfied fairy-tale conventions, which is already indicated in the title. As Greenhill notes, "Princesses are not limited to fairy tales, but are strongly associated with them, thanks in large part to the Disney Princesses franchise" ("Sexualities"). The three-minute video begins with a familiar scenario: a princess, dressed in an elegant golden dress, kisses a frog (see figure 2) and murmurs the age-old fairy-tale adage: "With one kiss, I will be reunited with my one true love" (Ashley).

The frog is obviously fake. This prop purposefully draws attention to the artificiality and self-reflexivity of the parody, as does the mixing of styles from different historical periods in the characters' costumes, the architecture, and the décor. Her plastic frog nonetheless turns into a handsome prince—this is, of course, not the ideal outcome for a princess whose desires are not recognized within the fairy-tale script:

FIGURE 2. Still of the first episode of *Lesbian Princess*. Brittany Ashley holds a fake frog in a lavish castle bedroom.

> PRINCESS: No, I can't, I'm sorry. I'm super-duper gay.
> PRINCE: You don't want to be with me . . . I am just not your type.
> PRINCESS: Yeah, you could say that.
> PRINCE: What would be your type?
> PRINCESS: Like . . . Rapunzel?
> PRINCE: I can grow my hair out! (Ashley)

This scene humorously contrasts the old-fashioned British prince—whose clean-cut appearance, delicate manners, and affected theatricality could in fact codify him as gay—with an American, down-to-earth, modern-sounding princess, heavily influenced by Ashley's online persona. It thus puts the traditional and the new in conversation. As in Manley's work, the video situates explicit queerness on the more "modern" side, highlighting the lack of queer characters within classic fairy-tale tradition. A union between a lesbian princess and Rapunzel has no precedent in the genre, after all. However, the video considers the possibility of subtextual queerness in fairy tales—imperceptible to the untrained reader—although it does so in a sardonic way. When the prince exclaims "I've never encountered a lady who lays with maidens," the princess responds, “Really? I doubt that” (Ashley). This leads to the prince listing several women in his life, including his mother’s chambermaid and the witch who enchanted him, to which the princess declares that they are, in fact, all gay due to stereotypical markers of identity:

> PRINCESS: What shoes does she wear to the stable?
> PRINCE: Homemade, low steel-toed boots.
> PRINCESS: Gay. (Ashley)

The virality of the first installment (at the time of writing, it has 4.2 million views) led to the expansion of the *Lesbian Princess* universe, turning it into a sitcom spoof that explores various aspects of modern lesbian life through an anachronistic fairy-tale lens. In this way, the titular lesbian princess visits a medieval lesbian “tavern” and falls in love with Cinderella, only to run into her *Maleficent*-inspired ex-girlfriend and lose her potential true love at midnight. Other subplots deal with the princess’s stepmother (who is only pretending to be evil to fit the expected script), being a closeted royal, and parental pressure to find a husband. The series thus does not address particularly mature topics. However, some of the six available episodes are still unavailable when using YouTube’s “restricted mode”—although only one of them (episode 5, “When You Have a One Night Stand with the Jester”) could reasonably be mistaken for mature content. This suggests that the algorithm is flagging these videos, like many others, simply because they contain the word “lesbian” in their title. Questionable platform policies aside, the web series will remain permanently unfinished. Ashley was fired by BuzzFeed in June 2016, reportedly due to a breach of a noncompete clause in her contract (K. Sutton). Although BuzzFeed offers its talent creative liberty and foregrounds marginalized voices rarely heard in mainstream media (such as racial minorities or LGBTQI people), it is first and foremost a company with economic interests, and it legally owns whatever their employees produce. Thus, *Lesbian Princess*, one of the most popular web series on BuzzFeedVideo, was left unfinished, and BuzzFeed rendered Ashley incapable of claiming ownership over her idea. Incidentally, this worked to further queer Ashley’s parody by truncating all possibility of continuing its narrative journey toward any kind of conclusion—much less the happy ending expected of the Disneyfied paratext.

Todrick Hall's Disney Parodies

Despite the popularity of Ashley's web series, the best-known queer parodies of fairy tales on YouTube are undoubtedly those by Todrick Hall, who built his online brand around Disney-influenced musical spoofs. He gained popularity as an *American Idol* contestant but is perhaps better known now for serving as a judge on *RuPaul's Drag Race* and a choreographer for artists like Beyoncé. Hall is also a prolific YouTuber who uses his channel to post personal video blogs, promote his music, and collaborate with other artists and personalities in elaborate, sleek musical parodies. His parodies combine elements of pop culture and filter them through a queer, Black, urban, and millennial lens. Some of his most notable Disney parodies—which have also been censored by YouTube's restricted mode—merge a Disneyfied fairy tale with a pop music diva. Examples include "Britney and the Beast" (2016), which casts Britney Spears as Beauty, and "Cinderoncé" (2013), which reimagines *Cinderella* through Beyoncé's songs. These videos assemble a medley of the chosen singer's catalog to fit the fairy-tale narrative, which several actors—including Hall himself—act out by dancing and lip-synching in Disney-inspired costumes and locations. These videos effectively bring together the traditional gay cult to powerful pop divas with the queer undercurrents of musical theater, or, as Doty calls them: "the musical's . . . camp and emotive genre characteristics [such as] spectacularized décor and costuming, intricate choreography, and singing about romantic yearning and fulfilment" (Doty 10).

Hall makes ample use of the excess of camp and the self-conscious artificiality of musical theater, so that although "Britney and the Beast" and "Cinderoncé" maintain the heterosexual love story of the Disney paratext, the heterocentrism of the tale is thrown into question. There is an inherent campiness to the musical genre, which is exaggerated, flamboyant, and draws attention to its own status as performance—including the Disney musical, which mixes realistic sequences with intricate, stylized musical numbers. However, other YouTube channels, like PattiCakes Productions, have taken a similar approach to the Disney musical parody, but the resulting videos are considerably more mainstream and downplay any queer possibilities. For example, their video "Cinderswift" (2017)—which uses Taylor Swift's songs to tell Cinderella's story—sticks closely to the Disney paratext without many playful departures. By contrast, Hall takes several queer detours on his way to the heterosexual ending. He routinely features beautiful male dancers (many of whom wear revealing costumes) in musical sequences that appear filtered through a clearly queer gaze, and which work to destabilize the apparent heterosexuality of some of the characters. Such is the case with Gaston, who, in "Britney and the Beast," can be seen pursuing Britney/Beauty, but also sharing a homoerotic sequence with several shirtless dancers to the sound of Spears's "Work Bitch" (see figure 3).

Another way in which Hall queers his own apparently heterosexual videos is through the inclusion of well-known drag queens. For John M. Chun, the "larger-than-life" personas of female performers in musical theater can be compared with the "exaggeration of femininity" one expects of drag queens (181–82). Hall effectively merges both into one: drag queens often appear in his musical videos, playing significant roles and cast on both ends of the good–evil spectrum. For instance, "Cinderoncé" features performer Miles Jay as one of the ugly stepsisters,

FIGURE 3. Still from "Britney and the Beast." Gaston, shirtless in the center, is surrounded by several background dancers. The women remain fully dressed while the men progressively lose their clothes in a queer inversion of heteropatriarchal expectations, by which women would typically have their bodies objectified instead.

and *RuPaul's Drag Race* alum Shangela as the Fairy Godmother—or, in this case, the Fairy Dragmother.

> SHANGELA: Cinderoncé! It's your Fairy Dragmother. Yes, Halleloo! Now, I see your heart, I see your grace, but honey you're gonna need some *fashion* to match that pretty face. Let's get to work! (Hall)

Shangela forgoes the matronly look of Disney's Fairy Godmother and instead wears a more appropriate sequined silver mini dress, flashy makeup, and big curly hair—a look inspired by one of Beyoncé's outfits from her 2007 tour, *The Beyoncé Experience*. Her appearance is one of the highlights of the video and marks the turning point in the story: after her magical appearance, Beyoncé's "Freakum Dress" begins to play, and Cinderella—emerging from a fog and surrounded by male dancers—sees her outfit transformed into Disney's iconic blue dress as they all break into highly choreographed dance. Like Cashorali, Hall draws a connection between the transformative skills of drag queens and the magic of donor figures, which often serve comparable cosmetic purposes in fairy tales. Moreover, both creators play with the parallels between the fairy godmother and the "drag mother"—usually an older or more experienced drag queen who mentors a younger queen, sometimes names her, and supports her through her initial steps into the drag scene. It is through this connection that Hall draws attention to the drag-like transformations of Disney princesses like Cinderella, who learns to perform luxurious hyperfemininity with the sartorial help of her fairy godmother.

Hall thus blends disparate layers of pop culture to engage in dialogue with a select group of viewers—namely, those who recognize the Disney paratext, those who appreciate obscure references to *RuPaul's Drag Race*,[9] and those deeply familiar with Beyoncé's repertoire and fashion choices (including specific tour outfits). Such esoteric references to various texts would presumably render Hall's parody somewhat ineffective, since, as Ulrich Knoepflmacher explains, our "awareness of a text before its comic refashioning is crucial to a parody's success" (762).

9 Shangela's catchphrase on *RuPaul's Drag Race* was "Halelloo!"

However, the video's 6.3 million views at the time of writing suggest both that Hall's parody is successful in making its multiple references ancillary to the narrative—so that they do not alienate less knowledgeable viewers but still delight informed ones—and that the Disney fairy tale, Beyoncé, and Hall himself are enough (separately or variously combined) to draw in a large audience.

Hall's presence is central to his parodies. Not only is he the creator of the videos but he also stars in them—usually in prominent roles. For instance, he plays both the Beast in "Britney and the Beast" and Prince Charming in "Cinderoncé." By his own design, these parodies appear alongside his video blogs in his YouTube channel, in which he speaks openly about his experiences as a Black gay man. Therefore, despite playing the heterosexual love interest in his videos, his queerness is always—if not directly referenced or implied—at least present around his parodies. In other words, the paratextual proximity of Hall's queerness is likely to color his audience's viewing experience, especially for those who would venture beyond one or two video parodies, ultimately drawing attention to the artificiality of the (seemingly straight) tales he stars in. His racial sensibility also significantly impacts his work. Of course, Hall's participation in his videos automatically ensures a degree of Black representation, but his parodies are also heavily influenced by African American culture. "Cinderoncé" has an all-Black cast, and he has set several videos in primarily Black neighborhoods (such as "Beauty and the Beat" and "Snow White and the Seven Thugs"), and he ensures his videos are always racially diverse at all levels—from the main parts to the background dancers—in direct criticism to their blindingly white Disney pretexts.

All the queer fairy-tale retellings explored in this study, including Hall's, are inescapably political insofar as they consciously include minoritarian identities rarely represented in fairy-tale texts. As such, they can be characterized as "activist adaptations," by which Bacchilega means those revisions in various media that "instigate readers/viewers/listeners to engage with the genre as well as with the world with a transformed sense of possibility" ("Adaptations" 80), and that "enact a politicized challenge to the hegemonic tropes of the genre" (*Transformed* 70). However, of the queer retellings analyzed so far, not many telegraph their political messages—and certainly not as boldly as Hall's "CinderFella." Hall himself plays the main part in this gender-flipped *Cinderella* parody, which is remarkable: although queer, non-white characters exist in retellings of fairy tales (such as Talia in Hines's *The Stepsister Scheme*), they are often secondary, or their identities are treated as discrete rather than intersectional. Hall never underplays his intersectional identity, and by placing himself at the center of the story, he projects a highly personal, political parody explicitly designed to support marriage equality. As Hall puts it:

> This story speaks volumes and I think that love is as classic as this fairy tale. It's time for us to legalize love in all shapes and colors. Please support this movement by posting this on your social media sites. ("CinderFella")

Hall thus uses "CinderFella" as a piece of online activism meant to transcend its origins in the queer and Black counterpublics of YouTube and effect change through peer-to-peer, web-based sharing. To make his message attractive and meaningful for people beyond his regular audience, Hall capitalizes on the interest accrued by Disney and the naturalized connection between romance and the fairy tale. He uses the assimilationist (and far-reaching) rhetoric of "love is love" while remaining faithful, as we shall see, to the codes and contestation styles of queer counterpublics.

Beyond its political effectiveness, "CinderFella" is possibly one of Hall's most successful parodies in terms of creativity and inventiveness. The video's concept is like other parodies in which Hall mixes "Top 40" pop songs with the Disneyfied fairy tale, but he rewrites the lyrics to make them work with Disney songs. In this way, the video opens with Hall playing a male Cinderella, singing a mashed-up version of the Disney song "A Dream Is a Wish Your Heart Makes" from *Cinderella* and "Who You Are" by Jessie J. Melodies and lyrics are integrated into a single, pop-sounding medley, and specialized knowledge is required to disentangle them. Some of the musical bits are intricately intertextual and reference several sources in the span of a few seconds—for example, the sequence in which a group of Disney princesses enter the ball:

> I kissed a girl and I liked it, the taste of her fairy Chapstick / A whole new world . . . take me away, on the magic carpet / It can't be wrong, it felt so right, can you feel that love tonight. (Hall, "CinderFella")

Hall makes use of one of the few pop songs released in 2008 to make overt queer references—Katy Perry's "I Kissed a Girl"—and changes certain terms to make it thematically appropriate (for example, "cherry Chapstick" becomes "fairy Chapstick"). He also references Disney's *Aladdin*'s "A Whole New World," the animated film's magic carpet (which also jokingly alludes to a woman's pubic hair), and the line "can you feel that love tonight," which references *The Lion King*'s "Can You Feel the Love Tonight"—a song, incidentally, sung by gay artist Elton John.

This constant stratification of references does not detract from the parody's energetic rhythm or its comedic dynamism. In fact, the rapid succession of musical references is comparable to the rapid succession of humorous cameos, some of them exceedingly brief: YouTuber GloZell plays a jaunty Fairy Godmother; Daniel Franzese shouts "He doesn't even go here!" in reference to his part in cult classic film *Mean Girls*; and gay ex–boyband member Lance Bass is revealed to be Prince Charming. One humorous highlight comes from Shangela, who appears again, this time alongside drag queen Willam, as they play CinderFella's stepsisters. They explain that CinderFella cannot attend the ball because he is a man, and the prince is, according to the well-known story, looking for a wife.

> SHANGELA: And that's why *you* can't go to the ball.
> WILLAM: Aw, I love balls. You're missing out! (Hall, "CinderFella")

Besides introducing an amusing double entendre, this exchange generates queer ironic tension, as two gay men in drag forbid another gay man from attending the ball for homophobic reasons. Homophobia and villainy are equated, and so the scene, purposefully ridiculous, criticizes the exclusion of queer people from the Disneyfied fairy tale. Through campy exaggeration, Hall exposes the seams of naturalized assumptions and shifts focus so Disney's heterocentric story is transformed into a pro-gay-marriage tale. At the end of the video, the clock strikes midnight as CinderFella and his Prince dance at the ball surrounded by distinctly queer attendees. In the traditional tale, this would lead to Cinderella's fevered escape to her carriage, but, in Hall's parody, CinderFella is right where he belongs, reclaiming his rightful place in the fairy tale. The clock's chime marks the end of an era, within and without the genre. "It's Time," read the sparkling words on the screen, "Legalize Love" ("CinderFella"). With this closing injunction, Hall urges viewers in no uncertain terms to take a political stance. Thus, the potential happy ending is visible on the horizon, but not a given, and thus requires the audience's political engagement.

José Rodolfo Loaiza Ontiveros's Pop Art Parodies

The final creator featured in this chapter is Mexican pop artist José Rodolfo Loaiza Ontiveros, who has gained international notoriety via his Instagram account (www.instagram.com/rodolfoloaiza), where he has 118,000 followers at the time of writing. He can also be found via his Flickr page (www.flickr.com/photos/rodolfo_loaiza). His work is heavily influenced by the 1970s lowbrow art movement—which formed as a reaction to the inaccessibility of the fine art world—and thus it shows "interest in more tangible and immediately representational forms" and is generally irreverent and rebellious in nature (Lowey and Prince 171). In Loaiza Ontiveros's case, this translates into a near-exclusive focus on subverting Disney's fairy-tale canon by placing its well-known characters in unorthodox or compromising scenarios, usually involving dark or adult themes such as drugs, sex, and violence. Loaiza Ontiveros's art style perfectly replicates Disney's stylistic conventions, down to the vibrant colors. Although he primarily paints on canvas using traditional materials such as acrylic or oil paint, technology has a flattening effect that disguises textures, brush strokes, and other marks of physicality. This technique ensures that his illustrations of Disney characters—as they appear filtered through the screen—effectively retain the two-dimensional animation style of classical Disney films. This resemblance adds to the shock value and parodic effect of his work, as it radically recontextualizes these readily recognizable characters. Grouped under an overarching theme of "loss of innocence" and unmistakably designed to provoke, Loaiza Ontiveros's art comments on the global impact of

American culture and sanitized fairy-tale imagery, as he distills both through a distinctly Mexican, queer gaze.

Loaiza Ontiveros shares Todrick Hall's fixation on American celebrity culture, pop divas, and classic Disney, and both of their parodies thus show a degree of overlap: they offer satirical reimaginings of iconic moments in pop culture, blend celebrities with Disney characters, and repeatedly revisit the same Disneyfied fairy tales—thereby engaging in multi-level conversations, including, presumably, between their own revisions. For instance, although Loaiza Ontiveros's artworks are not sequential, one can glean a degree of intertextuality from his Cinderella paintings *I'm Toxic* (2012) and *Like a Virgin* (2013). *I'm Toxic* shows a calm Cinderella shaving her head, in reference to Britney Spears in her 2007 photos, where the former child star can be seen shaving off her hair in front of a mirror. When Spears—who first became famous for her participation in *The Mickey Mouse Club*—shaved her head, she freed herself from one of her most clearly feminine signifiers and shattered a partially imposed image of herself. Cinderella is easily connected to Britney as a character for children who is denied "agency, sexuality, and corporeality" in the Disney tradition (A. Duggan, "Gender"). Depicted wearing her blue gown and with half her head shaved, suggesting her rebellion against her sanitized image is well underway, *I'm Toxic* points to a radical transformation not dictated by clocks or magic, but by necessity and personal conviction. One can arguably see the results of that transformation in Loaiza Ontiveros's *Like a Virgin*, in which a cartoonish Britney/Cinderella is depicted kissing a realistic Madonna. The mix of styles creates a textured, almost scrapbook-like effect that draws attention to the medium in parodic metareference. This piece references the much-discussed 2003 kiss between the two singers on the MTV VMAs but reframes and layers it with new meaning by connecting it to the Disney text. The image superimposes two emblematic moments: first, the aforementioned kiss between Spears and Madonna; and second, the closing image of Disney's *Cinderella*, in which Cinderella and Prince Charming are seen kissing through their carriage's window as they leave their royal wedding. Loaiza Ontiveros cleverly connects these disparate pop texts: Britney, who was also dressed as a bride, is substituted by Cinderella, who kisses the Queen of Pop rather than Prince Charming. The Britney–Madonna kiss was part of a performance designed to scandalize and titillate the audience, but the Cinderella–Prince Charming kiss is the ultimate symbol of true love, after which the camera pans out and the image transforms into the page of a book inscribed with the unequivocal fairy-tale declaration "And they lived happily ever after" (*Cinderella*). Loaiza Ontiveros thus activates a double reading, simultaneously suggesting that this kiss reinscribes the queer-as-spectacle of the MTV VMAs performance, and that this piece queerly challenges the exclusive, Disneyfied happy ending.

Nothing suggests that either interpretation is the correct one; in fact, Loaiza Ontiveros's work always invites simultaneous—even contradictory—readings, especially when one considers the body of work in its totality, as it obsessively engages with the Disney tradition from different points of view. He does not seek to substitute Disneyfied fairy tales by offering one stable alternative, or even to undermine them. As befits postmodern parodies, his work is concurrently situated as a loving tribute and a scathing criticism. Loaiza Ontiveros declares himself a Disney fan and considers the work of Disney to be his first visual school:

> The background watercolors, the balance of the colors and the outline of the characters impressed me a lot. My school notebook was filled with Disney characters. I tried to imitate the style. All of this definitely informs my development as an artist. (Loaiza Ontiveros, qtd. in Zaharuk)

However, the primacy of the Disney visual tradition during his formative years in Mexico raises other issues—namely, the Americanization of global culture and the hegemonic hold Disney has over the imagination of children around the world. This is a topic that Loaiza Ontiveros tackles in his work, as he consumes American icons, remixes them with his Mexican referents, and feeds them back to the United States with shifted emphasis.[10]

Many of his Disneyfied parodies thus integrate elements from Mexican culture, both high and low. For instance, *Reencuentro—Las Dos Blancanieves* (*Reunion—The Two Snow Whites*, 2012) remixes queer artist

---

10 Loaiza Ontiveros has had several exhibitions in the United States. His solo exhibitions in the lowbrow gallery La Luz de Jesus Gallery (Los Angeles), which is ironically located only thirty miles away from Disneyland, are also noteworthy.

Frida Kahlo's *Las Dos Fridas* with Disney's *Snow White*. Kahlo is a recurring figure in Loaiza Ontiveros's work, where she is equated to a Disney princess, after a fashion. In *Paloma Negra* (*Black Dove*, 2014), Loaiza Ontiveros forgoes the superposition of realistic and stylized figures he used in *Like a Virgin* and Kahlo appears in bold, colorful, Disney-influenced design, getting drunk with Cinderella, Snow White, and Belle. As a continuation of his criticism of Disney's cultural colonialism, he repeatedly casts Mickey Mouse in the role of Jesus Christ (see Loaiza Ontiveros's *The Incredulity of Saint Donald* [2014] and *The Veil of Clarabella* [2014]), suggesting that the iconic mouse has surpassed the visual influence of the religious figure. Religious imagery, fairy tales, and popular icons are all flattened by his work so that their narratives—elevated to different degrees by different groups—appear immediate and malleable, rather than distant and sacred.

Loaiza Ontiveros also uses this parodic blend of religion and pop culture to criticize the outdated morals of the Catholic Church, which are, after all, not so dissimilar from those of the Disneyfied fairy tale. One of his most notable pieces to do so is *Who Am I to Judge Him?* (2014). The picture shows Prince Philip (from *Sleeping Beauty*) and Prince Eric (from *The Little Mermaid*) getting married in a ceremony officiated by Pope Francis. In the work, Prince Phillip slides a wedding band onto Prince Eric's finger, both wearing their wedding attire from their respective films, while a Disneyfied Pope Francis looks on approvingly. The title references Pope Francis's statements during a 2013 press conference, in which he stated: "if someone is gay and he searches for the Lord and has good will, who am I to judge him?" (qtd. in Donadio). He was referring to gay priests at the time, but his statement was widely perceived as a gesture of reconciliation with the LGBTQI community, leading to the pope's nomination as "Person of the Year" by *The Advocate*, the largest LGBTQI magazine in the United States. In his work, however, Loaiza Ontiveros highlights the shortcomings of the pope's apparent acceptance of gay people. His discourse might be softer than that of his predecessor's views, but the pope still upholds Catholic doctrine, by which "homosexual acts" are considered sinful. The incongruous image of the Catholic pope marrying two Disney princes marks the pope's words as insincere—he would never, of course, officiate such a wedding, nor would he publicly approve of it, which clearly suggests a degree of judgment on his part. It is also highly unlikely that Disney would have two fairy-tale princes marry each other any time soon. It is only in the subversive artscape that Loaiza Ontiveros projects—one in which old prejudices, taboos, and hierarchies are blurred—that such a scene could take place.

Comparable to Hall, Loaiza Ontiveros deploys his revised fairy-tale images with political intentions. The flexibility of his medium allows him to constantly reuse his art. That is, he can routinely repost old pieces on his Instagram account and, through paratextual tagging, appeal to different counterpublics and recontextualize his work to comment on current events. For instance, he reposted *Who Am I to Judge Him?* in 2016 during the national debate that would eventually lead to marriage equality in Mexico, adding clickable hashtags such as #Mexico, #gaymarriage, and #nohypocrisy—the latter alluding to the pope's 2013 statement. Similarly, in 2016, he reposted an old illustration, *True Ending . . . Take 2* (2011), in which Snow White and Cinderella kiss tenderly, and tagged it #nationalcomingoutday. By strategically reposting his art, Loaiza Ontiveros expands his audience while using the technical affordances of Instagram to deliver textured, hybrid messages, in which current affairs, pop culture, and traditional Disneyfied fairy tales intertwine, resulting in ever-shifting possibilities.

Conclusions

Although these creators clearly identify Disney's filmic tradition as the canon to parody, they have also taken a leaf from *Shrek*'s book, which serves as a modern referent. As such, they engage the fairy tale with adult humor, rely on a mix of pop references and anachronistic elements, and seem to operate in a Disneyfied universe in which all fairy tales coexist to some degree. However, unlike the *Shrek* franchise, they also challenge the systematic exclusion of queerness from the fairy-tale tradition, reclaiming fairy tales even in their most hypercommodified and exclusive forms.

New technology is vital for this type of vernacular reclamation. Online social platforms promote the congregation of minorities in counterpublics, as they facilitate the production, dissemination, and popularization of counterhegemonic texts. Fairy-tale parodies that are born in alternative spaces remain freely accessible and independent from traditional capitalistic structures. On the other hand, as this chapter has made clear, online platforms that have fostered the creation of these texts regularly prioritize corporate and economic interests over the integrity of their user-generated content. There is an increasing pushback against queer content in digital spaces, which disciplines transgressive creativity and forces queer creators to navigate not only constantly shifting, homophobic intraplatform policies but also broader, inescapable homophobic structures of power. Although these obstacles are significant, these parodists persist in queering the Disneyfied fairy tale while remaining faithful to the distinctive, camp styles of contestation characteristic of queer counterpublics.

Adhering to these styles ironically opens new possibilities for financial security, as these creators take advantage of a hegemonic, capitalistic culture's tendency to absorb, appropriate, and commodify everything in its path. As Meyer puts it:

> Queer knowledge can . . . be introduced and incorporated into the dominant ideology because the blind spot of bourgeois culture is predictable: it always appropriates. And it appropriates whatever the [queer creator] chooses to place in its path. (Meyer 17)

Thus, queer parodists have pulled apart highly commodified fairy tales, installed counterhegemonic discourses within them, and resold them in consumable packages. For example, Loaiza Ontiveros is selling his paintings for as much as $5,000, and Manley's book was optioned for television by 20th Century Fox (Manley, "TV show"). These creators, therefore, benefit from the very system they criticize and seemingly resist. However, the fairy tales they give back have been infused with queerness and slowly erode the uniform, cisheterocentric, Disneyfied versions. Ultimately, their multimedia, kaleidoscopic parodies—which are endlessly productive—work to loosen up the hegemonic hold Disney has over the genre and throw the authority of these texts into question.

AFTERWORD

#GiveElsaAGirlfriend and a Queer Future for Fairy Tales

In 2016, the hashtag #GiveElsaAGirlfriend trended on Twitter (later known as X). This was by no means a rare occurrence: every day, in every corner of the world, new hashtags gain traction and sometimes manage to surpass the confines of their online bubble. Indeed, in the past ten years, we have witnessed the power of hashtag activism. Understood as the broad circulation of specific hashtags on social media to draw attention to a social or political issue, these online campaigns have a unique power to influence and shape public discourse. Guobin Yang points out that the hashtags that have mobilized the most people in recent years usually contain verbs expressing "a strong sense of action and force" (15), rather than just a single word. Among them, we find the widely influential #BlackLivesMatter or #OccupyWallStreet, and, on a comparatively smaller scale, #GiveElsaAGirlfriend. These hashtags contain "refusals, objections, and imperatives to take immediate action" and "often challenge narratives in mainstream media" (Yang 15). The mechanics of Twitter hashtagging allows people to easily find and interact with one another, uniting diverse and distributed users who individually might hold little power in communal, participatory online actions that can garner mainstream media coverage. #GiveElsaAGirlfriend was also not the first example of a fan-led hashtag campaign demanding better minority representation in popular media. Hashtag #PousseyDeservedBetter trended in 2016 following the death of a beloved character in the Netflix show *Orange Is the New Black*, but it also addressed broader issues pertaining to queer characters (and especially queer, non-white characters) who have historically been disproportionately prone to dying. A year later, the hashtag #SWRepresentationMatters was launched to celebrate the racial diversity of the new Star Wars trilogy, while other Twitter users employed it to request visible queer characters everywhere—including in a galaxy far, far away. However, #GiveElsaAGirlfriend was an exceptional case among these examples of online fan advocacy: it surpassed the limits of Twitter, sent ripples worldwide, gained a notable number of both supporters and detractors, and managed to reach (and perhaps influence) head creatives at Walt Disney Studios.

The movement started modestly enough. At first, it was just a comment stating a desire for a lesbian Elsa tweeted by user Alexis Isabel Moncada, who was immediately encouraged to turn it into a searchable hashtag by her Twitter followers—all of whom, she noted, "are overwhelmingly dedicated to supporting LGBT representation" (Moncada). Moncada tweeted the hashtag on May 1, 2016, three years after *Frozen* was released and a year after the company had officially announced there would be a sequel (Pulver, "Frozen 2"). Rather, Moncada's hashtag was in response to the release of the 2016 GLAAD Studio Responsibility Index, which gave Walt Disney Studios a failing grade, stating:

> Of all the studios tracked in this report, Walt Disney Studios has the weakest historical record when it comes to LGBT-inclusive films. . . . In 2015, Walt Disney Studios released 11 films, of which 0 included appearances by LGBT people, amounting to 0%. (GLAAD)

Although none of the studios analyzed that year obtained a passing grade, Walt Disney Studios was by far the worst rated. The hashtag was thus a means of criticizing the continued absence of queerness in Disney's films, but it was also responding to the queer subtext that many fans had identified in *Frozen*.

Elsa—who, in the first *Frozen* film, is forced by her parents to conceal her magical powers—has been often read as queer, particularly as her main song, Oscar winner "Let It Go," can be easily interpreted as a coming-out, liberatory anthem:

> Don't let them in, don't let them see
> Be the good girl you always have to be

Conceal, don't feel, don't let them know
Well, now they know

Let it go, let it go
Can't hold it back anymore (*Frozen*)

Her performance of the song marks the moment in which a newly outed Elsa effectively lets go of her old, constraining life to unapologetically explore her newly liberated identity—which temporarily turns her into the villain of the story. She is explicitly branded a monster in the film, further evidencing the alliance between fairy tales and the outsider-monster archetype. This places Elsa alongside other queer-coded villains in the Disney tradition, such as *The Little Mermaid*'s Ursula and *Aladdin*'s Jafar.[1] What sets *Frozen* apart from many Disney films—and, in fact, brings it closer to other queer fairy tales of the 2000s analyzed in chapter 3—is that Elsa reconciles her queer, monstrous identity with the normative world, represented here by her sister Anna and the kingdom Elsa inherits via normative succession. As such, she is ultimately positioned as the hero. This story of queer monstrosity resonates deeply with many queer viewers, as Elsa's arc explores themes of isolation, demonized difference one is born with, self-acceptance, and the ultimate assimilation of alterity into normative society via the taming of Elsa's queerness (here represented by her powers). If we also consider the fact that *Frozen* is not only one of the most popular Disney films in recent history but also one of the highest-grossing animated films of all time (alongside its sequel, *Frozen 2*), it is not surprising that Moncada's hashtag gained as much traction as it did among like-minded users.

It was not only LGBTQI viewers who identified queer tensions in the film. As tends to be the paradoxical case, queer critics and conservative pundits are similarly adept at reading queerness into nominally straight texts—an alignment that ironically serves to legitimize their queer subtext. Without referring to any particular element in the film, American right-wing pastor Kevin Swanson declared the

1 Elsa was originally meant to be a more straightforward villain, closer to Andersen's Snow Queen (after whom she is modeled), but the film's fraught production process led to severe rewrites (Hibberd).

film was "evil, pure evil," as "this cute little movie is going to indoctrinate [a little girl] to be a lesbian or treat homosexuality . . . in a light sort of way" (qtd. in Tashman). Thus the digital battlefield was set: at the same time as #GiveElsaAGirlfriend was trending, the reactionary #PrinceCharmingForElsa also emerged, arguing for the perpetuation of the exclusive, cisheteronormative Disney paratext. Ironically, conservatives all over the world begged for children's entertainment not to be "spoiled by an adult agenda about sexuality" (Moynihan), and several formal online petitions were launched in an effort to dissuade Disney from opening its filmic tradition up to queerness (Evans). Although none of these online campaigns accrued the desired attention, they represent the deep-seated anxiety that the mere *suggestion* of a nonstraight character present in a fairy-tale film awakens in some people. Some campaigns also used noteworthy strategies to instigate fear among right-wing constituencies. For example, a petition launched by Spanish ultra-Catholic group Hazte Oír (Make Yourself Heard)—which claimed that Disney was facing a historic decision "to continue transmitting the universal values on which generations have been brought up, or to become an ideological tool at the service of a minority" (qtd. in Estirado, my translation)—used a collage combining several of Loaiza Ontiveros's pieces. The collage mixed paintings in which same-sex Disney couples are shown kissing, such as *True Ending* and *Like a Virgin*, and placed them against a black background beneath ominous message: "Is this the Disney you want for your children?" (qtd. in Estirado, my translation). The right-wing group recontextualized Loaiza Ontiveros's art for political purposes—much like Loaiza Ontiveros often does himself, though with a decidedly different intent.

This fierce gatekeeping of the Disneyfied fairy tale would not have been as intense or as widespread had #GiveElsaAGirlfriend not reached some influential ears. By the end of May 2016, Idina Menzel, the actress who voices Elsa, responded to the online campaign and stated: "I think it's great . . . Disney's just gotta contend with that. I'll let them figure that out" (qtd. in Ungerman). Menzel would later confess, in conversation with the queer newspaper *Pride Source*, to being surprised by the campaign at first—"because it's Disney"—but added, "I can't promise anybody that's what's going to happen [but] deep down [I am] happy that it's causing people to talk about it" (qtd. in Azzopardi). While her response was not exactly an unequivocal endorsement, it raised alarm among conservative audiences and pleased queer fans. The intensity of the debate only increased when *Frozen* writer and co-director Jennifer Lee commented in 2018:

> It means the world to us that we're part of these conversations. Where we're going with it, we have tons of conversations about it, and we're really conscientious about these things . . . I always write from character-out, and where Elsa is and what Elsa's doing in her life, she's telling me every day. We'll see where we go. (qtd. in Bradley)

Lee's comment was, if possible, even more lukewarm than Menzel's, but mainstream media and fans (as well as detractors) took it to mean that there was a real possibility Elsa would indeed be given a girlfriend.

With the release of the first teaser trailer for *Frozen 2* in February 2019, the conversation was fully revived—though the trailer itself did not in any way reference Elsa's sexuality. There was a small window, between the release of the first *Frozen 2* trailers and the film's debut in November 2019, when everything seemed simultaneously possible: that Elsa would be paired with a man, that she would remain single, and that she would be revealed as queer. This last possibility, however distant, was full of promise. Such a bold move would have drawn definite attention to the #GiveElsaAGirlfriend campaign—not as a fun, fan-led, harmless online movement, but as a sophisticated use of online affordances "to force industrial attention on issues of inclusion" and "to secure industrial change in the treatment of LGBTQ+ people" (Navar-Gill and Stanfill 93). In other words, it would have marked the campaign as a queer counter-discourse, born in distinctly queer online counterpublics, that had managed to impact the exclusive and hegemonic fairy tale. If there were an openly queer fairy-tale princess (or queen), and if she also happened to be one of the best-loved characters in Disney history, it could significantly affect children's perception of queerness—which is, of course, why conservative critics were so vehemently opposed to the idea. It would be especially impactful for LGBTQI children, who, as Michael Warner puts it, might grow up in "families that think of themselves and all their members as heterosexual," a situation that can create "a profound and nameless estrangement, a sense of inner secrets and hidden shame" (*The Trouble with Normal*, 8). Supporting LGBTQI children was precisely one of Moncada's main objectives (as well as that of many supporters of the hashtag). In an open letter to *MTV*, Moncada wrote that no one "deserves to feel isolated and confused about who they are," alluding to her own feelings of isolation growing up, and emphasized the potentially reparative function of the queer fairy tale for queer children and adults alike: "All we need is someone to show us that there are other options, other kinds of princesses, and other ways to have the happy ending that you deserve." Like Ford, Moncada was advocating for queer fairy tales as a form of cultural therapy.

As the film's release drew closer, however, queer fans grew increasingly concerned that it would remain coy and equivocal about Elsa's sexuality—so as not to alienate conservative viewers—while still engaging in what Eve Ng defines as "queerbaiting." She describes this as:

> Situations where those officially associated with a media text court viewers interested in LGBT narratives . . . and encourage their interest in the media text without the text ever definitively confirming the nonheterosexuality of the relevant characters. (Ng)

Indeed, just months before the release, Lee revealed on *Entertainment Tonight* that Elsa "wasn't ready for a relationship at all . . . it just didn't fit with where she was in her life," only to add: "I don't know if it'll fit in the future" (qtd. in Boone). Such a statement is a prime example of queerbaiting: it aims assuage conservative film markets while remaining ambiguous enough about a potential queer future for Elsa that queer fans could remain invested in a hypothetical *Frozen 3*.

As it were, *Frozen 2* did not give Elsa a girlfriend. Perhaps predictably, it also did not give her Prince Charming. While Elsa's journey feels even more intentionally queer-coded in the sequel, she is primarily focused on growing into her powers and finding a community. In this way, while *Frozen* aligned with queer retellings of the 2000s—in which the queer monster and hero are one and the same, and the protagonist's alterity is often assimilated into normative society—*Frozen 2* falls thematically closer to earlier retellings from the 1990s. In the sequel, Elsa hears a mysterious female voice that beckons her to follow, and whose seductive call she tries to resist in the song "Into the Unknown:" "Everyone I've ever loved is here within these walls / I'm sorry, secret siren, but I'm blocking out your calls . . . I am afraid of what I'm risking if I follow you." This is a recognizable narrative for many LGBTQI people, who feel they must repress part of their identity to preserve their relationship with their (biological, heteronormative) family. However, this song is a turning point for Elsa, who must admit to herself that she feels like she does not belong in traditional Arendelle, where her sister Anna is so at home: "Or are you someone out there who's a little bit like me? / Who knows deep down I'm not where I'm meant to be . . . Don't you know there's part of me that longs to go?" Although it is eventually revealed that the voice she hears belongs to her deceased mother—and that the one she has been looking for is herself—Elsa meets a young woman named Honeymaren during her journey of self-discovery. Honeymaren and Elsa share a few scenes that could be regarded as Disney's tepid response to #GiveElsaAGirlfriend: they share an intimate moment by the fire, and Honeymaren quickly recognizes that Elsa belongs with her people in the forest. In the end, Elsa decides to abdicate the throne to a newly engaged Anna, who is much better suited to meet the normative requirements of the Arendellian crown. Elsa chooses to stay in the forest with the Northuldra people—and Honeymaren. While the resolution is not queer in any meaningful or explicit way, it aligns with the gay tales of the 1990s analyzed in chapter 2, which center on queer belonging—such as Scott's "Hansel and Gretel" or Bacchus's "Lily Boy," whose protagonist also finds community in the liminal forest. Elsa ultimately establishes herself among like-minded people, and presumably satisfies her need for belonging; or, to echo Freeman, her "longing to be, and be connected" ("Queer Belongings" 299).

Some critics have proposed that keeping Elsa single in *Frozen* and *Frozen 2* was the most revolutionary option, particularly as she is part of the lineup of Disney princesses whose stories have long focused on (heterosexual) romance (Davis 667). However, Elsa is not the only single Disney princess; recent princess characters seem to be mostly uninterested in romance, such as Merida (*Brave*, 2012), Moana (*Moana*, 2016), and Raya (*Raya and the Last Dragon*, 2021). None of them are openly queer, though they could be even while remaining unpaired. Considering that the American anti-LGBTQI organization One Million Moms boycotted *Toy Story 4* in 2019 over a background glimpse of two lesbian mothers (Reynolds), and that Pixar's *Lightyear* (2022) was banned in at least fourteen countries for an on-screen same-sex kiss (Tilly), yet single princesses have not elicited such backlash for being single, it is easy to see which of the two options—open queerness or female singledom—is regarded as the most confronting of the two. Most importantly, given Disney's corporate focus on profit, it is clear which would be the riskiest financial choice—and likely the reason why Elsa may never be given a girlfriend at all.[2]

Expecting an entertainment giant like Disney to make such a bold move might be regarded as naïve, but it is an understandable desire for queer people. After all, the intense interest that Elsa's possible queerness elicited across the political spectrum (and around the world) demonstrates that films like *Frozen 2* have a unique potential to influence public opinion on LGBTQI issues. It is also of particular interest to fairy-tale scholars, given that a queer Elsa would conceivably impact the fairy-tale genre and fairy-tale studies. This study has explored the many ways in which Disney has shaped the narrow fairy-tale canon in terms of corpus, aesthetics, morals, gender representations, narrative strategies, and more, from the twentieth century to the present. Lieberman's early feminist criticism of the genre—or rather, of "the best-known stories, those that everyone has read or heard, indeed, those that Disney has popularized" (Lieberman 383)—stands as a testament to this, as do the many retold fairy tales that allude to Disney's tradition or treat Disney as the contemporary fairy-tale canon-maker. If Disney is the canon-maker of our time, and if it dictates what the fairy tale *is* for a large portion of the global population—so much so that many of us must look past our Disney-given assumptions about the genre in order to see it for what it really is—then the appearance of a queer protagonist in the Disney canon would represent a fundamental revolution. If Disney has had the power to smooth out some of the most ambiguous edges of the fairy tale—to

2 This is compounded by the open letter that some employees at Disney's subsidiary, Pixar, released in 2022. The letter claimed that nearly every moment of openly gay affection had been cut out of Pixar films by Disney, thus severely curtailing Pixar's creative and political agency (Pulver, "Pixar").

disguise its queerest possibilities so that they become invisible to many contemporary readers—it is worth considering the possibility that Disney might also have the power to uncover queerness in the genre. Disney has exerted a remarkably retroactive effect on the fairy tale, changing the way we interpret historical versions of these stories. If this effect could be replicated (for instance, if Elsa was eventually written as queer), Disney might also make the genre seem less uniformly cisheteronormative.

Nonetheless, while the veil of normativity still covers the fairy tale, passionate, bottom-up campaigns like #GiveElsaAGirlfriend ensure that, at the very least, the industry becomes aware of minoritarian voices. Online, vernacular creators—independent from institutional control—will surely continue to question and unsettle the normative, hegemonic fairy tale in a more immediate manner. Scholars should thus monitor the fairy-tale web, particularly the unexplored queer counterpublics within it, where the queer fairy-tale subgenre is likely to flourish more rapidly and in more diverse, unexpected ways than anywhere else. It is equally necessary for future queer fairy-tale research to reach beyond the scope of the present study to include a wider range of identities. For instance, different linguistic traditions within the global web, as well as more traditional media such as literature, must be closely examined to fully trace the emergence of the queer retold fairy tale and its relationship to various historical, political, and geographical contexts. Similarly, transgender identities in fairy tales require dedicated attention. While this study has noted some of the transgender undercurrents in traditional fairy tales, the retellings analyzed here have been only minimally shaped by transgender sensibilities. However, since the mid-2010s, transgender retellings have emerged in various forms—novels such as *Cinder Ella* (S.T. Lynn, 2016) and *Cinderella Boy* (Kristina Meister, 2017); illustrated books like *The Royal Heart* (Greg McGoon, 2015); and YouTube videos like "Jamie, A Transgender Cinderella Story" (Pop'n'Olly, 2015). Scholars should therefore investigate how the transgender subtext of traditional fairy tales is decoded and reimagined by contemporary creators to explicitly articulate the modern transgender experience; how these works engage with the increased visibility of transgender people in society; and how they use the wonder mode of the fairy tale to negotiate the fraught political debates surrounding transgender identities. In any case, and whether Disney takes a bold leap in future releases and queers its own fairy-tale tradition—thereby easing the way for a widespread reconsideration of the genre—this study has shown that the magic mirror has been unshrouded, reflecting a queer future that is not only possible but inevitable in the realm of fairy tales.

ACKNOWLEDGMENTS

Once upon a time, this book began its fairy-tale journey as my doctoral thesis. I owe a special debt of gratitude to my main supervisor, Rebecca Scherr, for her incisive guidance, and to the members of the project *Literature, Rights, and Imagined Communities* at the University of Oslo, who first gave my research a chance. Their backing, alongside generous funding from the Faculty of Humanities and the Department of Literature, Area Studies, and European Languages, allowed me to carry out formative research stays at Brown University and Wayne State University.

My heartfelt thanks go to two dear fairy godmothers: to Carolina Fernández Rodríguez, who first sparked my love for fairy tales and inspired this lifelong journey, and to Anne Duggan, who not only supervised my thesis but also championed its magical transformation into a book. I am also grateful to the team at Wayne State University Press for expertly steering this manuscript, and to the anonymous reviewers for their suggestions.

Finally, I thank my family for their support; particularly my parents, whose constant belief in me kept this story going. I'm also grateful to Anna Campion (and Hermine!) for being such a stalwart travel companion for so long, and to all the friends I've gathered across the years and continents: thank you for the countless coffees, conversations, emergency Zoom calls, and margarita therapy sessions. I love you.

An earlier version of chapter 3 appeared in *Gender and Female Villains in 21st Century Fairy Tale Narratives: From Evil Queens to Wicked Witches* (Emerald Publishing, 2022).

BIBLIOGRAPHY

Aaron, Michele. *New Queer Cinema: A Critical Reader*. Rutgers University Press, 2004.

Adam, Barry D. *The Rise of a Gay and Lesbian Movement*. Twayne Publishers, 1987.

Alwakeel, Ramzy. *Smile If You Dare: Politics and Pointy Hats with the Pet Shop Boys*. Repeater Books, 2014.

Andersen, Hans Christian. *The Annotated Hans Christian Andersen (The Annotated Books)*. W. W. Norton & Company, 2007.

Anderson, Benedict. *Imagined Communities: Reflections on the Origins and Spread of Nationalism*. Verso, 1991.

Angelides, Steven. *A History of Bisexuality*. The University of Chicago Press, 2001.

Armstrong, Elizabeth A. *Forging Gay Identities: Organizing Sexuality in San Francisco*. University of Chicago Press, 2002.

Ashley, Brittany. "Lesbian Princess." YouTube, 11 Oct. 2015, www.youtube.com/watch?v=wuDgDF4poZw. Accessed 1 Jan. 2023.

Atwood, Margaret. "Bluebeard's Egg." *The Classic Fairy Tales*, edited by Maria Tatar, W. W. Norton & Company, 1999, pp. 156–78.

Azzopardi, Chris. "Idina Menzel on Working Toward LGBT Icon Status, a Lesbian Elsa & Angry Gays Who Oppose Her '*Beaches*' Remake." *Pride Source*, Sept. 2016, https://pridesource.com/article/78203-2. Accessed 1 Jan. 2023.

Babuscio, Jack. "Camp and the Gay Sensibility." *Camp Grounds: Style and Homosexuality*, edited by David Bergman, University of Massachusetts Press, 1993, pp. 19–38.

Bacchilega, Cristina. "Fairy-Tale Adaptations and Economies of Desire." *The Cambridge Companion to Fairy Tales*, edited by Maria Tatar, Cambridge University Press, 2015, pp. 79–96.

———. *Fairy Tales Transformed? Twenty-First-Century Adaptations and the Politics of Wonder*. Wayne State University Press, 2013.

——. "An Introduction to the 'Innocent Persecuted Heroine' Fairy Tale." *Western Folklore*, vol. 52, no. 1, 1993, pp. 1–12.

——. *Postmodern Fairy Tales: Gender and Narrative Strategies*. University of Pennsylvania Press, 1997.

Bacchilega, Cristina, and John Rieder. "Mixing It Up: Generic Complexity and Gender Ideology in Early Twenty-First Century Fairy Tale Films." *Fairy Tale Films: Visions of Ambiguity*, edited by Pauline Greenhill and Sidney Eve Matrix, University Press of Colorado, 2010, pp. 23–41.

Bacchus, Tom. "Lily Boy." *Happily Ever After: Erotic Fairy Tales for Men*, edited by Michael Ford, Masquerade Books, 1996. 329–52.

Baker, Dallas J. "Monstrous Fairytales: Towards an Écriture Queer." *Colloquy: Text Theory Critique*, vol. 20, 2000, pp. 79–103.

Basile, Giambattista. *Giambattista Basile's "The Tale of Tales, or Entertainment for Little Ones."* Translated by Nancy L. Canepa. Wayne State University Press, 2007.

Bauer, Robin. *Queer BDSM Intimacies: Critical Consent and Pushing Boundaries*. Palgrave Macmillan, 2014.

BBC. *BBC Equality Information Report 2017/18*. BBC, 2017, www.bbc.co.uk/diversity/reports/equality-information-report-2017. Accessed 1 Jan. 2023.

Beauty and the Beast. Directed by Bill Condon, Walt Disney Pictures, 1991.

Beauvoir, Simone de. *The Second Sex*, translated by Howard Parshley. Bantam Books, 1970.

Benderson, Bruce. "Pinocchio in the Port Authority." *Happily Ever After: Erotic Fairy Tales for Men*, edited by Michael Ford, Masquerade Books, 1996, pp. 5–16.

Benshoff, Harry M. *Monsters in the Closet: Homosexuality and the Horror Film*. Manchester University Press, 1997.

Benson, Stephen. "Introduction." *Contemporary Fiction and the Fairy Tale*. Wayne State University Press, 2008, pp. 1–19.

Bergman, David. *Gaiety Transfigured: Gay Self-Representation in American Literature*. The University of Wisconsin Press, 1991.

——. "Introduction." *Camp Grounds: Style and Homosexuality*, edited by David Bergman, University of Massachusetts Press, 1993, pp. 1–16.

Berlant, Lauren, and Michael Warner. "What Does Queer Theory Teach Us About X?" *PMLA*, vol. 1, no. 110, 1995, pp. 343–49.

Beukes, Lauren. *Fairest Vol. 2: The Hidden Kingdom*. Illustrated by Iñaki Miranda. Vertigo, 2013.

Blank, Trevor. "Toward a Conceptual Framework for the Study of Folklore and the Internet." *Folklore and the Internet Vernacular Expression in a Digital World*, edited by Trevor Blank, Utah University Press, 2009.

Bloomer, Jeffrey. "When Gays Decried *Silence of the Lambs*, Jonathan Demme Became an Early Student of Modern Backlash." *Slate*, 28 April 2017, https://slate.com/human-interest/2017/04/director-jonathan-demme-faced-down-silence-of-the-lambs-gay-backlash.html. Accessed 1 Jan. 2023.

Boklage, Evgeniya. "Safe Space, Dangerous Space: Counterpublic Discourses in the Russian LGBT Blogging Community." *LGBTQs, Media and Culture in Europe*, edited by Alexander Dhoest, Lukasz Szulc, and Bart Eeckhout, Routledge, 2017.

Boone, John. "*Frozen 2* Directors Reveal Why Elsa Doesn't Have a Love Interest." *ET*, 30 Sept. 2019, www.etonline.com/frozen-2-directors-reveal-why-elsa-doesnt-have-a-love-interest-exclusive-133425. Accessed 1 Jan. 2023.

Bottigheimer, Ruth B, editor. *Fairy Tales Framed: Early Forewords, Afterwords, and Critical Words*. State University of New York Press, 2012.

———. "Fractured Fairy Tales." *The Oxford Companion to Fairy Tales*, edited by Jack Zipes, Oxford University Press, 2000, pp. 209–10.

Boyer, Tina Marie. *The Giant Hero in Medieval Literature*. Brill Academic Publishers, 2016.

Bradley, Bill. "*Frozen* Director Gives Glimmer of Hope Elsa Could Get a Girlfriend." *Huffington Post*, 26 Feb. 2018, www.huffpost.com/entry/frozen-director-elsa-girlfriend_n_5a9388c5e4b01e9e56bd1ead. Accessed 1 Jan. 2023.

Brammer, John Paul. "I Fear Loss of Community: Tumblr's New 'Adult Content' Rules Worry LGBTQ Users." *NBC News*, 5 Dec. 2018, www.nbcnews.com/feature/nbc-out/i-fear-loss-community-tumblr-s-new-adult-content-rules-n944196. Accessed 1 Jan. 2022.

Brandes, Georg. "Hans Christian Andersen." *Eminent Authors of Nineteenth Century*. Translated by R. B. Anderson. Thomas Y. Crowell Co., 1886, pp. 104–5.

Bresler, Robert J. *Us vs. Them: American Political and Cultural Conflict from WWII to Watergate*. Scholarly Resources Inc., 2000.

Bronski, Michael. *Culture Clash: The Making of a Gay Sensibility*. South End Press, 1984.

Broumas, Olga. *Beginning with O*. Yale University Press, 1977.

Brundage, James. "Playing by the Rules: Sexual Behaviour and Legal Norms in Medieval Europe." *Desire and Discipline: Sex and Sexuality in the Premodern*

West, edited by Jacqueline Murray and Konrad Eisenbichler, University of Toronto Press, 1996, pp. 23–42.

Bullough, Vern. "Sex in History: A Redux." *Desire and Discipline: Sex and Sexuality in the Premodern West*, edited by Jacqueline Murray and Konrad Eisenbichler, University of Toronto Press, 1996, pp. 3–22.

Burt, Stephen. *The Forms of Youth: Twentieth-Century Poetry and Adolescence.* Columbia University Press, 2007.

Butler, Judith. *Gender Trouble: Feminism and the Subversion of Identity*. 1990. Routledge, 1999.

——. *Undoing Gender*. Routledge, 2004.

Cage, Ken. *Gayle: The Language of Kinks and Queens*. Jacana Media, 2003.

Canepa, Nancy L. *From Court to Forest: Giambattista Basile's "Lo Cunto De Li Cunti" and the Birth of the Literary Fairy Tale*. Wayne State University Press, 1999.

——. "From Court to Forest: The Literary Itineraries of Giambattista Basile." *Italica*, vol. 71, no. 3, 1994, pp. 291–310.

Capitanio, John P., and Gregory M. Herek. "AIDS Stigma and Sexual Prejudice." *American Behavioral Scientist*, vol. 42, no. 7, 1999, pp. 1130–47.

Carpenter, George. *The Intermediate Sex: A Study of Some Transitional Types of Men and Women*. George Allen and Unwin, 1908.

Carter, Angela. *The Bloody Chamber and Other Stories*. Vintage Classics, 1995.

——. "Notes from the Front Line." *Shaking a Leg: Journalism and Writings*, edited by Jenny Uglow, Chatto & Windus, 1997, pp. 37–43.

Cashorali, Peter. *Fairy Tales: Traditional Stories Retold for Gay Men*. HarperCollins, 1995.

——. *Gay Fairy & Folk Tales: More Traditional Stories Retold for Gay Men*. Faber & Faber, 1997.

——. "Let Me Tell You the Story I Heard You Tell: Fairy Tales in Therapy." *GoodTherapy.org*, 18 Jan. 2018, www.goodtherapy.org/blog/let-me-tell-you-the-story-i-heard-you-tell-fairy-tales-in-therapy-0118184. Accessed 1 Jan. 2023.

Chaperon, Sylvie. "The Foundations of 19th-Century Psychiatric Approaches to Sexual Deviance." *Recherches en psychanalyse*, vol. 10, no. 2, 2010, pp. 276a–285a.

"Child of the Moon." *Once Upon a Time*, created by Edward Kitsis and Adam Horowitz, directed by Anthony Hemingway, season 2, episode 7, ABC Studios, 2012.

Chun, John M. "Musical Theater and Film." *The Queer Encyclopedia of Music, Dance, and Musical Theater*, edited by Claude J. Summens, Cleis Press, 2004, pp. 181–84.

Cinderella. Directed by Clyde Geronimi, Hamilton Luske, and Wilfred Jackson, Walt Disney Productions, 1950.

"Cinderswift." *PattiCakes Productions*, 14 Jan. 2017, www.youtube.com/watch?v=g3SEX3xQk9E. Accessed 1 Jan. 2023.

Cohen, Jeffrey J. "Monster Culture: Seven Theses." *Monster Theory*, edited by Jeffrey J. Cohen, University of Minnesota Press, 1996, pp. 3–25.

Cox, Dan. "Are There No LGBT Characters in the Entire Fables Universe?" *Digital Ephemera*, 25 Oct. 2013, www.videlais.com/2013/10/25/are-there-no-lgbt-characters-in-the-entire-fables-universe. Accessed 1 Jan. 2023.

Craft-Fairchild, Catherine. "Cross-Dressing and the Novel: Women Warriors and Domestic Femininity." *Eighteenth-Century Fiction*, vol. 10, no. 2, 1998, pp. 171–202.

Crage, Suzanna M., and Elizabeth A. Armstrong. "Movements and Memory: The Making of the Stonewall Myth." *American Sociological Review*, vol. 71, Oct. 2006, pp. 724–51.

Creekmur, Corey K., and Alexander Doty. "Introduction." *Out in Culture: Gay, Lesbian, and Queer Essays on Popular Culture*, edited by Corey K. Creekmur and Alexander Doty, Duke University Press, 1995, pp. 1–11.

D'Aulnoy, Marie-Catherine. "Belle-Belle, or, The Chevalier Fortuné." *The Great Fairy Tale Tradition: From Straparola and Basile to the Brothers Grimm; Texts, Criticism*, edited by Jack Zipes, W. W. Norton & Company, 2001, pp. 174–205.

Davidson, Hilda Roderick Ellis, and Anna Chaudhri. "Introduction." *A Companion to the Fairy Tale*, edited by Hilda Roderick Ellis Davidson and Anna Chaudhri, D. S. Brewer, 2006, pp. 1–14.

Davis, Amy M. "On Love Experts, Evil Princes, Gullible Princes, and *Frozen*." *The Oxford Handbook of Children's Film*, edited by Noel Brown, Oxford University Press, 2022, pp. 649–70.

D'Emilio, John. *The World Turned: Essays on Gay History, Politics, and Culture*. Duke University Press, 2002.

Donadio, Rachel. "On Gay Priests, Pope Francis Asks, 'Who Am I to Judge?'." *The New York Times*, 29 July 2013, www.nytimes.com/2013/07/30/world/europe/pope-francis-gay-priests.html. Accessed 1 Jan. 2023.

Donoghue, Emma. "Interview." *Irish Women Writers Speak Out: Voices from the Field*, edited by Caitriona Moloney and Helen Thompson, Syracuse University Press, 2003, pp. 169–80.

———. *Kissing the Witch: Old Tales in New Skins*. HarperCollins, 1997.

Doty, Alexander. *Making Things Perfectly Queer: Interpreting Mass Culture*. University of Minnesota Press, 1993.

Dubin, Zan. "Poets Will Tell a Different Story: All-Male Fairy Tale Is Part of a Program at Chapman University That Will Explore Traditional Gender Roles." *Los Angeles Times*, 13 Mar. 1992, www.latimes.com/archives/la-xpm-1992-03-13-ca-3902-story.html. Accessed 1 Jan. 2023.

Duggan, Anne. "Charles Perrault." *The Greenwood Encyclopedia of Folktales and Fairy Tales*, vol. 2, edited by Donald Haase, Greenwood Publishing Group, 2008, pp. 738–40.

———. "Feminine Genealogy, Matriarchy, and Utopia in the Fairy Tale of Marie-Catherine D'Aulnoy." *Neophilologus*, vol. 82, no. 2, 1998, pp. 199–208.

———. "Gender." *The Routledge Companion to Media and Fairy-Tale Studies*, edited by Pauline Greenhill and Jill Terry Rudy, Routledge, 2018. Kindle edition.

———. "Marie-Catherine d'Aulnoy." *The Greenwood Encyclopedia of Folktales and Fairy Tales*, vol. 1, edited by Donald Haase, Greenwood Publishing Group, 2008. pp. 79–81.

———. *Queer Enchantments: Gender, Sexuality, and Class in the Fairy-Tale Cinema of Jacques Demy*. Wayne State University Press, 2013.

Duggan, Lisa. *The Twilight of Equality? Neoliberalism, Cultural Politics, and the Attack on Democracy*. Beacon Press, 2003.

Duncker, Patricia. "Re-Imagining the Fairy Tales: Angela Carter's Bloody Chambers." *Writing on the Wall: Selected Essays*. Pandora, 2002, pp. 67–83.

Dundes, Alan. "Fairy Tales from a Folkloristic Perspective." *Fairy Tales and Society: Illusion, Allusion, and Paradigm*, edited by Ruth Bottigheimer, University of Pennsylvania Press, 1986, pp. 259–69.

Dyer, Richard. *Gays and Film*. British Film Institute, 1977.

Edelman, Lee. *No Future: Queer Theory and the Death Drive*. Duke University Press, 2004.

Estirado, Patricia. "Más de 230.000 firmas, recogidas por HazteOír (España) y CitizenGo (a nivel mundial) piden a Disney que no se desvíe de los valores clásicos." *ElPeriódico*, 26 May 2016, www.elperiodico.com/es/extra/20160526/pulso-elsa-frozen-lesbiana-novia-5159183. Accessed 1 Jan. 2023.

Evans, Mel. "10,000 Sign Petition to Stop Elsa Getting a Girlfriend in *Frozen* Sequel." *Metro*, 14 Mar. 2018, www.metro.co.uk/2018/03/14/10000-sign-petition-stop-elsa-getting-girlfriend-disney-frozen-sequel-7388245. Accessed 1 Jan. 2023.

Eynat-Confino, Irene. *On the Use of the Fantastic in Modern Theatre*. Palgrave Macmillan, 2008.

Fabian, Renée. "6 of the Safest Spaces for LGBT Youth to Hang Online." *The Daily Dot*, 11 May 2016, www.dailydot.com/irl/lgbt-youth-safe-spaces. Accessed 1 Jan. 2023.

Farrell, Marcy. "The Heroine's Violent Compromise: Two Fairy Tales by Madame d'Aulnoy." *Violence in French and Francophone Literature and Film*, edited by James Day, Brill–Rodopi, 2008, pp. 27–43.

Farwell, Marilyn R. *Heterosexual Plots and Lesbian Narratives*. New York University Press, 1996.

Fink, Marty, and Quinn Miller. "Trans Media Moments: Tumblr, 2011–2013." *Television & New Media*, vol. 15, no. 7, 2014, pp. 611–26.

Ford, Michael. "Introduction." *Happily Ever After: Erotic Fairy Tales for Men*. Masquerade Books, 1996, pp. 1–4.

Foucault, Michel. *The History of Sexuality—Volume I: An Introduction*, translated by Robert Hurley. Vintage Books, 1990.

———. "Introduction." *Herculine Barbin: Being the Recently Discovered Memoirs of a Nineteenth-Century French Hermaphrodite*, translated by Richard McDougall. Pantheon Books, 1980, pp. vii–xvii.

Frank, Dian Crone, and Jeffrey Frank. *The Stories of Hans Christian Andersen*. Houghton Mifflin, 2003.

Fraser, Nancy. "Rethinking the Public Sphere: A Contribution to the Critique of Actually Existing Democracy." *Social Text*, no. 25/26, 1990, pp. 56–80.

Freeman, Elizabeth. "Queer Belongings: Kinship Theory and Queer Theory." *A Companion to Lesbian, Gay, Bisexual, Transgender, and Queer Studies*, edited by George E. Haggerty and Molly McGarry, Wiley Blackwell, 2015, pp. 295–314.

———. *Time Binds: Queer Temporalities, Queer Histories*. Duke University Press, 2010.

Frozen. Directed by Chris Buck and Jennifer Lee, Walt Disney Pictures, 2013.

Gaiman, Neil. *The Sleeper and the Spindle*, illustrated by Chris Riddell. Bloomsbury Publishing, 2014.

Gallant, Paul. "When a Right-Winger in Hungary Ripped Up a Book of Inclusive Fairy Tales, She Sent It Straight up the Bestsellers List." *Xtra Magazine*,

16 June 2021, http://xtramagazine.com/culture/books/fairy-tales-for-everyone-controversy-202844. Accessed 15 Aug. 2022.

Gambone, Philip. *Something Inside: Conversations with Gay Fiction Writers*. The University of Wisconsin Press, 1999.

Gavin, Steve. "Consciousness Raising Exposes the Orwellian Lies of Sexist Amerika." *Come Out!*, vol. 2, no. 7b, 1971, p. 19.

Geczy, Adam, and Vicki Karaminas. *Queer Style*. Bloomsbury, 2013.

Giffney, Noreen, and Myra J. Hird. "Introduction: Queering the Non/Human." *Queering the Non/Human*, edited by Noreen Giffney and Myra J. Hird, Ashgate, 2008, pp. 1–16.

Gilbert, Sandra M., and Susan Gubar. *The Madwoman in the Attic: The Woman Writer and the Nineteenth-Century Literary Imagination*. Yale University Press, 1979.

GLAAD. "Walt Disney Studios." *2016 GLAAD Studio Responsibility Index. GLAAD*, May 2016, www.glaad.org/sri/2016/walt-disney-studios. Accessed 2 Jan. 2023.

Goodman, Matt, and Seth Adam. "GLAAD Rates ABC Family and FOX as 'Excellent' in Ninth Annual Network Responsibility Index." *GLAAD*, 3 Sept. 2015, www.glaad.org/releases/glaad-rates-abc-family-and-fox-excellent-ninth-annual-network-responsibility-index. Accessed 1 Jan. 2023.

Gqola, Pumla Dineo. *Rape: The South African Nightmare*. MF Books, 2015.

Gray, Emma. "Fairy Tales for Twenty Somethings Tumblr Reveals the Truth About Growing Up." *Huffington Post*, 18 Oct. 2012, www.huffpost.com/entry/fairy-tales-for-20-somethings-tumblr_n_1980186. Accessed 1 Jan. 2023.

Greenhill, Pauline. "Sexualities." *The Routledge Companion to Media and Fairy-Tale Studies*, edited by Pauline Greenhill and Jill Terry Rudy, Routledge, 2018.

——. "Team Snow Queen: Feminist Cinematic 'Misinterpretations' of a Fairy Tale." *Studies in European Cinema*, vol. 13, no. 1, 2016, pp. 32–49.

——. "'The Snow Queen': Queer Coding in Male Directors' Films." *Marvels & Tales*, vol. 29, no. 1, 2015, pp. 110–34.

Greenhill, Pauline, and Sidney Eve Matrix. "Introduction: Envisioning Ambiguity: Fairy Tale Films." *Fairy Tale Films: Visions of Ambiguity*, edited by Pauline Greenhill and Sidney Eve Matrix, Utah State University Press, 2010, pp. 1–22.

Grimm, Jakob, and Wilhelm. "The Frog King or Iron Heinrich." *The Grimm Brothers' Children's and Household Tales*. Translated by D. L. Ashliman. University of Pittsburgh, 2005, https://sites.pitt.edu/~dash/grimm001.html. Accessed 1 Nov. 2022.

——. *Grimm's Household Tales*, translated by Margaret Hunt. William Clowes and Sons, 1884.

——. "Little Snow-White." *The Grimm Brothers' Children's and Household Tales*, translated by D.L. Ashliman. University of Pittsburgh, 2005, https://sites.pitt.edu/~dash/grimm053.html. Accessed 1 Nov. 2022.

Griswold, Jerry. *The Meanings of "Beauty and the Beast:" A Handbook*. Broadview Press, 2004.

Haase, Donald. "Feminist Fairy-Tale Scholarship: A Critical Survey and Bibliography." *Marvels & Tales*, vol. 14, no. 1, 2000, pp. 15–63.

——. "Framing the Brothers Grimm: Paratexts and Intercultural Transmission in Postwar English Language Editions of the *Kinder- und Hausmärchen*." *Fabula*, vol. 44, no. 1, May 2003, pp. 55–69.

Habermas, Jürgen. *The Structural Transformation of the Public Sphere: An Inquiry into a Category of Bourgeois Society*. MIT Press, 1989.

Halberstam, Jack (published Judith). *In a Queer Time and Place: Transgender Bodies, Subcultural Lives*. New York University Press, 2005.

——. *Skin Shows: Gothic Horror and the Technology of Monsters*. Duke University Press, 1995.

Hall, Todrick. "Britney and the Beast." YouTube, 7 June 2016, www.youtube.com/watch?v=je-UHCniqnk. Accessed 1 Jan. 2023.

——. "CinderFella." YouTube, 24 July 2012, www.youtube.com/watch?v=F9ZA7bn5ujk. Accessed 1 Jan. 2023.

——. "Cinderoncé." YouTube, 20 Aug. 2013, www.youtube.com/watch?v=7r7mGAxWB04&t=1s. Accessed 1 Jan. 2023.

Halperin, David M. "Reflections: The Normalization of Queer Theory." *Journal of Homosexuality*, vol. 45, no. 2–4, 2003, pp. 339–43.

Harries, Elizabeth Wanning. *Twice Upon a Time: Women Writers and the History of the Fairy Tale*. Princeton University Press, 2003.

Haynes, Suyin. "Why a Children's Book Is Becoming a Symbol of Resistance in Hungary's Fight Over LGBT Rights." *Time*, 8 Oct. 2020, www.telegraph.co.uk/news/2017/11/23/mother-calls-sleeping-beauty-banned-primary-school-promotes. Accessed 15 Aug. 2022.

Heilbrun, Carolyn G. *Reinventing Womanhood*. 1979. Norton. 1993.

Hettinga, Donald R. "Jacob and Wilhelm Grimm." *The Teller's Tale: Lives of the Classic Fairy Tale Writers*, edited by Sophie Raynard, State University of New York Press, 2012, pp. 135–51.

Hibberd, James. "*Frozen* Original Ending Revealed for First Time." *Entertainment Weekly*, March 2017, https://ew.com/movies/2017/03/29/frozen-original-ending/. Accessed 1 Jan. 2023.

Hines, Jim C. *The Stepsister Scheme*. DAW, 2009.

Hobson, Emily K. *Lavender and Red: Liberation and Solidarity in the Gay and Lesbian Left*. University of California Press, 2016.

Hourihan, Margery. *Deconstructing the Hero: Literary Theory and Children's Literature*. Routledge, 1997.

Hunt, Elle. "LGBT Community Anger Over YouTube Restrictions Which Make Their Videos Invisible." *The Guardian*, 20 Mar. 2017, www.theguardian.com/technology/2017/mar/20/lgbt-community-anger-over-youtube-restrictions-which-make-their-videos-invisible. Accessed 1 Jan. 2023.

Hutcheon, Linda. *The Politics of Postmodernism*. Routledge, 1989.

———. "The Politics of Postmodernism: Parody and History" *Cultural Critique*, no. 5, *Modernity and Modernism, Postmodernity and Postmodernism*, 1986–1987, pp. 179–207.

———. *A Theory of Parody: The Teachings of Twentieth-Century Art Forms*. University of Illinois, 2000.

Jasmin, Nadine. "Marie-Catherine Le Jumel de Barneville, Baroness d'Aulnoy: 1650/51?–1705." *The Teller's Tale: Lives of the Classic Fairy Tale Writers*, edited by Sophie Raynard, State University of New York Press, 2012, pp. 61–69.

Jones, Rebecca L. "Imagining the Unimaginable: Bisexual Roadmaps for Ageing." *Lesbian, Gay, Bisexual and Transgender Ageing: Biographical Approaches for Inclusive Care and Support*, edited by Richard Ward, Ian Rivers, and Mike Sutherland, Jessica Kingsley Publishers, 2012, pp. 21–38.

Jones, Steven Swann. "The Innocent Persecuted Heroine Genre: An Analysis of Its Structure and Themes." *Western Folklore*, vol. 52, no. 1, 1993, pp. 13–41.

Joosen, Vanessa. *Critical and Creative Perspectives on Fairy Tales: An Intertextual Dialogue Between Fairy-Tale Scholarship and Postmodern Retellings*. Wayne State University Press, 2011.

Kapurch, Katie. "Rapunzel Loves Merida: Melodramatic Expressions of Lesbian Girlhood and Teen Romance in *Tangled*, *Brave*, and Femslash." *Journal of Lesbian Studies*, vol. 19, no. 4, 2015, pp. 436–53.

Katz, Jonathan. *Gay American History: Lesbians and Gay Men in the U.S.A.* Thomas Y. Crowell Company, 1976.

Kenney, Zoe. "The Play's the Thing: Representations of Heteronormative Sexuality in a Popular Children's TV Sitcom." *Queer Media Images: LGBT Perspectives*, edited by Theresa Carilli and Jane Campbell, Lexington Books, 2013, pp. 71–84.

Knoepflmacher, Ulrich. "Parody." *Folktales and Fairy Tales: Traditions and Texts from Around the World*, edited by Hellen Callow, Anne Duggan, and Donald Haase, Greenwood Publishing Group, 2015, pp. 761–62.

Kohnen, Melanie E. S. "Tumblr Pedagogies." *A Companion to Media Fandom and Fan Studies*, edited by Paul Booth, Wiley Blackwell, 2018, pp. 351–65.

Kopcke, Robert H. "Foreword." *Fairy Tales: Traditional Stories Retold for Gay Men*, by Peter Cashorali. HarperCollins, 1995, pp. vii–x.

Koven, Mikel J. "Folklore Studies and Popular Film and Television: A Necessary Critical Survey." *The Journal of American Folklore*, vol. 116, no. 460, 2003, pp. 176–95.

Kristeva, Julia. *Powers of Horror: An Essay on Abjection*, translated by Leon S. Roudiez, Columbia University Press, 1982.

Kumin, Maxine. "The Archaeology of a Marriage." *POETRY*. The Poetry Foundation, 1978, pp. 3–4.

Lambe, Stacey. "*Alice in Tumblr-Land* Author, Tim Manley, on Internet Vices and Queer Fairy Tales." *Out*, 19 Nov. 2013, www.out.com/entertainment/popnography/2013/11/19/popnog-10-alice-tumblr-land-author-tim-manley-social-media. Accessed 1 Jan. 2023.

Lang, Nico. "Evil But Fabulous: In Praise of Films' Complicated, Queer Villains." *The Guardian*, 8 Nov. 2015, www.theguardian.com/commentisfree/2015/nov/08/praise-complicated-queer-villains-film. Accessed 1 Jan. 2023.

Laqueur, Thomas. *Making Sex: Body and Gender from the Greeks to Freud*. Harvard University Press, 1990.

Lassel, Michael. "*Beauty and the Beast*: Genius Remembered." *The Advocate* no. 600, 7 Apr. 1992, p. 77.

Leonard, Andrew. "How Disney Learned to Stop Worrying and Love Copyright Infringement." *Salon*, 23 May 2014, www.salon.com/2014/05/23/how_disney_learned_to_stop_worrying_and_love_copyright_infringement. Accessed 1 Jan. 2023.

Levin, Richard D., Stephan L. Buckingham, and Christina B. Hart. "Gay Men as Caregivers." *Caring for the HIV/AIDS Caregivers*, edited by Vincent J. Lynch and Paul A. Wilson, Auburn House, 1996, pp. 73–90.

Levin, Sam. "Who Can Be a Drag Queen? RuPaul's Trans Comments Fuel Calls for Inclusion." *The Guardian*, 8 Mar. 2018, www.theguardian.com/tv-and-radio/2018/mar/08/rupaul-drag-race-transgender-performers-diversity. Accessed 1 Jan. 2023.

Levine, Martin P. *Gay Macho: The Life and Death of the Homosexual Clone*. New York University Press, 1998.

Levy, Michael. "LGBT/YA/SF." In "SFS Symposium: Sexuality in Science Fiction." *Science Fiction Studies*, vol. 36, no. 3, 2009, pp. 394–95.

Lewallen, Avis. "'Wayward Girls but Wicked Women?' Female Sexuality in Angela Carter's *The Bloody Chamber*." *Perspectives in Pornography: Sexuality in Film and Literature*, edited by Gary Day and Clive Bloom, Macmillan, 1988, pp. 144–58.

Lieberman, Marcia R. "Some Day My Prince Will Come: Female Acculturation Through the Fairy Tale." *College English*, vol. 34, no. 3, 1972, pp. 383–95.

Liming, Sheila. "'Reading for It': Lesbian Readers Constructing Culture and Identity Through Textual Experience." *Queer Popular Culture: Literature, Media, Film and Television*, edited by Thomas Peele, Palgrave Macmillan, 2017, pp. 85–102.

Lin, Ming-Hsun. "Fitting the Glass Slipper: A Comparative Study of the Princess's Role in the Harry Potter Novels and Films." *Fairy Tale Films: Visions of Ambiguity*, edited by Pauline Greenhill and Sidney Eve Matrix, University Press of Colorado, 2010, pp. 79–98.

Lo, Malinda. "2014 LGBT YA by the Numbers." *Diversity in YA*, 10 Dec. 2014, www.malindalo.com/blog/2014/12/2014-lgbt-ya-by-the-numbers. Accessed 1 Jan. 2023.

Loaiza Ontiveros, José Rodolfo. *I'm Toxic*. 2012. *La Luz de Jesus Gallery*, laluzdejesus.com/jose-rodolfo-loaiza-ontiveros-disasterland-chris-bales-anthony-purcell-richard-meyer-ave-rose-click-mort-d-w-marino-byung-heather-oshaughnessy/im-toxic. Accessed 10 Aug. 2024.

———. *The Incredulity of Saint Donald*. 2014. *La Luz de Jesus Gallery*. laluzdejesus.com/jose-rodolfo-loaiza-ontiveros-profanity-pop-the-laluzapalooza-jury-winners/loaiza_the-incredulity-of-saint-donald-caravaggio-tribute. Accessed 10 Aug. 2024.

———. *Like a Virgin*. 2013. *La Luz de Jesus Gallery*, laluzdejesus.com/jose-rodolfo-loaiza-ontiveros-dishollywood-the-laluzapalooza-jury-winners/loaiza_lg_like-a-virgin. Accessed 10 Aug. 2024.

———. *Paloma Negra*. 2014. *La Luz de Jesus Gallery*, laluzdejesus.com/jose-rodolfo-loaiza-ontiveros-profanity-pop-the-laluzapalooza-jury-winners/loaiza_paloma-negra. Accessed 10 Aug. 2024.

———. *Reencuentro—Las Dos Blancanieves*. *Flickr*, 2012. www.flickr.com/photos/rodolfo_loaiza/7551946822/in/album-72157630533739678/. Accessed 10 Aug. 2024.

———. *True Ending . . . Take 2*. 2011. *La Luz de Jesus Gallery*. laluzdejesus.com/jessika-addams-walt-hall-derek-harrison-rodolfo-loaiza-miso-click-mort-jasmine-worth-lou-beach-alpha-lubicz-sam-lubicz/loaiza_lg_the-true-ending-second-version. Accessed 10 Aug. 2024.

———. *The Veil of Clarabella*. 2014. *La Luz de Jesus Gallery*. laluzdejesus.com/jose-rodolfo-loaiza-ontiveros-profanity-pop-the-laluzapalooza-jury-winners/loaiza_the-veil-of-clarabella. Accessed 10 Aug. 2024.

———. *Who Am I to Judge Him?* 2014. *La Luz de Jesus Gallery*. laluzdejesus.com/jose-rodolfo-loaiza-ontiveros-profanity-pop-the-laluzapalooza-jury-winners/loaiza_who-am-i-to-judge-him. Accessed 10 Aug. 2024.

Love, Heather. *Feeling Backward: Loss and the Politics of Queer History*. Harvard University Press, 2007.

Lowey, Ian, and Suzy Prince. *The Graphic Art of the Underground: A Countercultural History*. Bloomsbury, 2014.

Lurie, Alison. "Fairy Tale Liberation." *New York Review of Books*, 17 Dec. 1970, www.nybooks.com/articles/1970/12/17/fairy-tale-liberation. Accessed 1 Jan. 2023.

Maitland, Sara. *Angel Maker*. Owl Books, 1996.

Manalansan, Martin F. "Queer Love in the Time of War and Shopping." *A Companion to Lesbian, Gay, Bisexual, Transgender, and Queer Studies*, edited by George E. Haggerty and Molly McGarry, John Wiley & Sons, 2007, pp. 77–86.

Manley, Tim. *Alice in Tumblr-Land*. Penguin Books, 2013.

———. "There Are a Ton More Things That Would Have to Happen for It to Actually Become a TV Show . . ." *Fairytalesfor20somethings*, 15 Jan. 2015, fairytalesfor20somethings.tumblr.com/post/108226283259/there-are-a-ton-more-things-that-would-have-to. Accessed 1 Jan. 2023.

McIntosh, Mary. "Queer Theory and the War of the Sexes." *Feminisms*, edited by Sandra Kemp and Judith Squires, Oxford University Press, 1997, pp. 364–68.

McNeill, Lynne. "Digital 'Blood and Glitter': Fairy Tales as Text, Texture, and Context in Digital Media." *The Routledge Companion to Media and*

Fairy-Tale Studies, edited by Pauline Greenhill and Jill Terry Rudy, Routledge, 2018, Kindle edition.

Medhurst, Andy. "Batman, Deviance and Camp." *The Many Lives of the Batman: Critical Approaches to a Superhero and His Media*, edited by Roberta E. Pearson, Routledge, 1991, pp. 149–63.

MedlinePlus. "Bezoar." *Medical Encyclopaedia*, medlineplus.gov/ency/article/001582.htm. Accessed 1 Jan. 2023.

Meyer, Morris. "Reclaiming the Discourse of Camp." *The Politics and Poetics of Camp*, edited by Morris Meyer, Routledge, 1994, pp. 1–19.

Miller, Neil. *Out of the Past: Gay and Lesbian History from 1869 to the Present*. Vintage Books, 1995.

Miller, Sam J. "Assimilation and the Queer Monster." *Horror After 911*, edited by Aviva Briefel and Sam J. Miller, University of Texas Press, 2011, pp. 220–34.

Moncada, Alexis Isabel. "Why I Created the Trending #GiveElsaAGirlfriend Hashtag." *MTV*, 3 May 2016, www.mtv.com/news/zg5q9n/why-i-created-the-trending-giveelsaagirlfriend-hashtag. Accessed 1 Jan. 2023.

Monteagudo, Jesse. "The Prince and the Pauper." *Happily Ever After: Erotic Fairy Tales for Men*, edited by Michael Ford, Masquerade Books, 1996, pp. 283–94.

Morrison, Paul. *The Explanation for Everything: Essays on Sexual Subjectivity*. New York University Press, 2001.

Moynihan, Carolyn. "Give Elsa a Girlfriend? No, Give the Kids a Break." *Mercatornet*, 18 May 2016, https://www.mercatornet.com/give-elsa-a-girlfriend-no-give-the-kids-a-break. Accessed 1 Jan. 2023.

Muñoz, José Esteban. *Disidentifications: Queers of Color and the Performance of Politics*. University of Minnesota Press, 1999.

Namjoshi, Suniti. *Feminist Fables*. Virago, 1994.

Navar-Gill, Annemarie, and Mel Stanfill. "We Shouldn't Have to Trend to Make You Listen: Queer Fan Hashtag Campaigns as Production Interventions." *Journal of Film and Video*, vol. 70, no. 3–4, 2018, pp. 85–100.

Ng, Eve. "Between Text, Paratext, and Context: Queerbaiting and the Contemporary Media Landscape." *Transformative Works and Cultures*, vol. 24, 2017.

Nikolajeva, Maria. "Fairy Tales in Society's Service." *Marvels & Tales*, vol. 16, no. 2, 2002, pp. 171–87.

———. "Hans Christian Andersen." *The Oxford Companion to Fairy Tales*, edited by Jack Zipes, Oxford University Press, 2000, pp. 13–15.

Norton, Terry L., and Jonathan W. Vare. "Literature of Today's Gay and Lesbian Teens: Subverting the Culture of Silence." *English Journal*, vol. 94, 2004, pp. 65–69.

Nunokawa, Jeff. "'All the Sad Young Men': AIDS and the Work of Mourning." *Inside/Out: Lesbian Theories, Gay Theories*, edited by Diana Fuss, Routledge, 1991.

Once Upon a Time. Created by Edward Kitsis and Adam Horowitz. ABC Studios, 2011–18.

Orme, Jennifer. "Happily Ever After . . . According to Our Tastes: Jeanette Winterson's 'Twelve Dancing Princesses' and Queer Possibility." *Transgressive Tales: Queering the Grimms*, edited by Kay Turner and Pauline Greenhill, Wayne University Press, 2012, pp. 141–60.

———. "Mouth to Mouth: Queer Desires in Emma Donoghue's *Kissing the Witch*." *Marvels & Tales*, vol. 24, no. 1, 2010, pp. 116–30.

Palmer, Melvin D. "Madame d'Aulnoy in England." *Comparative Literature*, vol. 27, no. 3, 1975, pp. 237–53.

Palmer, Paulina. "Lesbian Transformations of Gothic and Fairytale." *Contemporary British Women Writers*, edited by Emma Parker, Brewer, 2004, pp. 139-53.

Pasquesi, Carina. "Of Monsters, Creatures and Other Queer Becomings." *The Journal of the Midwest Modern Language Association*, vol. 46/47, vo. 2/1, Fall 2013–Spring 2014, pp. 119–25.

Pearl, Monica. *AIDS Literature and Gay Identity: The Literature of Loss*. Routledge, 2013.

Perrault, Charles. "Cinderella." *The Great Fairy Tale Tradition: From Straparola and Basile to the Brothers Grimm; Texts, Criticism*, edited by Jack Zipes, W. W. Norton & Company, 2001, pp. 449–54.

Pershing, Linda and Lisa Gablehouse. "Disney's *Enchanted*: Patriarchal Backlash and Nostalgia in a Fairy Tale Film." *Fairy Tale Films: Visions of Ambiguity*, edited by Pauline Greenhill and Sidney Eve Matrix, Utah State University Press, pp. 137–56.

Picard, André. "How the Advent of AIDS Advanced Gay Rights." *The Globe and Mail*, 15 Aug. 2014, www.theglobeandmail.com/life/health-and-fitness/health/how-the-advent-of-aids-advanced-gay-rights/article20083869. Accessed 1 Jan. 2023.

Pretty Woman. Directed by Garry Marshall, Touchstone Pictures, 1990.

Pullen, Christopher. "Preface." *LGBT Identity and Online New Media*, edited by Christopher Pullen and Margaret Cooper, Routledge, 2010, pp. xi–xii.

Pulver, Andrew. “Disney Accused of Removing Gay Content from Pixar Films.” *The Guardian*, 11 Mar. 2022, www.theguardian.com/film/2022/mar/11/disney-pixar-employees-gay-content. Accessed 1 Jan. 2023.

——. “*Frozen 2* Officially Announced.” *The Guardian*, 12 Mar. 2015, www.theguardian.com/film/2015/mar/12/frozen-2-sequel-disney-to-be-let-go-jennifer-lee-chris-buck. Accessed 1 Jan. 2023.

“Queer Nation Manifesto” (1990). *History Is a Weapon*, www.historyisaweapon.com/defcon1/queernation.html. Accessed 1 Jan. 2023.

Radulovic, Petrana. “Tumblr Will Purge Most NSFW Content Under New Guidelines.” *Polygon*, 3 Dec. 2018, www.polygon.com/2018/12/3/18124039/tumblr-ban-guidelines-nsfw-content. Accessed 1 Jan. 2023.

Ranke, Kurt. *Folktales of Germany*. Translated by Lotte Baumann. University of Chicago Press, 1966.

Rankin, Walter. *Grimm Pictures: Fairy Tale Archetypes in Eight Horror and Suspense Films*. Jefferson: McFarland & Company, 2007.

“Red-Handed.” *Once Upon a Time*, created by Edward Kitsis and Adam Horowitz, written by Jane Espenson, directed by Ron Underwood, season 1, episode 15, ABC Studios, 2012.

Reynolds, Daniel. “A Pixar Film Has Drawn the Ire of the Antigay Group over a ‘Blink and You Miss It’ Moment.” *Advocate*, July 2019, www.advocate.com/film/2019/7/09/one-million-moms-boycotts-toy-story-4-over-lesbian-scene. Accessed 1 Jan. 2023.

Rich, Adrienne. “Compulsory Heterosexuality and Lesbian Existence (1980).” *Journal of Women’s History*, vol. 15, no. 3, 2003, pp. 11–48.

——. “When We Dead Awaken: Writing as Re-Vision.” *College English*, vol. 34, no.1, 1972, pp. 18–30.

Rich, B. Ruby. “New Queer Cinema.” *New Queer Cinema: A Critical Reader*, edited by Michele Aaron, Edinburgh University Press, 2004, pp. 15–22.

Ringu. Directed by Hideo Nakata, Omega, 1998.

Rio, Malcolm. “Architecture Is Burning: An Urbanism of Queer Kinship in Ballroom Culture.” *Thresholds*, no. 48, 2020, pp. 122–32.

Rodríguez, Randy A. “Richard Rodriguez Reconsidered: Queering the Sissy (Ethnic) Subject.” *Texas Studies in Literature and Language*, vol. 40, no. 4, 1998, pp. 396–423.

Rozin, Paul, Maureen Markwith, and Carol Nemeroff. “Magical Contagion Beliefs and Fear of AIDS.” Journal of Applied *Social Psychology*, no. 22, 2006, pp. 108–92.

Rozin, Paul, Carol Nemeroff, Marcia Wane, and Amy Sherrod. "Operation of the Sympathetic Magic Law of Contagion in Interpersonal Attitudes Among Americans." *Bulletin of the Psychonomic Society*, vol. 27, no. 4, 1989, pp. 367–70.

"Ruby Slippers." *Once Upon a Time*, created by Edward Kitsis and Adam Horowitz, written by Edward Kitsis, Adam Horowitz, and Andrew Chambliss, directed by Eriq La Salle, season 5, episode 18, ABC Studios, 2016.

Rupp, Leila J., Benita Roth, and Verta Taylor. "Women in the Lesbian, Gay, Bisexual and Transgender Movement." *The Oxford Handbook of U.S. Women's Social Movement Activism*, edited by Holly J. McCammon, Verta Taylor, Jo Reger, and Rachel L. Einwohner, Oxford University Press, pp. 665–84.

Scared Shrekless! Directed by Gary Trousdale and Raman Hui, DreamWorks Animation, 2010.

Schacker, Jennifer. "Fairy Gold: The Economics and Erotics of Fairy-Tale Pantomime," *Marvels & Tales*, vol. 26, no. 2, 2012, pp. 153–77.

Schildcrout, Jordan. *Murder Most Queer: The Homicidal Homosexual in the American Theater*. The University of Michigan Press, 2014.

Sedgwick, Eve Kosofsky. *Epistemology of the Closet*. University of California Press, 1990.

———. *Tendencies*. Duke University Press, 1993.

Seifert, Lewis C. "Disguising the Storyteller's 'Voice': Perrault's Recuperation of the Fairy Tale." *Cincinnati Romance Review*, vol. 8, 1989, pp. 13–23.

———. "The Fairy Tales of France." *The Oxford Companion to Fairy Tales*, edited by Jack Zipes, Oxford University Press, 2000, pp. 174–87.

———. *Fairy Tales, Sexuality, and Gender in France, 1690–1715: Nostalgic Utopias*. Cambridge University Press, 2006.

———. "Gay and Lesbian Tales." *The Greenwood Encyclopedia of Folktales and Fairy Tales*, vol. 2, edited by Donald Haase, Greenwood Publishing Group, 2008, pp. 400–402.

———. "Introduction: Queer(ing) Fairy Tales." *Marvels & Tales*, vol. 29, no. 1, 2015, pp. 15–20.

———. "The Marvelous in Context: The Place of the Contes de Fées in Late Seventeenth Century France." *The Great Fairy Tale Tradition: From Straparola and Basile to the Brothers Grimm; Texts, Criticism*, edited by Jack Zipes, W. W. Norton & Company, 2001, pp. 902–33.

———. "Queer Time in Charles Perrault's 'Sleeping Beauty.'" *Marvels & Tales*, vol. 29, no. 1, 2015, pp. 21–41.

———. "Sex, Sexuality." *The Greenwood Encyclopedia of Folktales and Fairy Tales*, vol. 3, edited by Donald Haase, Greenwood Publishing Group, 2008, pp. 849–53.

Sells, Laura. "'Where Do the Mermaids Stand?' Voice and Body in *The Little Mermaid*." *From Mouse to Mermaid: The Politics of Film, Gender, and Culture*. Indiana University Press, 1995, pp. 175–92.

Sexton, Anne. *Transformations*. 1971. Houghton Mifflin Company, 2001.

Sheppard, Simon. "The Ugly Duckling." *Happily Ever After: Erotic Fairy Tales for Men*, edited by Michael Ford, Masquerade Books, 1996, pp. 91–98.

Shimabukuro, Karra, and Kara Andersen. "European Horror Games: Little Red Riding Hood's Zombie BBQ and the European Game Industry." *Transnational Horror Across Visual Media*, edited by Dana Orch and Kirsten Strayer, Routledge, 2014, pp. 86–106.

Shippey, Tom. "Rewriting the Core: Transformations of the Fairy Tale in Contemporary Writing." *A Companion to the Fairy Tale*, edited by Hilda Roderick Ellis Davidson and Anna Chaudhri, D. S. Brewer, 2006, pp. 71–83.

Short, Sue. "Crime/Justice." *The Routledge Companion to Media and Fairy-Tale Studies*, edited by Pauline Greenhill and Jill Terry Rudy, Routledge, 2018. Kindle edition.

Shrek. Directed by Andrew Adamson and Vicky Jenson, DreamWorks Animation, 2001.

Simpson, Alan, and Rodger McDaniel. *Dying for Joe McCarthy's Sins: The Suicide of Wyoming Senator Lester Hunt*. WordsWorth Press, 2013.

Simpson, Kathryn. "'Queer Fish': Woolf's Writing of Desire Between Women in *The Voyage Out* and *Mrs Dalloway*." *Woolf Studies Annual: Special Issue: Virginia Woolf and Literary History: Part I*, vol. 9, 2003, pp. 55–82.

"Skin Deep." *Once Upon a Time*, created by Edward Kitsis and Adam Horowitz, written by Jane Espenson, directed by Milan Cheylov, season 1, episode 12, ABC Studios, 2012.

Sontag, Susan. "Notes on Camp." *Partisan Review*, vol. 31, no. 4, pp. 515–30.

Sorensen, Peer E. "Hans Christian Andersen." *The Teller's Tale: Lives of the Classic Fairy Tale Writers*, edited by Sophie Raynard, State University of New York Press, 2012, pp. 165–75.

Spencer, Leland G. "Performing Transgender Identity in *The Little Mermaid*: From Andersen to Disney." *Communication Studies*, vol. 65, no. 1, 2014, pp. 112–27.

Stein, Mary Beth. "Oral Tradition and Fairy Tales." *The Oxford Companion to Fairy Tales*. 2nd ed., edited by Jack Zipes, Oxford University Press, 2015.

Stone, Kyle. "Aquamarine." *Happily Ever After: Erotic Fairy Tales for Men*, edited by Michael Ford, Masquerade Books, 1996, pp. 353–68.

Straparola, Giovanni Francesco. *The Pleasant Nights*, edited by Donald Beecher, and W G. Waters, University of Toronto Press, 2012.

Summers, Claude J. "Homosexuality and Renaissance Literature, or the Anxieties of Anachronism." *South Central Review*, vol. 9, no. 1, 1992, pp. 2–23.

Sutton, Kelsey. "BuzzFeed Fires Two Amid Video Push." *Politico*, 15 June 2016, www.politico.com/media/story/2016/06/non-compete-agreements-buzzfeed-firings-004600. Accessed 1 Jan. 2023.

Sutton, Travis, and Harry M. Benshoff. "'Forever Family' Values: *Twilight* and the Modern Mormon Vampire." *Horror After 911*, edited by Aviva Briefel and Sam J. Miller, University of Texas Press, 2011, pp. 200–19.

Sweeney, Gael. "What Do You Want Me to Do? Dress in Drag and Do the Hula?: Timon and Pumbaa's Alternative Lifestyle Dilemma in *The Lion King*." *Diversity in Disney Films: Critical Essays on Race, Ethnicity, Gender, Sexuality and Disability*, edited by Johnson Cheu, McFarland & Company Publishers, 2013, pp. 129–46.

Tashman, Brian. "Swanson: Disney's *Frozen* Is a Satanic Push to Turn Kids Gay." *Right Wing Watch*, 10 Mar. 2014, www.rightwingwatch.org/post/swanson-disneys-frozen-is-a-satanic-push-to-turn-kids-gay. Accessed 1 Jan. 2023.

Tatar, Maria. *The Classic Fairy Tales: Texts, Criticism*. W. W. Norton and Company, 1999.

———. *The Hard Facts of the Grimms' Fairy Tales*. Princeton University Press, 1987.

Teal, Donn. *The Gay Militants: How Gay Liberation Began in America, 1969–1971*. St Martin's Press, 1971.

Teverson, Andrew. *Fairy Tale*. Taylor and Francis, 2013.

Thacker, Eugene. "After Life: Swarms, Demons and the Antinomies of Immanence." *Theory After Theory*, edited by Jane Elliott and Derek Attridge, Routledge, 2011, pp. 181–93.

Thompson, Stith. *The Folktale*. Dryden, 1946.

Tiffin, Jessica. *Marvelous Geometry: Narrative and Metafiction in Modern Fairy Tales*. Wayne State University Press, 2009.

Tilly, Chris. "Is There a Gay Kiss in Lightyear? Same-Sex Kiss Explained." *Dexerto*, 14 June 2022, www.dexerto.com/tv-movies/is-there-a-gay-kiss-in-lightyear-same-sex-kiss-scene-explained-1847320. Accessed 1 Jan. 2023.

Town, Caren. *LGBTQ Young Adult Fiction: A Critical Survey, 1970s–2010s*. McFarland & Company Publishers, 2017.

Travers Scott, D. "Hansel and Gretel." *Happily Ever After: Erotic Fairy Tales for Men*, edited by Michael Ford, Masquerade Books, 1996, pp. 311–28.

Treichler, Paula A. "AIDS, Gender, and Biomedical Discourse: Current Contests for Meaning." *AIDS: The Burdens of History*, edited by Elizabeth Fee and Daniel M. Fox, University of California Press, 1988, pp. 191–233.

Tribunella, Eric L. "From Kiddie Lit to Kiddie Porn: The Sexualization of Children's Literature." *Children's Literature Association Quarterly*, vol. 33, no. 2, pp. 135–55.

———. "Literature for Us 'Older Children': *Lost Girls*, Seduction Fantasies, and the Reeducation of Adults." *Journal of Popular Culture*, vol. 45, no. 3, 2012, pp. 628–48.

Trinidad, David. "How Anne Sexton Won the Pulitzer Prize." *Poetry Foundation*, 17 June 2014, www.poetryfoundation.org/harriet-books/2014/06/how-anne-sexton-won-the-pulitzer-prize. Accessed 1 Jan. 2023.

Turner, Kay. "Playing with Fire: Transgression as Truth in Grimms' 'Frau Trude.'" *Transgressive Tales: Queering the Grimms*, edited by Kay Turner and Pauline Greenhill, Wayne University Press, 2012, pp. 245–74.

Turner, Kay, and Pauline Greenhill. "Introduction." *Transgressive Tales: Queering the Grimms*, edited by Kay Turner and Pauline Greenhill, Wayne University Press, 2012, pp. 1–23.

Ungerman, Alex. "Idina Menzel Reacts to *Frozen* Petition to Give Elsa a Girlfriend: I Think It's Great." *ET*, 22 May 2016, www.etonline.com/news/189295_exclusive_idina_menzel_reacts_to_frozen_2_petition_to_give_elsa_a_girlfriend. Accessed 1 Jan. 2023.

Valente, Catherynne M. "Bones Like Black Sugar." *Sleeping Beauty, Indeed and Other Lesbian Tales*, edited by JoSelle Vanderhooft, Lethe Press, 2009, pp. 29–34.

Van der Veen, Evert. "A Global View of the Gay and Lesbian Press." *The Second ILGA Pink Book: A Global View of Lesbian and Gay Liberation*, edited by The Pink Book Team, Interfacultaire Werk-groep Homostudies, 1988, pp. 15–21.

Vernallis, Carol. *Unruly Media: YouTube, Music Video, and the New Digital Cinema*. Oxford University Press, 2013.

Wald, Priscilla. *Contagious: Culture, Carriers and the Outbreak Narrative*. Duke University Press, 2008.

Walker, Brian. "Social Movements as Nationalisms or, On the Very Idea of a Queer Nation." *Canadian Journal of Philosophy*, vol. 22, 1997, pp. 505–47.

Warman, Brittany. "I Am the Wolf: Queering 'Little Red Riding Hood' and 'Snow White and Rose Red' in the Television Show *Once Upon a Time*." *Humanities*, vol. 5.2, no. 41, 2016, pp. 1–11.

———. "YouTube and Internet Video." *The Routledge Companion to Media and Fairy-Tale Studies*, edited by Pauline Greenhill and Jill Terry Rudy, Routledge, 2018. Kindle edition.

Warner, Marina. *From the Beast to the Blonde: On Fairy Tales and Their Tellers*. Farrar, Straus and Giroux, 1994.

———. *Once Upon a Time: A Short History of Fairy Tale*. Oxford University Press, 2014.

———. *Six Myths of Our Time*. Vintage Books, 1995.

———, editor. *Wonder Tales: Six Stories of Enchantment*. Vintage, 1996.

Warner, Michael. *Publics and Counterpublics*. Columbia University Press, 2005.

———. *The Trouble with Normal*. Harvard University Press, 1999.

Warner, Sharon Oard. "The Way We Write Now: The Reality of AIDS in Contemporary Short Fiction." *Studies in Short Fiction*, vol. 30, no. 4, 1993, pp. 491–500.

Weems, Mickey. "Gay Communities." *Encyclopedia of American Folklife*, edited by Simon J. Bronner, Routledge, 2006, pp. 477–81.

White, Edmund. "Out of the Closet, onto the Bookshelf." *The New York Times*, 16 June 1991, www.nytimes.com/1991/06/16/magazine/out-of-the-closet-onto-the-bookshelf.html. Accessed 1 Jan. 2023.

Wills, John. *Disney Culture*. Rutgers University Press, 2017.

Winterson, Jeanette. *Sexing the Cherry*. Grove Atlantic, 2007.

Wittman, Carl. "Refugees from Amerika: A Gay Manifesto" (1970). *History Is a Weapon*, www.historyisaweapon.com/defcon1/wittmanmanifesto.html. Accessed 1 Jan. 2023.

Wittwer, Preston. "Don Draper Thinks Your Ad Is Cliché: Fairy Tale Iconography in TV Commercials." *Humanities*, vol. 5, no. 2, 2016.

Wood, Gaby. "Neil Gaiman on the Meaning of Fairy Tales." *The Telegraph*, 20 Nov. 2014, www.telegraph.co.uk/culture/books/11243761/Neil-Gaiman-Disneys-Sleeping-Beauty.html. Accessed 1 Jan. 2023.

Wood, Robin. *Hollywood from Vietnam to Reagan . . . and Beyond*. Columbia University Press, 2008.

Wright, Alexa. *Monstrosity: The Human Monster in Visual Culture*. I.B. Tauris, 2013.

Wullschlager, Jackie. *Hans Christian Andersen: The Life of a Storyteller*. Penguin Books, 2001.

Yamato, Lori. "Surgical Humanization in H. C. Andersen's 'The Little Mermaid.'" *Marvels & Tales*, vol. 30, no. 2, 2017, pp. 295–311.

Yang, Guobin. "Narrative Agency in Hashtag Activism: The Case of #BlackLivesMatter." *Media and Communication*, vol. 4, no. 4, Aug. 2016, pp. 13–187.

Yingling, Thomas E. "Wittgenstein's Tumor: AIDS and the National Body." *Textual Practice*, vol. 8, 1994, 97–113.

Yoshinaga, Ida. "Convergence Culture: Media Convergence, Convergence Culture, and Communicative Capitalism." *The Routledge Companion to Media and Fairy-Tale Studies*, edited by Pauline Greenhill and Jill Terry Rudy, Routledge, 2018, Kindle edition.

Zaharuk, Larissa. "Tribute Art." *Kid-In*, 9 Apr. 2014, www.kid-in.net/tribute-art. Accessed 1 Jan. 2023.

Zain, Ana Laura. "Will Tumblr Bring a Younger Audience to Yahoo! Sites?" *ComScore*, 22 May 2013, www.comscore.com/esl/Insights/Infographics/will-tumblr-bring-a-younger-audience-to-yahoo-sites. Accessed 1 Jan. 2023.

Zipes, Jack. *Breaking the Magic Spell: Radical Theories of Folk and Fairy Tales*. University Press of Kentucky, 2002.

———. *The Brothers Grimm: From Enchanted Forests to the Modern World*. Palgrave Macmillan, 2002.

———. *The Enchanted Screen: The Unknown History of Fairy-Tale Films*. Routledge, 2011.

———. *Fairy Tales and the Art of Subversion: The Classical Genre for Children and the Process of Civilization*. 1st ed., Heinemann, 1983.

———. *Fairy Tales and the Art of Subversion: The Classical Genre for Children and the Process of Civilization*. 2nd ed., Routledge, 2006.

———. *The Great Fairy Tale Tradition: From Straparola and Basile to the Brothers Grimm; Texts, Criticism*. W. W. Norton & Company, 2001.

———. *Hans Christian Andersen: The Misunderstood Storyteller*. Routledge, 2005.

———. *Happily Ever After: Fairy Tales, Children, and the Culture Industry*. Psychology Press, 1997.

———. "How the Grimm Brothers Saved the Fairy Tale." *National Endowment for the Humanities*, vol. 36, no. 2, March/April 2015.

——. "Media-Hyping of Fairy Tales." *The Cambridge Companion to Fairy Tales*, edited by Maria Tatar, Cambridge University Press, 2015, pp. 201–19.

——. *The Trials and Tribulations of Little Red Riding Hood: Versions of the Tale in Sociocultural Context*. Bergin & Garvey Publishers, 1983.

——. *When Dreams Came True: Classical Fairy Tales and Their Tradition*. Routledge, 2007.

INDEX